MORTAL

WOUNDS

Other Books in the Mining City Series

MORTAL WOUNDS

A MINING CITY MYSTERY

Marian Jensen

www.miningcitymysteries.com

Published by ABM

Copyright © 2016 Marian Jensen

This is a work of fiction based, to a greater or lesser extent depending on the story, on some actual events. Certain details have been changed and even more invented. The characters in this novel, even the most unsavory, are imaginary, or used fictitiously. The city of Butte, happily for everyone, is a real place. However, any resemblance to actual persons, living or dead, or organizations is entirely coincidental.

Cover Design by Mariya Peck
Cover Photos by Mariya Peck

Book Format by Luanne Thibault

Printed by CreateSpace

Printed in the United States of America

ISBN-10: 1533216754

Dedication

To women everywhere who have faced difficult decisions that often accompany bringing children into the world and to those who have helped and supported them so they would not feel alone.

Chapter 1

Butte has always operated in its own orbit, a city in another galaxy in the minds of many. Even Mesa Dawson could never have predicted exactly how dangerous that July's fireworks might become.

When Vivian Jobe called with an impromptu invitation to lunch at the Metals Bank Sports Bar, Mesa gladly accepted the excuse to get out of her office at the *Mining City Messenger*. In the main dining room that had once been the Metals Bank lobby, they sat together by the tall windows with a panoramic view of the East Ridge and the Summit Valley floor. Mesa briefly contemplated the Canada Day special, a.k.a. a Vault burger with peas and French Fries smothered with gravy, but thought twice. She would only pick at it.

"A curious guy came into the Archives this morning," Vivian said, toying with her gold necklace while she scanned the menu.

She wore a pearl gray blouse and scarf, and Mesa wondered where in Butte she could have bought something so stylish. One of her mother's closest friends, Vivian's reappearance in Butte that past St. Patrick's Day had sparked a strong connection. So much so, that Mesa confided in her often, especially after the unexpected death of her boyfriend, Shane Northey in March.

"He's from England," Vivian continued, placing the menu precisely on the corner of the table. "Some kind of filmmaker. Documentaries, I think."

Looking up, Mesa let out an audible sigh. "Vivian," she said, careful not to sound pesky, "you're not trying to set me up, are you?"

Just because she had refused to invite an attractive, software salesman into her office for an impromptu chat, everybody seemed to be turning into a matchmaker. She had told Irita, the office manager, to have him make an appointment for the next day, which he hadn't kept. She had told everyone who would listen, no doubt including Vivian, that Mesa had turned away another "golden opportunity."

Vivian's shoulders sagged and she looked out the window for a second as if to gather her thoughts. "Mesa, you should know me better than that by now." Then she smiled to soften the rebuke.

"So what's this Englishman making a film about?" Mesa asked after the waiter had taken their order. Mesa had decided to throw caution to the wind and ordered some sweet potato fries.

"I don't think he's entirely sure yet," Vivian said, "but your articles on the Internet about Elsie's Babies are what brought him here."

Mesa had to smile. Irita had been bragging that morning about the *Mining City Messenger* and her perception of it as Montana's, if not the world's, best community newspaper. "I suppose somebody there could have seen the blog," Mesa said.

"He says he has to convince his partners that coming to Montana to film is a viable project," Vivian continued. "So he's putting together a proposal with as many photographs as he can to tempt them with the possibilities. He went on and on about how the American West constitutes a deep allure for the British."

Mesa rolled her eyes and Vivian joined her in a quick chuckle. "Nana would love this guy," Mesa said. Both women had heard her grandmother refer to the "Gary Cooper spell" that she had fallen under when she had met Grandpa Ducharme, an American airman in Cambridge back in the fifties. "He was truly tall, dark, and handsome," she always said.

"You seriously think he came to Butte because of my articles? He never called me," Mesa said. "What else did he say about the film?" Butte had been the subject of more than a few documentaries in recent years. A couple of Hollywood actors had come to town to make a contemporary western. Matthew McConaughey had even been seen scouting the mine yards. Nevertheless, Mesa thought more outside interest was a pipe dream.

"He didn't actually say, but he struck me as serious. You should meet with him," she added. "He's only here until Tuesday. He's staying at the Finlen. Then it's back to London."

When Mesa did her best not to act interested, Vivian continued. "I was thinking we could combine a little business with international hospitality," she said, "and invite him to your grandmother's garden party tomorrow afternoon. She would enjoy meeting another Brit."

Again, Mesa had to agree, but then she became uneasy about what else she and this serious filmmaker could discuss. Her articles about Elsie Seppanen, Butte's infamous 'baby seller,' had followed the recent DNA match on an online genealogy site. One of the adult adoptees had discovered a half-brother in Butte. The New York Times had even picked up that story.

Once again, Irita's connections had triggered the story. Her best friend since childhood, Dolly Blinn, had registered her DNA almost on a whim and had learned that her prim and proper uncle Michael had fathered a child before heading off to the Vietnam War. Now she had a new cousin who was the spitting image of her long-deceased uncle. "We've invited him to come for Christmas!" Dolly had told Irita, who had promptly passed the tidbit along.

"Most of what I know is in those three articles," Mesa said. "Finding other people who will talk is a struggle. Everybody is drawn to that story partly because of how little actual information there is to substantiate what happened. Then there are the ones who don't want to bring up the uncomfortable past. If Elsa Seppanen did sell babies to barren couples, they certainly didn't want to talk about it, not even to their own children once they were grown.

"Is there a particular aspect of the story that he's so curious about?" she asked, unsure how much of the weekend she wanted to spend on this guy. Lately, she had been considering that a few days off might help her mood. After all, who read the paper in July? During the dark winter months, which in Montana meant from October to May, people paid closer attention to the news.

"He did mention the Dumas and the other houses in the red-light district," Vivian said. "We showed him the *Montana Standard* news articles about Elsie's trials back in the 1940s, and what we have about the madams. I told him I would try to get in touch with you, and meet him back at the Archives this afternoon. Maybe send him down to you then?"

Back at the *Messenger* office, Mesa picked up the business card that Vivian had given her, vaguely curious about D. Griffin-Jones and his film company. She had turned to her computer screen to check his background when she heard the lobby door fly open. Belushi, her behind-the-back nickname for Evan Llewellyn, sprinted into her office, pushing his hair back from his eyes. She had not seen her newest employee move so fast in the four months he'd worked there.

Breathing hard, he looked at her, his eyes dark and glistening with intensity. "Some woman jumped off the roof of the Finlen!" he said and turned and ran back out the way he came.

Belushi was not given to exaggeration, far from it. If anything, he tended to understate situations, a sign Mesa knew would someday make him a decent reporter. She jumped up from her desk and sped after him, leaving thoughts of the Englishman far behind.

She picked up speed by the Indian Alliance Building, turning the corner up Wyoming Street, and caught up with Belushi. A scattering of onlookers had gathered two blocks up, across from where the jumper had apparently come down. A police car had arrived and blocked off traffic at the intersection of Broadway and Wyoming, at the front of the hotel.

"She landed on top of that white Jeep," he said, breathing hard as they strode uphill.

The kid was barely twenty and already had a bit of a paunch, especially for somebody who claimed not to drink beer. Probably too many shakes and burgers from Matt's Diner where his mom worked. "Any idea who it is?" Mesa asked.

"Nope," Belushi said. "I just got a text from my sister. She was walking out of work, like right after it happened. Says she thought maybe somebody had wrecked their car."

Belushi's sister worked in the kitchen at the Uptown Café on Broadway, three doors from the corner. They stopped serving lunch at 2 p.m. Mesa looked at her watch and saw that it was 2:20. She and Belushi crossed Park Street and were half way up the block, walking in the middle of Wyoming Street, when a cop began unfurling yellow and black crime scene tape in front of them, cautioning them to stand back.

Mesa's breathing had slowed and she felt a growing wave of morbid exhilaration, the potential for a meaty story. She could see the Jeep parked on the incline, front and back windshields shattered and buckling, a gruesome pedestal. The body, clearly a younger woman, had landed with precision, lengthwise in the middle of the car's roof. Two shoes at the rear window's edge seemed improbably delicate. They looked like ballerina flats, the ones with thin heels. Mesa had a pair in her closet.

"I guess she fell from the roof all right," Mesa muttered, looking up. "None of the hotel windows are even open."

She scanned the seven floors of windows, her mind sharp as she searched the faces of the rooms' likely occupants. Clearly, word had spread inside the hotel. She considered each face as best she could in case she knew any of them. Could someone have seen something? Hard to imagine what—a shadow across the window and then light again?—unless someone was actually looking out the window at the exact moment the young woman had fallen. Even then, it would be hard to imagine what you were seeing until after the fact, when you'd be sickened by the reality of what it all meant.

More EMS and police were arriving. Mesa could see a police officer with white, crime scene gloves snapping photos from all sides. She turned on her cell phone camera and began doing the same. "Where's your sister?" she asked Belushi. "I want to talk to her. You go over to the crowd on the sidewalk, and ask if anybody else saw anything."

Surveying the street, Mesa realized that the *Mess* might beat the *Standard*, the local daily, to the scene. If they hustled, she and Belushi could post a breaking news update on the blog. She had already begun to mull over the feature they could put together about sudden death for the following week's issue. Maybe she wouldn't leave town after all.

Assuming this was yet another suicide, and a dramatic one, this felt like a big city catastrophe. After all, Butte only had three buildings with more than five floors. But they'd also had more than a half dozen suicides since she had returned to Butte the previous Labor Day.

"You're Evan's boss, aren't you?" said a tall, young woman who appeared at Mesa's side moments later. "I'm Sissy."

Dressed in a denim mini-skirt atop long legs, Sissy's thick curly hair constituted the only hint that she and Belushi were even distantly related. Evan's uncanny resemblance to the once famous SNL comedian had prompted Mesa to give him the nickname—though not to his face.

"Right," Mesa said. "You texted your brother about the woman over there?" She gestured toward the Jeep and then said, "What makes you think she jumped?"

Her face pale, Sissy looked around vacantly, appearing to show signs of shock.

"Let's stand over here in the shade," Mesa said and guided the woman by the elbow. "Can you tell me what exactly you saw?" she asked once they found a spot under the awning of the newest medical marijuana store.

"I'm totally creeped out. I, like, come out of work every day, look up and down Broadway and take a deep breath. Working in a kitchen can get stuffy, even when the food is good. I've looked up at the top of the Finlen dozens of times. I always did think that little building on top would be a super place to party."

"What little building?" Mesa said, looking up at the hotel's upper edge. She couldn't see anything beyond the parapets on the roof's edge.

"That's part of why it's so cool. You can only see it from certain sides. Lots of people never notice it. If you stand right in front of the Uptown though and look up, then you see it."

Mesa made a mental note to do just that. "So what did you see?"

"Well, I didn't see anything exactly," she said, steepling her fingers close to her chest. "I mean I heard somebody scream, and then this weird sort of thump and a loud crack," she said with a visible shudder to her shoulders. "A spooky scream," she said in a quiet voice, her memory seeming to take over, "high and long and then fading. I started walking toward the sound. I thought maybe somebody was in the car. But then when I got to the corner, I could see her."

"The woman?" Mesa said, gesturing again toward the Jeep. "You didn't see her jump?"

Sissy shook her head. "I could see her on the roof of the car, her arm and hand slack to the side, like she had decided to lie down."

Sissy lit a cigarette, her hands shaking, and Mesa made her sit down on the wide sill of the storefront. "Take it easy. You've had a shock." Butte was a tough town, infamous for its rough and tumble ways, but somebody jumping off a building was definitely unusual.

"You ever have that experience where you think someone's following you and you turn and there's no one there?" Sissy mumbled. "Like a ghost or somebody with super powers?"

Mesa bent down closer to be sure she could hear what the young woman was saying. People could come up with some off-the-wall ideas in the face of death.

"When I looked up at the Finlen when I first got outside, I thought for a second I saw somebody on the roof. Then I heard the scream, and I looked toward the corner. When I looked up again, there was nobody there."

"You mean like there might have been somebody up there?" Mesa said.

Sissy nodded timidly.

"This could be important, Sissy," Mesa said, her mind spinning with possibilities. "Did you see anybody leave through the front of the Finlen when you were standing on Broadway?" The hotel's double doors would have been clearly visible.

She stared back at Mesa with the same large green eyes as Belushi, eyes that didn't seem to comprehend everything they were seeing. She shook her head but then stopped. "There were a couple of guys crossing the street, I think."

Mesa began to scribble in her notebook. "What did they look like?"

Another shrug. "A construction guy and a guy in a suit."

"Were they together? Which way did they go? Did they get in a car?"

Sissy shrugged. "I didn't pay much attention. I was staring at the girl on top of the car," she said, her voice wispy with disbelief.

Mesa sighed, but she could understand Sissy's incredulity. She looked up at the roof again, wondering who might think to commit suicide that way. How could anybody even get up to the roof? The top five floors had long ago been remodeled into apartments with limited access. Maybe it was a tenant.

Leaving Sissy to the police, Mesa began to look for a way around to the front of the hotel. The sidewalks were now cordoned off. Then Belushi called to her, and she waited for him. For the better part of May and June, with her conscience sullied by her unproductive days at work after Shane's death, she had focused on training Belushi so that he could operate independently. The distressed look on his baby face surprised her. "What is it?" she said.

"It's not official or anything so I'm not sure what to say, but someone in the crowd thinks they recognize the woman." The young reporter gripped his lower lip with his thumb and first finger, pulling at the loose skin below it, a nervous gesture that Mesa hoped wouldn't become a tic. "They said it's—," he paused and then said, "It's Phade's sister, Danica."

"Are they sure?" she gasped. She looked again at the body on top of the car, the thin physique, the ebony hair, and a chill ran up her back. The paper's resident geek and local trendsetter, Phade Draganovich, was the *Messenger*'s badass blogger.

In the spring, Mesa had also spent time getting the blog up and running, working with Phade. The long hours involved had paid off. She knew he could handle the technical aspects, but she was stoked that he'd taken to the writing as well. She lived in perpetual anxiety that he'd get bored and move on. After lunch with Vivian, she had looked forward to teasing him with the news that people in England were reading the blog. If the young woman in front of her was Phade's sister, Mesa could not be sure how this would affect him.

"Damn," she said, pulling out her cell phone to call Irita. "Don't let Phade leave the building," she commanded when the older woman answered, but it was already too late. Mesa had turned instinctively toward Galena Street and saw Phade sprinting up the hill.

Back toward the Jeep, she could see the coroner had arrived and was climbing a short ladder with his assistant, Nick Philippoussis, to examine the body. A tidal wave of emotion engulfed her.

The dead woman was no longer the potential subject of a story but a relative of someone who worked at the paper. How would she be able to comfort Phade and at the same time remain detached while she wrote about what had happened? If she wasn't careful, both friendship and story could suffer.

She forced thoughts about the potential conflict to the back of her mind. For now, the story came first. Cataloging the scene in her mind, she saw the EMS workers emerge from the ambulance that had pulled up next to the Jeep, and put a stretcher in place. Thin trickles of blood from the young woman's nose and the corner of her mouth were visible in stark contrast to her ashen complexion. It was as though she had floated down from the top of the building and landed with nothing but her sunglasses askew.

Mesa took a deep breath and thought about how to prepare Phade for the unsettling scene, realizing she felt oddly at ease. She intercepted him at the spot where the police officer had stood at the south end of the street, but he fought through her.

"I need to get in there," he said to the police officer. "Somebody said it's my sister."

His voice sounded unnaturally flat as if he were on some sort of automatic pilot. He was staring straight ahead, his mink brown eyes rimmed with tears.

"You have to let me see her," he said, arguing with the cop who then went to seek permission from somebody.

Mesa took hold of Phade's arm, his tattooed bicep firm beneath her touch. He looked at her for a second and said, "What am I going to tell my mother?" He gripped his forehead and then staggered back a step. For an instant, Mesa thought he might collapse. But the cop returned and lifted the plastic tape to direct Phade toward the stretcher where the EMS workers were getting ready to move the body. He ran toward the Jeep and his sister.

As if expected for a summer picnic, she wore a white cotton sundress with a tiny yellow and blue flower pattern, short sleeves, and a scoop neck, perfect with her ballet flats. Mesa stopped taking photographs. She would not forget what Danica Draganovich looked like.

Even after talking with the police and watching as the EMS crew gently removed his sister's body, Phade could not be persuaded to leave. Finally, once all the vehicles were gone, he had walked with Mesa back to the office. She tread warily, wanting to give him comfort, but feeling tentative.

In recent months, Phade's flirting had gotten close to out of hand more than once. While nothing serious, his wily attentions were the kind she had needed— anonymous flowers she'd seen him sneak in, delivering her lunch, staying late at work until he knew she was the only one there. After the shock of Shane's accidental death, for weeks nothing had seemed normal. In the early days, the weight of her grief was palpable, like an anvil on her chest. She didn't eat or sleep. It took her twenty minutes to tie her shoes.

When she finally did come back to work, she couldn't think, let alone write. Schooling Belushi on the nuances of community news, watching Phade's progress with the blog was all she could manage. She was on automatic. Sometimes she thought that was all Phade was trying to do, make her realize that she herself wasn't dead.

One evening they had ended up in a clinch after a playful round of keep-away with a flash drive. Phade had planted a victorious, and unexpected, kiss on her lips, when the after-hours deliveries bell parted them. *Thank God for UPS* was what Mesa had thought later, even if it had all been innocent enough.

She'd had her share of office romances with the boss, and knew the up- and downsides. Only now, she was the honcho, and she was well aware that taking things too far could have disastrous results. But she couldn't deny chemistry. She felt a genuine attraction toward Phade, and they both knew it.

Once they were back in the office, Mesa told Phade to collect his stuff, and then she would drive him home. She could see he was exhausted—sapped like a balloon that had lost its air, while her adrenalin was skyrocketing. Her intuition was screaming that there was more to Danica Draganovich's death than they knew at that moment.

She was on the phone giving instructions to Belushi when Phade came into her office. He sat on the sofa, not moving or saying anything for the longest time. She wasn't sure what to do for him. It was nearly five by then and everyone who was on the clock had quietly departed, even Irita, who had signaled that she would call later.

"Here, have a shot of Neversweat," Mesa said finally and pulled the bottle of the locally distilled bourbon from her bottom desk drawer. Phade took the bottle. When they'd both taken a swig, she sat down next to him on the sofa. Wrapping her arm around his shoulder while tears streamed down his face, one thing she knew for certain, sadly, was there was nothing that she could say that would help.

Anxious that she might sink into a funk of her own, she turned her thoughts to Danica, recalling the bits and pieces she knew about her. Mesa might not have even recognized Phade's sister except for a family portrait he kept in his carrel, a testament to how close Phade was to his family. What unmarried, twenty something guy, who carefully cultivated a hipster persona, kept a Christmas photo of his extended family on his desk?

He had talked about her often enough. Mid-thirties, ten years older than Phade, Danica and her brother had shared enough of an age difference to spare them the usual sibling rivalries. Instead, he described his sister as a buffer to his ultra-conservative parents. She had always been able to explain her brother's penchant for what they thought of as strange music and even stranger friends. He had welcomed her recent return from California. And now she was gone again, only this time for good. Mesa had been looking forward to getting to know Danica, and the lost opportunity was oddly poignant. Rising to the status of lost loved one, she would become someone who would forever after be talked about in hushed tones.

Finally, Mesa drove Phade to his parents' home. They made the ten-minute drive in painful, if companionable, silence. The well-maintained but modest brick house on St. Ann Street stood down the block from Holy Trinity, the Serbian Orthodox Church, which was the heart as well as the soul of the Draganovich family. Mesa was mystified by much of its traditions, but she was relieved to know that she was bringing him to comforting arms.

Discomfort returned when she saw the coroner's car along with the Sheriff's. She knew they were inside to explain what had happened. But her heart went out to Phade's parents when she saw them, clinging to each other, while his grandmother sat nearby weeping softly.

Quietly in the background, the members of the Serbian Mothers Club were rearranging the furniture in the dining room, organizing china and cutlery, and laying out the comfort food—sarma, cicvara, priganica, povitica, and baklava—enough for a small army. Theirs was a church where food was definitely love.

Between the tears and the hugs, effort was in full force to make sure the Draganovich's had all the support they could handle with the certain knowledge that there could not be enough. Several older women approached and smothered Phade with kisses, squeezing his cheeks as if he was still a small boy.

Paying her condolences to Phade's parents, Nick and Tamara, along with his grandmother, his *baba* Vesna, Mesa felt embarrassed when they expressed their deep appreciation for his continued employment at the paper. His job at the *Mess* had largely been the result of his Baba's friendship with Mesa's grandmother, Rose Ducharme. She and the older Mrs. Draganovich knew each other from the Food Bank where they had volunteered together for years. Mrs. Ducharme knew about Phade's "trouble focusing," his failed attempts at college, and his reluctance to meet the rigors of an eight-to-five job.

Mesa could hear Phade mimicking his grandmother before he'd gotten hired. *He is strong boy with good mind. He work hard to help his parents and at church. Father Jovan says not to give up hope. The boy will find his way.* Phade had admitted to Mesa later that he was a twerp obsessed with video games and was lucky his parents hadn't given him the boot.

After his second disastrous semester at Montana Tech, Phade had taken over the *Messenger*'s layout job from a guy who had trouble even installing software updates. Rose Ducharme had made it clear that Phade's was a temporary job. He would format and oversea the paper's digital production, would troubleshoot any glitches, and make sure staff and their machines could work together. She didn't mind when he worked as long as he was available when the staff needed him, but he couldn't wear facial piercings at the office. Wondering if she would ever outgrow her tendency to blush, Mesa was touched that even now in the midst of horrendous grief, Phade's family wanted to be sure that she understood their gratitude and would convey it to her grandmother once again.

She told him not to worry about work that she would get Belushi to cover for him. When Phade's girlfriend, Stella, arrived, Mesa was relieved to turn Phade over and gladly made a quick exit. The open show of emotion brought up her own, which she struggled to keep in check. When she walked outside, tears ready to spill, she distracted herself with the cars pulling up onto the lawn, the outpouring of mourners evident. She drove to her grandmother's house on Silver Street where she would bury herself in the mundane 4th of July preparations and some stoic English peace and quiet where the stiff upper lip prevailed.

Her grandmother greeted her at the back door, red, white, and blue bunting in hand. "I was beginning to think I'd have to put these ribbons up by myself," she said with a smile that quickly vanished when she read the distress in Mesa's face. "What's happened?" she said, her tone somber, the decorations falling to the ground.

"Looks like Phade's sister jumped off the roof of the Finlen," Mesa explained and collapsed into a kitchen chair in tears.

Nana Rose stopped in her tracks. "Dear God," she said and then quickly recovered herself and turned on the teakettle. "Vesna has always worried so about her grandchildren."

Chapter 2

Chance had taken Mesa's call late that afternoon and was as shocked as she was when he heard about the jumper. He was also surprised that she was clearly on the trail of a story. Mesa's enthusiasm for her work had always impressed him. Not quite thirty years old, the up-and-coming editor would work double overtime, by herself if need be, to make sure she produced the best edition of the paper. At least that had been the case before Shane Northey had died. This was a good sign, that she wanted her older brother to try to get some details from his pal, the assistant coroner.

Not surprisingly, Nick Philippoussis was more than happy to accept the offer of a stiff drink. Once the body had been loaded into the ambulance destined for the Crime Lab in Missoula, he immediately agreed to meet for a quick beer. He was undoubtedly relieved that the coroner knew the Draganovich family personally, which meant he would make the obligatory official visit, the part of the job Nick was thankful to avoid.

When Chance finished up a coat of varnish on a stairwell at the Park Hotel, his current renovation project, it was close to 6 p.m. Curious for details about what had happened, he walked over to Mulligan's, commandeered the two stools at the far end of the bar, and ordered a couple of shots of Jameson, backed with Moose Drools.

When Nick walked in, even in the darkened interior, Chance saw by the dour expression on his friend's face that the removal of the body from the roof of somebody's shiny new Jeep Cherokee had been nerve-wracking. He wondered if it was the condition of the body or the looming arrival of the vehicle's owner who was sure to be pissed about the crushed roof of his SUV. "People got no sympathy for a coroner's job," Nick would often say.

Even he had never seen a jumper before, not in town anyway. Except for Spanky Spangler, the stuntman who'd dived off the top of the Hotel Finlen numerous times, once in flames, during Evel Knievel Days. Everybody in town had seen that. But this was different.

He downed the first shot before his substantial frame even hit the stool and then took a long swig from the Moose Drool. "God, I hate the holidays," he said. "Never fails that somebody decides to go over the edge." Then he took the second shot sitting in front of Chance and said with a smile, "literally and figuratively."

"Pretty gruesome, I'm thinking," Chance said by way of condolence. He couldn't even watch *The Walking Dead* on television and did not understand how the coroner's crew could do their jobs. There were four of them, the coroner and three part-time assistants, and they had all developed a gallows humor about what they saw. Even Nick could not account for how they were able to distance themselves.

"Not nearly as bad as the one we had a few years back. Kid took a nosedive off the railroad trestle next to

Roosevelt Drive. He was a real mess. He'd stuffed all this gravel in his pockets to speed up the trip. Course the bridge was a good deal higher than the Finlen, and he landed smack in the middle of the road. Talk about a bag of bones."

Chance grimaced, sipped his Moose Drool, and ordered up two more shots, glad his stomach was empty.

"The roof of the car tempered the impact on this one," Nick continued. "Plus the parachute effect of her dress, she only broke her neck."

"Better you than me," Chance said and tapped his Moose Drool bottle against Nick's. "I was surprised you're sending this one to the lab though. Isn't it obvious what happened?" He knew from Nick's complaints about the low pay and even lower budget for the Coroner's Office that bodies were only sent to the State Crime Lab when it was absolutely necessary.

Nick shrugged. "Need the tox screen. Manner of death appears obvious; a high dive off the roof, her laid out on that Jeep, but whether she jumped, fell, or was pushed, is a lot harder to tell. And if she had any drugs in her system that will be a crucial piece of the investigation."

Chance knew Nick was right. Sadly, speculation about suicide would seep into conversation around the Independence Day celebrations since the Draganovich family was well known. "Nothing on the body to suggest one thing or another?"

"You know I can't say anything about that," Nick winked at Chance.

"But if you had to bet?" Chance pushed, less out of his own curiosity than the realization that Mesa would be dying to know what Nick thought. When she had called, she was clearly in speculation mode, thinking about the story. Again, a good thing. Except for the feature about the death of a homeless man, written a month after Shane's death, Mesa hadn't written anything substantial since.

"You know the Draganovichs, right?" Nick asked with another shrug. "Hard working folks who've done well for themselves. Orthodox families, kids mean everything and they know it. If the daughter was in trouble, her family would have been there for her. Suicide, that's about desperation. Now that whack job son of theirs, that works for Mesa, poor kid. He was all torn up at the scene. Good thing your sister was there. She was going to get him home."

"Phade's not that bad," Chance countered, though the eyeliner did make him a little uncomfortable. "So he likes to wear eye makeup and play electronic dance music. He's a digital wizard. Mesa would be in deep shit without him," he mused. Then in a quieter tone, "I don't know much about his sister. She's a bit older than us, isn't she?"

Nick nodded. "Three or four years. I think she graduated in '99. Last I heard she was living in L.A. looking to grab the brass ring. She had big ideas, I guess. When they didn't work out, she was smart enough to come back to Butte where she felt at home."

Chance wondered how smart a decision it had been, or whether she felt so comfortable after all. "Another round?"

"Nah. I gotta get home and help Jeanne make potato salad to take to the in-laws tomorrow. It's her dad's birthday. Plus I'm on call tonight. Pray for peace."

৩৯৫

"People are nuts," Irita said. "Don't get me wrong, I'm really sorry for the kid, even if he looks like a pincushion with all those piercings. But life's not a fairytale—if you lose your shoe at midnight, you're drunk. What did his sister expect to happen if she went up on the roof of the tallest building in town?"

Mesa sat on her couch in her duplex looking out the windows across the valley, feeling restless. It was past nine and the sunset was beginning to fade. She had finally reached the point where she once again relished the last quiet moments of the day.

That she thought phoning her assistant was a way to enjoy those moments reflected how the day's event had affected Mesa's decision-making. Mostly she had called because Irita would rip her boss's throat out if she heard the details second-hand.

"The Draganovichs certainly don't think it was suicide," Mesa said, the distress of Phade's grief-stricken parents still fresh. "The idea of their child harboring suicidal thoughts is outside any Orthodox family's comprehension."

"Word on the street was that she had big plans for the Orphan Girl Theater this fall," Irita said, the word on the street coming from the half dozen women across town that she gossiped with every day. "Damn shame is what it is. She came up with a cute float for the parade in record time. All those little kids that were going to ride with her will be broken-hearted. Hope they find somebody else."

Mesa wrote *float?* on a sticky note next to the laptop, feeling that old familiar pique of curiosity. Had Danica talked to anyone about plans for the 4th of July? If she was intending to be in the parade, that didn't seem consistent with killing herself.

"That Englishman stopped by after you left," Irita continued. "We got to talking about the Dumas Hotel."

Everybody liked hearing the stories about the last brothel still standing that had managed to stay open until 1982. Its tour was a regular attraction for out-of-towners.

"When I told him that my mother used to be the housekeeper at the Windsor, he got all excited. Wanted to know all about what happened to the girls who got pregnant."

Mesa grinned to think of the stories Irita would have spun about the houses of prostitution. Growing up in Butte after her family had left the Crow reservation, her mother had struggled to keep a family of six kids together by doing whatever odd jobs she could find, no matter what business hired her. The stories Irita could tell.

"Did you expect me to ask him to come back around?" Irita asked pointedly. "After you stood him up and went ambulance chasing."

Mesa looked at her laptop screen next to her on the couch. Griffin-Jones' high-cheek bones and strong chin stared back at her confidently, gazing out over the city from tall windows in a big office. He was the real deal all right.

After leaving Nan's, Mesa had come straight home and taken a quick look on the Internet to check out Jones's background. Sure enough, Upper Clapton Films, Ltd. was a full-service film production company with studios in London and Newcastle. The web site boasted award-winning advertising campaigns, video commercials, and public service announcements for banks and high-end department stores and other businesses. Not to mention half a dozen digital shorts plus full-length feature documentaries that had also won awards.

"I didn't stand him up," Mesa said self-righteously. "I was covering a story. In case you've forgotten, I run the newspaper. Besides I don't have time to bother with some random guy." She had to admit he did have that ruggedly handsome look. Combine that with an English accent, he might be worth a look-see. Too bad the timing sucked. "Right now, the most important thing is to find out what happened to Phade's sister and help get him through this catastrophe."

"I know, keep your boots on," Irita said. "It's just that we've got way too many pasty-white, potato-faced, freckled Micks in this town. A tall-dark-and-handsome type could cheer us all up."

It was nearly four a.m. when Mesa woke to the banging on the back door of her duplex, her heart in her throat. Hardly anyone used that door except Chance, and he had a key. Mesa threw on an old sweater of Shane's and grabbed the miniature Cincinnati Reds baseball bat she kept at the top of the steps for reassurance. She had not lived through endless childhood tussles with her brother to become a shrinking violet.

He had installed a motion-detector light so bright that it lit up the entire back of the house including the alley. No way could anyone in their right mind expect to break into the house unseen. More likely, it was some misguided drunk, trying to get into the wrong house, which could present its own set of problems. She crept slowly down the stairs prepared for a confrontation and hoping there would be none.

"Mesa, it's me," a muffled voice called. "I'm sorry if I scared you but I need to see you. Please let me in."

She put down the baseball bat, immediately recognizing the coarse whisper and the handsome silhouette beyond the door's window curtain. She opened the door, and Phade fell into her arms.

Fifteen minutes later the two of them sat upstairs, bundled in a quilt on the sofa. Mesa had made some cocoa to try and warm Phade up, but his hands shook so bad, he couldn't hold the cup without making a gigantic mess. A pull on a bottle of Bailey's was equally ineffective.

Finally, despite her qualms about any physical closeness between them, she had sat down on the couch and wound her long legs around his firm but thin body. He clung to her like a lost child, and the immediacy of his distress made her feel all the more tender toward him.

"How far did you walk?" she asked, rubbing her warm hands on his cold biceps. It might be July, but Butte's thin mountain air meant nighttime temperatures could dip into the forties. And naturally, Phade had wandered out in shirtsleeves.

"I had to get out of that house. Stella wanted me to spend the night at her place instead, but like I couldn't deal with her either. She was only trying to help, I know, but I felt suffocated."

Stella Trbovich was Phade's on-again, off-again girlfriend, a bank teller by day and a clubber by night. Mesa only knew her through their occasional conversations when Stella stopped by the office to meet Phade after work. But she clung to him in the way typical of the tightly knit Serbian American community where there were only so many eligible guys. She was determined to hang onto Phade, her own kind, and his parents encouraged her.

"Does your family know you left?" Mesa did not want anyone panicking over Phade's absence.

"People have been coming in and out all night. Baba saw me leave. She doesn't sleep good any time. I couldn't sleep, and once I got up, I had to get out. I needed a break," he said, and then added, "but I didn't wanna be alone either."

He let out an enormous sigh. Mesa gave him a quick hug, all too aware of the same conflicting feelings since Shane's death. Even though she'd lost a lover and not a sibling, the territory was the same. She could not even bring herself to imagine the loss of her *brother*.

"Everybody is asking me how this could have happened. I don't have a clue, Mesa. She only came back from California a month ago, and she was totally glad to be home. She was stoked about the Orphan Girl job working with kids. She was sick of the L.A. rat race. It makes no sense."

"How often did you talk to her when she was living in L.A.? Was she being straight with you?" Mesa asked, trying not to imply that Phade might be in the dark about his sister. She would resent the hell out of anybody who suggested that about her and Chance. "I mean, do you think she sugar-coated the situation because she didn't want to burden you with her problems? Saying everything was fine when it really wasn't?"

Mesa recalled how her grandmother had downplayed the possibility of suicide. "It just isn't done," Nana had said. "The Orthodox don't call theirs the ancient faith on a whim. They keep to Old World standards of morality that are tightly held, albeit without fundamentalist judgment. Frankly, I admire them for their efforts, what with the arguments of modern science and the influence of the digital age. No, if she had a problem she was more likely coming home to get help from them."

"Maybe she felt she had to keep her real feelings hidden," Mesa reiterated to Phade.

"Maybe from Mom and Pop or Baba at first, but not from me. We were for real," he said, and then paused and looked at Mesa as if he were thinking of one or two little details he might not have mentioned to his sister, like how he felt about his boss, "most of the time, about the major stuff for sure."

He turned toward Mesa and closed his hands around hers. "Promise me you'll help me find out what happened to her, no matter what."

Mesa took a deep breath and pulled Phade close to her. She couldn't dismiss his questions, his fear. "I'll do whatever I can. You know I will." She also knew that Danica's death was a police matter, first and foremost. That was something she had to respect, not only as a private citizen but also as the editor of the *Messenger*.

Mesa let Phade's head rest against her chest as she began thinking about what he had said. If there were no apparent reason even to suspect suicide, then they needed to start thinking about alternate explanations. Phade's breathing had become quieter, steady. In the silence, the inevitable question, the tantalizing but grim possibility, rattled around Mesa's mind. If Danica didn't kill herself, then who did?

Chapter 3

Chance meandered around Adrienne's gallery, pretending to be a customer. He loved watching her, not only the graceful way she moved, but her quiet confidence and poise with people. She teased him after the first time she caught him, calling him a stalker in bed later that night. Not that he was yet telling anybody, he was completely smitten. He didn't care how much older she was.

By ten a.m. several tourists, staying over at the KOA on their way from Yellowstone Park to Glacier, had wandered in. Strolling along Park Street after shopping at the Farmer's Market, always big on a 4th of July weekend, they had found the gallery.

Adrienne and a retired couple from Wisconsin were admiring a watercolor of the Anselmo Mine yard, and so he angled behind the framing counter as if he belonged. Adrienne had spotted him, he knew. Hey, he knew as much about a miter box as the next guy. On the counter, he saw the *Montana Standard*, the daily paper, opened to the story about the remains of a dead baby that had been found in a house on Granite Street the day before.

Chance examined the paper's photograph of the hundred-year-old Queen Anne home in the midst of restoration. He thought about the new owners, Tola and Ward Landry. Fifty something attorneys who had taken early retirement, they had bought the house to open a bed and breakfast. He had talked to them about restoring their fireplaces and now was really glad he hadn't taken the job. Even for Californians the discovery was grisly. Still, he hoped they wouldn't change their minds and back out.

"…Wrapped in a hand-knitted blanket and a christening jacket, the baby did not appear to be the victim of foul play," the opening paragraph read. The infant was small, likely stillborn. Its decade-old remains had been found in the attic at the bottom of a dry cleaning bag, nested in a tuxedo jacket that had likely been hung there for storage. Jesus, that was Halloween worthy.

Chance felt a vacant chill, thinking about how the infant had died. Wonder why the authorities hadn't been notified? Not that he had ever thought that much about childbirth, but he could imagine all that could go wrong, given the nature of birth. Adrienne's warm touch at his back interrupted his thoughts.

"Peculiar, don't you think?' she said and gave him a squeeze of the arm.

He nodded. "Wonder how a baby's body could be hidden that long. What's it say, as many as ten years? I mean, wouldn't you notice the smell?'

Adrienne slapped him on the arm.

"I'm just saying," Chance said in mock distress. "Course, it was in the attic. I guess if it was born in the winter. I'll have to ask Nick. He was all caught up in that suicide when I talked to him yesterday. He didn't even mention this case."

Adrienne folded the newspaper. "My first thought was, who had been with the mother when she gave birth? And why didn't she go to the hospital? Was it her first child or the last of many? And how had she felt when she lost it?" She shook her head and sighed, "The endless woes that can happen when women have children."

Here Adrienne's voice faded to a whisper. She had never had children, as far as Chance knew, and rarely ever talked about kids, a circumstance not lost on Chance. Didn't every woman want to have children, at least the ones that got married? He wasn't sure. His ex-wife Stephanie had thrown around the possibility, but they hadn't stayed married long enough to get serious about it.

Adrienne and her ex, both physicians, had devoted their energies to busy medical careers, saving lives and making money, circumstances that she had walked away from when she had retired early to Montana. Kids hadn't been part of it as far as Chance could tell. "You don't talk much about kids," he said. "Did you ever think about having one?"

Adrienne stepped back from him and then chuckled. "You amaze me how you can go from the smell of decomposing fetus to my maternal aspirations in one breath."

Chance cocked his head in that way that always made her smile. "Open mouth, insert foot?" Then with his trademark misdirection, he said, "Here, the chai you wanted is getting cold," he said and slurped his coffee. "See, I'm not a complete brick."

Adrienne took the offered cardboard cup and headed toward her office. "Back in the nineties, I did a stint with Les Sages-Femmes International in sub-Saharan Africa, where beautiful big-eyed babies are fifteen times more likely to die before the age of five than children in our part of the world." She stopped for a second and straightened a couple of sample frames on the wall. "I never got over the delicate balance of life there, and how we take it for granted here."

She continued walking toward her office. "I wasn't much fun at cocktail parties when I got back. We did think about adopting at one time, but Angelina Jolie started getting all that press and I couldn't bare the comparison." She rolled her eyes and sat in her swivel, desk chair, dismissing any hint of further serious conversation. "Did Nick have anything curious to say about the jumper?"

Inwardly Chance was glad to change the subject. He had no interest in making Adrienne's life too introspective. Plus she enjoyed their conversations about Nick's work. She'd actually considered applying for the job of assistant coroner when she heard one of his compadres quit.

Except for the Christmas season, the winter months in Butte meant gallery customers were few and far between. She enjoyed painting but complained the daylight was so short in the winter, and sometimes she got antsy. He didn't think Adrienne needed extra money, but she did enjoy using her noggin. In his own self-interest, he had convinced her that the on-call shifts would be massively inconvenient, especially now they had committed to toothbrushes at each other's places. The last thing he wanted was her getting up in the middle of the night.

So she'd taken an *ad locum* position at the hospital where she filled in a handful of days a month for physicians, who were taking vacation, or on sick leave, and for way more money. As it was, that kept her away from his bed more nights than he liked.

"It's only the second jumper he's ever seen, and pretty mild by comparison."

"How's that?" Adrienne asked. "Splat in the middle of the street is pretty dramatic no matter what."

"That's just it," Chance said, leaning on the doorjamb. "The woman landed on the roof of a car, like an angel according to Nick, no splat, very little blood, only a broken neck."

"How elegant," Adrienne said with a smile. "Still have her glasses on?"

"As a matter of fact, she was wearing some trendy Ray Bans," he said. "What makes you ask that?"

"Saw it on *Inspector Morse* once, you know, PBS mystery show. Ask your grandmother, bet she'll know.

"She'll know what?"

"People who commit suicide by jumping off buildings usually take off their glasses—like they're going to sleep."

Chance shrugged. "Actually, the jury is still out on whether she jumped or not. The touchy part is the victim was Phade's sister."

"The tasty crumpet at the *Mess*?" Adrienne asked. "Mesa's dalliance?"

Chance straightened up, surprised to hear Adrienne talking as though she shared a confidence with Mesa that he didn't. "Her what?" Chance said, only half laughing. "No way."

Adrienne had put on a pair of purple-framed cheaters while she read the paper. "If you say so," she said looking over the glasses at him. "But last time I saw them, they were flirting like a couple of junior high kids."

"Where was I?" Chance said, wondering how he could have missed this.

Adrienne shrugged. "I don't think it's anything serious. I'm just saying…."

The next morning Mesa was thankful that Phade had gotten some sleep. She had left him dozing on the couch, made some coffee, and sat thinking about what their next moves should be. No chance of going back to sleep, finally she had jumped into the shower, aware that she seemed to have more energy than usual. When she pulled open the shower curtain, she had gasped at the sight of him in his Calvin Klein's, holding a large mug at chest height. "Your coffee, milady," he said.

"Get outta here," she had yelled but smiled at the possibility that this bit of lightheartedness might mean that Phade would find a way through the difficult days ahead. That said, she wasn't in the mood for any fooling around. The obsession that came over her, finding an angle for a story, how to attack the problem, had overtaken her. She reminded herself to tread carefully. If she was going to balance the needs of the story with Phade's heartbreak, her approach would have to be delicate.

She dressed and then sat calmly at the kitchen table where the two of them drank coffee. Then Mesa gently broached the subject of the investigation. "Tell me everything the Sheriff said to your parents about your sister."

Phade shrugged—his usual response to most requests. "Only that the police were asking around about what happened, and they'd tell us what they found out, or whatever. The sheriff was pretty chill. Everybody wants to give the cops shit in this town, but Sheriff Solheim has been really cool, especially to my mom and Baba."

Likewise, Mesa had mostly good things to say about Rollie Solheim. Chance liked to call him an old-time peace officer, the strong, silent type. That said, he held regular press conferences and if there was something she really needed to know, she would send Chance who seemed to be able to get more out of him than anybody else.

"He wants us to make official statements. Guess I'll go into the station with my parents sometime today," Phade added, his voice almost monotone.

"Can you think of any reason why Danica would have been up on that roof aside from what everybody seems to think?" Mesa asked, gingerly. She could come up with no logical reason why somebody would go out on the roof of a building unless they had a specific reason. She hated to ask but she had to hear Phade say he didn't know.

Phade shook his head. "I didn't even know people could get up there. Except for Spanky." For Evel Knievel stunt man buddies, all doors were opened.

"I guess they haven't found a note or anything," Mesa said, curiously. She knew that was the obvious indicator that the coroner would look for. But where would a note be if you decided to fly off a building? Could she have mailed one to somebody?

Phade shook his head. "The sheriff said their evidence people would go through her stuff first thing to see if they could figure out what was going on, but I'm thinking he meant to look for a note."

"Where was she staying?" Mesa asked. It would be hard to imagine a woman Danica's age, who had been accustomed to life in Hollywood, would come home to live with her parents, even for a short time. But then, when Mesa had returned to Butte nine months previous, she had stayed with Nana Rose initially.

"She was crashing around the corner at Baba's."

"I thought your grandmother lived with your parents," Mesa said, feeling slightly embarrassed about the police going through Danica's personal belongings, and simultaneously wondering if they could get a look in the house as well.

"She does. But she's never sold her house. She, or Mom, goes over there practically every day. Baba's got this old tabby cat, and it won't stay at our house, so they have to go over there to feed her. Plus it's an extra oven and fridge for holidays. Who knows why? Anyway, that's where Danica was staying."

"When was the last time you talked to her?" Mesa asked. As they talked, it became evident that Phade likely knew more about the comings and goings of his sister than anybody else did. Mesa felt hard-hearted pushing him for answers, but she wanted to get as much background as she could.

Phade stared down at his mug, running his long delicate finger and thumb along the edge of the handle. He sighed and then said, "She texted me yesterday morning. We were supposed to do lunch at that new fish taco place, but she cancelled."

"You have the text?" Mesa asked, wondering if he should show it to the authorities as yet another indication of a more positive state of mind, anything but suicidal.

Phade pulled his iPhone from the back pocket of his jeans which he had thankfully put on. He flipped though the texts and then showed the last one to Mesa. It read:

Hey squirt, something's come up. Rain check on lunch.

Mesa felt a tinge of melancholy. Phade's sister called him *squirt*. The affections of sisters and brothers—it was all too familiar to her. She sighed and said, "You'll want to show that to the police. It sounds like she definitely intended to see you in the future."

Phade's eyes began to tear up, and Mesa put her hands on his forearm. "You have to hang tough, Phade. If we are going to help the police figure out what happened, what you tell them will be key."

He put his hand on hers, nodded, and wiped a tear from his cheek. "But what the hell do I know. I'm so self-centered sometimes, I could puke."

Mesa gave him a gentle nudge to the shoulder. "Don't be lame." She pulled a legal pad out from a stack of books and papers on the table. "Call your parents and find out when you have to be at the police station. I'll get us some more coffee, and then we're going to make a list of all the people you can think of that your sister saw or talked to since she got back to town."

ॐ

Once Phade had left mid-morning, Mesa followed her usual Saturday routine and walked to the office, which was only five blocks away. She had rented the nearby duplex on Granite Street from Chance who had let her move in while he finished the renovation.

The sun was already high in a cloudless sky, blue and big as advertised. She walked down Montana Street, purposely avoiding the Farmers' Market a block further on. Though she had emerged from her three-month funk after the St. Patrick's week events that had led to the capture and arrest of a murderer along with Shane's death, Mesa mostly shunned crowds and continued to cultivate the single life, her flirtation with Phade aside. She suspected her friends were just glad she was well and truly back to some semblance of normal. Work was her refuge, and she liked to check in on the weekend, maybe pick up the snail mail.

At the office, she logged onto the computer and began to read The Mess, the newspaper's blog. Nana Rose wasn't crazy about the name. Mesa had drafted a formal proposal to her grandmother, still the publisher, outlining not only the reasons for devoting resources, particularly staff time—Phade and now Belushi—but also to explain its potential to attract a younger audience to the paper, not to mention the accompanying revenue.

Ultimately, Nan agreed that the primary audience for the blog would not see the abbreviated title as disrespectful but quite the opposite, unlike the readers of the print copy who were much more likely to mirror Nana's age range. She had sighed, but loosened her grip on her ongoing campaign to "raise standards rather than lower them."

Mesa admired her grandmother's philosophy and wanted to do the same. But in the case of the blog, the paper needed to have a cutting-edge web presence, and Phade had been nailing it. Now Mesa wanted to make sure the site didn't falter.

She had begun to make a to-do list for Belushi when the office phone rang. She thought about letting the call go to the answering machine. But most locals wouldn't call, knowing that the office was closed for business on the weekend, especially a holiday weekend. Could be potential out-of-town advertising business, so she answered, "*Mining City Messenger*, this is Mesa Dawson," her voice undeniably cheerful. Not yet a year in the job, Mesa felt proud of the improvements in the paper and wanted to put its best foot forward.

"Thank goodness," came a gravelly voice on the other end. The accent was crisp. "Griffin-Jones here. Vivian Jobe suggested I contact you. I stopped by yesterday and spoke with your assistant as you'd left unexpectedly. When I got back to the hotel, I realized I only had the office number. I wasn't certain of my next move if you didn't answer this call."

Mesa smiled at the Englishman's befuddlement. No doubt he could find his way across London, but plop him in the middle of small town America and he sounded slightly out of his depth. "Not to worry, Mr. Jones, or should I say Mr. Griffin-Jones, the front desk staff would have pointed you in the right direction."

She had forgotten that Jones was staying at the Finlen. Her mind was suddenly awhirl with the prospect of his presence there and the potential access to the scene of Danica's death, not to mention that he sounded extremely pleasant. "How is everything over there, by the way?" she said. "Yesterday was definitely strange, even for Butte."

"So I gather, and please do call me Griff," he said. He cleared his throat and then said, authoritatively, "Apparently the young woman was not staying at the hotel, nor was she a resident. The police inquiries have been primarily to do with how one gains access to the roof and whether those in the building saw the young woman with anyone, or anything else suspicious."

He sounded like a BBC newscaster and she wondered if he was making fun of her, but she was curious about what he said. It suddenly occurred to her that he might actually be helpful, but she didn't want to seem too eager. "I'm sorry to have stood you up yesterday. I hope you'll forgive me, the news, and all that."

"Absolutely, completely understandable," he said. "I was only sorry we weren't able to meet. Vivian spoke so highly of you. She said you might be able to give me a tour of some of the spots you mention in your well written articles—about the houses of ill repute in Butte."

Mesa felt her cheeks reddening, and she was glad she was on the phone. "Why not," Mesa said with sudden enthusiasm. The fact that he seemed to hang on her every word made her slightly fidgety, but an excuse to visit the Finlen's upper floors had suddenly dropped into her lap. "Why don't we start this afternoon?"

ঙ৵৻

"How's Phade coping?" Chance asked when Mesa stopped by Adrienne's gallery on the way to rendezvous with Griffin-Jones. She had hoped to talk to her brother about what he had learned from Nick the night before.

Elbow to elbow at the frame counter, sipping coffee, Chance and Adrienne were never far apart, a situation that no longer bothered Mesa as it once did. In fact, she was now embarrassed to say why she had objected to her brother's relationship with a woman who was fast becoming a pillar of the community.

Re-locating from California where she had sold a thriving but stressful medical practice, Adrienne had purchased and renovated an Uptown building, to the joy of the local urban renewal council. She had opened the Mountain Gallery where she exhibited her watercolors along with a good deal of local art. Her fondness for Butte had even pre-dated her interest in Chance. Adrienne was also a go-to person for info about all things medical. So what if her platinum hair was graying.

"I talked with him this morning," Mesa said, reluctant to share that Phade had appeared at her door at four a.m. "He's on his way to the police station with his parents about now to make their statements. What did Nick have to say?"

"Nothing you wouldn't expect," Chance said and gave a glance Adrienne's way. "It's only his second jumper, so they're taking it slow."

"So they are calling it a suicide?" Mesa asked with a grimace and then challenged, "They haven't found a note or anything, have they?"

Chance shook his head. "Easy, tiger. I misspoke. The only thing that's jumping is me—to conclusions. Hard to imagine, though, why else she would have been up there, you know what I mean?"

"There's no way Phade's family will accept suicide," Mesa countered. "It's majorly verboten in the Orthodox tradition. He says she was glad to be back in Montana, and he hadn't seen any reason that she might be the least bit upset, let alone suicidal."

She took a sip of her brother's coffee, and then said, "Did Nick say anything about personal effects, like her purse or her cell phone? Phade said he got a text from her yesterday morning around ten."

"He didn't mention it," Chance, said taking his cup back. "I think he was trying to shake off the visual of the angel on top of the Jeep. The cops would have started a search right away though, the scene being so open. Of course, you wouldn't catch Nick up on the roof. He doesn't even like to get on a ladder to clean his gutters."

Mesa sighed. The Butte Silver Bow police department saw only a handful of suspicious deaths each year, making their expertise limited. And there would be no budding Sherlock Holmes, only officers with on-the-job training who were recruited for an ad hoc evidence team. She took out her phone and texted Phade to remind him to ask the police when the family could have his sister's effects, especially the phone.

"You can imagine Phade's determined to find out what happened," Mesa continued to update them while she texted. "I had him make a list of everyone in town that she might have had contact with Danica since she came back. That should be manageable since she's only been home for three weeks. I emailed the two of you the list," she nodded toward Adrienne to be sure she knew she was included. "She had an eye for detail that sometimes escaped Chance. She might not know someone's name but she could often describe them down to the tiniest detail.

"Take a look and see if there's anybody on the list you know personally that you could talk to. Or even if you don't actually know them but have seen them around town, that's worth knowing too. That could be helpful. Then we can divvy up who contacts who. Something tells me that whatever detective is assigned to this case could use some help."

Chance saluted, looked at Adrienne who shrugged and then nodded in agreement.

"Sorry," Mesa said right away. "Was I barking orders?"

Chance rolled his eyes, and then said, "No worries. You can't help it if you're a natural born dictator, I mean leader. But let's agree to keep each other in the loop. No going off on wild goose chases," he admonished.

"Promise," Mesa said with a smile. "I knew I could count on you guys." She headed back out the door. "See you later. Nan still needs help putting up the banner out front."

"Where you going?" Chance asked, and put his hands on his hips in faux indignation.

"To the Finlen," she said with a smile. "I've got an inside contact," and left her brother and Adrienne looking curiously at each other.

Outside, Mesa took a deep breath and told herself her energetic attitude came with the perfect summer day, and had nothing to do with the likelihood that she might be onto a decent story. She gazed out toward the East Ridge that bounded the valley. Thanks to a rainy June, the mountain side was green and plush, and she reminded herself to be thankful for the little things.

Then she crossed Park Street, barely avoiding a string of firecrackers some troll tossed from the window of a wide ranging pickup. She did her best not to react, then rolled her eyes and muttered under her breath. "Dumb-asses."

Mesa had mixed feelings about Butte's Wild West attitude as far as fireworks were concerned. Risking fingers and eyes seemed to be a rite of passage for the local kids, particularly little boys, and parents had long ago given up fighting the losing battle since fireworks were legally sold. Dozens of overnight firework stands cropped up at the end of June, five days before the 4th, and would continue through the week. All men, many of them from out of town, seemed to turn into small boys for the duration, including Chance. She had to smile.

♀〜♂

Chance sipped his coffee and watched his sister leave the gallery. After Shane's death, Mesa had withdrawn much as she had done after their mother's death. Only this time, guilt had been intertwined with the grief. She seemed detached at times, but not this morning. "Mesa's definitely high energy this morning," he said.

Adrienne nodded and said, "Isn't that a new blouse she's wearing? That shade of green suits her. Maybe her dark spells are over."

Chance had to agree his sister did seem to be paying more attention these days to how she looked. Now that summer had finally arrived, her wardrobe had morphed from jeans, turtlenecks, and fleece vests to more colorful

T-shirts and shorts. He never knew her to like shopping, but her graceful, slim build allowed her to wear almost anything. He was just grateful that she had finally stopped wearing Shane's old baseball cap all the time.

He smiled when she looked hard at a pickup that had screeched past her while tossing firecrackers into the air. It was a long-standing tradition around the 4th of July, making girls jump out of their skin. Chuckling, he looked over at Adrienne, who was pulling up Mesa's email on her laptop, and made a mental note to stop by Jerry's Firework stand that afternoon for a few bottle rockets and Roman candles.

"There must be thirty names on this list," Adrienne said. "I'll print two copies."

Adrienne was nothing if not organized, which he admired, given his inclination to store his files behind the passenger seat of his truck. "Thirty people in three weeks," Chance mused. "That's probably average for a Butte girl who just got back to town. Let's have a look."

Adrienne handed him one of the copies and said, "Do you suppose Mesa's got herself another cause célèbre?"

Chance shrugged, and thought about Adrienne's question. He valued her counsel when it came to Mesa. Finally he said, "Beats me. When somebody dies under unusual circumstances in this town, seems like everybody takes notice."

"They always seem to come along at holiday time. Wasn't it St. Patrick's Day that Vivian's friend, Dowl Jessup, got killed?"

Chance looked at her quizzically. Vivian Jobe, a close friend of his mother's, had come to Mesa for help in finding an old friend who had ended up dead. It had all started out innocently enough given the crowds that flocked to Butte at holidays. "Lots of people come back to town then. St. Patrick's Day and the 4th of July are Butte's big homecomings. "

"More so than Christmas and New Year's?" Adrienne asked. "I would think that's when relatives would come home to family."

"It's too damn cold to get into that much trouble in December and January." He knew for a lot of people Christmas was the big family gathering. But in Butte's largely Catholic population, those holidays were religious and not a time for shenanigans. That was what St. Patrick's Day and fireworks in July were for.

"So you equate celebration with mischief," Adrienne said—more a statement than a question.

Chance gave her a quick squeeze around the waist and a peck on the cheek, knowing she was teasing him now. She'd seen both holidays for herself. "Well, what's a celebration without letting off a little steam one way or another?"

Adrienne shook her head and pecked him back.

"That's why there's always such a big crowd," he said. "Butte's the only place left that tolerates a little hell-raising. And you never know who will show up or what kind of stupid they'll get into while they're here."

Chapter 4

When Mesa entered the lobby of the Finlen Hotel, she felt like she was stepping into a scene in *Breakfast at Tiffany's*. Its ten-foot ceilings, chandeliers, and marble cocktail tables dwarfed by copper-burnished Corinthian columns, reminded her of some cosmopolitan hotel back east.

She liked to run her fingers along the marble columns simply because she couldn't do it anywhere else. In a town known for its grit and grime, the Finlen Hotel did its best to remind visitors of the glory days when Butte hosted the likes of Lindberg and Roosevelt and, later, Truman and Kennedy.

This Saturday afternoon, even after Friday's excitement, the foyer was strangely quiet. Mesa went over to the hotel desk with its deep green granite panels and asked the clerk to ring Griffin-Jones's room. She took a quick look down the hall toward The Gun Room, the hotel's bar, reconnoitering for a police presence, not that they were likely to answer any questions.

"Mr. Jones asks if you would like to come up," the woman said. Mesa recognized the clerk, a buxom woman with dyed red hair who had worked as a secretary at the high school. "He's in room 211," she added.

Mesa thought for a moment, wondering if she should meet him in the lobby instead. She didn't want to seem overly familiar and fuel what she knew Englishmen often thought about American women, that they were all hot to trot. When she hesitated, the clerk covered the mouthpiece and whispered, "It's a suite."

Mesa nodded and waited for the woman to hang up the phone, and then asked, "It's Mrs. Terkla, isn't it? You used to work up at the high school."

The clerk smiled broadly. "I did indeed. I retired last year, but I got so bored. I don't watch soap operas, and my grandkids are all grown. I started here part-time the first of the year." She broke into a broad smile. "And you're Mesa. Of course I remember you, and Chance, too. I really like what you've done with the *Messenger*. Bet your grandmother is pleased as can be."

Mesa nodded politely. The bigwigs might be making the decisions, but the foot soldiers, on the ground doing the work, were often the ones who really saw what was going on and were willing to talk about it. "Place crawling with police like yesterday afternoon?" Mesa asked in a lowered voice.

Mrs. Terkla looked cautiously to the right and then the left and said conspiratorially, "A couple of detectives talked to the staff that was here and some guests who had recently checked in. They set up tables in the ballroom to do their interviews." She nodded toward the right to the Treasure State Ballroom.

"You were working yesterday?" Mesa said. Mrs. Terkla was the kind of secretary who always remembered exactly what time you arrived at school when you were tardy. If she had witnessed something amiss, you could bet she would squawk. "Did you see the young woman come into the hotel?"

She shook her head. "The police asked me the same thing. I was no help."

"And you were at the desk at about that time?" The clerk nodded. If Mrs. Terkla hadn't seen Danica come through the lobby or from the parking lot to the east, then she had entered from the west side of the building from Wyoming Street. She could simply have walked up the west stairwell.

It's such a shame," Mrs. Terkla was saying. "I thought Danica had a real shot in Hollywood. She was talented and so pretty." Then she shook her head again and said, "Her poor parents."

Mesa nodded, feeling slightly guilty that her sadness about Danica's death was less a concern than her curiosity about what had happened. She could see that the ballroom's double doors were open now, suggesting unfortunately, as Mrs. Terkla said, and that everything was back to normal. A sign on an easel that stood at the edge of the shiny wooden dance floor announced the hours for complimentary breakfast in the morning as usual.

"They've mostly cleared out except for this one detective who's had the manager running back and forth all morning. This place is usually quiet except for festival time. We're not used to all this excitement."

The plump Mrs. Terkla fanned herself with a carry-out menu from the Chinese restaurant on the corner. Mesa nodded and left one of her cards in case the clerk thought of "anything else at all." Then she made her way to the wide marble steps up to the second floor, tracing the same route that Danica likely had taken.

She knew that Mrs. Terkla's assessment was correct. The Finlen's reputation as a quiet and secure environment meant there was no surprise that the forty or so apartments on the top five floors rarely became vacant. When they did, it was usually because the tenant died of old age.

And then the waiting list was long. After all, where else in Butte could you find a place that had a twenty-four-hour desk that handled mail, deliveries, maintenance, and housekeeping if you wanted it, and security. It was ideal for Butte's small community of cautious, usually single or widowed, snowbirds who could happily leave their Finlen apartments without worry and fly down to Phoenix or over to Seattle for the winter. Mesa was glad that Nana Rose had decided to stay put.

She couldn't deny a little energy in her step as she approached Griffin-Jones's room, nestled in the west corner. She knocked twice but not too curtly, to avoid seeming over-eager. "Mr. Griffin-Jones?" she said when the door opened.

Tall, dark-haired, and broad-shouldered like Irita had said, the Englishman wore a denim shirt and khakis that fit his svelte figure so well they had to have been tailored. He nodded ever so slightly at her and then flashed a blinding, mischievous smile. GQ handsome in a rugged sort of way, despite what she guessed were handmade leather high-top shoes, at least his shirt cuffs were turned up.

He offered his hand and said, "At your service, Ms. Dawson. Kind of you to take this trouble. Do come in, won't you. And please, call me Griff." Toothpaste ad smile again. "The blessings of hyphenated names are truly limited, I assure you. I try to downplay it as much as possible."

Mesa smiled and thought how impressed her grandmother would be with his manners. "We do tend to be informal here in Montana, Griff. Call me Mesa."

"It's early," he said, smoothly. "Can I offer you a coffee?"

Mesa hesitated. Part of her wanted to get going, but she was suddenly unsure whether to enlist Jones overtly in her search around the Finlen. Maybe it wasn't such a good idea to mix the personal and the professional.

Seamlessly he took up the slack. "However, I must warn you I woke up feeling like I'm finally over the jet lag. I'm ready for action if you'd like to go," he said and put his fists on his hips.

Truth be known, her early morning tête-a-tête with Phade was catching up with her. She suddenly worried that it might have left her looking ragged. She nodded to the coffee and walked over to the window to check her reflection in the mirror. Then she looked down to Wyoming Street. The white Jeep with its crushed roof had been removed, the shattered glass swept away. She wished she could erase the image of Danica's body as easily.

She returned to the faux suede sofa next to Jones's laptop. His camera lay next to a copy of the *Montana Standard*, the front page of which included a large photo of the hotel with the headline "Woman falls from Finlen." Mesa knew the *Standard*'s current editor did not assign suicides as news stories unless the victim was a public figure, his policy founded in the belief that too much attention might breed copycats. But given the spectacular nature of Danica's death, maybe the editor thought there was more to the story as well. Mesa thought of Phade and his mother and grandmother and hoped someone would keep the paper out of sight at the Draganovich household.

Jones presented her with a paper cup of coffee. "At least it's not Styrofoam," he said and rubbed his fingertips together as if to remove some offending object.

"The excitement yesterday didn't keep you from getting a good night's sleep then," Mesa said, trying not to seem to obvious about picking the Englishman's brain about what exactly the police had done the previous evening. Had they questioned the hotel's remaining occupants, she wondered. Hopefully he would be willing to talk about what he had seen and heard.

The Englishman shook his head. "A certain police presence was evident, if you will, going to and fro in the lobby last evening. Burly plainclothes fellows, badges, and handguns on belts, that sort of thing. Then this morning, a pleasant enough chap came knocking around 10 a.m. Wanted to know my 'wheres and whyfors,' and I told him where I was when events took a turn as it were. He made a note or two and then left me his card. I did receive the obligatory warning in case he had any follow up questions." Jones put his thumbs into the waistband and said, "*Don't leave town without telling me.*" This last statement was made in a lowered tone of voice with a swagger reminiscent of a John Wayne movie.

Mesa smiled again, wondering what impression the officer had gone away with. The Butte Silver-Bow police department's detectives spent most of their effort on casino and convenience store robberies and assaults, mostly domestic blow-ups or bar fights. Throw in an occasional missing person along with the usual DUI's and sporadic drug busts. Suspicious deaths, let alone homicides, were rare.

The only homicides that the *Mess* had covered in Butte, aside from the one that had occurred the day she flew into town ten months before and the arson death on St. Patrick's Day, was a shootout between two crack dealers the previous Thanksgiving. The day the verdict was announced in court, they'd shown up in solidarity. That was the first time she even realized the police department had eight detectives.

She was listening intently and when he finished their eyes met. "Right, then," he said and rubbed his palms together like he was preparing to tackle whatever she had to offer, but wasn't really sure what came next.

When he hesitated, she decided to return the favor and help him along. "I understand you've read about Elsie's Babies."

"Exactly," he said. "As Vivian probably told you, I'm in films, documentaries at the moment. Initially I was thinking about prostitutes in the West, red-light district, that sort of thing. But then I came across a file at the Archives about this woman, Elsa Seppanen, and her black market baby operation. I also read a number of news clippings from over the years, including your recent stories in the *Messenger*, which I'd seen on the Internet before I came to visit. I was hoping to ask you about some of the research you did. The staff at the Archives says you are scrupulous about attention to detail."

His hazel eyes were animated, rolling when he mentioned red lights and then moving side to side, as he continued. Mesa realized she was still focused on his perfectly arranged features when he had stopped talking.

Vivian or Irita could have warned her how good-looking he was.

"Mesa?" he said, his head tilted in her direction as if he wondered if she had heard him.

She cleared her throat and said. "Anything in particular you're hoping to find more about?" Griff seemed genuinely interested in Butte's unique aspects. She decided to combine reconnoitering the hotel with an impromptu walking tour that would interest him while she could touch base with a couple of people on that list she and Phade had put together.

"I was particularly interested in what one of the volunteers at the Archives said. That Elsa Seppanen kept a record of her, if you will, transactions in a small leather-bound ledger which she discreetly wielded when questioned by the judges those few times she was brought to court."

Clearly, Griff wasn't a total fly-by-night. He had learned something key while he was camped out at the Archives. He had grasped what many thought of as the heart of the matter as far as the adult "babies'" search for their parents. She shrugged, not prepared to discuss what she thought until she knew him better. "I questioned a half-dozen people about the notorious little ledger but nothing has come of it."

"Yet?" he said with a grin. "Your article ended rather nicely on that note. Of course, now with DNA tracking, maybe other, possible sources would see the truth is coming out one way or the other? Quite honestly, that sounds like an enormously good hook for a documentary."

She sipped her coffee. Jones's confident, unhurried demeanor made his pitch hard to ignore. Deciding to fuel his imagination, she continued, "My grandmother is fond of saying that, over time, conscience can burn into a person's soul. Maybe somebody will come forward, if in fact the ledger still exists, and if the person who has it realizes the significance of what it might contain."

"Do I surmise correctly that you have a theory about the best place to hunt for this treasure?" He leaned back into the sofa but never took his eyes off her, as if he were searching her expression in case she might give something away.

Mesa was tempted to tease him with a possibility or two but instead she silently strengthened her resolve. Why share her theories with a stranger, even one as charming as Griffin-Jones, at least not yet. He was no more than the latest in a long stream of pseudo-history buffs who like to swoop in and out of Butte. But she didn't want to disappoint him with Irita's more likely conclusion that "Those secrets are going to the grave with the people who've kept them for fifty years."

"Why don't we walk as we talk?" Mesa said to change the subject. "And if you'd like a taste of real Americana, you're welcome to join our family festivities this afternoon. I'm sure my Nan will rustle up a cup of tea for you in between the hot dogs and watermelon."

"How kind," he said with a genuineness that suggested he was curious to see what an actual Montana family was like. "But does this mean I have to eat with my fingers?"

She could tell by the way he rubbed his fingertips together he was only half-joking. "Only if you want to," she said with a smile. She had to admit his Hugh Grant charm with a touch of awkwardness was definitely attractive.

"I'll get my wallet, shall I?" Jones said and went into the bedroom.

Mesa turned her attention to the business card that lay on the table next to the coffee maker. The deep blue city-county seal stared up at her, the city's motto written in silver "The Richest Hill on Earth." Royal Macgregor, Detective Sergeant, a.k.a. "Mac the loner," if memory served, was the officer who had caught the case.

She knew Mac only by sight. His reputation bought him instant street cred in three-fourths of the state, including all of Butte. After four years in the Army, he had come home and decided to enroll at the Montana School of Mines, where he played defensive lineman for the football team that had come up short in the championship game back in the day. Macgregor, who had managed to serve a stint in Desert Storm unscathed, had left the game with an injury that many said had cost the Diggers the game. She'd once heard her grandfather say that the injury to his pride was far greater.

But Macgregor evidently made a decent cop, inspired most likely by his father who had been a Federal Marshal, guys who "always got their man." She had heard Chance say Mac was big and tough, and as age assaulted him, a bit slow, but he put his whole heart into whatever case he was assigned.

She immediately began to think about the best way to approach him. If there was one thing she had learned back East that also applied out West, it was how to treat police officers. The highlight of her first month on the job in Cincinnati as a rookie reporter at the *River City Current* had been the On the Beat program.

The Cincinnati Police Department had instituted the program to improve relations between officers and the media. She had ridden with on-duty cops every night for a week. By the end of the program, she had taken away what her editor confirmed as two important insights that would help her get information out of law enforcement for the rest of her career. First, appreciate that cops have a thankless job that most capable people wouldn't take, and second, smile at them because they take one hell of a lot of crap from the public.

When Jones reappeared, she said, "Mind if we take a quick look from the fourth-floor window in the hallway? I know it might sound a bit gruesome, but this incident yesterday is newsworthy, and we are *here*."

"Not at all, anything to help, in fact," he said with interest. "I understand someone on your staff was related to the victim?" he asked as they left the room.

Clever fellow, this Englishman, Mesa thought. He'd kept his ears open or had asked a few questions himself. She was thinking about how best to thank him when, two steps down the hall, Royal Macgregor came lumbering down the stairs.

He greeted Jones with a nod of recognition and then turned to Mesa. "You're not a hotel guest or a Finlen resident are you?" The words fell unevenly, one here, one there.

Mesa smiled, stuck out her hand, and introduced herself. Then she quickly added, "I'm acting as tour guide for Mr. Jones while he's here in Butte." Okay, maybe that was an exaggeration but she wanted Macgregor to see her presence as something other than a potentially nosey reporter.

"Aren't you also with the *Messenger*?" he asked. He wore a smile but put his arms across his barrel chest while he spoke. "Rose Ducharme's granddaughter."

Mesa nodded and said, "I am," wishing she had been more forthcoming. She had to assume he must have read the *Messenger* since they had never met. She could only hope the paper would stand her in good stead.

"Then you'll know Phadron Draganovich." He made this pronouncement with a solemn tone.

No one used Phade's full first name except his mother and Baba. "That's right," she said, her tone equally somber. She tossed the ball back to his court. "He was hoping to talk to you today. Was he able to get in touch with you?"

Macgregor nodded. "He's going to need a lot of support. These kinds of cases are always hardest on the family. They don't want to believe what's happened," he said, while he pushed his escaping shirttail into his khakis.

"These cases?" Mesa asked, wondering precisely what the detective would call it.

"Suspected suicides," the officer nodded, taking that moment to hike up his pants that seemed to prefer to hang below his beer belly. Like a lot of former football players, most of his growth in recent years had been around the middle. "We're canvassing the surrounding buildings' occupants, as well as the hotel, for witnesses, but it's hard to imagine another outcome at this point."

"When I talked to Phade this morning, he had some pretty strong suspicions otherwise," Mesa said, trying not to sound defensive or accusatory.

"I know," Macgregor sighed. "He mentioned he wants to talk to some of his sister's friends, see what else he could find out. He also said that you were going to help him."

Mesa shifted her gaze to the marble staircase so as not to give away her look of frustration. So that was how the detective knew who she was. Sometimes Phade could be a little too obliging.

"I'll tell you what I told him," the detective said and put his hand into his pants pocket and brought out a palm full of miniature jelly beans. Leaning back on his heels, he tossed a couple of the candies into his mouth.

They were the fancy, gourmet kind they sold at the Front Street market. Based on the color and pungent smell, Mesa guessed them to be orange and lemon.

"You wanna let the police do their job," he said with a slow chew. "If you do come across any new information at all, even minor details, then you need to have Phadron call me right away."

That full name again, it made Mesa shiver. "We'll do that, no problem," Mesa said. She had every intention of cooperating, but somehow she thought she might move a little faster than the detective might and decided not to think about the dilemma that might cause.

"I gotta keep moving," he said and started to walk away. But then stopped and reached out to her with a *one more thing* gesture. "I've handled this kind of thing before. No parents want to believe their child, even a grown one, would have reason enough to kill itself. Be careful you don't encourage the Draganovichs in ways that will only prolong their heartbreak."

She nodded knowingly. His concern for the family, even if it might be misplaced, did seem genuine. Better that, she reckoned, than if he put on a tough guy act, and didn't give a damn one way or the other. Mesa and Jones said their goodbyes and moved toward the stairs, Macgregor's eyes following them.

"Headed upstairs, are you?" Macgregor asked with a sly grin. "Not much to see up there."

Mesa ignored the policeman's last comments, waved, and quickly walked up the stairs past the third floor and on up.

"I thought you wanted to look out the fourth-floor hall window," Jones said with a nervous chuckle. He was signaling backwards with his thumb.

"While we're here we might as well see how far up we can get. I'm curious how the roof is accessed," she said, looking at him with an eye for mischief.

He laughed and said, "Why not. If there's a problem, I have connections at the British Consulate. And will you please stop calling me Mr. Jones. You make me seem far stuffier than I am. Griff will do," he said, huffing between the last few words.

"Americans like stuffy. You know, *Downton Abbey*, Maggie Smith? It's really big here in the States." She was teasing him, of course, but she didn't want him to get cold feet. Sixth floor and they hadn't seen a soul, not that she would have expected to. By now, any residents would have been well on their way to enjoy the spectacular summer day. She realized that was what she could be doing with good old Griff.

"British Consulate, eh? Never know, could come in handy," she bantered comfortably. "My gran really will enjoy meeting you."

They came to the ninth floor where the steps ended in the middle of a long hallway with deep red carpet. Only a large wall mirror, hand painted with a lassoing cowboy silhouette, brightened the passage. All the dark brown doors had numbers on them save one, down from the mirror, which had a red and white sign on it:

Roof Access. Authorized personnel only. Mesa turned the handle. "Damn," she said. The door was locked. "Wonder if there's another way up?" she muttered, only half to herself. She walked the length of the floor but saw no other access.

"You're really enjoying this, aren't you?" Griff said, his smile broad.

"My employee, as the detective calls him, is a valuable one and also my friend. I promised to do what I can to help him. Plus, as Gran would say, I can be a bit of a Nosey Parker."

Griff laughed again. "Likewise. Where do we go next?"

Mesa had to smile. Griff was turning out to be the quintessential Englishman—witty, polite, and game. She reminded herself he was only in town a few days and then tried not to think about Nana's inevitable matchmaking efforts for rear she'd begin to blush.

"Let's take the elevator down." She wanted to check inside it, on the odd chance the last stop was in fact the roof. No luck there. As she pushed the elevator button that would take them back to the lobby, Mesa let the impact of the last few minutes take hold. The specter of suicide had all but faded.

Danica would have had to have access to a key to get to the roof, or was with someone who did. Whoever had that key, or had given it to her, was likely the last person to see Danica Draganovich alive. And that was the person Mesa wanted to find.

❧

"We're not going to ride the little red trolley?" Griff had said with mock disappointment when she had announced she would be giving him a walking tour of the city. The Chamber of Commerce's revamped Butte trolley car, painted bright red and green with gold accents, was a convenient and popular attraction. But Mesa had her own agenda that included a different set of stops.

Phade's call came moments after Mesa and Griff had reached the corner of Broadway and Wyoming. When the caller ID on her phone popped up with Phade's name, she quickly resigned herself to the fact that her conversation would be extended. Just as she realized she needed someone to occupy Griff, Adrienne's gallery came into view. Mesa quickly readjusted. The first stop would have to be the Mountain Gallery. Griff would enjoy Adrienne and her artwork. She would enjoy his charm.

Listening to Phade's frantic description of the meeting with his family and the police, she steered Griff into the Gallery on Park Street. Using hand gestures and exaggerated whispers, she explained to him and then Adrienne that she needed to talk to Phade. With the smoothness Mesa was beginning to admire, Griff moved off with his newfound guide to look at the paintings in the far corner of the gallery while Mesa retreated to the back office.

"All my parents can talk about is how this can't be a suicide because we won't be able to have a service for Danica in the church," Phade said, his voice taut with tension.

Mesa was not surprised to hear this, given the Orthodox Church's traditional position on many of life's

edgier moments. At least now she could argue more
solidly that Danica might not have been up on that roof
alone. What that meant might not necessarily be any
more comforting, but at least that fact offered the
possibility of an alternative to suicide.

Phade's voice was rising, his mood even more
distraught. She had to interrupt him to tell him what she
had learned about the access door to the roof. "Did your
sister know anybody who works at the Finlen, anyone
who could help her get access to the roof?"

"Not that I know of," Phade said. "I know she went
to The Gun Room for drinks one night when she first
got back into town."

The Gun Room was a popular hangout, one of the
few upscale bars in uptown. But it didn't open until four
in the afternoon, so Danica could not have talked to
anyone on the premises the day she died.

"She could have known one of the bartenders
there," Phade said. "I'm not sure. I'd have to think about
it."

Mesa wanted to keep him thinking, as he seemed to
calm down when she asked him to give her details. "Tell
me what the cops had to say. Did they mention anything
about her personal items, you know, like her purse and
her cell phone? Did they find a key? What about her
car?" Mesa realized she was firing questions at him.
Jesus, he was a grief-stricken brother. She needed to dial
it down a notch.

"It was a Toyota. I told them what she was driving
when I identified her body. They found it yesterday
afternoon. At least, I was able to do that much." He
sounded really deflated. "They haven't found anything in
it."

Mesa sighed. He sounded so low it made her nervous. She had seen his mood swings first hand, and knew his tendency to brood all too well. "Where did they find the car?"

"On Washington Street next to the Mother Lode. Guess she went into work yesterday morning."

"Did the cops say who they talked to at the theater? That's somebody we should talk to as well. Who specifically was she working for? It might be worth tracking them down."

"She didn't exactly have a boss. I mean, the theater board hired her, but she kinda worked on her own. It's a small setup."

Mesa thought about the dogged, little theater community in Butte, always scrambling for money. The Mother Lode, despite the splendor of its venue, staged only a few productions on its own each year, opting to bring in touring groups like the Moscow Ballet or a regional company of a Broadway play or musical. God love them for trying to bring some culture to town, her grandmother would say.

Meanwhile, the Orphan Girl, a children's theater which was also housed in the Mother Lode building, mounted several productions a year and a theater camp. The director had to be both teacher and fundraiser. Previous directors had worked their butts off fundraising. Add to that casting and directing a couple dozen local kids and turning them, and hopefully their parents, into lovers of the arts and you had a tall order. And a recipe for burnout in Mesa's estimation, which was no doubt, why the position seemed to become vacant every couple of years.

Danica had taken on a job where she had to work independently, relying on volunteers she'd have to recruit to make the program work. Ultimately, it was the Theater Board, through its managing director, that she answered to. Most likely on a day like Friday, work would have been fairly minimal, since Danica had literally only been on the job for two weeks, and it was a holiday weekend. "Can you think of anybody in town who might have helped her get the lay of the land?" Mesa asked Phade who had gone silent on the phone.

"The last thing I remember, she was talking about a couple of old trunks of costumes she needed to go through." Again his voice was muted as if remembering their last conversation was painful. Then his voice gained some energy. "She did say she would talk things over with Hal." He paused, and then added by way of explanation, "her old drama teacher."

"From Butte High?" Mesa said her voice crackling with surprise. "Hal Winslow is still around?" She had fond memories of Mr. Winslow, the proverbial gay drama teacher, who had had the good grace to ignore the snickering of several decades of high school students and produce a couple of plays a year, mostly musicals.

He'd cemented his reputation—and fended off veiled homophobic criticism—by routinely clearing a profit from his high-quality productions, which allowed him to fund his program. When he had retired, the district school board had let the program die. She had assumed, sadly, that Mr. Winslow had, too.

"He bought that Piano Bar on Hamilton Street," Phade said. "He was the one who told Danica about the Orphan Girl job."

Chapter 5

Mesa finished her call and emerged from the Gallery office to a burst of laughter from Adrienne and Griff. They were leaning on the framing counter like bookends. Mesa felt obliged to apologize for the way she'd thrown them together.

"Don't worry," Adrienne said to Mesa softly. "Phade's in the midst of a crisis, and lucky to have your help. Besides, Griff seems to have a genuine interest in art of the American West. His family owns a Charlie Russell," she said with eyebrows raised.

"It's in one of the hunting lodges on the estate," he added with a wink.

Adrienne shot a knowing smile at Mesa and then added, "I gave him a quick tour of Butte on canvas."

"Well done, it was," the Englishman chimed in. "But I do feel badly for your friend. If it's inconvenient, Adrienne assures me I can hop on the trolley and continue my tour from there."

"No, no," Mesa said. She wasn't ready to let go of her Finlen Hotel contact yet. "To be honest, having you along is actually helpful. Showing a stranger around town is an ideal entrée. And I've got a few more stops to make."

"How's Phade holding up?" Adrienne asked. "Any revelations from his meeting with the police?"

Mesa shrugged. It was reassuring that Adrienne was so sympathetic to Phade's situation. She could be a solid counterweight if Chance took an attitude about Mesa's getting too involved. She explained about the roof access and how finding out who helped Danica get up there was a priority.

"The detective did find out that she was at work at the theater yesterday. I thought we'd wander over there next and see if anyone's around who might have talked to her."

Adrienne tapped an ad in the *Standard*, which was open on the counter. "Looks like this evening is the Yankee Doodle Sing-along," she said, and turned toward Griff and explained. "Patriotic songs performed to clever tableaus. Think big hair in red, white, and blue." Then to both of them, she said, "I would think there are all sorts of people around in the throes of last minute preparations."

Mesa grimaced. She had not a dramatic bone in her body, at least none suited to the stage, and the idea of being there in some over-the-top costume almost made her hyperventilate. Griff, however, seemed imperturbable, standing patiently in sartorial splendor, his hands clasped together in front of him. She felt his eyes on her while she and Adrienne talked.

She noticed he must have traded his three-hundred-dollar high-top wingtips for a pair of newly purchased navy Vann's when he had ducked into his bedroom. This attempt to downplay his appearance did make him seem less formal, and even more endearing. Nevertheless, he could easily have graced the cover of *Country Life Magazine.*

"It's a lovely historic theater that's been renovated," Mesa added with a smile. "It's even on the trolley route," though she hoped they didn't run into a busload of tourists.

"By all means, let's take it in," he said. Then he turned toward Adrienne and said, "It's been a delight talking to you, Dr. DeBrook. I'll look forward to seeing you again," and then he looked at Mesa and gestured toward the door with his hand. "Shall we?"

He offered his elbow and Mesa took it. They headed for the door, and Mesa, looking over her shoulder at Adrienne, said, "Cheerio."

‍৩৩৩

Chance had just pulled up in the Land Rover and entered the side door of the Gallery in time to hear the front door's bell clang as someone departed. It was nearly 2 p.m. and he hoped to convince Adrienne to close up shop early. One of the perks of owning your own business, especially a gallery, was that you could close any damn time you wanted. Or at least he thought that was a perk. He had made Adrienne a *Gone Fishin'* sign but had yet to get her to use it.

"You just missed Mesa," she said. "She's picked up this good-looking young Englishman somewhere, some kind of documentary film maker. Very charming," she said, the emphasis clearly on the *very*.

"Thought she was devoting herself to Phade and finding out what happened to his sister." That sounded a bit more self-righteous than he meant. He wanted to help

Phade, too, but he felt uneasy that Mesa might become overly invested in someone else's problems. The last time that had occurred, disaster had followed soon after.

"She is," Adrienne said calmly. "And get that worried tone out of your voice. This kind of story is what she needs. She feels useful."

"Good thing. I hear Royal Macgregor got assigned the case. He's slower than the spring thaw."

"I wouldn't think that any of the detectives have that much experience with sudden deaths beyond hit and runs or maybe a drug overdose," Adrienne said, offhandedly. "That's one of the reasons people like me move back to Montana—to get away from big-city crime."

Chance walked over to the water cooler and poured himself a quick cup and then another. The temperature outside was a balmy seventy-five degrees, and it was all he could do to be inside. "So what's with this Englishman?"

"He's considering the prospects of making a film about Butte's era of prostitution. He was telling me all about the *Messenger* office. I didn't realize the Cleveland Building was part of the Red-light district."

Chance rolled his eyes. "That's old news."

"Anyway, Mr. Jones is staying at the Finlen," Adrienne said, with a crisp, articulated pronunciation, "and Mesa went over there to meet him. They did a little reconnoitering. Mesa even made it up to the ninth floor. Apparently, a locked security door is the only access to the roof. She thinks Danica might have had a key, or was with someone who did. Can you think of anybody who works at the Finlen who might have that kind of access?"

"Wow," Chance said. "That throws a wrench into the suicide theory. Somebody else might have been up there with her." He started thinking about the hotel and if it might be possible to spot someone on the roof. Maybe someone had seen Danica and the person she might have been with.

"Has she talked to Phade about this?" he asked, and went over to the frame counter and started scanning the list of Danica's friends that Mesa had sent them.

"He called, fraught with angst about the police's use of the phrase 'suspected suicide'. His family is frantic to have some other explanation, but Phade has no idea about any key. He did mention that his sister had been working with a man named Winslow—retired teacher? Mesa's gone off to the Mother Lode to see if she can locate him."

"Hollywood Hal, eh? He should be a fountain of information. The guy must have a photographic memory. He probably knows the words to every Broadway show tune ever written."

Adrienne laughed. "What do you know about Broadway musicals?" she teased. "I can't imagine you'd be caught dead whistling 'There's no business like show business'."

Chance smiled. "Wrong. I played the Tornado in the *Wizard of Oz* one year. I had one line—*Whoosh!*" he said and made a quick circle around Adrienne and then grabbed her around the waist. "One of my buddies in high school though, Emmett Mallory, he was in all the musicals. They did *Music Man* one year, and he swore that Winslow knew the whole thing by heart."

∽∾

The distant notes of "A Grand Old Flag" filtered out on Park Street, and Mesa and Griff followed the music into the Mother Lode through the front double doors that were propped open. The red velvet upholstery and carpet in the lobby made for a perfect back drop for the red, white, and blue signs advertising the evening's performance of the Yankee Doodle Sing-along.

The foyer was empty so Mesa walked toward the right aisle entryway and looked inside. Her grandmother attended every production there, and Mesa had accompanied her many times as a teenager. The theater itself was dark, but the stage was lit. Several people were working on a set piece that included a gigantic Statue of Liberty with symmetry problems. She thought she would know Hal Winslow on sight, but none of the three men on stage looked familiar.

"Let's go down front," she said to Griff who was oohing and ahhing, muttering about the fantastic "Beaux Arts façade" and the theater's monumental columns. She nodded politely and promised to have Chance fill in the history of the theater. When she reached the proscenium, she realized Mr. Winslow was there, only a bit grayer than she remembered.

She motioned to Griff to sit down in one of the plush red velvet seats. "Take a load off," she said and wiped a thin layer of sweat from her forehead, a rare occurrence even in summer. In July's long days of sunlight and without windows, the auditorium created as large a hothouse as was likely to exist in Montana.

"That's our man holding up the Statue's arm. As soon as they take a break, I'll see if I can corral him."

She realized Jones was smiling at her again. "What?" she said, feeling self-conscious.

"These Western phrases," he said with a chuckle, "You really talk like that, don't you? It's not affected at all. It's quite charming," he added when she grimaced at him. He quickly changed the subject.

"The architecture in this town is really quite like nothing I've seen in the States," he said.

"A lot of it is from the turn of the early twentieth century," Mesa explained. "It's what a lot of America looked like before strip malls and Wal-Mart and Starbucks came along and built over it. Butte just didn't tear any of its old buildings down. We're waiting for the renaissance."

Griff nodded, "Well done. I look forward to seeing more of it."

"Is there anything in particular you'd like to see?" she said, trying to fill the wait time as Hal Winslow was still overseeing the set problems. "We've gotten a bit off the beaten path of the red-light district, but we can go back. Nothing is too far away."

Griff had stretched his long legs in front of him and turned to look at her for a long second, as though he had something serious on his mind. "Hamilton Street, the building where Elsa Seppanen had her office. I'd like to take a look at that."

"Absolutely," Mesa said, remembering Griff's questions about Elsie's Babies and the ledger. "Right after we're done here, that can be our next stop." She still hadn't worked out how serious he was about that story.

Then she saw Hal Winslow walking off stage and she called to him. Griff leaned in close to say he would take some photographs of the façade and the lobby and meet her there when she was finished. "Mr. Winslow," she called again, and Griff squeezed her elbow and walked back up the aisle.

Winslow moved toward Mesa's voice, then stopped at the curtain, stage left, and looked out. She trotted up to the stairs at the edge of the stage and said in a whisper. "I am sorry to interrupt, but could I speak to you for a few minutes? It's about Danica Draganovich."

His shoulders sagged when he heard Danica's name. Then he said, "I'm sorry. Do I know you?"

Mesa introduced herself and then said, "I'm Phade Draganovich's boss at the newspaper."

"You wrote that editorial in June about supporting the Pride parade," he said, his tone softening. "That was certainly a breath of fresh air, someone advocating celebration of diversity as opposed to simply tolerating it."

Mesa suspected Hal was a member of the PFLAG group in town, who had organized the parade. She had thought long and hard about what she wrote and hoped people in the group had read it.

"Phade and his family are trying to come to grips with what's happened," Mesa said, wanting to stay on point. "Finding out as much about Danica's last few days might give them some peace of mind. I understand she spoke with you yesterday?"

He nodded curtly, called to one of the men on stage that he would take a short break. "I'd rather not talk out here."

"I don't suppose Danica had an office or a particular place in the building where she hung out, so to speak?"

Hal nodded. "Danica's office is downstairs where it's a lot cooler. Let's go down there," he said and then motioned to the exit at the bottom of the aisle. She followed him out of the theater and through a narrow corridor to stairs off the main stage.

As they walked, he took the navy bandana from around his neck and wiped the sweat from his brow and his closely trimmed graying hair. Mr. Winslow was more handsome than she remembered with his styled haircut and his hundred-dollar Western shirt. He had aged well and looked more relaxed in retirement.

They went down two short flights of stairs, walked a few yards and through a half open door into a windowless, low ceiling room. It was hardly more than a large dressing room, closer than Mesa might have liked, and still stuffy. Winslow motioned for her to sit in a wooden folding chair. He sat in an overstuffed armchair at the small desk, reaching to turn on a small fan that was rigged above it.

Mesa took a deep breath and forced herself to focus on the items on the desk so the gnawing sense of claustrophobia would not increase. She could see a copy of the *Standard* tossed on what looked like a stack of applications for drama camp. A small calendar was pinned to a corkboard on the wall, several notations in red ink. She pulled her reporter's notebook out and began making notes of what she saw.

"How is her family doing?" Winslow asked, his blues eyes questioning.

Mesa described the distress of her meeting with them yesterday and then explained their concern about the possibility that Danica's death might be called a suicide. "What do you think about that?"

He sighed, and undid the top couple of buttons of his plaid shirt to a reveal a red tee with the words "I'm gay. Get used to it." emblazoned boldly. His expression grim, he said, "The police asked the same thing. They were here yesterday afternoon. I'll tell you what I told that Detective Macgregor."

Mesa could tell by his tone of voice that the officer had not inspired much confidence.

"Danica Draganovich was as full of life as anybody I know. She might have had some issues. Who doesn't? But she certainly wouldn't have jumped off a building for God's sake." He slapped his thigh with these last words.

"No, no, Phade doesn't think so, and neither do I. As a matter of fact, I think someone else might have been up on that roof with her," Mesa said quickly. She could see that Hal Winslow was upset, more than she had expected. "Phade says that you encouraged Danica to come back to Butte to take the job at the Orphan Girl. Did you talk to her often? Were you close?"

Winslow's expression softened and he looked at her over his trendy narrow glasses, much like the pair Phade wore. "As close as any drama teacher can get to a beautiful female student and not get in trouble for it," he said with a wink. "She used to tease me and call me Auntie Hal." He dabbed at the corner of his eye with the bandana.

Mesa smiled and patted his arm. "I'm sorry to upset you but if Danica's death is something other than a suicide or an accident, the sooner we find out what could have happened and who might have been up there with her, the closer we'll get to figuring out who is responsible."

Winslow sat back and glared at her. "What are you saying? Do you think somebody pushed her?" His voice rose on the last words.

"I'm saying that the only way up to the Finlen's roof is through a locked door and there's been no indication that Danica had a key. That means most likely, someone knew she was up there, or even went up there with her. We don't know yet. That's why it's important that you try to remember whatever she might have said to you in the past two weeks, particularly yesterday. Anything out of the ordinary that happens around a sudden death could be relevant. Was there anything or anyone in town that she talked about that might have had something to do with what happened?"

Winslow crossed his arms in front, rocking forward, hugging himself. But he said nothing.

Mesa sensed he had something to say but somehow felt he shouldn't. She decided to push, but gently. "We need to know what was on Danica's mind. You said she had issues. What did you mean by that?"

Winslow concentrated on turning up the cuffs of his shirt, gathering his thoughts. Maybe he was deciding if he could confide what he knew. It was all Mesa could do to allow the silence to linger, but he wasn't the only one who understood the power of the dramatic pause. Finally, he spoke.

"You know, Danica played the lead in half the productions we staged during her last three years in high school," Winslow began in a quiet voice. "She spent more hours in rehearsals and production with me than any other student. No teacher spent as much time with her. But her parents barely ever said more than a passing hello to me. I didn't really care, but it tells you how conservative they are. Don't get me wrong, I respect another person's religion, and I think her family is well-meaning people. But suicide, being gay, anything to do with sex really, even the theater was pushing the edge for them. That's why she had to get out of Butte for a while."

"Why do you think she finally decided to come back then?" Mesa asked. That seemed like an important question. Not that Danica's leaving was particularly unusual. Mesa understood her Butte rat friends who had spent their childhoods growing up here, and then felt like they had to get away. But it was usually not for long. Say what you want about the old mining town, the place was like no other, and the pull to come back was magnetic.

"Don't get me wrong. She loved her family and Montana," he said and then explained that, nevertheless, after she had finished two years at the U of M in Missoula, she had transferred to a California school. She had emailed him from time to time, letting him know how she was doing. After graduation, she had decided to stay and try to make it in the film business. "She had to take some risks somewhere else, where her family wouldn't worry, or even worse, feel ashamed. I guess she had done what she needed to do."

"She went to L.A., right?" Mesa asked. "What did she do there? What kind of work did she get?"

He chuckled and described how he had actually gone to visit her one summer. She was living in Studio City in what he described as the real-life version of *Melrose Place*. Four beautiful girls living in a tiny bungalow, they went to endless auditions for soap commercials, making ends meet by waitressing while they waited for the big break that never came.

"Story's as old as Myrna Loy, but I could understand, because I went through my own version of it years ago, only in New York." He sighed and rolled his eyes. "I was going to take Broadway by storm. But let me tell you, honey, you don't want to squash anybody's dreams."

The more Winslow talked, the more Mesa liked him. She had had her own dreams, still did—big-city journalism, Pulitzer Prize. But she knew how changes in the newspaper business, the technology, not to mention life events, could get in the way. "Was she hooking up with anybody?"

Winslow shrugged. "She hinted at someone a time or two when we were having one of our late-night phone chats after a couple of glasses of wine. A guy from around here, but she was always so coy about it. I never got a name."

Mesa was scouring the bulletin board behind Hal while he talked. "Looks like she had a card from somebody there." Mesa pointed to the postcard with a group of thatched huts on stilts, spreading out into an azure bay trimmed with white sand. It looked like paradise.

Winslow turned and pulled the pushpin from the card. He looked at the back and then said, "Oh, that's from one of Danica's old high school friends. She's a missionary in Africa somewhere."

"May I?" Mesa said and reached forward, resisting the urge to grab it from his hand. She could feel her curiosity growing and told herself to calm down, remembering Macgregor's caveat.

Winslow hesitated and then said, "I don't see why not. The police didn't even ask about her office." He handed her the postcard.

The handwriting on the back of the card was large and swirling, a combination of lower and upper case.

"It's a long way from Butte, but it's not bad. Email me, and don't let any of those kids break a leg!" It was signed Chloe and dated about the time Danica would have reached Butte. "Name's not familiar," Mesa said.

"Chloe Hardcastle?" Winslow said. "She's another Butte girl, one of the few I never corralled into one of my productions."

"Right," Mesa said, handing the card back. The surname did ring a bell, but she couldn't quite remember why. It hadn't been on the list Phade had made. She wrote the name in her notebook to ask him if he knew the name. "You were saying that Danica had tried to break into the film business but was unsuccessful. What kept her in California?"

Winslow crossed his legs, hands webbed at his knee and settled back into the chair, talking easily now. "Eventually her little set went their separate ways, finding real jobs. Danica got work as an assistant to an assistant producer and moved into production work. That's what led her back here. She had so many plans for this little place. Couldn't wait to start work with all the little ones."

"And the issues followed her?" Mesa spoke quietly, hoping her tone suggested a degree of confidentiality.

Winslow looked at her, tilting his head toward her. He sighed and then took off his glasses. "I don't know that it really matters anymore, but it's always bothered me." He paused, and then looked pointedly at her. "I want you to swear that what I say next never gets into the paper. I'm only telling you in case it might help her brother to understand."

Mesa found these moments awkward. She was not inclined to write exposés of local citizens, so she said what she always said to people who didn't want to see what they considered sordid details in the *Messenger*. "Mr. Winslow, we're not a tabloid. The *Messenger* doesn't print stories to be titillating or for the sole purpose of ruining someone's reputation." It was a hedge, but most people were satisfied by it. The truth was that if distasteful, but accurate, details were needed to get to the truth of a story, she wouldn't hesitate to mince words.

"The summer that I went to see her, I was in a relationship with a guy who wanted to have children. We decided to find a surrogate. Danica was the one person I thought I could truly trust. He was gorgeous like her, and they would have made beautiful babies. Back then, even in California, that was tricky business, but I approached her to see if she would do it."

Mesa's mouth dropped open. She couldn't hide her shock. "Did she agree to help you?"

Hal paused for a moment and then said, "Well, obviously I wouldn't have asked her if I didn't think she might say yes." Then he stared at his fingernails, all ten spread out before him "Danica loved children, and I had told her it was one of my dreams. I think she was willing to do it because it meant so much to both of us.

"When was this?" Mesa asked, wondering how that would have gone down with her conservative family. She might be doing a good deed in the eyes of some, but for others, her involvement might be construed as a major religious no-no.

Winslow paused, calculating mentally. "I wanna say 2005. It was when she was still struggling to make ends meet. We were going to pay her, as well as all her expenses, while she was carrying the baby. The money would have been enough to pay her rent for a good year or more. She was definitely considering the idea, but it wasn't to be."

"What happened?" Mesa asked, admiring Danica's ability to have a close relationship with someone whose lifestyle was so far on the other end of the spectrum. She was nonjudgmental all right.

"She called me and said she couldn't do it. Initially I thought it was because of her family. Open-minded as she was, I thought maybe she had gotten cold feet because she was afraid they wouldn't approve if they found out. But she made a point of telling me that wasn't it. She'd gone to the fertility clinic for the initial round of testing and found out she wasn't a viable candidate."

Mesa considered how healthy and vibrant Danica had looked. "Wow. That must have been a surprise. What was the problem?"

"She didn't exactly say, only that she'd had an infection at some point previously that had scarred her female parts."

"So they said she was infertile?" Mesa wondered out loud.

Winslow shrugged. "I guess so. It was more medical explanation than I wanted to know, really. But I was worried about Danica because she was clearly upset. When Anthony and I went to the clinic for our appointment, the nurse practitioner explained that the problem was irreversible and that we would have to look for another volunteer."

He stopped there, looked around dramatically, and then said, "She told us that Danica couldn't ever have children."

Chapter 6

Mesa gasped imperceptibly. She hadn't considered the possibility that Danica might have health problems. Could that have contributed to some depression that no one, not even Phade, knew about? Mesa wondered how to broach the subject of his sister's health or how they might get her medical records. She would have to talk to Adrienne. "So you didn't really get to hear the cause of her infertility?" Mesa asked.

Winslow shook his head. "It was an emotional conversation. She knew I was disappointed, and of course, I didn't feel right pressing her. Trust me, she wasn't acting. Something happened to that girl, and she had lost her ability to bear children. You could see the heartbreak in her eyes."

"Did she give you any indication that she knew what might have caused the condition?" Mesa asked, trying to imagine the shock of learning such news and how it could upend her world.

Hal shook his head. "Again, I didn't feel like I should pry. If she did know, she hid it well."

"How about any health problems she might have had in the past?" Mesa said, trying to remember Danica's birth date, the math that might shed light on when something awful might have happened. All she could think of was the STD pamphlets at the doctor's office. Herpes, chlamydia, couldn't one of them lead to sterility? She felt slightly irresponsible that she didn't know. Not that she was having unprotected sex, or any other kind, for that matter.

"I don't know that she'd ever been in the hospital," he said and then he sat up, slapping his hands on his knee. "I need to get back upstairs." Then he added, "In the end, it was for the best. Anthony and I broke up the next year and I met Walt, my partner now, the year after. I was too old to be a dad anyway. Any parental instincts I have, I lavish on our pair of Scotties." He smiled, stood up, and then said, "I'm glad we talked. If I can be of any help, don't hesitate to get back in touch."

Mesa smiled and stood up as well. So Danica had considered acting as a surrogate. Now that was a departure from the Orthodox Church's teaching. What could have made Danica consider such a thing, even if it hadn't worked out?

Taking another look at the desktop, Mesa noticed a part of the *Standard* had been torn away. She made a note of the page number, and then gave Winslow a card as he led the way out the office. She followed him back into the hallway and said, "And if you think of anything else that might help, please call me anytime. I'm working on this round the clock, holiday, or no."

They walked back upstairs into the auditorium where she could see Griff hovering near the entrance to the aisle. When she reached the Englishman, he pulled her out into the lobby and to a wall of photographs of the Mother Lode's staff. Mesa's heart sank when she saw the newly framed head shot of Danica Draganovich, director of the Orphan Girl Theater.

"Is this our victim?" he asked. He pointed to the photo of a brunette woman in a soft white blouse with stylish shoulder-length hair, dark eyes, high cheekbones and a killer smile. The resemblance to Phade was haunting. Mesa nodded, not looking forward to telling him what she had learned.

"No wonder she went to Hollywood," Griff muttered. "She's stunning, really drop-dead gorgeous." Then he gasped and said, "That was the most unintended pun. I am so sorry. That said, I can't believe she didn't get snapped up by some auteur."

Mesa thought about this. It did seem surprising that Danica had not left a trail of broken hearts, not even in Butte. Maybe she had in L.A.

Admirers of good-looking young women like Danica in a town the size of Butte could not have escaped notice. Phade might have been too young to pay attention. She needed to talk to Irita who was always good for a steady stream of what Mesa liked to call historical gossip. Irita could always remember who dated who. Maybe Danica's issue, or the cause of it, was still in town.

Mesa and Griff headed back out into the sunny, blue sky, where she found herself taking his arm again. Oddly, she felt the need to be close to another human being, as if the knowledge of the sad news that Danica brought home with her was too much to bear alone, at least in that moment. Griff stopped and looked at her, obviously sensing the change in her mood. "Are you all right?" His voice sounded protective. "Did you learn something upsetting?"

Mesa tugged his arm, but said nothing. Just as quickly, the moment passed, as if his acknowledgment of her humanness was enough. She shrugged it off and said, "Not really. Some stories are tougher than others." Then she pulled him across the street.

She fell into an easy banter then as they walked, guiding him along the scenic route up Idaho Street on the way to Elsa Seppanen's former office. They passed the once-prosperous Presbyterian Church where Griff had stopped to take photographs of the rose window and discuss the use of abandoned churches at the Edinburgh Festival. Every time he looked at her with that sincere gaze, she became a little more comfortable. Not only was he handsome, she felt an intellectual attraction, which she rarely found in a guy.

They moved on to the Copper King Mansion a few minutes later. Mesa was describing its new paint job and the bed and breakfast's return to its former glory when she got a text from Alexis:

Where the hell r u? The party's started and I can only drink so much tea. Plus Phade is here asking for you.

Mesa felt the mood disappearing, and texted back,

Pick up in 15?

and gave Alexis the Hamilton Street address of Elsa Seppanen's onetime office.

Griff was suitably impressed by the gaudy Victorian mansion, but by the time they passed the Courthouse, Mesa could see he was focused on the Elsie's Babies story. In the final two blocks, he had asked her a dozen questions. "So only two of all these babies that Elsa Seppanen delivered and then sold have ever found their birth parents or any relatives. That's an amazingly well-kept secret."

"Now it's three," Mesa said and she expected there could be more. She fully intended to revisit the story. Initially, she had used the occasion of the anniversary of *Roe v. Wade* back in January to write a feature about Elsa Seppanen. And hard writing it was.

Quoting from the Berton Braley poem that described Butte, "Her faults and her sins are many to injure her fair repute," Mesa acknowledged that many readers would find the story uncomfortable. Unquestionably, Elsie was a controversial figure in Butte's past. But the more Mesa had learned about the nurse turned chiropractor, abortionist, and seller of babies, the more she was determined to write a balanced story.

"The research was fascinating and heartbreaking," she told him. Thirty-one known abortionists had operated in Montana during the period from statehood leading up to the Supreme Court decision in 1973. Elsie had offered poor and socially ostracized women who couldn't raise another child, whether for economic or social reasons, an alternative. Mesa felt the label of black marketer was too harsh.

True, Elsie had taken money for the babies she delivered into the hands of willing, adoptive parents who were desperate enough to never reveal the baby's origins. But Elsie also took the risks. Not to mention, more than twenty babies had been saved from the orphanage or, worse, from mine shafts, sinkholes, and wells where the bodies of unwanted babies were routinely dumped by desperate women in Butte.

The medical people, typically those on the periphery of the profession—chiropractors, naturopaths, and midwives—who had performed abortions, garnered the respect as well as the silence of the people they helped, at least privately. "Seppanen's clients had every reason to protect her," Mesa had written. "For the babies, the adoptive parents, and the mothers that felt they had no other choice but to give up their babies, she was their last resort."

While Seppanen was also reviled publicly by some for her unethical practice of adopting out the babies she delivered for a fee, complete with falsified birth certificates, no one had complained at the time. As far as Mesa could find out, most people in Butte simply looked the other way.

Never mind that the practice of using falsified certificates for adopted children took place all across the country for years. In Florida, a doctor had delivered and falsified the records of hundreds of babies, and in Tennessee, the head of an orphanage had sold thousands of babies. But in Butte's orbit, deeply Catholic, Elsie's sins took on greater proportions.

Meanwhile the men who paid the bills, many of them supposed pillars of the community—politicians, judges, lawyers—managed to avoid not only the consequences of their ill-conceived behaviors but the controversy altogether. All these years later, it was the anguish of those with falsified birth documents, adults now searching for their birth parents, which had brought Elsa Seppanen's name back into the news.

As she and Griff talked about Elsie, Mesa felt a chill standing at the very spot where one of the exchanges of money and baby likely took place. Remembering the adult account of one of Elsie's Babies who had questioned her aging adoptive mother, Mesa thought about what had happened. The mother's only memory was of parking for a few minutes, waiting in a dark side street within blocks of the Courthouse. That was Hamilton Street.

She and Griff leaned companionably on the railing that surrounded the inconspicuous entry to what had once been Elsa Seppanen's office. Nothing had been bulldozed and built over in this part of town. "Goodness, you do make a case for Elsie as a victim of bad press," Griff said and smiled at her.

Mesa smiled back, and said. "It wouldn't be the first time that powerful men used the newspaper to protect their reputations by smearing those that threatened them."

"When she did run afoul of the law? Did that happen in Butte?" he asked. "Who finally turned her in?"

"In the three instances that she was arrested for manslaughter, the victims had families who were the last to know what was going on. The women ended up dying in the hospital or at home. The coroner had to be called in, and so the deaths triggered official inquiries."

"I'm surprised more charges weren't filed," Griff said and snapped several photos of the building and its discreet lower level entrance.

"That's because a lot of her clients came from the houses in the 'twilight zone', as the miners liked to call it. The madams looked after their employees and made sure

Elsie was around to safeguard their investments. They would have protected Elsie to the last."

Mesa could never verify any breakdown of the demographics of Seppanen's patients, but the consensus was that a fair number of them were well-kept prostitutes who worked in the houses of prostitution on Wyoming, Galena, and Mercury Streets. She had spoken to the granddaughter of Dr. Kane, a long time Butte physician who tested the women of the houses for STDs on a weekly basis. He refused to terminate any pregnancy, though he would refer women to Elsie.

She was a necessity in the red-light district. If the least little problem cropped up after a procedure, they sent for Elsie. Patients from upstanding families might not have realized what was even wrong, but the women in the houses were all too familiar with possible complications.

"Do you suppose any of those women came to term and delivered babies that were eventually sold too?" Griff asked his tone doubtful.

Mesa nodded. "Not that you'll ever find any evidence of their confinement, but I interviewed numerous people who knew pregnant women worked at the houses—the Victoria, the Windsor, and the Dumas. Irita, my assistant at the paper, for one. Her mother was a housekeeper at several of the establishments and every week saw the women who worked there."

Irita had an enviable memory for details, much of which she had learned from her own mother. "Her mother cleaned the Victoria and the Windsor, two of the larger houses, on Tuesday and Thursday, and the Convent of St. Mary's on Wednesdays and Fridays." Perversely, she always liked to mention the second job, and the fact that her mother had left her the "whorehouse china," a gift from Blonde Edna, the madam at the Windsor when it closed.

Irita's mother could name a handful of girls that she had seen pregnant and described the madams as protective. They didn't like to see a girl get thrown out on the streets, especially if she had a large and regular clientele. "A girl like that could do other jobs in the house—cleaning, laundry," Mesa explained. "Not to mention the well-heeled patrons who compensated the madams for their cut of the soiled dove's lost wages."

"Ah yes, the patrons, the influential ones with deep pockets that were likely listed in the infamous ledger."

Mesa nodded. "Once the women got close to delivery, they took up residence in one of Tony the Trader's flophouses a few blocks away. Elsie tended them there."

"Beg your pardon, Tony the what?" Griff asked.

"Another of Butte's more colorful characters, he ran a junk shop up on Park Street. His is a tale for another day," Mesa replied as a large white pickup truck, with remnants of a bale of hay fluttering out of its bed, pulled into Hamilton St.

"That was quick," Mesa called up to her favorite wing woman Alexis Vandemere who sat tall in the driver's seat, her blonde ponytail flipping as she leaned toward the passenger window and called out.

"At your service, hop in."

Griff looked at Mesa and said, "What have we here?"

"Our chauffeur," Mesa announced with a grin. "We're going to a party."

৽৵

Mesa hoped Alexis would take to Griffin-Jones, and vice versa. The Vandemeres had cousins in England, who Alexis visited regularly, horse people, she called them. She figured they could compare family crests on their signet rings. Anyway, his time, at least at the garden party, would be taken up by Nana Rose who would enjoy some conversation with a fellow countryman. After that, well, Mesa would have to see.

"Welcome to the Wild West," Alexis said with a wink, after Mesa introduced them.

"I don't believe I've ever ridden in one of these," he said when he climbed in.

"A pickup?" Mesa said, trying to disguise her disbelief.

"Amazing how much more one can see from up here," Griff said as they made the short drive to Silver Street.

Alexis turned into the alley off Excelsior Street and parked behind the side yard. It was just past four in the afternoon, and thirty or so people stood in the garden amidst lawn chairs and tables covered with billowing tablecloths and tea trays stacked high with cucumber sandwiches.

Rose Ducharme sat in the shade in a high-backed wicker wing chair, one of a pair that usually decorated the front porch in summer. Vivian Jobe, who knelt next to the chair engaged in conversation, waved when she saw Mesa with Griff. Sam Chavez, long-time family friend and Nan's handyman, hovered between the sandwiches and the petit fours, ready to do her bidding.

The trio entered through the back wrought iron gate. Alexis headed straight for the back door and the kitchen, where she no doubt had a bottle with a bow on it. But she knew better than to drink alone at Mesa's grandmother's house. Hence the text.

Mesa escorted Griff to introduce him to her grandmother, nodding to each person she passed while scouring the rest of the group for Phade. He was nowhere in sight. The minute Mr. Jones bowed and thanked Nan for inviting him to the party, the smile on her face said it all.

Sam provided a chair so that Griff could sit in the favored spot next to Nana. They were already in a deep discussion about what part of England "his people" hailed from. He glanced quizzically in Mesa's direction when she started to move away. She mouthed *I'll be back* and reversed her steps to look for Alexis in the kitchen.

Irita stopped her on the way and presented her with a 1999 Butte High yearbook. "I was over at one of my nieces' house this morning. She's in a state of shock about Phade's sister. Apparently, they graduated the same year. Who knew? Anyway, she had out the yearbook and I borrowed it. I went through and added a couple of sticky notes to pertinent pages. I'm leaving the rest of the detective work to you," she said and rolled her eyes.

Mesa smiled and gave her assistant a gentle hug. Despite her bluster and hard-nosed attitude, Irita would lay down in traffic for her boss if that's what required. The yearbook was her way of saying she would do what she could to help, even if she got nervous about what Mesa was up to.

Inside the house, Alexis wrestled with the cork on a bottle of Proseco. "Saving the hard stuff for later," she said with a wink. "Who's the crumpet?"

"Tell you later," Mesa said, winking back, and moved toward the dining room where she could see Phade leaning against the doorjamb, dejected. She took him by the forearm and dragged him into the front parlor where they could talk undisturbed. He practically tripped over his own feet.

"What's going on? I was a little surprised when Alexis said you were here," Mesa said quietly. Her concern sounded more judgmental than she intended, and Phade was quick to react.

"Why? Have your hands full with Sir Lancelot?" Phade said, and took a swig from the longneck he had been nursing. "I heard Vivian telling your Nan that he was hot to talk to you."

She ignored his dig. "What I meant was did you have some new information you wanted to tell me? We just came from the Mother Lode. I agreed to show Griff around along the way."

"Griff?" Phade said in a smarmy voice.

"Stop," Mesa said and gave him a quick punch in the arm. "I'm serious. I talked with Hal Winslow, who doesn't think Danica would have killed herself either. He showed me into Danica's office. I found this postcard there from Chloe Hardcastle. Who is she?"

"Chloe and Danica were BFF's. They used to hang out in high school. What else was in her office?" Phade said. "I guess I'll need to get her stuff out of there, too."

"I wouldn't worry about it for the time being," Mesa said. Phade could get responsible at the oddest times.

"Mr. Winslow won't let anybody touch anything. He was a big fan of your sister."

Phade sighed. "Yeah, I know. She was big on him too, not that my parents were any too happy about that. They thought she would never have gone to L.A. if it hadn't been for his encouragement. If they'd had their way, she never would have left Butte."

"So he mentioned," Mesa said. "And he told me something else that was a bit of a surprise." She paused trying to think of an appropriate way to begin the discussion, and finally just dove in. "Did you know Danica couldn't have children?"

Phade looked at Mesa with a start. "Hell, no. How would I know that? And how does he? That creeps me out."

"You never heard her or maybe your mom talk about it?" Mesa couldn't begin to imagine how that conversation would even come up.

"No," he said emphatically. "And what's that got to do with anything anyway?"

"We were talking about any issues worrying Danica that could point to someone in town who might have been the source of some conflict." Mesa didn't like beating around the bush, but she felt weird asking Phade if he thought there was a guy in town who might want to hurt his sister.

"What are you saying?" Phade asked. "You mean like a guy she was into? You got that list I made. There was hardly any guy's name on there unless it was with a girl he married. It was mostly old girlfriends from school and church."

Mesa shrugged. "Well, if she wasn't on that roof alone, she probably wasn't up there with a total stranger.

It must have been somebody she knew. And why would you go up there except to talk about something in private. Or to be sure not to be seen." Mesa started pacing as her mind ran through the scenarios that fit. "Who are her closest friends that are here in town?"

"I told you. Girls she used to hang with in high school, I guess. I mean she didn't exactly keep up with that many people as far as I know. Most of her friends who stayed here have gotten married and had kids. Chloe was the only one who didn't, but she's off some place in Africa I've never heard of."

"Right," Mesa said, "now I remember." The second mention of Africa brought it all back. Dr. Chloe Hardcastle had gone to Gambia as part of a World Health Organization's program to address childhood malnutrition. The *Messenger* had run an article about her parents' reaction to a national magazine article called "Forty under Forty." Chloe Hardcastle had been recognized for her work with a nonprofit she had helped found. Her parents in Butte were proud, but worried about their daughter's proximity to the Ebola epidemic.

"What about guys? Your sister was an attractive woman, in case you hadn't noticed. Did she have any serious relationships here in town? Hal said something about there being somebody that she was hung up on, but she didn't really talk about him."

"I don't know that kind of stuff," Phade said, his voice apologetic. "She was graduated and gone to college before I was even in junior high. I mean she always was going out with somebody but just not the same somebody at least as far as I remember. Look, I gotta get back to my parents. I just stopped by…" he paused. "I needed a quick break. That's all."

Mesa put her arm around Phade's shoulder and gave him a quick squeeze. Just then, Chance walked in.

Her brother gave her an odd look and then said, "Hey, Phade, how you doing? Sorry to interrupt but Nana's looking for Mesa." Then he motioned to his sister. "Nan wants you to show something to the English guy."

Phade stood up. "I gotta get going anyway. Tell your Nan I said Happy 4th. I'm gonna duck out the front."

Mesa and Chance watched him go. Then she followed Chance as he walked outside. "You wouldn't be fishing in the office pool by any chance?" he asked almost in a whisper as they walked out on the porch.

"Seriously?" Mesa rolled her eyes. "You didn't just ask me that."

Chance shrugged but was saved from more brow beating when Adrienne approached. She wore a lavender sundress, a color she always looked unnervingly good in. "Exactly the person I need to talk to," Mesa said and turned her back on Chance. "Female questions."

The two women linked arms and walked out into the garden. "What's going on?" Adrienne asked.

Snagging a couple of crustless cucumber sandwiches from a picnic table along the way, Mesa explained Winslow's revelation about Danica not being able to have children. "What could have caused that?"

Adrienne sipped her glass of pinot gris and the two women sat down on a concrete bench near a flowerbed lush with purple pansies. "Infertility is often unexplained," she said between sips. "But if you narrow it down to something a doctor would be able to diagnose from an internal exam, the answer includes irregularities or abnormalities in ovulation, endometriosis, PID."

Mesa made a face at the unknown abbreviation while she pulled apart the tiny sandwich.

"Sorry," Adrienne said. "Pelvic inflammatory disease, which is caused by all kinds of bacteria, the most prevalent of which is chlamydia."

"Ouch," Mesa said. "What a cliché, a dose of clap from some would-be actor?"

"Happens to four or five million unsuspecting women in America every year," Adrienne said and sipped her wine. "Of course, the insidious part is that there are often no symptoms for the woman, so the infection comes and goes without treatment."

Yet another situation where the women get the short end of things, Mesa thought, remembering her conversation earlier with Griff about Elsie.

"Want my entire lecture on the Perils of Unprotected Sex?" Adrienne teased.

Mesa shook her head and finished off the sandwich. "Don't ask me why, but I can't believe that Danica Draganovich would have been that careless, let alone slept around that much."

"Epidemics of STDs come in waves, subsiding, and then coming back again. You'd be surprised at the demographic of women I treated in my time—sorority girls, country club mavens, first-timers, seventy-year-olds in nursing homes."

"Eew! Adrienne!"

"I'm simply saying that it can happen to anyone," she said with a grin. "Of course, it could have been a completely different set of circumstances, maybe a birth defect, but you'll never know now unless you get permission to talk to the doctors who treated her, or if there is an autopsy."

৩৵৶

The rest of the afternoon unfolded predictably, and Mesa tried to put Danica Draganovich's death out of her mind for at least a few hours. Nana's peeps from various social circles, the Episcopal Church, and Homer Club – the longstanding Butte women's club she had been a member of for years. Then there was her War Brides Club as well as staff from the *Messenger* who had been invited to stop by and toast two hundred years of goodwill since the independence of the colonies. Mesa mingled while she kept an eye on Griff.

He had become a bit of a celebrity as Nana had introduced him to every person with English ancestors in Butte, all of whom had been invited to the party. Mesa found her heart melting as he had graciously stayed by her grandmother's side. Meanwhile, the cucumber sandwiches, miniature pasties, and shortbread biscuits had flown off the plates.

At four, the sherry had appeared, and by six, Nana and her set were saying their goodbyes. Vivian and Adrienne sat under the weeping willow deep in conversation. Sam and Chance seemed to be schooling Griff in the nuances of pitching horseshoes in the pit at the end of the garden. On her way out the door, Irita had agreed to quiz her niece about Danica's previous romantic involvements.

Around eight, Alexis had reluctantly agreed to help Mesa with kitchen duty. They stood over the double sink washing and drying silverware, teacups, and saucers. Alexis wasted no time getting to the heart of the matter, the elephant in the room, so to speak.

"So Phade's sister didn't off herself. What gives then?"

Mesa shook her head. "I wish I knew. My instinct is that she went up there for a specific reason, or to meet a specific person, and things went south."

"Well, it's the week for weird crimes. First, the dead baby in the attic and then a high dive off the Finlen. Even for Butte, those are doozies." Alexis shook water off a pint glass. "You don't think they could be connected, do you?"

"Crap, I hope not," Mesa grimaced. "I can't imagine how. But who knows. What we need is more information about what Danica Draganovich was doing once she got back to town, which I'm not exactly sure how to get." Mesa sighed and let the water out of the sink. Then she added, "4th of July weekend isn't exactly an ideal time to talk about sudden death. Not in front of the kiddies and all that."

Alexis pitched her dish towel onto the counter. "It's a showstopper all right," she said and walked over to the fridge to grab yet another bottle of Proseco.

"And speaking of showstoppers, where'd you find the English guy?" Alexis said with a smile. "You wouldn't be thinking about getting back on that pony?" she said, and moved her hips in a back and forth motion that caused Mesa to cringe.

"Stop," Mesa said and threw the tea towel at her friend. "I only met him today!"

"Well, he's certainly kept his eye on you all afternoon," Alexis said with a grin." He's totally into you."

Mesa stood on her tiptoes to see out the window into the garden. Griff was still pitching horseshoes. "You think?"

Vivian and Adrienne entered with more dishes from outside which Mesa and Alexis quickly dispatched. Then the foursome adjourned to the parlor.

Over the past four months, helping Mesa deal with her depression after Shane's death, the four women had developed this intergenerational connection. Mesa didn't exactly know how it had happened, except that between Vivian and Adrienne she felt like she had a couple of guardian angels quietly watching out for her.

The four had regular "all girl" dinners at Nan's. Chance's hurt feelings were easily assuaged with leftovers. On Mother's Day, they had fixed dinner at Nana's and talked late into the evening.

"Adrienne was telling me about the baby they found in the Granite Street house," Vivian said once Alexis had poured sparkling wine all around. "What a heartache. Makes you wonder what could have happened."

"What do you think?" Mesa asked Adrienne. The question had been in the back of Mesa's mind since she'd seen the story in the *Standard*, but her curiosity about Danica's infertility had taken precedence when they'd talked earlier. "Why wouldn't you call a doctor if it was a home delivery that went wrong? Or an ambulance?"

Adrienne sighed. "Eager mom enters the hospital and gives birth to a bundle of joy is only one scenario. You'd be surprised how many other ways there are, especially when the mother's not so thrilled and the child not so desired."

Vivian nodded toward Alexis and Mesa and then said, "I like to believe that your generation has had the benefit of more enlightened views about choice, but I imagine that's my wishful thinking."

Alexis and Mesa exchanged a glance. They had both known more than one classmate at Damascus College, back in Ohio, who had gotten pregnant mid-semester, one particularly well. Mesa had always worried it would be Alexis, who admitted that the college's decision to stock the bathrooms with condoms was the only thing that had saved her. Instead, Lindie Guskin, a go-getter with a heart of gold who didn't even date that much was the unlucky one.

It was an all too familiar story. Lindie had agonized for weeks, first about telling her family. A first-generation college student, she had scrimped and saved with her parents' help to get into Damascus. Their disappointment aside, Lindie said she couldn't bear the thought of an abortion and decided to have the baby. Then the guy bailed, a whiz kid who had gotten a Fulbright to study some obscure bacteria in a foreign land, and left Lindie all alone.

Alexis and Mesa had talked to her into the wee hours of the morning, right before Spring Break. Finally, they all agreed. The three of them would drive to Columbus, stay with Lindie through the procedure, bring her back, and take care of her during the break.

But trying to get into Planned Parenthood had been a nightmare. A wall of protestors with giant posters of aborted fetuses had surrounded the clinic. Alexis had cursed at the demonstrators and chided the cops who did almost nothing to help. Guilt overtook Lindie, and the three women had turned around and driven back to the college.

Lindie had left school at the end of the quarter and gone to live with an older sister, a nurse in Oregon, to have the baby. Three years later Mesa had seen Lindie in Cincinnati where she had gotten into law school. It had been a joyful reunion at first.

They had gone to the Wooden Nickel, a beer joint near campus, sat in a corner booth, ordering beer and burgers and laughing about old times. After a few pints, Lindie had told Mesa the details of the last months of the pregnancy, most of which went well, except that Lindie had to work two jobs to save up to pay her hospital bills since she had no health insurance. She worked in a daycare center and then did medical transcription at night.

The tears came, for both of them, when Lindie described how she had initially found a way to keep the baby. The daycare center had agreed she would be able to bring the baby to work. She had even picked out a name. Mesa had begun to think Lindie had made it all work.

She had listened quietly and was thankful her reaction was muted especially when she realized the story did not have a happy ending. In the last month, Lindie had gotten laid off when the State had cut back support for the daycare center, and she had no choice but to give the baby up.

Lindie and Mesa had parted on the street outside the bar with a long hug, Lindie's parting words etched in Mesa's head. "Giving up my baby was the hardest decision I've ever made. I wonder if the pain of it will ever go away. "

Mesa had gone back to her apartment, called Alexis, and bawled her eyes out.

"I don't know, Vivian," Alexis said. "Unless you've got money or a family with a big heart, the choices remain limited."

Mesa wondered how the mother in the Granite Street house must have felt. "It sounds like the baby hadn't lived long," Mesa said. "Isn't that what it said in the article?"

Adrienne was sitting next to the coffee table with the newspaper on it. She opened the first section and quickly scanned the article and confirmed what Mesa said. "So that means somebody in that house probably delivered a stillborn," Adrienne said. She handed the article to Mesa. "Who lived there then?"

Mesa thought for a minute, but couldn't come up with a name. The house was regularly on the Historic Preservation's annual tour. And the families who could afford the upkeep that went along with owning a hundred-year-old home were relatively few.

"Your Nan would know, don't you think?" Adrienne said. "Not that it necessarily matters at this stage. I doubt any charges would be brought."

"It's against the law to hide a corpse?" Alexis said, and then when she saw everyone wince, "I mean, to not report a death?"

"If a physician or a midwife or a nurse was involved, they could be sanctioned, even lose their license for not reporting it," Adrienne said. "That's what makes me think this was some kind of home delivery without benefit of medical care."

"Don't forget, this is Butte where we don't necessarily follow the rules," Vivian half-chuckled. "You're talking about the stomping ground of Elsie's Babies." Vivian looked at Mesa, "When Griff asked me about them at the Archives yesterday, all I could think of was a volunteer who said, as a girl in elementary school, her mother scolded the kids in the neighborhood by saying, 'Better be good or you'll get sold'."

෨ᢀᨇ

Once the garden party had moved inside with only a handful beyond the usual suspects, Griff had suggested a nightcap at The Gun Room, clearly keen to treat his newly made American friends.

Vivian had a long drive back to her place, and Chance and Adrienne had begged off as they tended to do more and more. In exchange for no guilt trip for their early departure, Adrienne had agreed to peruse the yearbook to see what other information she could gather about Danica, which Mesa appreciated. If Adrienne was interested, then Mesa was less likely to get any pushback from Chance about investigating a story he thought was best left to the police.

When Nana had encouraged Mesa to show the young Englishman a good time, she was more than happy to oblige. Griff had cemented her high opinion of him when he spent the afternoon graciously submitting to her grandmother's attention. The attraction of genuine, good manners in a man being so rare, it could not be overlooked.

Alexis was staying the weekend so she wanted to tag along, promising that she would disappear on command. In the meantime, she goaded Mesa, saying "let the games begin." But good manners or no, Mesa needed to make it home at a reasonable hour. She had promised to go over to Phade's grandmother's house the next morning to see if they could find anything that might explain what Danica was doing on that roof. She had no immediate intentions of getting frisky with Griff.

The Gun Room at the Finlen was relatively quiet when the trio entered. They sat at one of the round tables, discussing frontier life, as Griff called it. He had a flurry of questions after realizing that Sam, with whom he and Chance had been playing horseshoes, was an Apache transplant from New Mexico. Mesa did her best to keep Alexis from skewering him for his naiveté.

They had all the makings of a decent night out, no drama, when a cowboy, most likely in town for Butte Vigilante Bull-a-Rama that weekend, decided he wanted to buy Alexis a drink. He left his buddy standing at the bar and plopped down beside Alexis, presenting her with a Corona like the one in front of her. "Didn't we meet in Dillon last year?"

Mesa smiled, giving credit to the cowboy for playing the odds. She kept a running log of lines that guys used to try to pick up Alexis. The Labor Day Rodeo in Dillon was the largest in the state. Every cowgirl in Southwest Montana would have been there, many sporting long, blonde ponytails.

"Wrong ponytail," Alexis said with a smile. "I was in Paris."

The cowboy was lanky and handsome, with a thin toothpick in the corner of his mouth. He smelled faintly of barbeque. "Texas? I competed in the Red River Valley one year," he said.

"France," she said, and leaned her chin on her upturned palm.

"That a fact," the cowboy said, not the least intimidated. He looked at Mesa and Griff and then said,

"Hope you won't mind if I invite this young lady to join me at the bar. I wanna introduce her to the man who's gonna win the bull-riding competition this weekend."

Alexis gave Mesa a quick glance and one thumb up, their usual *let's give this about half an hour and then hit the road* signal. Two thumbs signaled a definite *don't bother to leave the porch light on.*

"Why not?" she said.

"Knock yourself out," Mesa mumbled under her breath. Sadly, cowboys buying drinks for Alexis often ran out of good sense before money.

"I take it that's the real McCoy," Griff said, his voice betraying a hint of amazement. "No sign of side arms though."

Mesa chuckled. "Rodeo cowboys get thrown off horses and bulls all the time. They are notoriously tough," she said and added, only half-facetiously, "They leave their six-shooters in the pickup."

"You sound like you've seen them in action," he said with a smile.

"Butte's not really a cowboy town. We do have this one rodeo in the summer, sometimes a National Rodeo event in the fall, but that's about it. I'm surprised to see these guys up here at the Finlen. They usually stay out at the rodeo grounds in somebody's trailer or on the flat at the Comfort Inn or the Super 8."

Griff nodded inquisitively and sipped his Neversweat and water. Nursing her Corona, she was slightly disappointed when he turned the conversation back to black market babies. "I keep hoping you'll share your theory about Elsa Seppanen's ledger."

Mesa smiled, considering if she was ready to ask him to continue the discussion upstairs in his room, knowing that she ought not to abandon Alexis. "How interested are you?"

He smiled and said, "Do I seem obsessed? I was thinking how you seem to be the expert on the subject. I don't mean to seem forward, at least not here." He looked around and smiled.

"One idea has occurred to me," she said, unsure how serious Griff was, but she was starting to feel the effects of her afternoon glasses of Proseco and her second Corona. "This is my pet theory, and I haven't told a soul. Promise you'll keep it to yourself?"

Griff smiled and shifted in his seat. "Do tell." He opened his eyes wide, but she couldn't tell if he was genuinely curious or simply flirting with her.

"Elsa Seppanen died at home alone," Mesa began, looking conspiratorially around her to be sure no one was listening. "She had a couple of poodles that put up a fuss and attracted a neighbor, but she was afraid to go in because of the dogs. So she called the police who called the coroner who found Elsie, long gone, in her bed. Stroke."

"You think the ledger ended up in official hands, never to see the light of day?" Griff suggested, swirling the ice cubes in his glass.

Mesa crooked her head. "This was in the early seventies. Butte had a really colorful coroner back then, Einar Mortensen. Mortie, everybody called him."

"Does everyone in Butte have a nickname?" Griff asked with a smile. "Is it some sort of rite of passage?"

Mesa smiled. Irita was fond of saying that she had so many friends with nicknames she couldn't tell you their real names if her life depended on it. "Lots of names get passed down," she said, and then went on to explain the confusion that custom could lead to in big families, which Butte was famous for. It was nicknames or a lot of juniors, or Big Mike and Little Mike. "Anyway," she added, "Mortie had a history of taking advantage of what the old-timers liked to call *first count*."

"Meaning?" Griff said, rocking on the back legs of his chair. Now he looked dead serious.

"Never worked retail?" Mesa said, with a teasing voice. She wondered if Griff had ever had to work at all. He definitely gave off that aristocratic air. She was surprised Alexis hadn't sniffed him out already.

"Before you start the day, you count the cash in the register, the till as you might say, to compare with the day's earnings at the close of business. If you were inclined to do any skimming, that would be the ideal time."

"So he took advantage of being the first one to go into the house?" Griff asked, nodding his head.

"Apparently. Mortie had a cocaine habit, and money was always an issue. So if there was no one else in the house, he had a tendency to remove any cash left around, prescription drugs, jewelry. According to my grandmother, it was no secret what Mortensen was up to. Eventually he was taken down for it by a political rival.

"Special prosecutor was appointed to investigate. The charges were ultimately dropped, but Mortie lost the coroner's election that next year."

"And you think he could have found Elsie's ledger?"

Mesa shrugged and sipped her Corona. "Elsie's second husband was a policeman, but he was older and had died long before she did. But it makes sense that she had some kind of protection that allowed her to operate unimpeded not two blocks from the Courthouse. So the ledger could have been well-known to people in law enforcement."

"What do you suppose he might have done with it?" he asked, his chin now resting on both fists, genuinely enthralled.

"According to Chance's pal who is an assistant coroner now, Mortie lived out his retirement playing golf in Butte in the summer time and traveling to Arizona in the winter—courtesy of contributions from the men named in that ledger."

"And you believe that?" Griff said with a smile and raised eyebrows, and then leaned again onto the back legs of his chair.

Griff could say a lot with an eyebrow, she decided. "If anything, Mortie was an opportunist—pragmatic but not greedy. He wouldn't have asked for too much, which could have gotten him hurt. Only enough to keep himself to himself, and others out of trouble."

"I don't suppose Mortie is still around," Griff asked, half-heartedly. The left eyebrow went up this time.

Mesa shook her head. "Heart attack on the eighteenth green on a golf course down in Tucson in 2008."

Griff let his chairs legs fall to the floor. "This story could be tough to bring to the screen without the ledger. What about his family, anybody who might have taken care of his estate?"

Again, Mesa shrugged and grinned at the word *estate*. "You mean the clothes on his back when he died?" she said with a chuckle. "His wife divorced him in the 80s, and he never remarried. They had a couple of daughters. One is still around. I've talked to her, but she didn't have much to say. Apparently, Mortie wasn't a sterling father.

She saw him at Christmas, sometimes Easter. He supposedly has a nephew who's also in town. I've yet to track him down."

He was silent for a moment and then said, "Have another?" He pointed to her empty Corona bottle.

Mesa looked at Alexis who seemed to be perking along nicely. It was that time of the evening when a person would commit to a few more drinks, maybe a little adventure. This was the first time since St. Patrick's Day that Mesa was actually considering it. "Why not," she said.

While Griff went to the bar, she watched the ease with which he talked to Rooney Boylan, a bartender she liked. He was usually in a decent mood, probably because he didn't own the place, but simply did his shift and went home.

Griff was gone long enough for Mesa to consider what kind of adventure she could squeeze in. She thought about what Alexis had said at the garden party, that while British men could basically charm the pants off most women, they were likely to run away when they saw your knickers. She was in the middle of trying to remember which knickers she'd put on that morning when Griff sat back down.

He sat her Corona on the table and then lifted his tumbler of bourbon, said, "Cheers" with that devilish smile, and they clinked glass to bottle. Then he said, "You think the ledger is essentially a wild goose chase then."

"Not entirely," Mesa said, drinking daintily. "But best case scenario, it's in some bottom drawer, maybe a trunk or a box in the house, unbeknownst to the nephew, if he ever even had it. Eventually Mortie got sober but I doubt seriously that he would have confided in anybody else, plus the majority of the people in that ledger are either dead or long past caring. Besides, I think the DNA tracking is much more likely to provide direct results to the grown babies looking to identify long-lost family. Maybe interviewing several of them might give you some ideas for your documentary. I could probably arrange it."

Griff thought for a moment and then said, "I bet you could."

Over Griff's shoulder, Mesa could see Rooney filling a line of shot glasses with Patron in front of the cowboys. The last time she had seen that happen at the Irish Times on St. Paddy's Day, the outcome had not been pretty.

She was about to go to the bar and orchestrate a stand down when to her surprise, Belushi entered the lounge from its front door on Broadway. He strode over to the table in a rush, the sound of his sagging jeans brushing along in time to his step. "I need to talk to you right away."

Griff nodded almost imperceptibly to Belushi and then Mesa. Reluctantly, she excused herself and Belushi took her by the arm and herded her out the bar's other exit that led into the hotel hallway. He had never so much as touched her before, so Mesa knew something was definitely up. "What's the matter?"

They were standing next to the glass-encased shelves in the hallway that were filled with hotel memorabilia of then-Senator John F. Kennedy's visit. "I found the phone," he mumbled, nodding down to his hand. He was holding an iPhone with a mangled screen.

Mesa wasn't sure what the fuss was about. A couple more cowboys from the lobby pushed past, and Belushi, half their size, turned protectively toward the wall, pulling the phone to his chest. "What are you talking about?" Mesa said.

Belushi whispered between clenched teeth. "I found Danica's phone." Then in a normal voice, he said, "I think."

Chapter 7

Chance cuddled next to Adrienne on the sofa in her loft apartment, her feet on the coffee table with a Butte High yearbook propped on her knees. He watched the moon rise above Table Mountain at the south end of the valley and thought about old school annuals filled with endless montages of poorly composed and fuzzy black and white photos. They reminded him of an awkward time he'd as soon forget.

Adrienne, clearly curious to wander down someone else's memory lane, stared at an eerie pair of computer-animated eyes emblazoned on the front of the book. "That's an odd emblem for Butte High back in 1999, don't you think?" she said. "But, what do I know? I can't remember anything about that year. Maybe Japanese animation made a big splash then."

Chance sat up. "Where were you then?" he asked. Adrienne rarely talked about the past, and he wasn't about to let this occasion go by. Staying in the moment was her catchphrase, and she applied it to most parts of her life. But once in a while, he got a peek into her past.

She looked over at him, and slowly a grin spread across her face. "I know what you're up to."

He chuckled and then said, "Ah come on. Where were you? I like to imagine your boring life before me."

She sighed and then smiled. "I had just finished my residency at Stanford and full of hope and glory, joining Devlin and his father in their practice."

Her voice was flat, and she began flipping through pages in the yearbook. She had just started looking at senior class photos. He reached out and stopped her from turning another page. He took her hand into his.

"That was the year I got married," she added and wove her fingers into his. Then she muttered, "Biggest mistake I ever made." She stuck her tongue out at him. "That's all you're getting."

He had heard all the details he wanted to know about her womanizing husband who had slept with his patients as well as the nurses that worked in their office. He had no desire to have her retell any of that. She wasn't bitter about her divorce, but he knew from his own experience that the scarring never went away. "Right," he said and kissed her. Eventually the yearbook fell to the floor.

Once they sat up again, Chance joined Adrienne in scanning the senior photos, where each student had the opportunity to summarize the highlights of four excruciating years of public high school. Chance thought about how he'd spent those days—hanging out with Tyler Fitzgerald and taking flying lessons.

He found himself reading the nicknames, the lists of clubs and athletic teams, and fragile future plans that seventeen-year-olds dreamt of. At least these photos were in color.

The blurbs he read ranged from funny to bizarre. A guy nicknamed "Killer" intended to join the World

Wrestling Federation, win the cruiserweight championship, and then come back to Butte and own a bar. A blonde nicknamed "Spook" planned to move to Sweden where she would churn butter and live on peaches and Prozac.

"Was I ever this juvenile? Probably worse," Chance thought to himself. He looked at Adrienne, who seemed completely enthralled, and decided comments about age were definitely to be left for another day.

Danica's photo was easy enough to find. She had already begun to blossom into the beauty she would become. Her nickname was Huey. She was president of the Thespian Troupe and had won several state drama awards. Her plans were to always make her family proud, to go to the University of Montana, room with Dewey, whoever that was, major in theater, and maybe make it in the movies. Clearly, Danica was more focused than a lot of her classmates, Chance thought.

They reached the Senior Poll pages where pairs of seniors were singled out for some outstanding achievement. Full-page, posed shots, they showed some creativity. Danica's dark-eyed beauty was on display again, sitting coyly atop a grand piano being played by a guy Chance recognized from the Courthouse. The duo had been selected *Most Likely to Be in Movies*.

"Destined for Hollywood from the beginning, I guess," Adrienne said. "Wonder if it was her own ambition or everybody else's that made her decide to go to California."

"I'm bettin' it was her own confidence," Chance said, with a sly grin. "The guy playing the piano never left Montana. He works in the County prosecutor's office, and he's lost most of his hair."

They continued flipping through the pages and saw Danica in the spread for the Thespian Troupe. She appeared in the group photo and then in the officers' photo, sandwiched between a tall, well-dressed—not T-shirt and blue jeans—male student and Mr. Winslow. And that was about it.

Chance and Adrienne reminisced about the list of top ten songs for the decade, most of which she hardly remembered except for "My Heart Will Go On," which everybody knew. And the top ten video rentals, a category Adrienne didn't see the use in. "You know, for making out," Chance explained.

"That's what we had drive-ins for." Adrienne said with a knowing smile.

"We have a drive-in," Chance countered. He had spent more than a few cozy evenings there, but Butte temperatures at night got cold even in summer. "But we had to find something else to do somewhere else the other ten months of the year. *Scream* was a big favorite, and *Titanic*, of course."

"Okay, I get it. How to get the girl into your safe and loving arms," Adrienne said with a smile.

"See, you're not so old," Chance said and immediately began to nibble at her ear. Adrienne continued to flip through the pages and ended back at the senior photos.

She kissed Chance once and then said, "More, after we find out who Dewey is."

With renewed intensity, Chance found Dewey a mere three pages away. "There she is," Chance said. "Chloe Hardcastle." Her plan was to get into med school in record time, learn to fly her own plane, travel all over the world, and fly back to Butte "whenever I want."

"These Butte kids like to think big," Adrienne said and closed the book.

"Definitely gotta love a girl who wants to learn to fly. They'll try anything," Chance said and began to kiss Adrienne.

§◦◦§

"Can you go over to the office?" Mesa said, trying to act casual while she looked at the phone Belushi held. "I want to take a quick look at this before we turn it in."

She looked at the young reporter. "You do know that we need to turn this phone in to the police as soon as possible, right? It's material evidence in a likely homicide."

"We don't know that for certain, do we?" he asked.

Belushi's wide-eyed expression was always confusing. She couldn't tell if he was really that naïve or if he was worried he might get into trouble.

"We'll take a quick look," Mesa said reassuringly. "If anything's on this phone, it might help Phade figure out what was going on with Danica, and then he can tell the detective."

Belushi nodded in agreement.

"But I don't want to discuss it here," she said, lowering her voice as a handful of people were milling about the hotel's lobby.

Belushi nodded to the pair of disheveled but harmless look-alike pals who were sitting on the stairs to the mezzanine. "I'll get them to drop me off."

"Give me five minutes," Mesa said. "I want to let my friends know where I'm going."

"We can wait for you," Belushi said earnestly. "At the side entrance."

"That's okay," she said and gave him her key to the office. "You let yourself in," then she glanced at Belushi's friends and said, "Just you. I'll be there in two shakes." Then she gave him a quick slap on the shoulder and said, "Good work."

Mesa ducked back into The Gun Room and saw that one of the cowboys was chatting with Griff. Alexis and another cowboy were shoulder to shoulder at the jukebox, mulling over the tunes. Reluctant to leave Alexis, given her affinity for ending up in the middle of something she always said she hadn't started, Mesa was conflicted. Several more women came into the bar. So at least the odds were evening up.

And then there was Griff. Damn, damn, damn. She took his arm and moved with him toward the table closest to the door. "Something's come up," she said to him. "I've got to go over to the office."

Griff put his drink down and leaned closer so they could hear over the two-step music that was now playing. "Will you be coming back?" he asked, his tone suggesting he hoped she would.

She was torn. "I'll try. If not, will you tell Alexis I had to go and that I'll see her at the apartment later?"

"Right," he said and looked like he wanted to say more, but the cowboy was back with another drink for Griff, and asking about some rodeo in England.

"If you like, tomorrow night we can get together to watch the fireworks. It's quite a show," she said, feeling oddly self-conscious, "for Montana, anyway."

"I'd like that," he said, and looked down at his drink and then back at her.

The two stood there looking at each other. Now they were both self-conscious. "Good," Mesa said, kissed him quickly on the lips, smiled, and left the bar.

Mesa returned to the lobby, trotting across it toward the side door. Her mind was spinning, the look on his face after she kissed him, but she couldn't get distracted by Griff, at least not tonight. The words of her former editor echoed in her head, "The best reporters don't let anything get in the way of an important story, not friends, family, or relationships." Which was how he rationalized their sleeping together, since they were professionals who understood their priorities. Yeah, right.

What was important now was that the phone could be the key to what had happened to Danica, even if it looked beyond repair. Belushi had geek potential. Maybe he could retrieve the text messages and the list of phone calls. But they needed to do what they could quickly.

She wanted to avoid any hint that the paper had interfered with the investigation, like concealing evidence. Good God, she said under her breath. Maybe they should simply turn the phone in to the police station. But wait, she rationalized, nobody who would know what to do with it would be there at this time of night. She put the police out of her head.

She was almost to the stairwell and the exit when, as though her conscience had conjured him up, Royal Macgregor came lumbering down the stairs from the mezzanine. Damn, Mesa thought and slowed her pace. She took a deep breath and told herself she wasn't doing anything wrong. Pray he doesn't stop, she told herself, and if he does, stick to the truth and hope he doesn't mention telephones.

Macgregor nodded and walked right up to her as if they'd known each other for years. He was popping jelly beans and offered her some, which she gratefully accepted. They were orange and lemon as she had suspected earlier and she tried to focus on their unusually tart flavor instead of her pounding heart.

Act like a journalist, fool, she told herself. What would she say to him if she were simply covering the story of the investigation? "Working overtime?" was the best she could come up with.

Macgregor gave her a sideways nod that she interpreted to mean *sort of*.

"A little business and a little pleasure, let's say. My mother-in-law is in town for the 4th, and she's staying here."

Mesa nodded and thought of a couple of snide mother-in-law comments but decided to forego them. "Have you heard anything from the Crime Lab yet?" she asked. That was a sincere question, the answer to which would be newsworthy. Phade seemed to think his sister would never do drugs—that she'd left that all to him. Macgregor, on the other hand, would probably say the families often were the last to know.

"This ain't CSI Montana," he said, shaking his head. "We'll be lucky if we get tox results in six weeks." Then he followed with his own question. "How did your tour end up this afternoon? Find out about anything I should know about?"

Mesa thought for a minute, trying not to choke on her final jelly bean, then recovered. "I did see the door to the roof was locked. Doesn't that suggest Danica had someone with her when she went up to the roof, or did you find the key on her?"

Macgregor smiled. "We're checking into that, don't you worry. Have you seen Phade today?"

Mesa nodded and said, "For a short while this afternoon." She wondered why the detective was asking, but she didn't want to offer too much information for fear she might look overly concerned and have him begin to wonder what she might be up to this very moment.

"Put a call in to him this evening and haven't heard back," Mac said, between jelly beans. "You see or hear from him, would you remind him to check his messages?"

"Sure," she said, desperately trying to act all nonchalant when she wanted to tear out the door. "Anything I can help with?"

The detective shook his head and said, "Just some follow-up from the interview this morning," and then he made for the front entrance, calling as he left, "Have a good one."

As soon as he was gone, Mesa sprinted out the side entrance, giving a quick glance outside in case Macgregor was walking her way. The last thing she wanted was for him to wonder where she was racing. The thought occurred to her that she should have mentioned Danica's infertility, but she was too nervous about the phone. She would call him tomorrow. It would be a good excuse to check in with him.

She retraced her steps from the afternoon before, down Wyoming and then across the block to the *Mess* office. The lights were on and the door unlocked. She locked it behind her and walked back to the newsroom where Belushi sat at his cluttered desk with his laptop open, struggling with the phone. He turned to her and said, "It's messed up."

Then he sighed and said, "I hear there's some software that you can use to recover messages and contacts."

"You're sure this is her phone?" Mesa said.

He stared at her blankly. "Who else's would it be, do you think? I mean it was right there next to where the Jeep was parked."

"You're kidding me?" Mesa couldn't believe the kid's luck. The police would have scoured the area looking for anything that might be considered evidence. Or at least she assumed they had. Why hadn't they recovered it? "How is it that you found it and the cops didn't?"

Belushi shrugged. "Well, it wasn't me. Spike found it. It was in that concrete planter."

Spike? Mesa thought back to Belushi's two friends who looked more like Sponge Bob and Patrick.

"You know those two concrete planters on the sidewalk next to the hotel, the ones with the petunias in them? Well, it was in the one right down from the Jeep. He and Sled wanted to see where she fell. So we were standing there. That's how I figured you were in The Gun Room. We saw you walk by on Broadway. Anyway, Spike, he was leaning on the planter. He puts his hand down on the edge of it and feels something under the heel of his palm. The phone had lodged straight down into the dirt."

"Seriously?" Mesa said, but surely, the whiz kid wasn't making this up. It was too bizarre. "Okay, download this software and let's see what we can find."

ৎৡ৶

"Just because there's a Huey and a Dewey, doesn't necessarily mean there's a Louie," Adrienne said, having returned her attentions to the search for background information about Danica's friends in the yearbook.

"My money's on the brother," Chance said, tapping the photo one row below.

"You don't even know for sure that they're brother and sister," Adrienne countered. Simply because they have the same last name, plus they're the same age. Give me the magnifying glass."

"Maybe one of them flunked seventh grade like I nearly did," Chance added. "You don't think Nathan Louis Hardcastle could be nicknamed Louie?" He and Adrienne had been going back and forth like this for five minutes.

"It could be Louie, but the fact is he already has a nickname—Major Tom—Adrienne said and tapped under his photo with her fingertip. " And there's nothing that he says about himself that suggests a connection, no Donald Duck for example," Adrienne pointed out. "Not that any of this can be considered remotely serious." She had turned on the small desk lamp next to the futon so she could examine the photographs. "I guess they could be half-siblings."

Chance had pointed out Nathan Hardcastle's cryptic plans: "Going to get a degree in aerospace engineering and rebuild the GH so I can become a lifetime member of the 'Air Defense Team'." Whatever the hell that meant.

"We can solve this by getting on the Internet," Chance said. "These people have to be on Facebook or in the *Standard*, somewhere."

"You know it's past midnight," Adrienne said.

They were both sitting up in bed, backs resting on pillows leaning against the wall.

"I know, I know," he said.

"And it was your rule." Adrienne said matter-of-factly.

"You agreed right away," Chance countered. "No laptops after midnight."

Adrienne had put down the magnifying glass and had gone back to flipping through the annual. At least they could tell Mesa that Danica and Chloe had been good pals in high school, which she probably could have found out simply by asking Phade.

Adrienne had come to the end of the student photographs and was speeding through the ads at the end of the yearbook until she realized that some of them were personal ads from families and employers. She began to look more closely at the photos with good wishes from moms and dads, rather than advertisements from businesses.

On the next to last page, she cried, "Aha." A half-page ad containing three photographs read, "Congratulations, Chloe and Nathan!" The first as infants in the cradle in matching, hooded onesies; the second in grade school, again with matching outfits; and then in their caps and gowns. "Well, I'll be damned. You win," Adrienne said with faux disappointment. "They must be fraternal twins."

"Thank God for that," Chance said and laid back down.

Adrienne turned out the lamp and snuggled into his arms.

Mesa and Belushi scanned a half-dozen websites before they finally found some free software that claimed to recover lost or deleted messages, phone logs, and contacts. But they couldn't figure out how to upload anything from the mangled iPhone to the laptop. Mesa decided to call in Phade.

She debated briefly whether to disturb him, partly because she suspected he was exhausted, remembering the inertia of grief all too well. After Shane's death, she had pulled the covers over her life. Either she was sleeping for days at a time, or if she was upright, she was sleepwalking.

Her reluctance also grew out of the uncertainty of what they would discover on the phone—maybe nothing at the rate they were going, which would be a big letdown. But what if there was something on the phone that might provide a clue to Danica's death. She couldn't be sure what Phade would do with that information. Maybe it was best that she see the data first and then call him. Finally, her frustration won out.

She had just texted him when five minutes later Belushi yelled, "Got it!" He had finally figured out that the damaged phone needed to be charged. Once the phone was plugged in and charging, the software was able to recognize the device.

With a couple of clicks, Belushi had them into the recovery part of the software program. A white screen popped up, listing the data contents of the phone. Nearly three hundred contacts, a couple a dozen text messages, thirty-four calls. Like Mesa and the rest of her generation, Danica had made prolific use of her cell phone.

"Open the text messages," Mesa said, her voice hushed, tense with the possibility of what they might find, or more likely what they wouldn't. She disliked the possibility of having to turn over the phone to Macgregor and eat crow for nothing.

She watched Belushi move the cursor on the screen, but loud banging at the door preempted any discovery. That was quick, she thought, and then to Belushi she said, "That's probably Phade." She sighed. She could see how much Belushi wanted to be in on the story. To dismiss him now would be precious little reward for his evening's effort. He had sought her out and acted in the best interest of the story. Too bad—this was personal, a story that Phade couldn't be left out of.

"It might be better if he and I do this," she said. Disappointment fell over Belushi's soulful eyes. His shoulders drooped, but then he nodded.

The two of them walked toward the lobby and the front door. "I'll call you tomorrow and update you if we find anything. I promise."

"If you want, I can be the one who turns the phone in to the police department," Belushi said. "That way you don't have to risk getting jammed up for anything. I can turn it in at the station in the morning. I did that once with a wallet I found. I just had to fill out a form."

Mesa wasn't sure what to do. She certainly didn't want to get accused of impeding the investigation. But if she let Belushi follow through on his plan, the phone might end up in Lost and Found for weeks. "Let me think about it," she said. "And thanks, Belushi, this could be huge."

"What did you call me?" he said.

"I mean, Evan. Thanks, Evan," she recovered quickly and then had the sudden urge to hug him, except that Phade had started banging on the door again. She nodded and then yelled, "Coming."

Phade tore into the reception room, without so much as a *Hey, how are ya.* A whiff of ganja came with him. "Where's the phone? Let me see it."

Belushi looked at Mesa who piped up, "Evan got the software to work. It's up on his computer."

Phade looked briefly at Belushi as if he had only just noticed him but then acknowledged him with a nod. The two worked together on the digital side of the paper, Phade more technical, Belushi more on content. But Phade clearly held the reins, not that Belushi seemed to mind. Mesa suspected one bully or another had been leaning on Belushi most of his young life.

But there was no discounting Belushi's natural instincts for a story. Consistently he was the one who came up with the juicy angle, a tidbit, a factual anomaly, a catchy headline.

Belushi nodded back, and Phade headed to the newsroom. Mesa bid an abbreviated goodbye to Belushi and then followed.

She walked over to the desk and stood next to Phade who sat at the laptop, staring at the screen and a list of phone numbers with dates, times, and duration of calls. A few of the numbers were replaced by names, like *Phade* and *Mom*, from the phone's list of contacts. Suddenly the mundane seemed poignant.

She didn't want to upset Phade, so she told herself to concentrate on the details. "Who is Donuts?" Mesa said, "There are six calls to that number in the last ten days."

The first call had lasted a minute and a half; the rest came in around twenty seconds, the length of an answering machine message, more or less; but the sixth and last call had been longer, nearly five minutes. "We need to find out whose number this is," Phade said.

"Check the messages," Mesa said. "Maybe there are some to that number. If somebody's not answering the phone, maybe she texted them, right?"

There were three texts on Friday: one to Phade about lunch, which they had seen on Phade's phone that morning; and two to that number with the six calls. The first text said

I saw the story. How could you lie to me like that?

The second said:

I'll be at the GH at 1. Be there or I'll come find you.

There was one text response after Danica's ultimatum:

You have to believe me. I couldn't see another choice.

And then on the next line, after Danica's second text:

Okay.

"We need to find out who this number belongs to," Mesa said. Her mind was racing. Someone had lied to Danica and she wasn't having it. But whoever she was talking to had their back against the wall. This had all the makings of a serious confrontation. But what the hell was GH?

Phade had already pulled out his phone and begun to punch in the number. Then he put his phone on speaker.

"Wait, wait!" Mesa cautioned. She wanted to think their approach through, but it was too late.

"Yeah," said an irritated, male voice.

Holy shit, it was a man. Big surprise. In the background, Mesa thought she heard a couple of high-pitched voices—children playing? Mesa looked at the clock. It was barely ten p.m.

Phade was super cool. "This is the emergency room at St. James Hospital," he said in a matter-of-fact but assertive tone. We have a patient who had this number in his pocket. Could you please identify yourself?"

Mesa was impressed with Phade's ruse. If it had been her answering the phone, she would have been too flustered to be suspicious. Who was hurt? Was it somebody she knew? Why did they have her number?

But the man on the other end of the line paused for only a second and then said, "Sorry," and hung up.

"Bastard," Phade said and then began punching in the number again. This time the call went to an answering machine. "You have reached Summit Valley Power and Light Technical Services. Please leave your name and number…." Phade hung up.

"Who did Danica know who works at the Power Company?" Mesa asked and thought about the two men Sissy Llewellyn had seen leaving the Finlen yesterday afternoon, one in a hardhat, the other wearing a suit. The Power Company's headquarters was only a block away. They could have both come from there.

Phade shrugged. "I don't know. But he's a pretty smug bastard if he can dodge the ER call. That usually shakes most people up."

Mesa reran the man's responses. What could you tell about a person from two words and a little background noise? No greeting, just "Yeah." It was a safe guess he wasn't happy about the call. He certainly didn't recognize Phade's number. Then the pause and "Sorry." He hadn't simply hung up, he'd apologized, and his tone had changed. He wasn't irritated anymore. He sounded genuinely sorry, but why, for what?

While he talked, Phade entered the phone number on Facebook and then through a series of reverse number lookup websites—anywho.com, Google, Yahoo, and even a site called SpyDialer.com that Mesa had never heard of. No joy.

Finding out where a phone number led was not rocket science for a journalist. Contacts were what it was all about. But Phade did seem to have a knack for it. "How did you learn all this?" Mesa asked.

Phade shrugged. "Study Hall, senior year." He sighed and ran his fingers through his thick black curls. Then he pulled up the Power Company's website. Dozens of pages led to even more pdf documents and way too much information to wade through at that time of night. No page or number existed for "Technical Services," and nothing came up when he searched the website using the phone number.

"The name's bogus," Phade said finally, then added with sarcasm. "I always use Domino's Pizza."

When Mesa gave him a confused looked, he continued. "In case your girlfriend goes through your contacts while you're in the shower, you don't want her to see some other girl's name and get curious."

Mesa shook her head slowly. Phade always had an angle. But this was Danica's phone. So she was the one who didn't want the caller's name to come up. Who could she be calling that she didn't want other people to know about?

"Who do we know at the Power Company? I'm going over there right now," Phade said emphatically.

"It's a holiday weekend," Mesa said. "We're not going to find anybody but a night watchman and the number for an emergency crew. Besides, you said yourself that it's bogus. It's most likely not a Power Company phone.

Phade leaned back in the desk chair and rubbed his hair with his hands as if he were trying to rid himself of the frustrations in his head.

"Either way," Mesa said, trying to speak calmly, "Monday's the 4th. We'll have to wait until Tuesday. I'll go over there in person and see what I can find out." Then she added, "Unless Detective Macgregor finds out before we do. We have to give him the phone, you know. Why don't you call him and tell him you found it?" she said, and poked him in the chest right where several strands of curly black chest hair peeked over the vee of his T-shirt.

Phade was sullen, rocking on the back chair leg.

"Apparently, he's been trying to get in touch with you." Mesa added. "And when you talk to him, ask him if he's looking at the tapes from the traffic cams on the light at that intersection in case the two people Sissy Llewellyn saw leaving the hotel crossed the intersection. Maybe you might recognize them."

Phade let his chair rock forward, and the wooden legs hit the concrete floor with a crack. "I don't wanna deal with this," he said with the same bleakness she could remember feeling after Shane's death. It was the desire to close the door and not have to face the reality of what was happening now, let alone what had happened yesterday.

The sudden wave of sorrow surprised her. She remembered saying the same words to herself after Shane died. Part of her feared getting drawn back into the paralyzing grief, even if there was the comfort of sharing such an awful feeling. She held him by both shoulders, and said, "Look at me, Phade. I'd give anything to change what happened yesterday, but I can't. And I know how hard this is, but you have to start to accept what's happened, painful and unfair as it is. Your family needs you."

He looked up at Mesa and said, half-heartedly. "Why can't we just run away?"

She gave him a sympathetic rub on the shoulder while she tried to think of what to say that she truly meant. "Sorry, Phade," was the best she could come up with. Useless words.

His flights of fantasy were flattering and she knew that's all they were, undeniable as their attraction was. The last thing Phade needed was to feel more guilt, and it would be too easy to become maudlin and stupid and risk the *Messenger*'s reputation. She had to keep his feet on the ground, hers too.

"You have to call Detective Macgregor and give him the phone." She tapped his shirt pocket where he had put it. "Then tomorrow we're going through your Baba's house. We're going to figure out what happened to Danica, by God."

They turned off the laptop and headed for the door. A siren blared close by, maybe a block away and then was cut short. "Oh damn, that better not be at the

Finlen," Mesa said, half in aggravation and half in resignation. "Will you lock up, Phade? I think I better check on that siren."

Chapter 8

Once again, Mesa found herself speed-walking up Wyoming Street to the Finlen, spurred on by the reflection of a squad car's revolving red light on the buildings at the intersection. The Gun Room had its own front entrance so she decided to walk up to Broadway and peek around the corner to see how far along trouble had traveled.

Thankfully, only one cruiser stood outside the hotel, empty. An officer on the sidewalk was talking to a hatless cowboy with his arms out pleading his case. Mesa recognized him as the one who had offered Alexis that first Corona. A couple of the other cowboys stood nearby, though Alexis was nowhere to be seen. Mesa sighed with momentary relief.

Clinging to the hotel's wall, head down, to avoid anyone's attention, she made a quick entrance through its double doors. The lobby was empty and quiet, the night clerk keeping an alert posture at the desk, stretching to look out the windows and see what the cop was up to. Mesa nodded at him like she belonged and headed for the lounge's hallway entrance which was a glass door.

She could see the bar was nearly empty. Another cop stood talking to a patron, who was leaning on a bar stool.

Where in the hell was Alexis? Griff, too. Mesa looked at her watch. It was almost eleven thirty. She was surprised how much time had gone by while she was fooling around with that phone.

She pushed open the door and sidled in as though she was an unsuspecting patron, looking for a nightcap. Rooney was halfheartedly wiping down the bar's counter. She sat on the nearest bar stool and nodded to him.

"Welcome to the Swinging Cowpoke Saloon," Rooney said with a smile. "I was about to pour myself a pick-me-up. You look like you could use one, too." Then he poured Mesa and himself a shot of Jim Beam. "On the house," he said.

Mesa didn't have to think twice. She downed the bourbon and savored the momentary warmth and sense of calm it provided. Then she dove in, sort of. "I'm almost afraid to ask what happened."

Rooney welcomed all comers to the bar—women in particular, since their presence was usually good for business. But like most Butte bartenders, he was also acutely aware of the effect an attractive, confident woman could have on men who were drinking more than their fair share. Mesa expected him to be philosophical—to a point.

He shook his head slowly. "Things got stupid a short time after a couple of the cowboys decided they were both going to give Alexis two-step lessons. Then another cowboy ponied up for more shots of Patron and some limes. Next thing I know, somebody kicks over a chair, a Corona bottle goes flying, and the swinging starts."

"And Alexis, what happened to her?" she asked, looking around the lounge to see the extent of the damage.

Rooney shrugged. "I'm not sure. I was trying to get the crazies to take it outside. I think she left the way you came in, along with that guy you were with."

"She been gone long?" Mesa asked, checking her phone. No messages. She looked around again, and nothing expensive appeared to have gotten smashed, so settling up wouldn't be too painful. Hopefully, Alexis would show up at the duplex.

Another shrug. "Maybe twenty minutes. You know how it is, once the fight starts. It seems like an eternity to get people separated, but then you realize it's only been five minutes since all hell broke loose."

"Can I settle up for us?' Her ID and a credit card were in her back pocket.

Rooney nodded and walked over to the cash register.

"And for the Englishman, too," she said, calling after him. She tried to imagine what Griff would have done in the midst of the chaos. She couldn't see him in a corner, which was where she would be. Would he have entered the fracas to protect Alexis? Not that she needed it.

Rooney brought the tab to the bar. Mesa paid the bill and left him a hefty tip.

He thanked her and then said, "Maybe next time you two come in, she should put her hair in a bun. That swishing pony tail, it does things to guys."

෨෧

The next morning, deep in thought about where next to go with the story about Danica, Mesa had finished her first cup of coffee before she realized she was alone in her duplex. While she was a notoriously heavy sleeper, Mesa usually heard Alexis stumble through the door.

More often, this was followed by her friend flopping down on the bed beside her. No matter what time she got in, Alexis always felt the need to report her night's activity to Mesa immediately, often falling asleep where she lay. But not last night.

Mesa didn't have time to think about where Alexis was. She was a grown woman, and if she chose to lay her head somewhere else on the spur of the moment, it wouldn't be the first time. In fact, if it hadn't been for the little dust-up at The Gun Room, Mesa wouldn't have thought twice about it. Instead, she got dressed, telling herself that if anything really bad had happened, she would have heard by now. She couldn't wait around, as she had promised to meet Phade at 9 a.m. at his Baba's house.

By the time Mesa pulled into the driveway of Phade's grandmother's house, she had been mulling over whether to give Alexis a jingle. But there was an unwritten rule between them that basically prohibited ANY early morning calls, especially on the weekend. Not that it mattered to Mesa, who had put a temporary moratorium on any intimate entanglements, a decision Griffin-Jones had her re-thinking. Mesa took the high road and simply texted her BFF, "What's your 20?" using the old-fashioned CB code for location.

The trouble with texts was that other people could read them. The simple variation on out-of-date police codes worked better. Alexis would answer if she were awake. What eventually came back in mid-morning was "10-6," which was basically, "I'm busy," as in hooked up, unless it's super urgent. This really had Mesa wondering. Who had Alexis, that fox, spent the night with—one of those cowboys?

Mesa finally put her phone away and walked up to Baba's house. The neighborhood had been built on the east side of town in the mid-seventies when the Anaconda Mining Company was still making a profit. When the Orthodox Church moved to Continental Drive, many of its parishioners had followed. The elder Draganovichs fit right in and had moved into this home when it was new. Vesna's immigration from Canada had followed the turbulent post-war years and prompted her escape as a humanitarian refugee from Communist Yugoslavia and religious oppression. The idea of owning her own home must have seemed like a dream come true, and the house showed it—spotless and neat as a pin. Her gratitude was evident.

Nana Rose had told Mesa the touching story of how Vesna had been taken in by the Orthodox Church Community, meeting her husband at her first Christmas Eve service. Vesna had likely lived in this house for most of her adult life, until her husband passed away. Mesa wondered if it was possible for two people to become so devoted to each other in this day and age.

She gave a gentle knock and then opened the storm door, calling a muted 'hello.' Phade answered back, and she stepped inside the modest brick home that smelled faintly of incense. Mesa called out to Phade again. He answered with an expressionless "yeah" from the kitchen, which was about half the size of the living room. He was sitting at the gray Formica and stainless steel kitchen table, staring at the list of names they had made the morning before.

"We should talk to Suzana Petrovich," he said, not even looking up. "She and Danica were always tight, and her number is on the phone log at least three times. She does hair at that shop across from the Silver Dollar. She might even own it by now." Phade was definitely focused. He hadn't even looked up.

Mesa looked around Baba's kitchen which was squeaky clean. Her only pause came when she saw a recipe for some Serbian delicacy that she could not pronounce, typewritten on paper, yellow with age. A handwritten sticky-note read "for Danica," the script halting with age. "Where are the cups?" Mesa said after a moment, looking for a second infusion of coffee.

Phade pointed to one of the white metal cabinets. Mesa retrieved a mug decorated with what she suspected was the Serbian flag—red, blue and white with a gold crest—and poured coffee into it. "Did you get to talk to Macgregor yet?" she asked quietly, trying not to press.

Phade nodded. "After I turned the phone in to the station first thing this morning."

She looked at the clock. It was barely 9 a.m. "What did he want?"

"Only to say that there was no trauma to her body beyond what happened in the fall."

"Hopefully, that means she didn't suffer at someone else's hands, right?" Mesa had resolved to keep Phade's spirits up, or at least try.

"He also said to forget the traffic cams. They're put up by the State Department of Transportation, for looks, you know. They're bogus."

"You mean like a deterrent?" Mesa said, puzzled, "to make people think photos are being taken when they're not?" She shook her head and smiled. Montana DOT was making the best of a budget short-fall.

"I don't know, Mesa," Phade said with the ever-present sigh. "If I don't find out what happened to her, I am well and truly fucked."

"Phade, language! This is your grandma's house!" Mesa said.

"Yeah, well, if the coroner's report says her *unuka* committed suicide, my Baba won't care because she will die of shame."

"Phade, don't say that," Mesa pleaded, though she understood what he was saying. Mrs. Draganovich was a pillar of the Serbian Mothers, but as Nana Rose had made clear, Vesna faced another kind of challenge—the stigma of suicide. She would have to summon all her considerable courage to deal with it.

"She's from the old country, Mesa. She left everything to come here and make a new life. How could anything have been harder than that? She always talks about how your faith gives you the strength to go on. She can't understand why Danica wouldn't have come to the family for help, whatever was wrong."

"Assuming Danica knew that, all the more reason to wonder why she was up on that roof," Mesa countered. "And who she was with."

Mesa looked around the kitchen for anything that was personal to Danica, but saw nothing, not even mail. "Where's her stuff?" Mesa said.

Phade got up. "I haven't looked around yet. Let's go into the back bedroom. That's where we used to sleep over when we were kids."

Though she wouldn't say it out loud, Mesa couldn't deny the palpable adrenalin she felt at that moment. Coming to grips with Danica's death was important. This was not a community filled with strangers. Quite the opposite. Butte was a tight-knit bunch, who thrived on their immigrant heritage and the bonds it built among families. You didn't need to have read John Donne, to know that when one person died in Butte it affected everyone.

They walked through a hallway with icons, bright paintings of saints, on both sides of the wall—gold and white vestments decorated with black crosses. Next to one was a red and gold portrait of the Virgin Mary and Child. Mesa walked solemnly, seeing that Phade was not exaggerating about his grandmother's religious devotion.

The bedroom was simple but cozy with its dark walnut chest of drawers and a Byzantine cross above it. The double bed, with a dark purple and red comforter, reached almost from wall to wall. There was hardly room to turn around, which made Mesa feel slightly claustrophobic. In the corner, there was a small desk which Mesa headed directly toward. She wanted to search through Danica's belongings quickly and get out.

Several books about teaching drama to kids and set design were on one corner. A stack of forwarded mail from L.A. lay unopened, mostly bills, nothing personal. As Nana Rose pointed out regularly, only old people use the regular mail these days.

A cosmetic bag with gobs of makeup took up the rest of the space. She picked up the bag and under it was an address book, which made Mesa perk up. Tattered and falling apart at the spine, it looked like a holdover from before cell phones. She began leafing through it. "Let's take this with us," she said to Phade.

"What if the cops want to see it?" he asked.

Mesa shrugged. "They haven't exactly made a beeline over here. If they ask if she had an address book, we can give it to them. If you're uncomfortable, we can go over it today and make copies, and then put it back."

She moved to the closet, opened the door, and was surprised to find a floor-length, framed mirror attached to the inside. Tucked into one corner was a photo of three people, all dressed in skiing gear and smiling broadly at the camera. They posed in front of a snow-covered mountain peppered with pine trees, maybe at Discovery Basin? Mesa took it down to look more closely at Danica, who stood in the middle between another young woman and a guy, all obnoxiously good-looking. "Who's this?"

Phade took the dog-eared photo, and turned it over. He read from the back, "*Big Sky, 1999*. That's the year she graduated high school. That's Chloe, the one you asked me about yesterday. The guy's name, I'm not sure but I'll think of it. It's her brother."

For a guy with a particularly difficult moniker to pronounce and remember, Phade was lousy with names. Maybe that was why he was so forgiving when everybody botched his. "She have the hots for him, ya think?" Mesa asked, wondering why of all the photos Danica might have kept after all this time, this was the one she wanted to see every day. And not where just anybody could see it. Here it was out of sight, on the inside of the closet door.

"Not that I remember. I think she was best friends with the sister and he tagged along to meet chicks."

Mesa turned to the interior of the closet. She went straight for the shoe boxes on the top shelf. Wasn't that where everybody hid their precious mementos? She tossed a couple of the boxes on the bed and examined the closet shelf underneath, not that she necessarily knew what she was looking for. Nada.

Phade meanwhile had found a couple of pieces of luggage under the bed which he began to search. Mesa's phone rang right after she opened a Jimmy Choo shoe box to find a pair of red pumps, size eight. Six hundred bucks easy.

"What's up?" Alexis said, sounding more chipper than a typical Saturday morning. "Sorry to go MIA on you last night," she said, "But all's well."

"Really?" Mesa said, "That's not what I heard from Rooney Boylan," deciding to let her friend share a little of the worry.

"Oh crap," Alexis said, her cheeriness gone. "I didn't think we broke anything that couldn't be easily replaced. Did he call the cops?"

Why was it rich people figured money could fix everything, Mesa thought with a sigh. Then she returned to being Alexis's conscience, "Not sure. It might have been a girl friend of one of the bull riders. But what if he did? Who could blame him? I swear, Alexis, you need to start bringing a handler when you go into a Butte bar. I'm getting tired of the job." Mesa could see Phade looking her way with a curious grin.

"I didn't start anything," Alexis said matter-of-factly, a testament to the many scrapes she got in and out of. "Where did you disappear to, anyway?" Alexis countered. "What happened to the 'never leave your wing woman' pact?"

"I didn't leave you totally alone," Mesa said, feeling only a tad at fault. "Griff was supposed to tell you I had to go over to the office because Belushi found the dead girl's phone."

"Good job, little man," Alexis said with more interest than she usually expressed in any of Mesa's investigative endeavors. "Anything helpful?"

"Maybe. Phade and I are going through his sister's belongings right now." It was a random thought that went through her head and out again that Alexis had not mentioned where Griffin-Jones had gone in the midst of The Gun Room melee.

"So where DID you spend the night?" Mesa asked, only half curious. She had found nothing of interest in Danica's closet except a lot of high-end clothes that must have cost a bundle. She made a note to look into where and for whom Danica had last worked in L.A. Apparently she had done all right for herself.

"Ah, listen," Alexis said in a distracted voice. "I'll have to get back to you on that. I'm off to brunch now. I'll catch up with you later." She hung up.

But before she did, Mesa thought she heard someone say, "Ready, then?" in a decidedly English accent.

Adrienne had barely put the Stars and Stripes in the newly-installed flag holder on the front of the building, to signify the gallery was part of the Summer Art Walk, when three different sets of customers had entered and made purchases. Chance, who had returned from a coffee run, could only shake his head. "What's wrong with people?" he said. "You come to Montana to camp and fish and hike."

Adrienne chuckled and then handed him a painting to put into a large cardboard carton. "Help me with this.

That couple from Pennsylvania is coming back in an hour to pick it up." Chance obeyed.

Adrienne had been preparing for the Art Walk all week, but Chance figured it was pretty much a no-brainer. It was mostly deciding what to serve: food that people would eat or food that was good for them. Chance had done his best to make sure fudge brownies were involved.

Adrienne went back to the laptop and the list of names Mesa had given them the day before. They were checking the names against the yearbook to see if there were any other candidates for "Louie" when Alexis Vandemere came in. "You seen Mesa?" she asked. "She's not answering my texts."

Adrienne, who had given Alexis a long stare when she entered, said. "This lack of communication wouldn't have anything to do with the fact that you have on the same clothes that you wore yesterday?"

Alexis shrugged and said, "Now Adrienne, don't be judgey." Then she added, "Maybe, but it shouldn't. As a matter of fact, if she is irritated, it could be a good sign. You know, that's she's thinking about getting back in circulation. Right?"

Adrienne thought for a second and then nodded.

"Thank you," Alexis said and then looked at Chance over her shoulder. "So, do you know where she is? I talked to her a couple of hours ago. Now I can't find her anywhere. I've checked the apartment and the office, and I called Nana Rose. I don't know where else to look."

"And a fine good morning to you, too," Chance said with a smile. He and Alexis had seemed to reach a kind of détente. He wasn't crazy about some of her bullshit, especially her *party 'til you drop* attitude, but she had the good sense not to ignore his concern. Much had improved as he had seen her struggle to support his sister in the months of grieving after Shane Northey's death. Numerous times he had gone to Mesa's apartment to check on her only to find Alexis doing the same thing. He had come to the realization that their friendship was more than a simple convenience.

"Is there something wrong?" he asked, his enthusiasm suddenly tempered.

When Alexis didn't answer immediately, Adrienne pressed, "Can we help?"

Alexis leaned on the frame counter and sighed, more resigned than relaxed. "It's only that I got to talking to the Englishman last night, and I'm thinking he's not totally for real."

Chance's ears perked up. Say what you want about Alexis, she wasn't naïve, far from it. The Vandemeres were high society back in New York, and while Mesa described their family as "a nest of dysfunction," they had given Alexis every opportunity to travel all over the world and rub elbows with the wealthy and eccentric. Chance figured she could spot a poser.

"It's not like Mesa and this guy have any business arrangement," he said. "At least from what I heard, he's simply doing some ground work for a possible documentary," Chance said and looked at Adrienne. "Right?"

Adrienne nodded. "The conversation I had with him yesterday afternoon seemed fairly benign. We talked about Butte before the mines closed. He was interested in the Elsie's Babies story, that's all. Fairly innocuous, I would say."

"I don't suppose you heard him mention that he's the son of a baronet then," Alexis said, "or that he has a cousin who's one of the most controversial members of Parliament in England?"

"Well, what is he doing in Butte then?" Chance asked, offhandedly. "Keeping a low profile?"

Alexis shrugged, "If what I found in his room is any indication, it feels like he's interested in more than making a documentary."

Mesa pulled up in front of the Petrovich home on Paxson Street, glad she had come alone. Much as Phade wanted to accompany her, she had forced him to go back to his family. "They need you," she had said, "Plus I want you to chat up anybody who turns up to pay their respects. You can get people in a corner and see what, if anything, they might know." She didn't really expect him to learn anything new, but you could never tell. It was hard to predict where pieces of a puzzle might turn up.

After they had finished at Baba's, they had walked across the alley to Phade's parents' house. Mesa had hugged Mrs. Draganovich whose longing look toward her son confirmed the decision. Even if he made no headway, he'd be there where his family knew he was all right. She could see the Draganovichs needed to know that what was left of their family was safe.

She had just parked her Subaru when she got another text from Belushi. First thing that morning, he had texted about Danica's phone, volunteering again to turn it in. She had explained that Phade had taken care of it and that she would call him when she'd finished going through Baba's house. She had to admire the rookie's enthusiasm. At least somebody else was interested in this story, even if it was disrupting the biggest holiday weekend of the summer. She called him. When he answered, she could tell he was surprised to hear from her.

"I didn't mean to bug you," he said, meekly and then added, "Anything you want me to do. I hate July 4th."

"What do you mean?" she said, genuinely concerned. "You're supposed to be drinking PBR and setting off fireworks."

"Not my style," he said quietly. "I don't drink, remember."

"Sorry, I forgot," Mesa said, wondering if the kid would ever loosen up. "Well, in that case, there is something you could do for me."

"Sure," he said, his voice eager.

"Pull together some background on Nathan Hardcastle. He and his sister, Chloe, were close with Danica Draganovich. Find out if he's in town, what he does, where he lives—the usual."

"Didn't his dad run for Senate a couple of campaigns ago? Republican, I think," Belushi asked. He sounded like he was typing on a keyboard already.

Mesa had found little reason to pay attention to Montana politics, at least the campaigns, while she was living back east. Back in Butte, she hadn't paid much attention either. She didn't see it as a particular area of interest for a lot of the *Messenger* readership. If they wanted political coverage, they could read the *Standard*.

Not that she thought politics weren't important, far from it. She was eager to cover the issues. It was politicians and their campaigns that aggravated her. She could hear the click-click of a keyboard. "Where are you anyway?" she said.

There was a pause, and then Belushi cleared his throat and said, "At the office. I hope you're not mad. I had the key in my pocket when I left." Then another pause as if he were waiting for the other shoe to drop. "I wouldn't let anybody else in, unless you told me to." He paused again, no doubt waiting for her reaction. When she said nothing, he added, "I can bring the key back to you now, if you want."

She smiled to herself, remembering a similar conversation she had once had with her first editor when she wanted to take solace in the newsroom. That was what an in-depth story could do. Nothing like the search for what had happened to someone else to fill empty hours. She knew what it was like to be obsessed with getting the pieces to fit, to feel the completion of the whole, the energy that builds from not knowing something to figuring it all out. The press toward the answer created a natural narrative thrust for a great story. "Okay, make yourself a copy," she said, "then give mine back. And remember, there's no overtime."

"I know. I'll get a copy made today," he said, and then he went back to his assignment. "There should be plenty to dig into if the Hardcastles were on the campaign trail." Montanans had a well-developed sense of privacy. But politicians' families were fair game.

To make Belushi feel like he was in the loop, she let him know what she was up to. "I'm here at the Petrovich's'. Remember, Danica had made several calls to her? I wanna see what they talked about. Then I'll swing by the Mountain Gallery and catch up with Chance and Adrienne. They went over the Bulldog yearbook last night and want to fill me in. As soon as you finish with Nathan, see what else you can find out about Chloe. Text me anything significant. Okay?"

She got out of her car, and was met with the smell of newly mown grass, charcoal, and grilling hamburgers as she strode up the driveway of the ranch-style home. The picnic was set up inside the garage, out of the wind and a possible thunderstorm. For most Butte families, the 3rd of July was one long wait until darkness, around 10 p.m., when the largest display of fireworks in the state would erupt. Why wait 'til the 4th, right? That was Butte—in its own orbit.

Like any reporter worth her salt, Mesa had no trouble wading through a crowd of locals. She smiled at the half a dozen people who were milling the horseshoe of tables, replete with the usual potluck potpourri. Several elderly folks sat in lawn chairs off to the side while a trio of men stood around a couple of coolers of Moose Drool and Bud Light. While Mesa didn't actually know any of the immediate Petrovich family, she was willing to bet she knew someone at the picnic.

She had barely approached a large bowl of potato salad when she saw a couple of forty-something women come through the door that connected the kitchen to the garage. She knew them both. She greeted the nurse from Nana Rose's cardiologist's office and gave a hello to a woman who worked at the Court House and was a friend of Irita's.

Not that knowing anyone mattered. Everyone was welcome, and like St. Patrick's Day, no one was really a stranger on the 4th of July weekend in Butte. It would be that way at anyone's house at holiday time. Nana Rose had held her party the day before, so she was spending the afternoon at the home of one of her Homer Club friends along with her current escort, Philip Northey, Shane's grandfather.

The rest of Shane's family had retreated to their cabin at Canyon Ferry, north of Helena. Mesa had cringed when her grandmother explained that the Northey's weren't ready for much celebration, barely three months since Shane's death.

The Northey family would have welcomed Mesa without question, which only made her feel more guilty. She was relieved that covering the story of Danica's death provided her an excuse not to join them. She couldn't do anything to comfort Shane's family, but she could help the Draganovichs. Maybe it made her feel like less of a coward. Whatever it was, getting to the bottom of Danica's death was where she wanted to put her efforts.

She politely moved through the garage and out into the backyard where another dozen people were enjoying hamburgers and Bud Light, while keeping tabs on kids playing with sparklers. She steered clear of the handful of prepubescent boys lighting the occasional firecracker, delighted by the accompanying squeals of nearby girls. She was pleased when she finally spotted a woman about Danica's age, talking with a couple of teenagers.

She had purposely decided not to text Suzana to give her a heads up. When she was training Belushi, she had warned him that such a tactic was a major *no-no*, at least in normal circumstances. Yet, Mesa knew there was no way to truly justify disturbing the family holiday with talk of death. But if something criminal had happened to Danica, the more diligently they worked, the quicker they'd figure it all out.

Mesa was counting on the strength of the women's friendship to get Suzana to open up. Phade had shown Mesa a scrapbook in his grandmother's house with a photo of a whole group of kids at church, Suzana and Danica being a couple of the older ones. Mesa had no trouble recognizing Suzana. Easily fifteen years older now than in that photo but, like Danica, she was an attractive woman, not as striking, but like all hair stylists, keenly aware of the importance of appearance. Well-tanned, she looked picture-perfect with a red and white designer blouse and a denim skirt just the right length, casual but not too short.

Mesa slowly wormed her way into the conversation, introducing herself and being surprised when Suzana brought up the fact that she knew that Phade and Mesa worked together. Nana Rose had not been exaggerating when she said everybody in the Holy Trinity congregation must have been thankful when Phade had gotten a job at the *Messenger*.

Once the teen-aged girls wandered off and the two women were alone, Mesa fessed up. "I imagine this is the last thing you want to talk about right now, but Phade and I were going through some of Danica's things this morning. He mentioned you and Danica had been close. So I decided to take a chance and stop by. He and his family are reeling, as you can imagine, and I've been trying to help Phade come to grips with what happened. I was wondering if you could answer a few questions and maybe help piece together her last few days." That sounded more dramatic than it needed to, but Mesa didn't want Suzana to underestimate anything she might know.

Suzana studied her beautifully manicured fingers, nails painted with bright red polish that matched her blouse, and then folded her arms. Suddenly Mesa thought she might be about to get the cold shoulder and was ready to backpedal toward an interview later in the week. But instead, Suzana sighed and said, "It's all I've been thinking about for the past forty-eight hours. " I can't believe she's gone." Her voice quivered, but she quickly recovered. "Let's get a beer and go sit in the shade."

For the next forty-five minutes, Suzana quietly talked about the best friend she would ever have. Mesa kept her questions to a minimum, allowing instead for the helpful bits of information to spill out on their own. It was almost like a eulogy, but Suzana was controlled and seemed genuinely perplexed. In her mind there was no way Danica had killed herself. "It had to be some sort of freak accident," she said.

Suzana and Danica had met for drinks Thursday night at The Post, a trendy new watering hole where you could actually sit down in a comfortable chair and have a cocktail and a conversation. "If she had had a problem, she would have told me," Suzana said adamant.

After all, they had shared their ups and downs their whole life, mostly about their social lives. It wasn't easy to navigate high-school years in Butte when you were taught that serious dating should lead to marriage. Why even bother, the girls had agreed.

But now that Suzana had finally found the right guy and was engaged, Danica had agreed to be in the wedding. "I wanted her to be my maid of honor, but I have a ton of cousins and the oldest one has talked about having that job since we were in elementary school.

Danica totally didn't mind though. She said she'd be happy to do whatever. That's the way she was, always accommodating."

Mesa pressed her about whether Danica had talked about any problems, even minor. Someone who had come into her life recently, maybe in California? Suzana shook her head at both suggestions.

"We mostly caught up on what was going on in town. She was so happy about her job. She sounded like she was really looking forward to settling back into Butte. After you've been away, it's a relief to be back. There's simply no place like it."

Mesa had to agree. The city was like a pair of well-worn shoes that fit perfectly, no matter how long since you'd put them on. That said, something had gone wrong somewhere.

Remembering that list of names that Phade had come up with, she asked, "What about guys in town?"

Suzana rolled her eyes. "I've spent my whole life being Danica's cock block, pardon my language. She attracted a lot of guys. Most of them weren't interested in only being friends."

"So where did Nathan Hardcastle fit into the picture?" Mesa asked, explaining about the photo she had found that clearly meant something to Danica.

"Not at all really, not anymore," Suzana said. "She did say she talked to him a couple of weeks ago when she first got to town, sort of a welcome home. But that's it."

So why did that photo still seem important, Mesa wondered. "You don't think there was anything special between them anymore?"

Suzana shook her head. "Sure she had a crush on him in high school, but it was never going to happen. His family is as close to old money as you can get in Butte. But Danica was the beautiful Orthodox girl who needed to find herself a decent Orthodox husband. They seriously could not have been farther apart in that way. There were always expectations about the kind of life they were both headed toward, and those expectations didn't overlap."

"You don't think that mind-set has loosened up?" Mesa asked. She thought about her friends in Butte who had gotten married, and she didn't feel like their choices were necessarily restricted. Granted she knew few people her age in the Holy Trinity congregation.

Suzana smiled and then said, "Maybe for some. But in our little community, it's more complicated. The traditions are what keep us strong. We might play the field a little, but in the end, commitment trumps casual sex every time. We're like swans, we mate for life."

Mesa nodded and the women sipped their beers. Suzana added, "Maybe it seems old-fashioned but that's how we're brought up, to respect those beliefs. They might have had a thing at the end of senior year and then hung out at the U for a while, but he joined a fraternity and started dating this sorority girl. That was pretty much it."

Mesa thought back to her first year of college and the exuberance of dorm sex, worries about getting pregnant and late night discussions about who was hooking up with whom. That might have seemed natural back east, at a place like Damascus College, liberal stronghold, but not necessarily the norm in the flyover states.

"She came home for Spring Break that first year," Suzana continued. "I'll never forget it. I had started working on my stylist's license and she stopped by the shop where I was working on Harrison Avenue. My boss got mad at me for taking off to talk to Danica."

Mesa could imagine the two friends, deep in discussion. Suzana had that earnest, straightforward expression, following every word.

"We sat in her car and she poured her heart out. She told me that Nathan said he cared about her, but that he didn't want to get serious. She realized then that he didn't have the capacity for intimacy that she did. It was awkward, you know."

Mesa did know. Guys that age were a-holes. Okay, that wasn't fair. Chance hadn't been a jerk at that age. Still, life could be a roller coaster, and finding someone to share the ride wasn't easy. At least that was the case outside the Orthodox community.

"Did you know she couldn't have children? Mesa asked, knowing this was a bombshell but feeling there was no easy way to ask. "Could that have had an impact on her relationships?"

A twelve-year-old darted past where they were sitting and the predictable *bang bang* of a couple of firecrackers that followed made both women jump. Mesa recouped. "It had to be upsetting for her given her expectations about marriage."

When Mesa looked up, she thought Suzana had really been spooked by the firecracker. Then she said, "That can't be right. Are you sure about that?"

"That's what she told Hal Winslow."

"I had no idea," Suzana said, a frown across her face. "I guess maybe there were some things we never talked about."

Chapter 9

"I don't know why you're so pissed," Alexis said. "Nothing happened." They were sitting at a table under an event canopy in the parking lot next to the Mountain Gallery. The Art Walk Committee had set up the tent for people who needed to rest their feet or get out of the sun. So far Mesa and Alexis were the only takers.

"Who said I was pissed?" Mesa answered, admiring one of Butte's many ghost signs on the side of the Imperial building, and trying to decide why, in fact, she was so irritated. Her connection with Griffin-Jones couldn't be more temporary. She knew it. He knew it. Kiss or no kiss.

"Mesa, I can always tell. Listen to yourself. You sound like you did that time you thought I slept with Robbie Cornwall. Nothing happened that time either."

Mesa sighed. Robbie had had a crush on Mesa since the day they met their first year at Damascus, though she had never given him a single bit of encouragement. Even so, the fact that he and Alexis had ended up together the night before graduation annoyed her to this day. It was the principle of the thing.

Truth was, she didn't want to admit that she found the Englishman attractive, that she looked forward to seeing him later, but that she knew the timing was bad.

Distracted by a cell phone message from Belushi about the Hardcastle twins, she said, "All right, all right. Let's drop it."

Alexis turned her chair out toward the sun, closed her eyes, and stretched out. "I wasn't going to say anything except I got such a weird vibe off him and I felt like I ought to tell you. Sometimes I should just keep my mouth shut."

"Let's get real," Mesa said. "You act like it's the first time anybody ever gave you crap for sleeping with somebody you had no business being with."

A couple walked by and sat down at the next table.

"Well excuse me, but that's not what happened," Alexis shot back in a whisper. "I told you, I slept on that lumpy pullout couch. God, can you not understand plain English?"

Mesa rolled her eyes. She and Alexis had a long history of communal hook-ups, going so far as to even compare notes. So this wasn't the end of the world, aside from the annoying reality that every man seemed to find Alexis attractive. Mesa had to accept that she'd missed her chance with Griff by leaving him in The Gun Room, even though she had thought he might wait for her to return, thinking about the kiss again. "So whose idea was it to go back to his room?"

"Well, it was sort of the obvious choice," Alexis said and then stopped talking when Chance walked past them, carrying two plastic glasses of white wine which he served to the recent arrivals at the next table.

He talked with them for a few moments, and then turned to the table where Mesa and Alexis sat. "I'm gonna have to chuck you two unless you can act civil," he said with a fake smile. Then he looked at Mesa and said, "And don't leave without telling me where you're going."

"So where's *our* wine?" Mesa said with her own fake smile.

"Yeah," Alexis agreed. "A little hair of the dog could do wonders for my thought processes. I don't suppose a cold beer would be too much to ask?" Alexis took off her ubiquitous cowboy hat and fanned her face.

"Sounds even better," Mesa agreed. This was her first full summer back in Butte, and she'd forgotten how the hot, dry wind made a cold beer sound so good.

"Couple of freeloaders," Chance said and left to go back inside the Gallery.

"Continue," Mesa said, gleeful at Alexis's discomfort as she tried to talk her way out of her latest indiscretion. She stared at her cell phone, waiting to see the email Belushi had promised.

"We ran for the door when the swinging started," Alexis explained. "After all, you'd left me, and I didn't have a car. I wasn't too excited to hang around and talk to the cops. When we heard the siren, Griff made for the stairs and I followed him. It was totally innocent. When we got to his room, we both collapsed in a fit of laughter. I think he was pumped to check 'bar fight in historic western town' off his bucket list."

Why hadn't she thought to check his room, Mesa chastised herself, still curious to find out what else went on. "And the reason that you didn't come back to the apartment once the excitement died down?" Now she was simply giving her friend a well-deserved hard time.

Alexis sighed. "It was early and since I did have the presence of mind to grab the bottle of Patron off the bar on the way out, we decided to toast our escape. And then we kept going. You know how tequila is. We finished off the bottle. Then he went his way and I got the lumpy sofa." She raised her right arm. "I swear."

"So what's all this crap about him having some ulterior motive for being in Butte?" Mesa did find this slightly exasperating as she considered herself a decent judge of a bullshit story, and that wasn't what she had picked up. Far from it.

Alexis warmed to this part of the conversation, no doubt sensing that the previous night's behavior had been forgiven. "When I woke up this morning, I started nosing around."

Mesa could totally believe this. Alexis had no boundaries when it came to other people's property. Walk into somebody's house and, first thing, Alexis would be opening drawers and cabinets like they were in some product demonstration home. The minute the host's head was turned, she began acting out what she tried to pawn off as some bizarre form of kleptomania. It was compulsive, she would say. She didn't know why she did it.

Chance reappeared with three bottles of Moose Drool, dripping wet, and sat down with them. Alexis had stopped talking. "Don't let me interrupt," Chance said after distributing the bottles and taking a long pull off the one he'd kept for himself. "I might learn something."

Alexis shrugged and then said, "He'd left his briefcase unlocked. I sort of knocked the clasp, and the lid popped up."

Mesa took a swig of her beer and slowly shook her head, "Just one big accident."

"I happened to see these folders inside," Alexis said. "One was labeled *birth certificate* and had a report from a private investigator about the search for the original birth certificate for Reginald Griffin-Jones. That was when it hit me where I'd heard the name before."

Chance looked between the two of them and then said, "This is the Englishman? You've been snooping around in his briefcase?" He nodded in approval.

Mesa gave her brother a faux slap on the arm. "Don't encourage her," she said, though in fact she was curious about what Alexis had learned.

"When I was in London last fall, the tabloids were filled with headlines about 'Rabid Reg' and his anti-abortion campaign. It's like the pro-life movement had suddenly skipped across the pond."

Mesa had to stop and think a minute. As far as she knew, abortion in the first two trimesters had been available through the UK's National Health Service since the nineties. She wondered if Alexis's dyslexia had crossed her up yet again. "I thought abortion was mostly legal in the UK."

Alexis sighed. "I didn't get the details, but the headlines were catchy. You know how they write them in the big letters on those sandwich boards. Anyway, while I was there, we stayed with great aunt Rosaline," Alexis nodded at Mesa. "You've heard me talk about her."

Millicent Vandemere, Alexis's grandmother, and her two sisters, Rosaline and Athena, came from a wealthy

New York family, who were as sought-after by aristocratic English families in the 1950s as the American women in *Downton Abbey* had been at the turn of the century.

Mesa did remember some tale about one of the sisters marrying an English earl, but with Alexis you could never be sure how much was exaggeration. "Is she the one who married the cash poor aristocrat who died young and she came out of it smelling like a rose?" Mesa tried not to sound snarky, but she did have a deep-seated prejudice against rich people who always seemed to get richer.

"Exactly," Alexis said. "According to gran, the guy was strapped for funds to renovate the family estate that had been bombed during WW II. I think they actually did like each other, but he died before he was even forty. The younger brother couldn't inherit because the will stipulated that he marry. Only he was living in Ibiza with a guy who had been an art forger."

"Guess the family wanted to keep that under wraps," Chance said, looking at Mesa in mock horror.

"Gotta love those Bohemians. They simply wanted to get by, live the artistic life," Alexis countered, "so Aunt Roz ended up inheriting this pile of rock which she eventually had torn down. She built luxury flats instead. She did give the brother a percentage to keep him solvent."

"So what was the story on Rabid Reggie?" Chance said, savoring his cold brew.

"You'll have to check it out on the Daily Mail website," Alexis said off-handedly. "I do remember that the current baronet, Lord 'whoever' was about to croak, and Reg was next in line to inherit the estate, the assets of which he was planning to use to bankroll his right wing agenda. According to gossip Aunt Roz heard, the rest of the Griffin-Joneses were none too happy about any of it."

"Bit of a sticky wicket, eh?" Chance said in his best English accent.

"That's the British upper class," Alexis said, nodding. "All that public airing of grievances gets their knickers in a twist. Reggie's a bit too out there for them."

"So why the interest in an original birth certificate?" Mesa wondered aloud, "Why come to Montana of all places?"

"Got me thinking too," Alexis said. "I remember Aunt Roz saying she was glad her brother-in-law loved the Mediterranean and had the good grace to stay out of the limelight. She didn't have to hire a gaggle of lawyers to argue for years over who should inherit. Maybe that's what Griff intends to do."

"Where is his lordship now?" Mesa asked. If in fact he hadn't done the dirty with Alexis, he could make things right with a more direct conversation about his family when they met up later. And why the ruse about some documentary and his interest in the Elsie's Babies articles? Why hadn't he been upfront about whatever the hell he was trying to find out?

"He said he was going to check out a few possible shooting locations," Alexis said. "Of course that could be complete bullshit. I told him we would hang out in Nan's yard for the firework show tonight, and that I was sure he was welcome. And he said you'd mentioned it."

This last comment Alexis had made with a coy expression. Mesa ignored her and answered her vibrating phone. It was Belushi.

"Did you read my email?" he asked.

She smiled to herself. It was Saturday afternoon of the 4th of July weekend, and Belushi was all over the assignment she'd given him. He had the makings of a real workaholic. "I've been talking with Alexis and Chance. I haven't had time. So what have you sent for me," she said with a smile. Had she created a Bernstein for her Woodward?

"Nailed it," Belushi said. "Hardcastle went to University of Montana after high school and then law school in California. And then, this is the kicker," he said with breathless enthusiasm. "He comes back to Butte after graduation and guess where he goes to work?"

"You're seriously going to make me guess?" she said, more surprised than annoyed. She realized she was beginning to think Belushi might have a sense of humor, or at least irony, after all.

"The legal department of Summit Valley Power," he said without skipping a beat. "It could be a coincidence, but I'm thinking he's the Donuts number."

Mesa stood straight up, startling Alexis, who almost fell out of her folding chair. "Let's pay him a visit and ask," Mesa said. "Where's he live?"

"Out by the Country Club with a wife and two kids, but they're not there," Belushi said matter-of-factly.

"How do you know?" Mesa said, bewildered.

"I'm sitting in front of his house," he said, again without skipping a beat. "I figured I would get a reaction from him about Danica's death, but nobody's home."

"Dammit," Mesa said. "Maybe he's back on Monday," she said with a sigh, "though the way our luck is running, he's probably taken the kids to Disneyland for the week."

"Georgetown Lake," Belushi answered calmly.

And before Mesa could even ask, he finished with, "I talked to the next door neighbors. The Hardcastles have a family cabin out there by Denton's Point. The whole family goes out for the month of July every summer. I got the address."

Mesa had no trouble convincing Alexis to drop everything, hop in her pickup and head to Georgetown Lake. Having a wing woman like Alexis, with no family and no job except keeping track of her trust fund, meant that she was ready to go at a moment's notice, all disagreements put aside.

The forty-five-minute drive through mostly wide-open spaces, mountain ranges across the horizon, reinforced for Mesa what she loved about the West—endless vistas devoid of urban sprawl. Nearby Discovery, the local ski resort, aka Disco, was a central attraction of the Georgetown Lake area in winter, but few people lived there year-round. Aside from two restaurant/bars, amenities were few. The closest grocery or drugstore was fourteen miles away, not to mention a gas station. Suffice it to say, Georgetown was mostly a seasonal community with July and August seeing the most overnight visitors.

While residents were sparse, the number of fish was another story. More trout were caught out of Georgetown than any lake in Montana, and the area would be lousy with anglers around July 4th. The Hardcastles would not be alone. That said, a crowd by Montana standards meant more than five people standing on a street corner. They would have no trouble finding the address and Mesa guessed if they drove around long enough, they'd find Nathan without too much problem as long as he hadn't headed into the mountains.

After crawling through the one-time company town of Anaconda, Highway 1 sported a steady, though certainly not heavy, stream of traffic. While Alexis drove, Mesa thought about whether it would be possible to recognize Nathan Hardcastle's voice from one conversation. After all, it had been nothing more than a two-word exchange she'd overheard twenty-four hours before with Phade. "Yeah" and "Sorry"—that was all she had to go on.

But then there were the background sounds. Hardcastle had two daughters. Was that what she had heard in the background of that phone call—children playing? Had he simply left town to celebrate the holiday with his family? But why would he have taken that phone, if it was him? And why would he have even answered? Maybe he didn't know Danica was dead. Simply having a phone with a number that Danica had called and texted didn't prove anything by itself.

What if Mesa came face to face with Nathan Hardcastle and had to tell him what had happened to her? How distraught might he be? For sure, his initial reaction to Mesa's questions would reveal plenty.

They passed the Brown Derby, a local roadhouse known for its thick steaks and chocolate pie. Alexis had to slow down to make the turn off the highway to Denton's Point. She had only been to the Lake once, when her foreman and sometimes hug buddy, Jessie, had taken her ice fishing in March. "First time I've ever seen bourbon start to freeze in the bottle," Alexis had said, "and I've been to Antarctica."

As they slowed to turn, a motorcycle pulled toward the road's shoulder from the Brown Derby parking lot, revving its engine and ready to pull out in a cloud of dust. The driver wasn't wearing a helmet; few did in Evel Knievel country. Maybe they thought the mirrored sunglasses would save them. At least his passenger wore a helmet, one with a charcoal tinted visor that obscured his face. But the creased shirt sleeves, khakis, and blue Vann's were quite visible. Alexis turned and looked at Mesa and said, "Was that our Englishman?"

Mesa craned to look out the back window and saw the bike receding down the highway toward Anaconda. Apparently, Griff had made friends with some other local and decided to scout locations after all.

Alexis's revelation about Griff's deception was unsettling, though Mesa felt like there would be a reasonable explanation, or at least she hoped there would be one. She fully intended to ask Griff what was up, once she figured out how to do it without busting Alexis for rifling his briefcase. But first, she wanted to talk to Nathan Hardcastle.

Georgetown was not really a town but two small clusters of houses near the highway, one to the east toward Discovery, and the other right on the lake. They turned toward the west onto Denton's Point Road, past a large campground full of RVs and campers, and drove along the lake's south shore where numerous speedboats were in use. Mesa shivered. A brave few in wet suits were on skis, which Mesa had to admire. She had spent many a summer weekend with her childhood friend, Tara

McTeague, at her family cottage on the north end of the lake. She knew how cold the lake water could be.

In another five minutes they were pulling into a circular driveway in front of what was easily the largest house in sight. Some family cabin, more like a lodge. Mesa was betting this was the place. At the center of the driveway a space widened to form an impromptu parking lot, filled with numerous pickups and SUVS, of various sizes and colors, mostly new, and all with Montana license plates, several with Griz motifs from the University.

Mesa admired the rambling two-story cedar home, with newer wings off a central section and picture windows on each side. Backed up against the Deer Lodge National Forest, the house commanded a stunning view of a pristine alpine lake with the snow-capped Pintlers and the Flint Creek mountain range in the background. This was the playground of Montana's one percent.

Half a dozen swimsuit-clad kids of assorted ages ran in circles around a metal flagpole on the lower lawn, Old Glory fluttering in the wind. Mesa could see a clutch of women at a table with a red umbrella on the second-story deck. No men were in sight, probably all on the lake boating or fishing.

Most of the people who frequented the lake had roots in Butte or Anaconda, whether present or past. So when one of the women stood up and came to the deck rail, Mesa assumed it would be a member of the Hardcastle family. The woman moved to a stairway that led down to the drive watching the pickup park. Still, she gave Mesa and Alexis a hard look as they approached.

Mesa wasn't worried. If this wasn't the Hardcastle's property, this woman would know where it was.

Mesa had deputized Alexis for the day and introduced themselves as reporters working on a story. A stack of free copies of the *Messenger* appeared every Wednesday at the Seven Gables restaurant as well as the Brown Derby, the ski resort, too. The name of the paper would afford them some legitimacy.

Mesa apologized for interrupting a holiday afternoon and said they were looking for Nathan Hardcastle. The woman was willowy and blonde, much like the little girl who had quickly approached and hugged her mother. "I'm his wife, Francine. What do you need to see him about?" the woman asked in a serious, though not defensive, tone.

Mesa had run the possibility of such a question through her head. She was conscious of the sensitive nature of her interest and didn't want to create any problem for Hardcastle, at least not yet. She cautioned herself to tread softly. "This past Friday afternoon a woman fell from the roof of the Finlen. The story is still developing, and we're talking to a number of her high school classmates."

"Still developing?" Mrs. Hardcastle interjected. "What does that mean?"

The wife was no pushover that was for sure. "There's been no determination about how she actually died," Mesa answered succinctly. "We were told that Nathan and Chloe Hardcastle were two of the victim's close friends from high school." Mesa had no intention of suggesting anything else until she talked to Hardcastle. Hopefully she would find him before his wife got even more curious, in which case *he* could answer the questions. "Is he around?"

"He ran up to the Derby to have a drink with a guy who's only passing through."

"What about Chloe? Is she here?" Mesa asked, looking up at the women on the deck, hoping they hadn't driven all this way only to come up empty-handed.

The woman gave a chuckle. "Chloe hasn't been out here in years. She works in Africa, in case you didn't know."

Mesa nodded, registering a hint of disdain about the sister-in-law. Chloe's absence didn't sit well?

Francine added, "Nathan should be back in a few minutes. You're welcome to wait," she said sincerely.

"That's okay," Mesa said, not wanting to impose, especially if Nathan Hardcastle turned out to be fooling around on his wife. "Maybe we can catch him at the Derby."

"He rode up there on a red ATV," the woman said, turning back toward the house, "in case you see him coming up the road as you go down."

Francine Hardcastle was so earnest that Mesa almost felt bad. Then she reminded herself that there was no direct link between Danica and Nathan that wasn't at least ten years old. Maybe she and Belushi were completely off base.

Back in the pickup, they headed down the road, reaching the Derby parking lot in time to see a tall, tanned man in plaid golf shorts and a navy polo shirt stand up from a plastic table on the porch. He emptied a Coors Light, put the bottle on the table, and calmly pulled a set of keys from his pocket. Then in a single athletic move, he stepped off the porch and reached for a nearby red ATV.

ᔤᔥ

"You seen Mesa?" Evan Llewellyn asked Chance and Adrienne when he walked into the Mountain Gallery in the late afternoon. Chance thought the young reporter seemed particularly eager, not at all like a slow loris. He had looked up the animal when he had heard that Cinch, the *Mess*'s circulation guy and resident grouch, frequently referred to Evan as such.

The annual 4th of July weekend Art Walk was almost over, and Chance knelt on the floor stuffing the rods of the event canopy into its carrying bag. He looked up at Evan and said, "You know, you're the second person in here today asking for her. She was here, but she left to go out to Georgetown Lake a couple of hours ago. I'm starting to think we should call this the Mess Office Annex."

Evan nodded slowly and slapped his reporter's note book on his palm.

At times Chance couldn't quite figure out Mesa's protégé though his writing had definitely elevated the *Messenger*'s reportage. His story about the number of churches in town that had closed and what leading architects on the west coast thought of their potential for other uses had impressed Chance. It wasn't that it was about architecture that appealed to him, but that Evan had actually gotten comments from well-known experts. The kid was thinking big, which was good, because sometimes, like now, he seemed almost tongue-tied.

"You tried her cell phone?" Adrienne said and then answered her own question. "She's probably outside cell range up there."

Evan pulled at his lip and then nodded.

"Is there something I can help you with?" Chance asked when Evan remained standing at the counter, biting his lip and smacking his reporter's notebook against his hand again.

"It's just that I asked around about that key to the Finlen roof, and I think I might have something."

"Yeah," Chance said, tying the tent bag's drawstring in a bow, "like what?"

"I was talking to my buddy, Spike, who's a summer intern up at the Archives. He came across this box of old stories about Butte, mostly written by high school students over the years. You know, they did the research up there and left a copy for the Archives when they were done. Anyway, Spike saw a paper about how they used to have this observatory up on top of the Finlen during the Cold War. Way back, you know, like in the fifties."

Chance smiled thinking of the absurdity of it. "You mean spotters were up on the roof of the Finlen looking for spy planes. You gotta be kidding me."

Evan smiled slightly, and said, "We sent that U-2 plane over Russia and it got shot down."

"That we did," Chance said, remembering fondly a display at the Smithsonian he'd seen with his dad. "So you think there were keys to the roof made for these observers fifty years ago. Don't you think they might have changed the lock since then?" Chance thought about the Park Hotel building he was currently working on, and for which he had been given an ancient set of keys, and said, "Then again, maybe not."

Evan shrugged. "I was trying to think of who might have a key and how come. Mrs. Terkla, you know, the hotel receptionist, she told me that only the maintenance man has one now, and the owner, of course. All those keys in the office behind the desk, they're only extras for the rooms."

"So who's the maintenance man?" Chance asked.

Chapter 10

Nathan Hardcastle leaned on the seat of the ATV, his legs crossed at the ankles, his wrist nonchalantly resting on the rubber grip of the handlebar. Mesa explained that his wife had suggested they could find him at the Brown Derby. Then she made clear why they had sought him out. "You heard about Danica Draganovich's death?"

She paused ever so slightly to gauge his reaction. Her attempted casual manner did not fool him. He looked directly at her and nodded while she spoke, as if they were meeting in the middle of a fight ring.

So be it. "When was the last time you saw her?" Mesa asked, delivering an exploratory opening jab. Still trying to keep her tone light, she explained that she was looking for a quote for a story.

He shook his head slowly, pursing his lips, "Couple of years ago maybe. I can't remember. She was really closer to my sister." His manner was relaxed, measured, but direct.

So he hadn't seen her? Had she misheard Suzana Petrovich, or was this the first lie? "She didn't call you when she got back to town recently?"

Hardcastle's hazel eyes drilled into her, and he crossed his arms. "Yeah, now that you mention it, I did get a call from her about a month ago, asking how to get in touch with my sister. She works abroad. But I didn't see Danica. Like I said, she's been gone from Butte for quite a few years. We lost touch."

He had parried her attack without losing a beat. Mesa kicked herself for the missed opportunity. She should have simply confronted him with Suzana's statement and at least made him think she knew he was being evasive.

Mesa jotted down what he said and then closed in for the next punch. "The police recovered Danica's cell phone and one of the last numbers she called, several times in fact, ended up being a cell phone with a Summit Valley Power number. We thought since you work there, maybe it was yours."

He smiled and pulled a cell phone from his pocket and then said, "Over a hundred people work at the Summit office in Butte." He held her gaze while he talked, not showing the least concern over the question's implication. When he finished talking, he ran his tongue over a pinch of hair below his lower lip, a faux Leonardo DiCaprio.

"The number was somebody in Technical Services," she said unblinking.

Hardcastle crossed his arms in the other direction. "I'm in Finance. I know those guys who go out on the line carry company cells. Maybe it was one of them," he said and traced over the tuft of hair again.

"Maybe," Mesa said, lingering, and made another note on her reporter's pad. What did they call those whiskers, Mesa thought, surprised by her growing irritation.

"Danica was a beautiful girl," Hardcastle said and stood up, ready to get back on the ATV. "It's a real tragedy what happened to her. You can quote me on that."

Mesa closed her notebook, dropping her pen in the process. She reached down to pick it up just as Hardcastle did the same. They bumped shoulders on the way down.

He came up with the pen, looking her in the eye when he handed it to her, and said, "Sorry."

༄

"Riordan Gillette is the name Mrs. Terkla gave me," Evan said. "He only works three days a week, usually one day on the weekend."

"You mean Razor?" Chance said. "That guy that used to work out at the Country Club, always trying to weasel into the money games?"

Evan nodded. "Mrs. Terkla, she remembers everybody by their roll book name, I think," he said and gave Adrienne another hint of a smile. "She said he graduated same year as Danica."

"That's a bit of a coincidence, don't you think?" Chance said, not that he could imagine Razor even knowing someone like Danica. "She seem sure about that, too?"

In the time it took for Evan to shrug, Adrienne had ducked into her office and returned with the Bulldog yearbook. She had turned to the senior class pictures, going immediately to the Gs. "There he is—Razor

Gillette," she said, tapping the portrait of a fresh-faced kid with a shock of scraggly, sandy hair, a square jaw, and a cleft in his chin—his photo a couple of rows above the Hardcastles.

Adrienne came around to the front of the counter and put the large volume between the two men. Chance, who towered over Belushi—a.k.a. Evan—and Adrienne, read aloud. "Nickname—Rocket Man; Future Plans—Score a Winnebago and sell prescription drugs to fund my Twinkies addiction while sky watching with Major Tom."

Chance let out a groan. "In his dreams. He spent the last ten years cutting grass at the Country Club and oiling golf carts. I'm betting he started up at the Finlen to make extra cash in the winter."

"I've seen him around town lately," Evan said. "Not in a Winnebago," he said seriously. "He rides a Fat Boy."

Adrienne looked at Chance who translated, "Harley-Davidson."

"What if he and Nathan Hardcastle are tight somehow? He's a Country Club type, right?" Belushi said. "I mean if Nathan is the guy who got the calls from Danica, maybe Razor could have unlocked the door to the roof for them."

Adrienne nodded. "You think Danica went up on the roof to meet Nathan? Or maybe Razor?" she said and began flipping back and forth between the photographs. "But why the roof? You think one of them might know what happened to her?"

"Maybe I could try to track this Gillette guy down," Belushi said.

Chance nodded but Adrienne countered with, "Why don't you give a call to Phade and see if he knows this

Razor Gillette and whether Danica knew him. His name's not on the list Mesa gave us. See if he wants to give that bit of information to Detective Macgregor. If he's working half as hard as you and Mesa, I would think he'd be glad to know what you found out."

"Except I don't think he is," Belushi said, looking only slightly deflated, but he nodded, and pulled his phone from his back pocket. "On account of it's the weekend. I mean, unless he gets called out on a homicide, I don't think the department has detectives working overtime on deaths that aren't tagged suspicious." He added this last comment so seriously it made Chance think the kid really did want to find out what had happened to Danica. He wasn't simply trying to impress Mesa.

Belushi began to scroll through his phone contacts, then stopped and asked, "Do either of you know if Mesa told Phade about Hardcastle working at the Power?"

Chance and Adrienne looked at each other, and both shook their heads. "She only found that out this afternoon from you," Chance said, with a nod of approval.

Adrienne added, "She didn't say anything about telling Phade before she left."

Chance could see why she might want to wait, given Phade's inclination toward drama. It made sense—having Phade close to home and working directly with the police. "I wouldn't say anything yet."

Belushi went back to tapping numbers on the phone's keypad. His conversation with Phade was mercifully short. "S'up," Belushi said, and followed with, "Got something for you." He explained about the key and Razor Gillette. Then he said, "Okay, cool," nodding while he listened. Then he said, "Yeah, later," and hung up. He immediately began texting on his cell phone.

"And so?" Chance said with arms outstretched, when Belushi didn't offer any other information.

Belushi looked up from his phone, clearly distracted, and saw both Chance and Adrienne looking at him. "Sorry. Phade said Detective Macgregor was there for a short time this afternoon with his wife, to pay his respects, not anything official. He did say he knew about the key from the owner, Mr. Kinder, who says he's been thinking about canning Gillette anyway, and if he is the one who let Danica up on the roof, he'll fire him for sure. He said some other stuff too but Phade didn't say what. He says why don't we all meet at Mrs. Ducharme's before the fireworks tonight and compare notes?"

Chance could tell Belushi was happy to be included in the *we*. "He said all that, did he?"

Belushi nodded and then his phone pinged again, and his thumbs immediately sprung into action. Chance and Adrienne began closing up shop. Belushi cursed aloud, and then seconds later a tall, thin girl stuck her head in the front door of the gallery and said, "You better come now. He's getting out of hand."

"Okay," Belushi said, and then turned to Adrienne and Chance, "I gotta go home to take care of something, but I'll be back. Will you text me when the boss gets back into town?"

"Sure, kid," Chance said, stifling the smile that came when he heard Mesa referred to as *boss*. And then he added, "Is everything okay? You need help?"

Belushi shook his head, "Nah, just another 4th of July," he said, his voice resigned as if whatever was happening was nothing new.

ɷ·ᴄᴗ

"Son of a bitch is lying," Mesa said to Alexis as they walked back to the pickup. She tossed her reporter's notebook on the dashboard, surprised how angry she felt. She thought about Hardcastle's wife, clueless, waiting at home, his daughters playing in their swimsuits. How long had he been lying to them?

Alexis nodded, cranked the engine and shifted into reverse while they watched Nathan Hardcastle roar off down Denton's Point Road back toward his lake house. "You sound certain," she said.

"What do you call that stupid triangle of hair under his lip?" Mesa said. That was his tell, all right. And she was sure it was his voice on the phone when Phade had called, using the ER ruse. That single word "sorry," sincere but controlled, was what she had heard then, and just a few moments ago.

That and something else about him, his self-satisfied attitude, his conceit, Mesa couldn't put her finger on it exactly. But it was him. She could feel it in her bones. Nathan Hardcastle had been Danica Draganovich's "Donuts," the one she had called five different times since her return to Butte, the secret someone she didn't want anyone to know about.

"It's a soul patch, flavor-savor in the Midwest. It's so nineties," Alexis said. "He was working it though, with those close trimmed sideburns. He's still turning heads. But a bit of a cold fish, if you ask me."

Unquestionably, Hardcastle was a good-looking guy and he knew it, something that aggravated Mesa even more. His smugness pressed up against Mesa's journalistic standard to put emotions aside and gather the facts. "Let's head home," she said, looking at the time. It was past five and would be six by the time they got back into town.

She thought about the motorcycle they'd seen Griff on and wondered what else he was up to. "I want to catch up with Belushi and Griff. It sounded like he was coming over to Nan's tonight, right?"

"More or less. Of course, he and his motorcycle buddy might have something a little wilder in mind."

Mesa thought about the guy driving the motorcycle. He looked vaguely familiar—like a lot of people she saw on the streets of Butte. She had spent chunks of her childhood living with her grandparents, and then attending Butte High after her mother had died. If she didn't know most people in Butte by name, she usually knew them on sight. Even the motorcycle looked familiar. It was the color that set it apart—beige. What testosterone-filled motorcycle jock owned a bike that color?

She sighed and looked at the reception bars on her phone— no cell service. She would have to wait until they got into Anaconda before she could see if Belushi had emailed her anything new.

Her thoughts turned to Phade. When she had left him at his grandmother's house that morning, he was leafing through his sister's dog-eared address book. She wanted to know what or who he might have discovered, and she wanted to know more about Chloe Hardcastle and if there was someone else in town they could talk to who was a mutual friend of hers and Danica's. She knew there was more to Danica and Nathan's story. She could feel it. They needed to cast a wider net.

Alexis had just sped past the outskirts of Anaconda, and The Haufbrau, a restaurant with a German name that served Italian food, when Mesa's phone began to ping with notifications. The first was an involved text from Belushi saying that he had a lead on the maintenance man with a key to the Finlen roof access door, including a detailed description of him and his vehicle. He had also talked to Phade, and they would be waiting for her at Nan's. Mrs. Terkla was the person who had come up with the name, Razor Gillette.

"No shit," Mesa said aloud when she finished reading. It had just hit her.

Alexis looked over at her, "What?"

"This guy named Razor Gillette is the maintenance man at the Finlen.

"Somebody you know?" Alexis said.

"Know *of* is more like it. He could be the guy on the motorcycle with Griff."

Adrienne would have preferred to forgo the entire red, white, and blue fireworks extravaganza. When she had returned to Montana, she had envisioned a quiet, bordering on reclusive, existence—time to paint and read. But quiet reflection did not enter into Butte's Independence Day celebration, which would soon begin less than a mile away.

Fireworks sales were brisk and available to one and all, despite a call from some locals, not to mention the fire marshal, that grass fires were already a concern. But when it came to fireworks in Butte, reason went out the window. The Council of Commissioners was not inclined to incur the wrath of the community by shutting fireworks sales down. The little boy in everybody had won the day.

So while Adrienne felt like she had been transported to the middle of Baghdad for the last three days, everyone else nodded indulgently when the kids across the street began lighting up rockets, cherry bombs, and whatever else they'd saved their allowance to purchase for the occasion. Meanwhile, the clock ticked relentlessly toward the appointed hour when "the big show" would begin on Big Butte, the outcropping to the north of the college.

Chance alternated between conversation with Sam Chavez about aspects of the Park Hotel restoration and running out into the street to help the neighbor kids with troublesome fuses. One of the ten-year-olds was trying to light a cone rocket. When he leaned in close to examine the fuse that appeared dormant, Chance had grabbed the boy, and pulled him away right before the rocket went off. Adrienne could see Chance giving the kid a talking to. Then at the end, the two bumped fists in mutual understanding.

Adrienne smiled. There was something special about a guy who genuinely cared about kids not even his own. Nana came into the garden and Adrienne turned her attention to learning more about the house on Granite Street where the baby's remains had been found the previous Thursday. That was the story that was niggling in the back of her mind.

"Who was living in that house in the winter of 1995?" Adrienne asked Nana Rose after she joined her to sit under the willow tree. According to what Nick Philippoussis had told Chance, a ticket to the Winter Ball of that year had been found in the pocket of the jacket in which the body had been wrapped. Presumably the baby's corpse had been placed there sometime after that.

Nana sat in her wicker chair, still and calm, except for adjusting the silver bangles on her thin wrist occasionally, ever the well-turned-out matriarch. "That would have been the Armisteads," she said, straightening the surface of her skirt as she thought. "He was the last of Butte's old-fashioned general practitioners, like his father before him. I knew his wife, Clarice, from Homer Club."

Adrienne enjoyed hearing Rose Ducharme talk about Butte and its families. Though Rose would always be an outsider herself, especially since she had married an Ojibwa Indian, she was a keen social historian and took pride in keeping track of the city's social events. That was partly what had interested her in buying the *Messenger*, according to Mesa. "Nan sees the newspaper as a vital historical record."

"They traveled a good deal after he retired," Nan said, tightening the light shawl around her shoulders against the evening breeze. "I remember her giving a travelogue at Homer Club one year about their trip to the Vatican. They had one of the last audiences with Pope John Paul before he fell ill." She paused for a moment as if remembering some curious aspect of the trip. Then she said, "Not long after that, they became snowbirds, spending the winters in Phoenix, I believe it was. The winters here can be awfully hard on these old bones," she said and rubbed her long slender fingers together playfully.

Adrienne smiled at the older woman and patted her arm. "You seem to do fine." She meant it, too. Her heart attack aside, Rose Ducharme's overall health seemed to be good.

"I remember we had a conversation about the winter of 1947 in England being the coldest in fifty years. I was only seven, but I remember how coal was still rationed. Clarice was rather a delicate type, not sure she could have hung on. She ended up staying in Arizona after her husband died."

"What happened to the house then?" Adrienne wondered aloud.

"I would have thought it would have stayed in the family after she passed away. But apparently none of them wanted to live in it. It stood empty for quite a while. Finally they had an estate sale, and then sold the house *as is* a year or so ago."

Adrienne was quietly doing the math while Rose talked. According to the paper, the infant's body was ten-plus years old. "So by about 2000, the house would have been empty for part of the year while its owners were in Arizona?"

"Seems likely," Rose said. "For a while they had one or two of the grandchildren living in it. They had a lot of heirlooms, beautiful Wedgewood tea set, French furniture, that sort of thing. Clarice did have an eye for an antique. I'll say that for her."

House-sitting grandchildren, Adrienne thought, now that could be a healthy, fertile group. She had hardly shown at all for the first four months of her single attempt at pregnancy. The miscarriage had come not long after that. She knew other women who had almost completely concealed their pregnancy. If you weren't having sex with anybody, the layered look, especially in winter, made concealment deceptively easy.

It would have been possible to keep the pregnancy secret, but then did that mean the birth had to be secret, too? Having delivered babies in tribal huts in Africa and several in ambulances when she was a resident in the ER, she knew it was possible to deliver a baby anywhere if you had to. But in this case, she had to wonder if this was an emergency birth, or a clandestine home birth that had gone wrong.

The Freedom Fest was in full swing at Chester Steele Park—balloon artists making hats, a cover band playing Bruce Springsteen, vendors selling hot dogs and cotton candy. The aromas actually made Mesa lick her lips.

As they drove along Alabama Street, Alexis complained, "There's no place within a mile to park, I tell you. Why did Belushi insist on meeting you here? Why can't he come up to your Nan's? It's only a block away." Alexis was ranting now.

"I don't know," Mesa said, exasperated, looking for the house numbers. "He said he'd be right around here." Mesa had received a stream of texts from her young reporter as soon as she left Anaconda. He had thoughts about the key to the Finlen roof and could she meet him right away.

They pulled up to the corner of Alabama and Diamond. Mesa could see no identifying numbers, and the cover band was playing "Hungry Heart" at an obnoxiously loud level. Then, like that, Belushi stepped out from the cover of a large lilac bush overgrowing a white picket fence. Belushi was wearing a pair of metal-framed aviator glasses but they couldn't completely conceal the red mark that cascaded down his left cheek.

Mesa rolled down the truck's window and was about to ask him what had happened when a door slammed inside the house beyond where he stood. Then a man's voice roared, "Get me another beer."

"Everything okay here, Evan?" Mesa said in an even tone. She didn't want to embarrass him but the tension in the air was obvious.

"Swell." he said with a forced smile, and got right to business. "This maintenance guy at the Finlen, Gillette, went to school with Danica. I talked to Chance and Dr. DeBrook and they think he might be a friend of Hardcastle's, too."

Mesa's mind was racing. Now they were getting somewhere. "Do either of them happen to know this Gillette?"

Belushi shrugged. "Chance said he used to work at the Country Club fixing golf carts, but that he thought he got fired. Adrienne found something in the yearbook about him that connects him to Hardcastle." He paused and then added. "I've seen him around town. He's always on his Harley Low Rider."

Mesa sensed that Belushi had had more than one fantasy about the motorcycle, which would fit his short frame well. It would also be a darn sight cooler than the bicycle he used to get around town.

Alexis, who had been listening with one ear, looked at Belushi and then Mesa. "Like that bike we saw the Englishman on this afternoon."

Mesa looked at Alexis and then turned back to Belushi. "You're sure it's beige?" was all she said.

"Sand denim, the manufacturer calls it."

Mesa nodded. "I think we better get up to my grandmother's and talk to Chance and Adrienne. The Englishman, too." She wondered if Griff's connection to this Razor guy was more than coincidental. She looked at Belushi again. "You want a ride up?"

He shook his head perfunctorily and gestured at his cheek. "Better not." Another loud bang came from the house behind the lilac bushes. This one sounded like a dish breaking. "My old man doesn't like loud music."

Chapter 11

Nana Rose's shivering cued Adrienne to move inside to await the fireworks. Despite a sweltering ninety degrees earlier, the temperature had dropped quickly once the sun had set. She smiled, watching Chance through the picture window in the front of the house. She loved his gentle playfulness. Overseeing firework safety out front, that was what *he* said, he was cradling a timid little girl who buried her face in his chest when the blasts got too loud. Meanwhile his laughter was as exuberant as the kids.

When Mesa and Alexis arrived, they were quick to ask Adrienne if she could show them the yearbook and what she and Chance had learned about Belushi's latest discovery—the key man, Razor Gillette. Adrienne called to Chance who dutifully left the fireworks and the kids, much to their protest, to retrieve the tome from his Land Rover.

He quickly turned to the appropriate section. "I recognized his name and then when I saw the yearbook picture, it's this guy who was the greens keeper at the Country Club, general maintenance guy, too. Then I got to thinking that Hardcastle might have been one of the Country Club officers. So they probably would keep up with each other. I don't pay much attention to the politics out there, but it seems to me Gillette got the sack at the end of last summer."

"His nickname *Rocket Man* dovetails nicely with Nathan Hardcastle's *Major Tom*, a la the David Bowie song," Adrienne said. "Then in 'future plans', Nathan says 'aerospace engineering and rebuilding the GH so he can become a lifetime member of the Air Defense Team'. This seems to connect to Gillette's 'becoming a Skywatcher with Major Tom'." As she presented her analysis aloud, she found herself smiling at her seriousness. After all, she was talking about the inane banter of eighteen-year-old boys. She couldn't help imagining what Chance must have been like then.

"Air Defense Team? Skywatcher? This makes no sense," Mesa said. "I don't even think I put anything in my yearbook, but I'm pretty sure if I did, it wasn't as bizarre as all this."

"Don't look at me," Alexis said. "I went to Drug Rehab Boarding School. We had mug shots instead of senior pictures."

"Where's Evan?" Chance asked. "He said something earlier that's got me thinking." He looked at Adrienne. "Remember he was talking about the kid who's working at the Archives this summer?"

Adrienne clasped her hands together in comprehension. "That's right, something about an observatory on the roof of the Finlen during the Cold War."

And with that realization, the first, ear-splitting *kaboom*! Made her jump a half-inch. The annual fireworks display, which the entire town had been anticipating all day, had begun. The subsequent volleys made conversation impossible without screaming at each other. Everyone but Nana Rose went out to the porch to watch the show. She had long ago declared the cacophony intolerable.

Adrienne looked around the garden at the various people who had gathered to watch the fireworks showering down on them. She wondered if Mesa had noticed that neither Phade nor the charming Englishman had yet to show up.

The show lasted a full half-hour, filled with incredible color that lit up the entire neighborhood. Mesa couldn't help but enjoy the spectacle that never seemed to lose the excitement of childhood. The collective *oohs* and *ahhs*, when a clever combination of pyrotechnics formed a red heart inside a giant blue circle, were magical. And then there was the finale—a thunderous, five minutes of orchestrated pandemonium that easily invoked the image of the "rockets' red glare, the bombs bursting in air."

When the end came, Mesa didn't feel any more patriotic than before, but she was certainly thankful that she had never had to live through a real bombing. It was then that she looked through the window to see her grandmother sitting quietly in her rocking chair in the living room, no doubt relieved that the spectacle and the noise were over. Mesa was about to join her when Phade appeared at the front gate.

Quickly her thoughts shifted to the reality of the Draganovich family, steeped in grief. She couldn't imagine that they saw town's celebration as anything but something to avoid.

Mesa went down the path to greet him alone. He looked as haggard as when she had left him hours ago at his Baba's house. She gave him a quick hug and put her arm through his and led him up to the front porch. The others had all gone inside, most likely to the kitchen to warm up.

Phade slumped onto the wicker loveseat on the porch and Mesa sat next to him. "How's the day gone?" she asked. "Your family, how are they?"

Phade let out a long sigh. "Still in shock. Father Jovan stopped by. He prayed with Baba and my parents and reassured them about how the funeral would be handled. Helped them not worry so much about the church service."

Mesa felt a sense of relief for them, but she knew that Phade's attitude was much more secular. "And what about you?"

"I'm mad. I wanna find this Gillette guy and beat the shit out of him until he tells me why he let my sister up on that roof."

"Something tells me he wasn't necessarily the only one up there with her," Mesa said quietly, "if he was up there at all."

"What makes you say that?" Phade said, his eyes searching her face.

"I talked to Nathan Hardcastle," she said, cautiously gauging Phade's reaction, trying to anticipate how much to tell him. If she painted Hardcastle in too harsh a light, she worried that Phade might decide to do something drastic.

"Where'd you find him? Did he talk to Danica Friday?"

"Georgetown. He said he didn't. But I recognized his voice. From the phone call. It was him."

Phade sat up straight, as if a bolt of electricity had passed through him. "You mean, he's the guy who answered the phone last night?"

Mesa nodded and said, "I think he's Donuts."

"Shit," Phade said. "Belushi says the dude's married with a couple of kids."

"I know," Mesa said calmly. "And Suzana Petrovich did confirm your sister and Hardcastle had a thing when they were in high school and the year after. She also said Danica said she talked with Hardcastle when she first got back to town." Mesa flipped through to the notes in her phone to look at the texts between Danica and Hardcastle. She showed her phone to Phade. "Remember what her text said:

> Danica: I saw the story this morning. How could you lie to me like that?
>
> Donuts: You have to believe me. I couldn't see another choice.
>
> Danica: I'll be at the GH at 1. Be there or I'll come find you.
>
> Donuts: Okay.

"Sounds like she was upset with him about lying," Mesa said. "It didn't sound like they were looking to hook up."

"Depending on where the GH is," Phade said sarcastically. Then he sighed. "God, what's wrong with me? My sister was as religious as Baba. Danica wouldn't do anything that could hurt someone's marriage, not in a million years. How could I even think that?"

"It does sound like he felt threatened though," Mesa said. "Otherwise, why be evasive about talking to her?" Mesa sighed. "There's so much we don't know. Like, what story is she talking about, and what the hell is the GH anyway, and where is it, and why did she end up on the roof instead."

Phade had pulled out Danica's address book from his back pocket. "Here's this. I been through it a couple of times. Nobody popped out at me except Brendan Fife."

Mesa began flipping through the dog-eared book. "Who's that?"

"Next-door-neighbor kid. They moved to Seattle after the old man retired, to be near their daughters. Brendan and Danica were tight growing up, high school, too. Another drama queen." Phade rolled his eyes. Then he said, "I suck. That wasn't fair. He is gay, but he's cool. He lives in Bozeman now, I think."

Mesa opened the address book to Fife's name. Half the page was filled with crossed-out addresses, a couple of which were APOs. "Was he in the military?"

Phade nodded, "He was gonna go to med school, but he ended up in the Air Force instead. I think he was in Germany for a while."

Next to the last entry, an address outside Bozeman, she saw a giant asterisk next to a repeated underline of a cell phone number. Mesa was almost certain it was among the ones Danica had called in the final days before she died.

Soon after midnight Phade left the Ducharme house with Mesa's promise that she would call him as soon as she talked to Brendan Fife. Since it didn't look like Griff wasn't going to show, she went inside to gather up Alexis and head back to the duplex. Chance and Adrienne were getting ready to leave as well. Mesa reminded her brother of their plans to meet at the *Mess* office an hour before the parade began the next morning. They were discussing logistics of their coverage when a loud knock came at the front door.

Chance frowned at his grandmother and then Mesa, saying, "Who the hell could that be?" and then he went to the door.

For half a second Mesa thought it might be Griff, but then her breath caught when she saw Sheriff Solheim following Chance back into the dining room.

Oh my God, she thought. There was no good reason for him to be calling at this hour. What could have happened now? An image of Belushi, his dark glasses, and his father's loud voice flashed in her mind.

"It's Griffin-Jones," Chance said in a flat voice. "He's been shot."

The house suddenly became quiet with Mesa the first to recover. "Has he been able to tell you what happened?" Mesa finally asked, after she had shaken off her initial shock. *How could this have happened* was all she could think. Griff might be a stranger in town but he was not the type who might be looking for any trouble. Quite the opposite. She couldn't help feeling somewhat responsible. Why hadn't she called him when he didn't show up for the fireworks?

The Sheriff shook his head. "He was found in the alley between the Mai Wah Society and the Silver Dollar Saloon," the Sheriff said. They were all in the parlor, drinking strong coffee that Adrienne had helped Nana make. "He's lucky that somebody used that alley to take a leak, or he might have bled to death.

"He was gut shot so they took him straight to surgery. There was no gun at the scene, so we don't think the wound was self-inflicted, and his wallet was empty. Course nobody saw or heard anything, except fireworks."

Then he took a long look around the room, ending with Mesa. "Royal says you know this fellow." He nodded toward her.

Mesa felt her heart in her throat, and for a second she wasn't sure she could speak. So she simply nodded back.

Then he said to the group, "Anybody else met him?

Alex, Adrienne, Chance, Sam, and Nana all answered in the affirmative.

The Sheriff sighed, rubbed his close-cropped white hair, and said "Ah, hell," under his breath. Then he turned to Nana Rose, "Mrs. Ducharme, mind if we use another room so I can ask a few questions in private? Otherwise, everybody'll have to come up to the station. I wouldn't ask, but it's late, and it's a bit rowdy down there 'bout now."

"By all means, Sheriff," Nana said and gestured toward the double doors to the dining room.

Mesa watched with appreciation at her grandmother's composure, how she took bad news in stride, simply looking to do what needed to be done. "I learned it from my mother, stiff upper lip and all that," she would tell Mesa.

"Everybody will have to stay put in here," the Sheriff said. "Chance, get the officer on the porch to come inside and wait with you. I'll have to ask you not to discuss anything pertinent to the case until I've met with everybody individually."

"Mind if we have a drink while we wait," Alexis said with a pout as the Sheriff got up from the sofa, standing nimbly to his full six feet plus.

"Nope. I'd have one myself if I wasn't working."

"When was the last time you saw this fella?" was the first question Solheim asked.

Mesa sat across from him at the well-polished, mahogany dining table where most of the Ducharme family dinner celebrations had taken place through the years. She felt both comforted and slightly intimidated by the specter of her grandparents and parents sitting around the table. Despite her desire to protect Griff, she knew it would be a mistake to tell anything but the truth, and so she told it.

First, that she'd seen him late that afternoon at Georgetown Lake riding on the back of a Harley, likely owned by Razor Gillette. Then she explained how she'd met Jones, and the later reservations that had arisen based on the information that Alexis had discovered. Here she did hedge, hoping not to say anything that might contradict the story that Alexis would no doubt concoct that would leave her in the most innocent light.

"But you can't think of any specific motive for why anyone would want to harm Mr. Jones?" Solheim asked, now stretching to put his hands behind his head.

"I thought you said his wallet was empty." She sensed the Sheriff was tired and knew he had a room full of other people to interview. She decided theorizing would not be welcome.

Sheriff discounted her comment with a doubtful nod. "We're not sure how long he'd been down before somebody called us. The cash could have disappeared after the shooting."

Mesa shook her head, genuinely perplexed. "He's only been in town a couple of days. He's a pretty low-key guy, polite, smart. Can't imagine he could piss off anybody in that amount of time." Then she thought about the dust up at The Gun Room, but as far as she knew, he and Alexis had gotten out of there without drawing attention to their involvement. Mesa decided to leave it that way.

Solheim paused before asking the next question. She could see why he was such an effective law officer. He seemed to know just how long to allow someone to become uneasy and start babbling. It was a technique she used when interviewing Hardcastle, only he hadn't fallen for it either. Finally the sheriff said, "The officer who was first on the scene said that the vic kept muttering something about a book. 'Get my book. It's mine.' Something like that. Any idea what he might have meant?"

Mesa thought for a moment about the conversations she'd had with Jones. The only book they had talked about was Elsa Seppanen's ledger. That seemed too far-fetched a possibility, and she hesitated to mention it, for fear the Sheriff would accuse her of an overactive imagination which he had done in the past. She shook her head again, and said nothing.

"Then it's down to some random encounter as far as you would know?"

"'Fraid so, sheriff." She stopped here, deciding not to muddy the waters with Griff's interest in Elsie's Babies.

It was nearly 2 a.m. before the Sheriff left. By then he had issued an "attempt to locate" for Razor Gillette. Mesa felt compelled to wait around until the Sheriff was gone. Nana had gone to bed as soon as she had finished talking to the Sheriff and vouching for the Englishman's good manners and breeding. Adrienne and Chance had left soon after.

It was Alexis who spent the longest time talking to the Sheriff. Whether it was the two beers she had drunk while waiting, or simply her suspicions about Griff's true interest in Butte and perhaps, its red-light district, she had managed to keep the Sheriff's attention. Of course, it could have been the ponytail.

Chance's cell had awakened them both right before 9 a.m. Adrienne was the one who found the phone, buried under a mound of hastily removed clothes. They hadn't gone straight to sleep after Saturday night's excitement. Adrienne had paced the apartment, what with the fireworks and dealing with Solheim. "Imagine that Englishman lying in that alley listening to all those fireworks," she said. "He must have thought he was in the middle of World War III."

"Take it easy. Can't let that overactive imagination get away with you," Chance had said and made her some chamomile tea. "Here, chug this," he said, and then proceeded to employ all manner of ways to get her to relax and fall asleep. Adrienne hadn't complained. After all, if she was going to be awake anyway, how could a hot oil massage not help?

Now Chance was supposed to be meeting Mesa at the *Mess* office before the parade which started in two hours, and he was barely awake. She got up to make him some coffee and found herself thinking about what she had told the Sheriff about her conversation with Jones.

Based on the questions the Sheriff had asked, Adrienne couldn't quite tell if the shooting had anything to do with Jones and why he was in Butte, or something more sinister. She was inclined to believe that Griff had been the victim of random violence, a sad enough consequence of America's gun culture, happening all too frequently, though Adrienne had learned, as an outsider in Butte, not to draw attention to it.

Even if Montana had one of the lowest rates of violence in the country, from what Chance said, the average Montana household contained about fifteen guns, which was considered completely normal and aboveboard. Adrienne thought it was beyond the pale, though she had to admit she'd never seen anybody with a sidearm in town and only the occasional rifle on a rack in a pickup during hunting season.

Adrienne had not been alone in her concern for Griffin-Jones. Mesa had cornered her once Solheim had finished his questioning. She had asked if Adrienne would be willing to check up on Jones in the morning. Her *ad locum* privileges at the hospital meant she could check his status while everyone else was at the parade, which she had no plans to attend. After all, he was a long way from home, and Adrienne shared Mesa's concern.

Adrienne had put her mug of tea on the table when Chance came into the kitchen, poured himself some coffee, and sat down next to her. He had a perplexed look on his face. "That phone call was Tyler out at the airfield. You'll never guess who just flew into town."

"Special guest for the parade?" Adrienne said, responding seriously. "The governor decide to march after all?" It wasn't unheard of, she knew. Even Barack Obama had been to Butte for the 4th of July parade during his first campaign.

"More curious than that," Chance said. He rubbed his chin and said, "Dewey."

ⷎⷎ

Alexis padded out of the bedroom in flip-flops, walking like a zombie. She wore a faded Griz basketball jersey and her blonde hair gathered atop her head in a bandana, one good looking zombie. Her eyes were barely open, so Mesa called out to give her focus. "Coffee. Over here."

Mesa sat at her makeshift dining table where she and Phade had conspired on Saturday morning, to outline a strategy for who to talk to about his sister's death. Now she was contemplating how to sneak into the hospital and see Griff. She felt terrible about what had happened to him. But she also wanted to ask him a few questions.

Alexis plopped down next to her, pouring Bailey's into her coffee. "Happy Birthday, America," she said and took a sip. She looked at Mesa and then said, "You've got that determined look on your face. Tell me what's going on in your head, but don't forget you promised to go to the rodeo with me tonight."

Mesa twirled the pen she held around her thumb. "Okay. It's been forty-eight hours since Danica

Draganovich came off the roof of the Finlen Hotel, and I'm pretty sure she didn't jump. I wanna know what happened to her." Mesa detailed what they knew. Danica had texted someone to rendezvous with her at 1 p.m. She had known someone who had a key that accessed the door to the Finlen's roof and that someone might have been her one-time crush, Nathan Hardcastle, but he was denying it. And they had no way of proving anything different. At least until they found Razor. She was now sure it was no coincidence that he and Hardcastle had been at the Brown Derby. "I'd like to know if Griff being there had anything to do with him getting shot. But maybe we have to let the Sheriff figure that out."

By now Alexis appeared to actually be paying attention. "You think the Englishman could be involved in this?" she said skeptically.

Mesa shrugged. "Seems like a big coincidence if he's not. I called Vivian first thing when I got up. She told me Friday at lunch that Griff had agreed to come back to the Archives Friday afternoon, but he never showed. He could have been back at the Finlen about the time Danica died."

The other puzzle piece that was niggling at the back of her mind was this business about Danica not being able to have kids. What that might have to do with anything, other than to add to the argument of suicide, she didn't know.

"Have you talked to Phade this morning?" Alexis said with a yawn. "Has he come up with anything new?"

Mesa picked up her notepad and looked at the phone number Phade had given her the evening before. "As a matter of fact…," she said, her voice trailing off as she picked up her phone. She punched in the number for Brendan Fife, the Draganovich's one time neighbor.

He answered on the first ring, which caught Mesa by surprise. She half expected most people to be far from their phones on the 4th, even cell phones. Not to mention the fact that she felt like everywhere she looked for a lead about what might have happened to Danica, she got nowhere. Now here was a crisp, alert voice at the other end of the phone.

"I'm afraid I have some bad news," Mesa said after her initial introduction, saying that she'd gotten his number from Phade.

"It's okay," Brendan said, "I've heard." He sounded resigned. "The Butte grapevine reaches across the mountain to Belgrade." A bedroom community of trendy Bozeman, the small town was now the fastest growing city in Montana and only seventy miles east of the Divide.

Mesa went on to explain her conversation with Phade about connecting with Brendan and did he know that he had been among the last people Danica had talked to.

"We were making plans to get together during the Folk Festival, that's all. She sounded excited about her new job. I don't know what to tell you."

Mesa sighed. Brendan was telling her the same story everyone else had. She decided to dig deeper. "You guys were pretty close growing up, right?"

"Totally. She was the first person I ever came out to. She guessed, actually. She wouldn't give up on wanting me to ask Chloe Hardcastle out. Finally Danica figured out it wasn't going to happen. It didn't bother her at all, even with her Orthodox background. Maybe because of it. They don't judge, you know. And we stuck together—Huey, Dewey, and Louie."

"Say what?" Mesa said, remembering Chance and Adrienne talking about their search in the borrowed yearbook. They had never found Louie, only now it seemed she was talking on the phone to him.

"Danica, Chloe, and me—that's what we called ourselves."

"I was hoping you could tell me more about Chloe," Mesa said, trying not to sound too excited out of respect for Brendan's friendship with Danica. "I'd like to talk to her about what happened."

"Well, this is your lucky day. She called me last night from Phoenix. She's flying into Butte today. We're getting ready to drive over there right now to meet up with her after the parade. I don't see why we couldn't catch up with you later today as well."

"Fantastic," Mesa said aloud, suddenly rejuvenated. She hung up the phone. "Alexis, gets your boots on. I need you to be my chauffeur for the parade. And no, I won't forget about the rodeo."

Chapter 12

When Mesa walked into the *Mess* office, she smiled to find Belushi at his desk working on a blog post for the paper's website. He was twirling a Tootsie Pop in his mouth, which he removed the second Mesa appeared.

"Got any more of those?" she said, surprised at the sudden tenderness she felt toward him. Before the previous night, when she had known nothing of Belushi's home situation, Mesa had given little, if any, thought to the reporter's personal life.

To the contrary, she had decided that anything except his work persona was mildly annoying. Her attitude toward his friends on Saturday night had been dismissive. Realizing now how important Belushi's go-to peeps must be when he needed to get away from home, she regretted her snap judgments.

He opened a desk drawer to reveal a large sack of the candy. Mesa picked a cherry Pop. "You could take another one for the road if you want," he said and nodded back to the drawer.

She reached in and ferreted out a grape-flavored version and then an orange, "And one for Alexis?"

"Absolutely," he said his voice clear and enthusiastic.

The mention of Alexis's name, let alone knowing she might want something you possessed, was a way to brighten any guy's spirits. "What are you working on?" she said and unwrapped the candy.

Belushi tilted his screen so she could see the masthead of the blog. "I'm checking for comments. Last night I posted a follow-up to the entry you made yesterday about Danica. I said we wanted to do a feature on her and encouraged anybody who had talked to her before Friday to text us."

"Good idea," Mesa said. Why hadn't she thought of that? Belushi was scoring points right and left. "I'm headed over to the Civic Center to see if anything is brewing at the parade lineup. Irita heard that someone was going to show up with a flaming crucifix. That should cause a stir, open flames prohibited on the city streets and all."

Belushi was nodding his head. "Sweet," he muttered.

"Chance is running late, so he's going to meet me there. I was planning to get some quotes farther down the route toward the end, you know, when everybody is tired, sweaty and worn out."

She paused and savored her Tootsie Pop. She noticed Belushi had gone back to his. Then she said in a collegial tone, "But I might get a call from this guy named Brendan Fife. He was a childhood friend of Danica's. Hopefully Chloe Hardcastle will be with him. So I may have to split before the parade is over."

"I could cover the route where the crowd widens, by the mall, maybe get a few shots with my phone. Or anything you want me to do," he offered. "I got my mountain bike so I could ride to the end of the parade quick if you needed to leave."

"Why not?" Mesa said. It was clear that Belushi would do anything that would keep him occupied. He was no longer wearing the dark glasses, at least not indoors. His left eyelid was slightly puffy and a purplish half moon lay beneath his eye, but the redness on his cheek was gone. "You hear about the shooting last night?"

Belushi nodded. "On the *Standard's* website in the breaking news banner. It was the Englishman that was at your grandma's party, wasn't it, and at The Gun Club, right?"

Mesa smiled and nodded, only half surprised that Belushi was apparently keeping tabs on her.

"I walked over to the Silver Dollar to see if the cops were still around. But it's closed. Must have been a lot of blood. You can see a big stain in the alley. I took a couple of pictures if you want to see." He nodded toward his laptop screen.

Mesa smiled at Evan's initiative and looked over his shoulder at the photos. The bloodstain was large enough to make Mesa feel queasy. Griff might not have dodged a bullet, but he had been damn lucky. Someone had left him to bleed to death.

She patted him on the shoulder and said, "Good work. Hang on to those and let's see what else develops. Meanwhile, while I'm gone, why don't you spend five minutes and see what you can dig up on Brendan Fife, and get me Chloe Hardcastle's parents' address. Email me what you find, and I'll read it while I'm catching up on parade entries.

She would have deep-sixed the parade coverage altogether if she thought she could get away with it, preferring to visit Griff. She had stopped by the hospital before coming to the office and had gotten as far as the surgery floor, only to find a detective in Griff's room. She had skedaddled when a nurse had looked her way.

Coverage of the parade was important, Irita would be quick to remind her. Readers looked forward to the page of photographs they would run. Not that Mesa didn't like parades, but meanwhile, the person involved in Danica's death was roaming free, not to mention people taking pot shots at strangers. Even if Danica's death was an accident, if someone else was involved they ought to come forward for the sake of the family. In Mesa's experience, that someone often needed a nudge.

She began to walk toward the lobby and the door, sucking the Tootsie Pop for all she was worth. She'd forgotten how good they tasted. Then she said, using the Pop as a pointer, "I'll text you when I get called away to meet with them. Okay?" She left Belushi beaming at his keyboard.

Adrienne took a deep breath and walked into the spacious, hospital lobby and spoke to one of the volunteers at the Information Desk about where Griffin-Jones was currently resting his head. When she heard he'd been transferred from recovery to the surgery floor early that morning, Adrienne knew that his injury had likely not been life-threatening on the face of it. She relaxed, thankful she would not have to be the bearer of bad news. That said, her experience had taught her that anytime a human being underwent surgery in a hospital these days, complications and infection, especially from a bullet wound, were common.

The hospital lobby was quiet with the clinics closed for the holiday, and she took the elevator up to the third floor, easily finding his room. She peeked around the privacy curtain and saw the Englishman dozing on the bed with a bandage around his head, dark circles under his eyes, and the ubiquitous IV in his arm. Evidently, he had a head wound along with the gun shot.

She looked toward the nurse's station where she saw Evie Menucci, a nurse she'd worked with before. "How's the gunshot?" Adrienne asked, referring to the injury rather than the patient by name as the nurses so often did.

"Hey, Dr. DeBrook," Evie said, leaning on her elbows. "Came up from recovery around 5 a.m. Then a detective showed up to talk to him a bit ago," the nurse said with a conspiratorial air. "I'd be more excited except the cop used to cut our grass when he was a teenager. I know too much about him to get too worried."

"No complications at all then?" Adrienne asked. Griff had bypassed ICU, an excellent sign. She was beginning to wonder if Jones didn't have some Irish blood.

"He won't be doing a jig anytime soon," Evie said, "but he's able-bodied and relatively young. I give him another forty years at least, but you didn't hear it from me."

Adrienne smiled at the dark-humored nurse, knowing what it was like to work the holidays as an *ad locum*. Filling in for physicians on vacation had allowed her to keep her diagnostic skills sharp and provided some added income. It also meant that in slow periods, like holidays, when medical procedures were not scheduled, she got to know the staff. If Adrienne needed any more updates, she could call Evie easy enough.

Evie finished a note she was making and then said, "The bullet bounced off his pelvis, cracked a rib and lodged next to it. Picked it out of him with only a small scar to remember it all by. He'll need a good week of bed rest after he's out of here in a day or two. You know him?"

Adrienne nodded. "Met him on Saturday. He's a long way from home, so I thought maybe he could use a visitor."

The nurse nodded approval, and Adrienne headed back down the hall. She poked her head into the room again and saw Griff had opened his eyes.

"Doctor," he said with a forced smile, "I did hope to see you again but not under these circumstances. Please excuse my wardrobe," he spoke again, his voice becoming raspy.

Adrienne reached over to the outsized plastic cup bearing the hospital's logo, and put the straw to Griff's lips. "Drink up," she said. "Surgery at this altitude is a double whammy as far as dehydration goes."

He lifted his head and sipped gingerly from the straw. "Bit tender in the tummy," he said and put his hand on his right side.

Adrienne nodded, "Well, that's to be expected." She sat in the chair next to the bed. "I hear you had a close call, but they got the bullet out of you." She was glad to see he'd come through the surgery without too heavy an anesthetic hangover.

"Odd feeling, really, getting shot, just like the Old West. This will see me through endless, boring cocktail parties once I'm back in London," Griff said and then grimaced as he tried to rearrange himself in the bed.

Adrienne had to admire his bravado. "Is there anyone I can call for you, someone in England? I promised Mesa I'd do whatever I can. She's covering the parade at the moment, but she's planning on stopping by later."

"So she asked about me, did she?" he said with an animation Adrienne was surprised he could muster.

"The Sheriff came over to the Ducharme house last night and told us what happened and to ask some questions."

"Ah," Griff said. "So that's what precipitated this visit. And here I thought you were the angel of compassion."

Adrienne smiled. "I'm glad to see you haven't lost your sense of humor."

"Unfortunately, however," he said, "I do seem to have lost my short-term memory. The police had all manner of questions for me as well, and I can't seem to remember anything after I left my hotel in search of a chop and a pint."

Having agreed to act as transportation captain for the day, Alexis dropped Mesa off behind the Civic Center at 10:30 a.m. This in exchange for Mesa's giving her word to take in the last night of action at the Freedom Fest Bull-a-Rama, making good on a promise Alexis had made to the cowboys she had met at The Gun Room.

Navigating Butte streets during the 4th of July parade was best accomplished by having someone who could drop you off in one place and pick you up in another. Thank God for cell phones. Alexis could then use the city's perimeter roadways to get from one side of town to the other without having to cross Harrison Avenue, which the slow-moving parade had commandeered.

Depending on the number of entries, the procession, moving about half a mile an hour, would take nearly three hours to complete, depending on how many politicians stopped to chat with the crowd. If the temperature rose above eighty degrees without cloud cover, those walking would move even slower. At least that was what Chance had informed Mesa would happen since she'd not been in Butte for a 4th of July parade for a good fifteen years. Back then, she had sat on the curb, watched the parade go by, and then waited for the traffic jam to untangle itself like everybody else. After all, it wasn't New York City.

Irita and Chance already had their heads together at the back lot of the Civic Center next to the county Democrats' float, which was displaying a red, white, and blue sparkled donkey with a moving tail, surrounded by a host of large photographs of candidates.

"The bunch with the burning crosses didn't show, thank God," Irita explained, "but this yahoo across the street kept us plenty busy." Irita had been a member of the parade committee for years, a position of influence, or a pain in the butt, depending on what mood she was in.

Irita pointed to a camo-painted pickup with the words *Montana—Living Free* stenciled in black around a seal on the door. On a pole in the bed of the truck, and waving overhead behind the cab, was the Confederate flag. "It took three of us, plus the under-Sheriff to convince this nut job that his First Amendment rights weren't being usurped. His organization never applied to be a parade entry, or paid the fee, pure and simple—and oh, by the way, he's an idiot," Irita said with a shake of her head. "Where do these people come from?"

Chance shrugged. "He was happy to pose next to his pickup. Thankfully, the wind is down so the flag isn't particularly visible. Not that I was thinking you would want to run the photo."

"Land of the free, home of the brave," Mesa muttered and then answered her vibrating cell phone.

"What happened to calling me after you talked to Brendan Fife?" Phade's voice sounded tired, and bitchy.

Surprised, Mesa took a deep breath and made a deliberate effort to modulate her tone before she spoke. She had made that promise the night before and forgotten. A big mistake, given that Phade clearly was getting too little sleep, and the mystery around his sister's death had only gotten greater. "I'm sorry, Phade. I did talk to him this morning, but then I had to get over here to the Civic Center for the parade." Not to mention stopping by the hospital, plus the alley where Griff had been shot. She decided not to mention that to Phade.

The remnants of a large blood stain in the alley behind the Silver Dollar Saloon had made her realize how thankful she was Griff was alive. He had planned to be in town for three days and now he was in the damn hospital. So much for her prospects. The instant connection she had felt with him unnerved her. Okay, he was hot and he was English. Why couldn't she leave it at that?

"Well, Brendan was just here," Phade went on, interrupting her musings. "And I would have appreciated a heads-up that he was on his way."

She heard a big sniff on the line and for a second she thought maybe he was crying.

"Are you okay?" she asked. "Phade?" she said when he didn't answer.

He cleared his throat and spoke as though his teeth were clinched. "No, I'm not okay. I'm about ready to lose my shit."

"Sorry, poor choice of words. Of course, you're not okay. I'm sorry I didn't realize Brendan was planning to stop by your house. He said he was coming to Butte to meet Chloe Hardcastle." Sometimes she was amazed at her lack of sensitivity. Of course, Fife would want to pay his respects to his former neighbors. Why hadn't she realized that?

"Yeah, well he came here first, didn't he?"

Mesa hated not knowing what to say. She stuttered as she tried to think of something comforting.

Then Phade finished with, "It's too hard, doing this," he said and hung up.

"Shit," Mesa said and shook her phone in frustration. She didn't like the way Phade sounded, and she made up her mind to stop by the Draganovich household to see him after the parade.

She wasn't sure what grief might do to him. In the nine months she had worked with Phade, she had seen his defiant side, and knew he could become volatile. Mostly the defiance erupted when he would get into it with Cinch, the paper's admittedly cranky old guard who liked to refer to Phade as "a snot-nosed punk." Or if he was having girlfriend problems with Stella, he could do his share of drawer slamming and book throwing. And who might he feel that way toward now—the police, who always moved at their own meticulous, but slow, pace? Hardcastle? The whole situation? Or what concerned her most—himself.

Mesa meandered down Harrison Avenue at a pace slightly faster than the parade, taking photos with her phone and getting quotes from onlookers while turning down offers of Bud Light about every hundred yards. Human interest was the name of the game, especially in Butte and especially on holiday weekends. But despite the festive atmosphere and reconnecting with some old friends in the crowd, Mesa couldn't stop thinking about Phade.

It wasn't that her drive to find out what had caused Danica's death exceeded the grief she felt for the fact that Phade's sister was the victim. But Mesa's tunnel vision for the truth led her to some dark places, and she quickly became obsessed, no matter who was involved. That didn't mean she didn't care about Phade, or his family. But her job, the paper's mission, investigating whatever had gone wrong, and putting it in perspective for the community took precedence.

For Phade it was personal. He felt responsible for finding out answers for the sake of his family. Mesa hoped whatever she found would give them, and the community, some closure. She needed to make Phade believe they could accomplish both goals together.

Mesa had walked three-quarters of the parade route when she saw Belushi working the crowd at the corner of Holmes and Harrison by the Town Pump gas station.

He was smiling and talking to his sister and a couple of her friends. Maybe he was capable of a good time after all.

She was trying to decide if he would be embarrassed if she joined them, but then a text from Brendan distracted her. Could they meet after the parade around one p.m. at Sparky's Garage in Uptown? That would be a welcome relief after the parade. They could sit on the deck and actually enjoy the weather and the view.

She texted Alexis, who had parked at Starbuck's, waiting to be summoned to pick up Mesa. Then she walked over to join Belushi, to tell him that she was leaving and that he was on his own.

Immediately, he excused himself from his sister and her friends to tell Mesa that he had seen Nathan Hardcastle. He was talking to yet another woman, who wasn't his wife, in front of the Montana Club restaurant. Mesa was about to ask what the woman looked like when two loud cracks, gunshots, rang out and all hell broke loose.

❧

By noon, the last of the parades' 120 entries had been pulled or walked out of the Civic Center parking lot, and Chance hopped on his Bianchi and pedaled away from the parade. The best part of the assignment was that he didn't need to deal with the traffic at the end.

He had photographed all the floats in contention for prizes, which amounted to four professionally made floats paid for by Summit Valley Power, Montana Resources, Town Pump, and some tech company that had recently moved to town. He much preferred the amateur efforts, of which there were considerably more. His vote would have to go to the Forest Service "Carry your Bear Spray" float, where the rangers were taking turns squirting one of their own in a bear suit.

He had cycled up Arizona Street to the *Messenger* office on Galena in ten minutes and was uploading his photos to Mesa's computer when he got a call from Irita. He had last seen her flying down Harrison in a golf cart to encourage one of the gubernatorial candidates to stop posing for selfies and pick up the pace.

"I can't get hold of Mesa," Irita was yelling into the phone. "Where is she?"

Chance could hear all kinds of yelling and general hubbub in the background, but he kept his cool, not wanting to push Irita any closer to hysteria. "What the hell is going on? It sounds like you're in the middle of a riot."

"Somebody took a couple of shots, with a pistol, not a camera, along the parade route. Honest to Christ, I don't know what is wrong with people. It was probably one of those Vow Takers or whatever they call themselves, getting back at us for not letting them in the damn parade."

"Was anybody hurt?" he asked, wishing he had paid more attention to Mesa and where she had said she would be. "Where did it happen exactly?"

"Hell, I don't know. I thought it was a cherry bomb or one of those mailbox explosives, and then when everybody started running toward me, screaming *gunfire* I turned the golf cart around and headed the other direction. I'm at the judges' stand right now, where every living soul with a walkie-talkie is jabbering. Cop cars are swerving down the street driving like circus clowns to avoid all the abandoned floats. Personally, I'm beginning to think it's all smoke and no fire. I can't tell what the hell happened, but I haven't seen any ambulances, so apparently no one was hit."

Belushi and Mesa, along with his sister and her friends, had crouched behind the Hampton Suites' brick planter. The shots weren't necessarily menacing, but most Montanans recognized gunfire when they heard it and knew to take cover. Almost immediately, police cars at the front of the parade had turned back in the direction of the shots. Mesa sent Belushi on his mountain bike to see how close he could get to the scene, while she quickly rendezvoused with Alexis, parked two blocks away behind the hotel. *Why's everybody gotten trigger-happy all of a sudden*, Mesa thought. *First Griff gets shot and now this?*

"Don't tell me. Everybody in this town finally lost their mind," Alexis said when Mesa jumped into the front seat.

Mesa had to chuckle. Alexis could be blasé at the oddest times. "Didn't you hear the shots?"

Alexis shrugged. "I had the radio turned up. Where to?"

"Make a quick right and then a quick left onto Paxson and head toward the blinking red lights."

They drove approximately 500 yards before they were turned away by one of the parade marshals on an ATV who was apparently now in charge of traffic control. He assured them that law enforcement had swept the area and whoever had been the shooter had vanished into thin air. Though how he could assert that, Alexis questioned. "He could be anywhere around us."

"All the more reason you girls should head in the other direction," was all the ATVer said.

"That's okay, Alexis," Mesa said judiciously. "Evan is on the scene. I need to get back uptown anyway. I was thinking I'd make a quick stop at the hospital." She wanted to check in on Griff, if only for a few minutes, and she did not want Alexis to get into a pissing contest with the wannabe traffic cop.

"Prick," Alexis said. "If he'd had a different attitude, I might have told him what I saw from my stellar point of observation while sitting in my pickup. Who's Evan?"

They were passing the Municipal Golf Course, heading back uptown. Mesa was thinking about what she wanted to say to Griff and so was only listening with one ear. Then Alexis' comment sunk in. "What did you see?"

"Well, I can't say he was the shooter, but I saw that beige motorbike again. This time it was tearing across that open field in a cloud of dust."

"What field?" Mesa said, wondering now if they should have sought out the Sheriff.

"I could see right across those two vacant lots across the street from where I was parked, where the old rodeo grounds used to be. He sure as hell looked like he was making a fast getaway."

Chapter 13

"Think he's telling the truth?" Chance asked Adrienne. They were pulling up to Nana Rose's house. He had promised to help Sam pack up the tables and chairs from the previous two days of celebration. Nana was a stickler for neatness in her side garden which, with its well-tended flowerbeds and rattan furniture, was the envy of the neighborhood.

"Why is it that everyone thinks people with amnesia are always faking?" Adrienne said, as she got out of the Land Rover and walked toward the back porch of the house. "He got cracked on the head to the tune of three stitches. Retrograde amnesia is completely within the realm of possibility."

Chance carried a case of red wine that Adrienne had ordered from Hennessy's and wanted to keep at Nana's since they seemed always to be at her house eating and drinking. "Easy now, no need to get defensive on me."

"But why would he lie," Adrienne pressed. "I would think he'd want his assailant behind bars as soon as possible."

"Seems mighty convenient is all." Chance said, thinking about what Sheriff Solheim had said the night before about a book that it sounded like Jones had lost, and the cash. His wallet had been emptied. "What if he recognized the jerk that attacked him and wants to get back at him in his own way?"

Adrienne shook her head. "Recommending the vigilante approach, are you? He's an Englishman. Honestly, Chance, how many people do you suppose Jones knows in town, particularly someone who would rob and shoot him? Most of the people he knows were right here on Saturday night. "

Chance had to admit Adrienne had a point, which was what he was mumbling as they entered Nana's kitchen. She greeted the couple with kisses to the cheek. "I take it Mr. Jones is the subject of this conversation. How's he doing?" She looked at Adrienne, "I want a full report."

Chance put the box of wine on the counter and stretched his back. He nodded in Adrienne's direction. Guy has an English accent and suddenly the women are falling all over him.

Adrienne leaned on the counter next to Chance. "He'll make a full recovery. He had a single .22 removed from his torso. It grazed the edge of his hip so he'll be in the hospital for another 48 hours to make sure he doesn't develop any infection. And he has a concussion and three stitches in the back of his head. He'll need a few days rest before he's ready to fly back to England, that's for sure."

"Has his family been notified?" Nana Rose asked with concern. She sat at the long kitchen table, sipping tea.

"He doesn't seem worried," Adrienne said, shaking her head. "I asked if there was someone to call, but he said no."

"Goodness," Nana Rose said, clearly concerned. "Then we'll invite him to recuperate here," Nan said. "Don't you think, Adrienne? He can have Chance's old room unless you think the stairs are too much for him. That hospital is so sterile. I know, I've spent enough time there. But I shouldn't want him to have to go back to that hotel room, and you can keep an eye on him here. What do you say?"

"Now Nana," Chance began, though he wasn't sure why he was hesitant. Nan's offer was not a surprise. She didn't like seeing anyone on their own have to struggle, especially someone from overseas, and a Brit too. "Maybe we need to take it slowly, see what Jones wants to do."

Adrienne sat down across from Nana. "That's wonderfully generous of you, Rose. I have to agree that this is a far more comfortable environment than the hospital or the hotel. I'll bet Jones would jump at the chance to be someplace else."

"That way we can help him sort out what needs to happen to get him back home without any further damage." She looked at Chance. "No need to check with Mesa, do you suppose?"

Chance grabbed a biscuit from the plate of shortbread on the table. "Okay, I know when I'm overruled."

❧

By the time Mesa and Alexis had tracked down Sheriff Solheim to tell him about her sighting of Razor Gillette's motorcycle, or one that looked like it, it was well past one. She didn't want to miss Fife while he was in town, so she decided to delay her visit to Griff and to the Draganovichs.

Sparky's was about half-full, mostly out-of-towners, or people who didn't have family picnics to go to. The aroma of barbecuing pork kept the restaurant busy during the summer, especially with the Folk Festival coming up. Even Mesa wasn't immune.

She headed for the deck, while Alexis was ready to peel off to go sit at the bar. But Mesa could see Brendan Fife, sitting with another good-looking, clean-cut guy about the same age. "Come with," she said to Alexis. "Looks like Brendan brought a friend along, and it isn't Chloe Hardcastle. If he wants to talk privately, you can keep the other guy company."

"Use me and abuse me," Alexis said with her usual sarcasm.

"At least you're getting something to eat," Mesa taunted.

"And drink," Alexis added.

Turned out the other guy, Colin Vance, was Brendan's partner from whom he had no secrets and who was well aware of Danica's role in what turned out to be Brendan's "tumultuous teen-aged years." He stayed his ground and so did Alexis, who immediately ordered a pitcher of Cold Smoke Scotch Ale.

Mesa introduced her as one of her assistants, which resulted in a swift kick under the table. Once they'd placed their orders of pulled pork sandwiches, Mesa asked about Chloe. "Have you seen her yet?"

Brendan sighed. "We were supposed to meet up after the parade at the end of the route. Then she texted me that she had to see her brother and that she would catch up later. In case you haven't heard, there was an incident out that way. It took us forever to avoid all navigate the drama and come uptown. I told her about this meeting with you, and she said she would try to make it."

Alexis and Mesa exchanged glances. Nathan, the sack-of-shit brother who was lying to his wife. That brother. "We've been trying to find out more about Danica's relationship with Nathan," Mesa said, deciding not to sway any opinion Brendan might have.

Brendan sat back from the table like someone had slapped him. "How did you find out about that? It's always been double top-secret confidential." He said this in a tone that suggested he didn't see what all the fuss was about.

"We've spent the last 48 hours finding out everything there is to know about Danica. Her family is worried that her death will be classified a suicide, but they feel strongly that's not the case, so we're pursuing every possible angle. She texted someone she wanted to meet at one o'clock the day she died. We're trying to verify who that someone might have been."

Brendan looked at Colin, whose green eyes got bigger as Mesa talked. If they had come to Butte thinking she was looking for some tribute story about Danica, they were probably in a state of shock.

"So what did you know about Danica and Nathan?" Mesa asked.

Brendan sipped at his beer and then shook his head dismissively. "Danica and Nathan were a pipe dream. He was Catholic. She was Orthodox. Those girls either date someone in their church, or they don't get serious. They are brought up to think there's no sense dating anybody unless you actually think you could marry them. Nathan wasn't in that category, or at least he wasn't going to be for a long time."

"Who else knew about them? Did Chloe know as well?" Mesa pressed. "I'm assuming they're close, being twins and all."

Brendan nodded. "They were when we were all growing up together. Now that she's flying around, saving the world, not so much." He paused and stared out over the deck.

Mesa got the feeling that Chloe had left a lot of people behind. Then the waitress appeared with their order, mounds of pulled pork and sweet potato fries, and a tossed salad for Mesa, whose appetite was mostly for the story.

They finished the first few bites and Brendan said. "The four of us did a lot of stuff together back in the day. But it was mostly so Nate and Danica could have their little flirtation that wasn't going to go anywhere, any more than mine was."

Here Colin looked up from his sandwich and poked Brendan in the shoulder. He tilted his head and then said, "I was young once, you know."

"You sound like you don't necessarily approve of Chloe's high-profile career," Alexis said while she poured another round from the pitcher of beer.

Mesa was curious about it herself. She remembered reading what Chloe had said in the yearbook about coming back to Butte to take over her grandfather's medical practice. "Seems like she was being groomed to come back to Butte. Were you surprised she didn't?"

"I have to say I was," Brendan said. You know, her grandpa was old-school. He actually made house calls. Even let her ride along sometimes. Hell, by the time she was fifteen, she had helped deliver two babies." Brendan shook his head again. "Even twenty years ago, obstetricians were getting the life sued out of them. But old man Armistead didn't give a damn. Plus, the families he was helping had nothing to begin with. His own mother died in childbirth, so it was a real calling for him. Chloe would say he wasn't going to let any woman face childbirth alone because she couldn't afford decent care. I think she got her crusader spirit from him."

Dr. Armistead. Mesa thought about that name as she entered notes into her iPhone. She would have to ask Nana Rose what she remembered about him. "But she was originally going to join him in his practice?"

"Yep, she was his protégé. He was hanging on, keeping the practice going, even though he was close to retirement. Then she was finishing medical school, and the next thing I hear she was joining some NGO in West Africa. I was doing a tour in Germany at the time, so I never talked to her, but I was really surprised."

"Weren't you going to medical school yourself?" Mesa asked. Brendan seemed like a bright guy, and Butte, like most of the state, struggled to recruit physicians.

"Yeah, but I wasn't a whiz kid like Chloe or from a well-to-do family. Med school was going to cost a small fortune. The Air Force's physicians' training program is a great deal financially, but that was going to mean a career in the military, and *don't ask/don't tell* really wasn't my style. I opted for the physician's assistant training so I could shorten my years in the service. I've got no complaints," he said and looked toward Colin with a smile.

"You ever ask Chloe what made her change her mind?" Mesa asked. Chloe could have opened her clinic in Butte—Montana being closer to a Third World country in terms of medical care than a lot of people would believe.

"I was here at Christmas about three or four years ago, before Colin," Brendan said, with a nod to his partner. "She invited me to this holiday reception her grandmother was throwing. I think she was looking for somebody she could pass off as a date."

"Couldn't rustle up one on her own?" Mesa asked, curious about other liaisons Chloe might have had.

"You kidding me? Half the guys at the Country Club would have been glad to cozy up to her. She could have had any guy she wanted, but she married her work instead. Those were her words after a couple of glasses of champagne. We were sitting in the solarium of her grandmother's house. When I asked her why she couldn't do that in Butte, all she said was too many bad memories."

Mesa thought about this for a minute, making a quick note to follow up with Chloe. "You have any idea what she meant?"

He shrugged. "Something that must have happened after I left town. That girl led a charmed life, if you ask me. I mean, she always did have an overdeveloped sense of responsibility. She was always pulling somebody out of a scrape, usually her brother. She would joke and say it was because she was the oldest, by about ten minutes."

"So tell me about your last conversation with Danica," Mesa said and picked at Alexis's sweet potato fries.

"Like I told you on the phone, we were making plans to get together at the Folk Festival. I told her that I had traded shifts with somebody so I wouldn't have to work. We were going to stay at her place Saturday night. That was it."

"When was this conversation?" Mesa asked. She had the list of calls at the office, but she couldn't remember whose was whose.

"Thursday night," Brendan said. He had stopped eating again. "The last thing she said was that we would dance the night away like old times." His voice trailed off and then he cleared his throat.

"And what about this—the GH?" Mesa asked, printing the abbreviation in box letters on a napkin. "I don't suppose you know where that is?"

"Sure. The glass hut," Brendan said matter-of-factly. "*Keep watching the skies!*" he added and then saluted with a smile.

౿౭

"You were right. He was lying," Alexis said as they got into her pickup in Sparky's parking lot. "Nathan did meet her on the roof."

According to Brendan, he, Danica, and the Hardcastle twins had spent a good part of their senior year in high school sneaking out onto the roof of the Finlen, inspired by stories told by the Hardcastles' grandmother. "She had a pin and a certificate and a letter of gratitude from the Defense Department," Brendan had explained in the only light moment of their interview.

When she was a high school student, Dianna Hardcastle, then Culligan, had joined numerous Butte Central students who, along with about three hundred other Butte residents, were recruited into the US Ground

Observer Corps. During daylight hours, she had watched for enemy planes from a glass hut that had been constructed on top of the Hotel Finlen's elevator equipment room on the roof. With pictures of planes for identification, binoculars, and a red phone, they had cataloged planes that flew across the valley to report suspicious flight patterns, particularly those headed north.

"We did this research project about it in English class," Brendan had said. "Go to the Archives. They have a whole file of stuff."

The glass hut was long gone by the time they had snuck onto the roof in high school. All that was left were the remnants of the wooden staircase that led from the roof up to the hut. They had sat on the steps and watched the stars.

Mesa sighed and put on her seat belt. "We have to find a way to get Nathan Hardcastle to admit he met her up there. As long as he denies it, it's his word against the victim's text message unless the police have come up with some evidence he was there."

"What if this creep Gillette was who she met?" Alexis asked.

Mesa shrugged. According to Brendan, Razor had not been in on the rooftop escapades, at least not when Danica had been around. Brendan had said, "The one and only time I ever saw Danica even raise her voice was at that dweeb. He could be a bully. He liked to call me *Brenda*. Clever, huh? She hated that he always had grease on his hands and dirt under his nails. Plus, he smelled like old oil rags half the time."

Alexis sat behind the steering wheel, picking her teeth with a toothpick. She smiled and said, "It's kind of a sweet, silly story really, some goofball high school adventure. Too bad it has this downer ending."

"I've never even heard of a glass observation room on top of the Finlen or talked to anybody else who has," Mesa said, envious. "If it weren't for Brendan Fife saying he'd been up there himself, I'd say the whole thing sounds like an episode of that old science fiction show. You know, like Twilight Zone."

Alexis chuckled and said, "Only in Butte." Then she cranked up the engine and said, "So what do we do now? Tell Macgregor what we know and hope that he can wheedle the truth out of Hardcastle?"

"I'm pretty sure Macgregor is at some picnic with his feet up, but I can at least leave him a message. Then I want to go over to the hospital."

Alexis rolled her eyes while Mesa picked up her cell phone and saw that she had a text from Belushi.

Found Chloe at her parents' house. Nathan too. He left bent out of shape.

"On second thought," she said, showing Alexis the text, "maybe we can talk to his sister. Maybe she knows what happened or she can persuade her brother to tell us." Mesa called Belushi. "Is she still there?" She could hear street noise and the flutter of wind in the background. Belushi must be on his bicycle.

"Yep. They got a picnic going in the backyard," he said. "I didn't get it 'til I got over here that she is the woman that Nathan Hardcastle was talking to at the parade."

"You mean before those shots were fired?" Mesa said.

That made total sense. Families often congregated to watch the parade, having sat in the same spot along the route year after year. "What did you mean about Nathan leaving bent out of shape?"

Belushi stuttered and then said, "Well, I could see them talking and he started like pointing with his fingers, you know, waving his arms. Then he turns and kinda stomps off. She called after him, but he kept going. He jumped in his car, slammed the door hard, and roared off."

Wow, Mesa thought. That sounds like a major disagreement between siblings who, she suspected, didn't often see each other. "Where exactly is the house?"

"Just north of the airport, Burning Tree Lane."

"You on your bike?"

"Yeah, but it's not a problem. I'm tucked behind a neighbor's Winnebago."

"I'm gonna pick up my car and then I'll come out."

"Where to?" Alexis said when Mesa was off the phone.

"Chloe Hardcastle's out at her parents', back off Elizabeth Warren Avenue."

"Belushi track her down?"

Mesa nodded. "I should probably get my car and drive out there myself."

"That little bloodhound," Alexis said with a smile. "He's getting to be like you. Doesn't want to let go of that scent."

Mesa ignored Alexis's comment, thinking instead about what needed to happen next. She did not want to miss talking to Chloe Hardcastle. And then there was Phade who she definitely wanted to see in person. And

Griff, who she was beginning to think, would feel completely ignored.

"Maybe you could check on our English pal. I'd go myself but I don't know if I'll get another chance to talk to this Hardcastle chick, plus I wanna stop off and see Phade. Tell Griff that I'll stop by later." Then she smirked and said, "And no funny business!"

"I guess I can squeeze him in," Alexis said, "but don't forget the rodeo later. I want to catch the bareback riding and the saddle broncs. No later than eight."

Mesa smiled and nodded. Alexis never cared a damn about being on time except when it had something to do with horses.

༺⚬༻

By the time Mesa had picked up her SUV and driven back out toward the airport, it was nearly four in the afternoon. She considered stopping by the Draganovichs', then thought better of it. Phade would not appreciate a quick in and out, and that was all she had time for. She'd text him and let him know she'd come by later. Trying to decide how much she wanted to tell him was worrisome, especially about Hardcastle's likely involvement.

The elder Hardcastles lived in a well-appointed ranch house that backed onto the Country Club's golf course next to a house with a tennis court where it appeared that some amateur tournament was going on. The good news was that there were plenty of people enjoying the holiday and Belushi could keep an eye on things without drawing attention.

She found him on his bicycle, finishing a slow loop around the lane which circled back around the subdivision and back up to Elizabeth Warren. She parked along the street and walked over to him as his bike coasted to a stop.

"That's her in the blue shirt, sitting in the lawn chair near the deck."

Mesa gave a quick glance, making sure she had her bearings.

"Did the meet with Fife give us anything new?"

Mesa smiled. She could tell Belushi was into this story as much as she was, like Alexis said. She nodded and said, "He confirmed what we already know, or at least suspected, that Danica and Hardcastle had a thing but it was mostly innocent and long over. But the real blockbuster is that Fife says 'GH' in the text stands for glass hut which is, or was, on the roof of the Finlen." She explained about the Ground Observer Corps.

Belushi started nodding his head.

"You know about this?" Mesa said in awe.

"I told Chance and Adrienne about it yesterday," Belushi said in an unassuming manner. "My friend Spike, he read about it at the Archives. The Ground Observer Corps. It sounded kinda cool."

"I guess so, if it didn't have something to do with Danica's death. Right now we need to find out what happened up there, glass hut or no. I'm hoping I can get an explanation out of Chloe."

"Want me to wait for you?" Belushi said enthusiastically. "Or anything."

Mesa smiled again. "No, you've done a great job today, Evan," she said, resolving to stop using her cheeky nickname for him. "You head on back uptown, or wherever. Chill. If I get anything breaking, I'll call."

With a reluctant grin, he swung his leg over the bike. Mesa knew he wasn't looking forward to heading home. Then she remembered she was supposed to go out to the rodeo grounds with Alexis. It might be tough to squeeze Phade in after this interview with Chloe.

"Well, there is one more thing you could do." St. Ann Street was on the way back up the hill, more or less.

Evan stopped in his tracks. "Sure."

"Want to cycle over to the Draganovichs'? Give Phade a heads-up about what we've been doing. You wouldn't have to stay too long." She knew Phade could be prickly around his younger coworker, and she didn't want to create any awkwardness for either of them. "Tell Phade I'm interviewing Chloe and that I'll try to swing by afterwards, but it might be late."

"You betcha," he said with the usual Butte enthusiasm.

Mesa watched Evan cycle quickly down the street, and then she walked across the Hardcastle lawn for her third picnic in as many days. Once again she recognized several faces. The crowd was older and from a slightly elevated economic status. A Councilman, one of the owners of the Uptown Cafe, and Nana's lawyer were among the guests.

Mesa exchanged greetings and grabbed a glass of Chardonnay, eventually sidling over to Chloe Hardcastle. The only kids at the party, a couple of pre-teen girls, most likely someone's grandchildren, were fascinated by native bracelets that Chloe wore. Bright orange, green, and pink stripes and checks were intricately woven against a black background. She was explaining that village women in Gambia had made the bangles out of recycled plastic bags and water bottles.

Eventually she gave each of the girls a bracelet and even offered one to Mesa who gratefully accepted. "Full disclosure here," Mesa said. "I'm not an invited guest. I spoke with Brendan Fife at lunch and I thought I'd try to follow up. I knew this was where your parents lived, so…."

Graciously, Chloe didn't let Mesa dangle too long on her pitch to ask a few questions. "Brendan called me after lunch," she said with a resigned smile. "I understand what you're trying to do. Why don't we go around to the front of the house so we can talk without being interrupted."

Mesa followed Chloe around the house. Tall and fit, her walk was unhurried as though she had nowhere else to be. She was tanned, and the tips of her light brown hair that hung to her shoulders were bleached by the sun. Life in the African bush seemed to suit her.

"Do you get back to Butte for the 4th often?" Mesa started with an easy question, hoping to ease into the difficult subject about the death of her long-time friend.

She shook her head once. "I typically only get stateside a couple of times a year and usually only to New York. But I had a fundraising event in Phoenix. When I heard from Brendan what had happened, I felt like…," she paused.

Mesa scribbled in her notebook that Chloe had not heard about Danica's death from her brother or family, but rather from Brendan. She wondered how significant that might be.

When the doctor looked up, her deep blue eyes were rimmed with tears. "I felt like things had come full circle. I needed to come home."

"Full circle? How do you mean?" Mesa said, watching as the doctor wiped her eyes quickly and then went back to toying with her bracelets.

"I know who Danica was going to see Friday and why she was so upset."

Chapter 14

"As soon as I hear from her, uh, Evan," Chance said, almost calling him Belushi to his face, "I'll have her call you. You did what you could. Okay, later then."

Chance hung up and sat back down on the sofa next to Adrienne, draping his arm around her. "I tell you, that Belushi kid, he is one devoted little drone. Apparently Mesa sent him over to the Draganovich house to update Phade on what's happened. Except nobody has seen him since this morning. And Mesa isn't answering her phone and Belushi's worried because he doesn't know what to do, and since he can't get hold of Mesa, he figured he should call me."

Chance hung his head in mock supplication, and then looked at Adrienne who had a wide grin on her face. "What?" he said. "I know, you think I'm too laid back. Right?"

"Not at all," she said. "I think it's sweet the way Mesa has all these men vying for her attention."

Chance thought about this for a minute. "You mean Phade and Evan? Okay, I get that Evan follows her around like a puppy. You think Phade's pulling some stunt to get her attention? That's harsh."

Adrienne sat up, reached for her glass of wine and said, "Let's hope not, but I wouldn't be surprised, if he's frustrated by the lack of progress on the case. I think he sees Mesa as his one confidante, and she's been so busy trying to cover all the bases, she's hardly had time for him."

Chance rolled his eyes. He had mixed feelings about his sister's connection, if you could call it that, with Phade, who was first and foremost an employee. "He needs to look to the police to figure out what happened. Don't get me wrong, this whole deal with his sister is terrible, but the last thing I wanna see is Mesa getting too close to another homicide investigation, if that's what this is. The last time that happened she was lucky she didn't get shot. She's a journalist and that is as far as her investigations should go. I wonder sometimes if she knows where to draw the line."

Adrienne sipped her wine dutifully and said, "And then there's Griff."

"What about him?" Chance said, recalling his ineptitude when they were playing horseshoes at Nan's party on Saturday. "Some Englishman comes to town, starts nosing around, and ends up in the wrong place at the wrong time. What's that got to do with Mesa? He say something to you about her at the hospital?"

"Not in so many words, but there's some interest there, too."

Chance shook his head and put his arm back around Adrienne's shoulder. "I swear, you women and your intuition."

"And then there's you with your big brother act." Adrienne pinched his side.

"Stop that," he said and jumped toward the edge of the sofa. "I only think that Mesa shouldn't get too involved in a police matter, even one that involves an employee. I get that this is a story that has a high level of community interest, a death like Danica's, from a close-knit community. That resonates with everybody, no matter which community it is. Your heart goes out to the family, that's for sure."

"Chance, you forget that Mesa has a clever head on her shoulders and a lot of heart for the people here. Whatever she's up to, I'm sure she's got good reasons for what she's doing."

"I hope you're right," Chance said and stood up, pulling Adrienne up by the hand as well. He was all about family business and a community with heart, but sometimes Mesa could get in over her head. "Because I do not want to have to pull her butt out of a sling in the middle of the night," and he led Adrienne toward the bedroom.

Mesa sat in complete amazement as the story unfolded. Chloe told it with the efficiency you might expect from a physician who spent her days seeing one sick baby after another. Without anything extraneous, she summarized the heart of the matter like a blurb for a TV show. "That Friday, Danica realized the baby she thought she had delivered twelve years ago, to be adopted by a loving family desperate for a child, had died instead."

"Baby?" Mesa whispered. It took her a minute to process what's she'd heard. Then she pulled out her notebook and began scribbling.

The narrative poured forth. After college Danica, Nathan and Chloe had all been in California at the same time. Danica was trying to break into the film industry. Nathan was at Loyola Law School, and Chloe at UCLA in med school. Despite Danica's best efforts to be true to her Orthodox faith and with Nathan already engaged to Francine, they had succumbed to proximity and biology.

Mesa could see the connections now. The facts she and Evan had pulled together now had a context.

When Danica discovered she was pregnant, Chloe had been the first person she had called, even before Nathan. He would want an abortion, Danica felt sure, but she was adamant that she would carry the baby to term.

"She never wavered and I wasn't surprised," Chloe said. "Sleeping with Nathan was forgivable on some level. Even Orthodox girls dabbled outside the faith on occasion. But it would have been against everything Danica had been brought up to believe to terminate a pregnancy. Such a thing could only have happened in extreme circumstances. The curtailment of her career didn't matter. That was simple inconvenience. What mattered was the baby."

Chloe told the next part of the story with a poignancy that came with the knowledge of its tragic ending. At first Danica had explored finding a home for the baby in L.A., but the idea of leaving their offspring to be adopted in La-La land didn't feel right. It was Nathan who had come up with the Elsie's Babies approach.

Couldn't they quietly find a family in Montana who would want the infant?

Chloe had heard all about Elsie's Babies from her grandfather. "One Halloween weekend, I went with him to attend a birth on a ranch out along the Big Hole, practically to Wisdom. We were there 'til about three in the morning, and then on the drive home, a storm came up and it started to snow. Took us forever to get back to Butte. He told me all about Elsie on the white-knuckled drive home. Of course, I passed the story along to Nathan."

According to "Doc," as she liked to call her granddad, all the physicians knew about Elsie and even referred patients to her. For women who were so poor they could not feed an extra mouth, or who would suffer untold shame, even be ostracized, or who worked on Mercury Street, Elsie was the only option. He claimed he knew well-to-do men who had fathered children with mistresses and willingly paid to have Elsie find a home for the newborns, no questions asked. "When Nathan said we ought to 'take a page out of Elsie's playbook', I naively agreed."

Finding a family who would take the child had been deceptively simple. Chloe had done an Ob/Gyn rotation in Montana the previous summer, working in a rural clinic in Jefferson County between Butte and Helena. She knew a rancher and his wife who had struggled with infertility that she could contact.

They had considered adopting a baby, but there was no way they could afford it. Adopting a child cost upwards of fifteen thousand dollars, paying medical and legal expenses at the very least, and then there was a waiting list. "The couple had no trouble accepting an alternative approach. Danica even had thoughts of being able to keep track of the child growing up."

"But why didn't she at least deliver the baby in a hospital in Los Angeles?" Mesa asked. She understood why she decided not to come home to Butte while she was pregnant. Even if her own family would have understood, she could see Nathan wanting to protect his reputation.

Here Chloe's voice quivered. "I kept thinking about the deliveries with gramps, how you got on with whatever needed to be done. I was so sure I could deliver that baby without a problem. The three of us were going to handle everything. For Nathan, I think it was his way to assuage his guilt, to make sure Danica felt like the baby would have a good home. In the end, it was arrogance. If I hadn't been so full of myself, Nathan and Danica would have had to find a different way to do things. They couldn't have kept going without me."

Mesa shook her head, "That's quite a story," she said, trying to imagine herself in that situation. "That had to be a difficult decision for Danica to make. I mean, don't you think she'd have wanted to find the baby sometime down the road."

"You have to understand," Chloe said. "Danica was never afraid, never indecisive, once we had the details worked out. I was the one that started getting cold feet. But she was so grateful to me for offering a way for her to atone for getting pregnant in the first place by giving that ranch family a gift, even if it was an anonymous one. Don't you see? No other doctor or clinic was going to give her a forged birth certificate. I felt like I couldn't go back."

"How did you think you could fool everybody?" Mesa asked, trying to mask her disbelief that three otherwise intelligent people had been so naive. "Didn't the neighbors see you in the house?"

"We had the timeline figured out. Danica had told her roommates she had a job out of town. Then she came to stay with me for the last two months. They never even realized she was pregnant.

"Our grandparents went to Phoenix for the winter. Nathan and I were done with the semester by mid-December. He had arranged for us to house sit, which we'd done before. We were so full of superiority on that drive to Butte, the three of us, like we were on some mission of mercy. We made sure we got into town after dark and snuck Danica upstairs to wait for the baby. She was well into the last trimester. The worst we would have had to wait was another couple of weeks."

Mesa had begun to see how the plan could work out, at least on paper, if everything had gone perfectly, which obviously it hadn't. "What went wrong?"

Again Chloe's approach was clinical. The baby arrived in the middle of a driving snow storm two days later. Danica's labor lasted nearly twenty hours. A partial breech delivery, Chloe had trouble turning the baby. It was stillborn. Chloe had relived the birth a thousand times and still wasn't certain what caused the child's death. "The cord was wrapped around its neck, but I've seen that happen hundreds of times since and the baby survived." She stopped talking and shook her head.

Mesa stopped writing and looked around. She was worried that someone would call Chloe away before she could finish the harrowing story.

"I've forgiven myself finally," Chloe continued. "At least I thought I had. I've lived in fear of what she would think if she ever found out the baby died. I only wish I'd found the courage to explain to Danica what I understand now."

"What's that?" Mesa asked, realizing her voice was a mere whisper. "You mean you never told Danica?" Now her last text to Nathan made sense.

"Childbirth is a magical, miraculous thing. It's both simple and complicated at the same time. Even if we had been in a hospital with all the advanced equipment in the world, that baby might have died. Sixteen percent of babies are stillborn. It simply wasn't meant to be."

"She had a right to know," Mesa said, unclear why Chloe and Nathan had kept the child's death a secret.

Chloe nodded. "Looking back on it, even now I think we did the best we could in difficult circumstances. Poor Nathan was all but useless, he was so distraught."

Once the baby was born, Danica was exhausted and bleeding and barely coherent. Chloe had all she could do to make sure her friend survived. When she realized the baby was stillborn, she didn't have time to help Nathan, because she had to attend to Danica. She told him that he would have to decide what to do. Involving Danica in deciding how to deal with the baby's body would have been too cruel. "I know he was frantic. The one thing we hadn't planned for, and couldn't control, was the weather and the heaviest snowstorm in a decade."

Lastly, Mesa pressed on about how the baby's corpse ended up in the attic. "I can only tell you the first part of that story," Chloe said. "Until my mother showed me the story in Friday's paper, I had no idea that was what happened."

"So you can't be certain that the remains found Friday actually were those of the stillborn child you delivered?" Mesa said. The two women looked at each other, their doubt a surprise to both.

Finally, Chloe said, "No, I guess I can't," she said. "I just assumed so. I never asked Nathan what he did, and he had the good sense never to tell me. You'll have to get those details from him."

Alexis could tell that her rodeo outfit had the desired effect when she walked into Jones's hospital room. His eyes grew wide and the otherwise, articulate Englishman was speechless.

"Mesa asked me to stop by before I head out to the rodeo grounds," she said nonchalantly. Maybe Mesa was right that Alexis did not realize the subliminal effect her looks had on men.

"You look remarkable," he finally said. "Are those rhinestones then?" he asked and gestured to his own chest where the points of a shirt collar would be.

She nodded. "I had this shirt hand embroidered. The key is simplicity," she said, holding up one cuff and pointing to the delicate, flower design and vintage piping around it the cuffs, the collar, and her hatband. The black shirt and hat contrasted perfectly with the cowgirl bling. "Sorry you won't make the rodeo," she said sincerely.

Jones shrugged gingerly. "You'll give my regards to our bull riding compatriots from the other night?"

Alexis nodded and smiled. She almost liked Jones even though she wasn't entirely sure what he was up to.

"We could share a little pick me up." She pulled the silver flask, which had the Headframes logo engraved on it, from the back pocket of her black jeans.

Jones gave her a hesitant look and a half smile and then held up a hand to refuse. "Probably not wise in my current condition."

Alexis took a swig of the bourbon and then said, "No worries. I'll have one for you," and took another. She was sizing him up, feeling fairly sure that his amnesia was more convenience than anything else. He didn't want to talk about what had happened.

"So I hear from Adrienne you're going to move over to the Ducharme house in the morning."

Griff nodded, "Terribly kind of them, isn't it? Not that I haven't been well-treated here, but Mrs. Ducharme has promised me tea and biscuits, a bit of comfort food for one who is on the mend far from home and hearth."

"I'm glad you brought that up," Alexis said and took off her hat, resting it on her thigh as she leaned onto the hospital bed. "The Ducharme family, the Dawsons, they're like family to me. I wouldn't want to see anything unseemly go on in their house."

"Nor would I," Griff answered, sounding slightly offended. "Whatever gives you the idea—?"

"I think we both know you haven't been entirely forthright about your reasons for coming to Butte. And frankly, I don't like the implication that you take everybody around here for rubes, which they most certainly are not. That would be a mistake."

Griff's expression had changed from mild amusement to slight irritation. Alexis knew he'd let his guard down while she wowed him with her rodeo get up. Like so many guys, they saw nothing but her blonde hair.

"And what exactly do you suppose we both know?" he asked with some concern.

"My grandmother owns a terrace house in Russell Square, Griff. And her sister, an estate in Essex. I've been reminded all my life how class distinction is alive and well in old Blighty. Background, education, and family crests cloud people's judgments across the pond, especially in families like yours. I know, because I've checked yours out."

"Look here, I certainly haven't done anything wrong." Again Griff's expression darkened. "I'm the one lying here with a bullet wound."

"Exactly my point. I understand your situation, and you need my help," Alexis said, enjoying Griff's squirming. "So for starters, why don't you tell me what you were doing out at Georgetown yesterday afternoon with Razor Gillette?"

For a moment Griff looked stunned. Alexis knew he was used to Mesa asking all the clever questions. She had surprised him.

"And please don't insult me with your memory problems. I've already told the Sheriff about your cousin, Rabid Reg, and the potential jealousy and resentments around the family inheritance. So explain to me why in God's name would Reg have a Montana birth certificate? I saw a copy of it in your briefcase on Saturday. I can only begin to imagine the complications that troublesome detail could be generating. So come clean, and then maybe I can help you get out of whatever mess you've gotten yourself into."

∽✑∾

It was nearly seven on Monday night when Mesa knocked on the door to Adrienne's loft. "Hope I'm not interrupting," she said, thankful that Adrienne had answered her phone.

"Chance is out for the count. He actually did not sleep well last night. I think we've all had a little too much excitement this weekend. And he's getting up at 5 A.M. to work with the Festival sound crew."

"No worries," Mesa said. "This is definitely girl talk." She could tell her brother anything but he got downright gamey when it came to talking about "female stuff," a fact that amused Adrienne no end.

"You look like you could use a glass of wine," Adrienne said, and walked toward the bottles of red that lay in a rack on the kitchen counter. "You know Evan Llewellyn's been looking for you."

Mesa walked over to the couch and collapsed into it. "I saw his text. I have no idea where Phade could be, and before I can even begin to think about him, I need to sort out my thoughts about what I've learned from Chloe Hardcastle."

"This is the Butte woman who runs the mission in West Africa, right?" Adrienne said, and came over to the couch with a bowl of toasted almonds to munch. She was wearing a mauve caftan that hit her in the middle of her well-toned thighs, which reminded Mesa that she could stand to do more to stay in shape. She grabbed a handful of the almonds and told herself to eat them one at a time.

Mesa nodded assent to the question and took a hefty gulp of the Beaujolais Adrienne had given her. Her taste in wine was also spectacular. "You've heard of her?"

"Her name comes up occasionally at the hospital," Adrienne said and sat down next to Mesa. "I hear her grandfather was a local legend, a GP who used to make house calls and forgave his poor patients' bills, practices that haven't existed since the 19th century. Supposedly she takes only living expenses as a salary and raises money tirelessly to keep her clinics in Africa stay open. Clearly, she's a saint."

Then looking at Mesa, Adrienne leaned over and squeezed her hand. "What's wrong? What's upset you so?"

Mesa took a Kleenex from the coffee table and began wiping the tears that had started to fall in a steady stream. Shaking her head and then letting out an embarrassed laugh, she said, "I don't know. It's all so sad and useless."

Adrienne moved closer and put her arm around Mesa's shoulder while she spoke. "Chloe Hardcastle gave up everything to work in Africa out of guilt. She's atoning for what happened a dozen years ago at the Granite Street house when they lost the baby."

Adrienne's mouth fell open. "She was the one who delivered that baby?"

Mesa nodded and told Adrienne the entire story, the stillbirth and then Danica's eventual sterility. How Chloe had failed to remove a portion of the placenta and six weeks later, back in California, Danica went to a doctor thinking she had some kind of infection. How Chloe learned later from the Fertility Clinic that Danica couldn't ever have children because of permanently scarred Fallopian tubes. "I guess this is all making sense to you."

Adrienne nodded and sipped her wine. "That is sad. So Danica's burden was a baby she felt she had to give up." She shook her head. "And Chloe was saddled with the guilt of a botched delivery, not to mention Danica's sterility."

Mesa sipped her wine and tried not to sniff too loud lest she miss a single word of what Adrienne was saying.

"They don't teach you how to deal with mistakes in med school. That's on-the-job training, if you're lucky. Otherwise you learn it in the lawyer's office before you're being deposed in your first malpractice suit." She refilled their glasses while she talked.

"You lose a baby in delivery, and suddenly excitement and anticipation turn to despair," Adrienne said. "I've cried in stairwells and hallways, let me tell you. And with a stillborn, it's heart-wrenching."

Mesa wiped her tears, listening as Adrienne's voice filled with tenderness. "When you're a physician, you're not allowed to grieve. You deliver the bad news and go on to the next patient. But you don't forget the patients you lose. It becomes a scar that never goes away. It shapes the person you become."

Mesa thought about the tears that Chloe had wiped away. Unquestionably, she had been shaped by the death of Danica's baby. She'd devoted her career to ensuring the safest possible deliveries for some of the poorest women in the world.

"And then there's the cover up, and it's your best friend," Adrienne continued, almost in a whisper. "Why did they decide not to tell Danica?"

"In Chloe's case, it was a default. Danica's labor had lasted nearly twenty hours and with the difficult delivery, she had slept the better part of the next day after Chloe's frantic efforts to stem the bleeding. Neither of them had been in a position to know what Nathan had done."

"So he decided Danica shouldn't be told?" Adrienne pressed.

"Chloe said she didn't have the heart to tell Danica after what she'd been through. And Nathan didn't say anything."

"Then fast forward a decade, the chickens come home to roost," Adrienne said, "Danica finally finds out about what really happened. What a nightmare."

"And she finds out about it in the newspaper," Mesa said, more in control now that the wine was having effect.

Chloe had explained how several times in the last years, Danica had asked the name of the ranch family so she could find a way to see how the child was doing. Staying in Africa made it easier to avoid those questions.

But once Danica saw the article in the paper, it must have all come into focus. She called Nathan for answers, and he agreed to meet her and explain.

"That's why she ended up on the roof?" Adrienne asked in a disbelieving tone.

Mesa shrugged. "Chloe wouldn't say. She said she tried to get Nathan to tell her what happened after he met with Danica, but he got defensive and they ended up in an argument. He said he had more important things to worry about—like those shots at the parade. Apparently Nathan believes they were meant for him.

"Chloe told Nathan she was going to talk to the Sheriff in the morning. Nathan warned her that was the last thing he needed and left."

Adrienne filled their wine glasses yet again. "What do you think happened?"

Mesa sighed. "There are so many threads to this knot. I'm having trouble keeping them apart. I can only trace one at a time."

She did think Chloe had told her the truth. Her last conversation with Danica had taken place ten days before on Skype. Upbeat and full of plans, she looked radiant. Ten years since the death of the baby, Chloe thought they had come full circle. Danica was coming back to Butte. She was done with Hollywood. She would settle down, find a good Orthodox husband, and adopt babies. That was what she wanted. No one would have to know about the first child. That was between Danica and God.

Adrienne sighed and finished the last of her wine. "And now that Danica is gone?"

Mesa put her empty glass on the coffee table. "At least Chloe doesn't have to struggle with her guilt anymore. For years she'd wanted to tell Danica what really happened. She always thought she could make Danica understand, but Nathan had made her promise she would never tell. Maybe now she'll come back from Africa."

Chapter 15

"His girlfriend says sometimes Phade goes up to the newspaper to work at night. I'd like to check," Macgregor said. "Can you meet me at your office?"

Mesa looked at the microwave clock which read a bit after nine in the evening. She had arrived at her duplex moments before, collapsing onto the couch when her phone rang. "You working the night shift?" she said, stalling while she thought about a good reason to tell the detective no.

"Technically, I'm not working at all. It's a holiday. Can you meet me or not?"

She could tell by the tenacious tone in Macgregor's voice that he wasn't going to take no for an answer, but that didn't stop her from trying. "I drove by there a few minutes ago, and there were no lights on."

Her phone pinged with the third text from Alexis at the rodeo, wondering where Mesa was. She took a deep breath and went over to the refrigerator, hoping Alexis had not already depleted her stash of Red Bull that she always brought along. Mesa hated the taste but it was too warm for coffee, and she knew the high-energy drink would have the intended effect. At least, it was cold.

"How can you tell if there were lights on? It's nowhere near dark," Macgregor said. "Nobody's heard from him all day and I'm starting to wonder where he is. This town's not that big. He better not be doing something stupid."

Mesa suspected Macgregor's instincts were not far off. She knew enough about Phade's moodiness and what it could lead to—not sleeping for a couple of days and walking into the office looking like it, driving all night to get home from a punk concert in Seattle so he wouldn't be late for work, refusing to speak to Cinch for weeks.

Mesa was only reticent because she wasn't sure what Macgregor might find in Phade's desk. If Irita was to be believed, a couple of joints could be lying between the pencils and pens. Of course, the detective was only asking to look around for signs of people. She could stop him from opening drawers, but that wouldn't stop her from sweating.

Chugging the Red Bull, she put on her jeans and cowboy boots and headed out. She'd spend five minutes at the office with the detective and then on to the rodeo. There was no way she'd be able to sneak into the hospital to see Griff tonight, which was what she really wanted to do.

Alexis sat between Rowdy and Hank, the two cowboys she had met at The Gun Room Friday night. It hadn't taken long to meet up with them. In fact they had found her.

Armed with a twelve-pack of Coors, everybody's favorite rodeo beer, which the Vigilante Saddle Club was conveniently selling at the entrance, she had climbed twenty bleacher rows to the top of the stands and taken a seat at the far end of the ring where the crowd was sparse enough that she could be seen. She could also reconnoiter inside the arena and keep an eye out for Mesa arriving in the parking lot.

Alexis had learned early on when she first came to Montana that nothing made a rodeo cowboy happier than having some friendly faces in the audience cheering for him. She figured the least she could do after Friday's mess was to actually show up to root the boys on. On top of which, she was considering an investment in a rodeo stock company and wanted to check out the bucking stock for the events that night.

The cowboys were surprised by her appearance. Walking alongside several of the petite, barrel racers, whom they dwarfed, both cowboys had seen her at the same time and broken into smiles. The cowgirls had kept going, but the guys had climbed up to her perch and sat down, one on each side. Alexis enjoyed Rowdy's bantering which she was pretty sure was for her benefit. He knew every competitor by name and most of the animals as well. The tall quiet one, Hank, seemed happy enough to sip his beer and let his pal do the talking.

Once the bareback riding and the steer wrestling competition had finished and the beer had been depleted, she began to wonder about her wing woman. She'd heard about all of the Brooks and Dunn she could tolerate and began to text Mesa in earnest once the sun had begun to set.

Alexis was looking forward to telling Mesa about what Griff had finally confided. Her suspicions about troubles with the family inheritance had been spot on. And the story about the Montana birth certificate was worthy of a screenplay, though she doubted seriously that Jones's family would ever want it to see Hollywood. The big secret—and it was a whopper—was that the heir apparent, cousin Reg, was one of Elsie's Babies.

That was what Griff had come to Butte to prove. The fact of the Montana birth certificate alone was not enough to keep Reginald from inheriting. His parents were British citizens who were living in the United States in 1966, Reg's father being a junior member of the British consulate. His mother, a highly-strung English aristocrat, found her confinement just that—too confining.

The couple had taken up the invitation of somebody in the State Department with a family ranch outside of Three Forks, Montana. When their own infant died soon after birth, the mother was bereft. Her husband was beside himself as well. In a strange country, far from home, he was prepared to do anything to help his wife. It was Griff's own mother, who had traveled to attend the birth, who found a way to soothe her grieving sister.

"My mother died last year but not before she told me that they had gotten a baby from Butte," Griff had told Alexis, seeming almost ashamed. His mother was also in America with her husband who was at the University of Chicago. She had helped broker the baby deal through the local midwife who had attended the original birth and who knew someone in Butte. The "someone" had been Elsa Seppanen.

Once the young family returned to England, the husband died in a car accident and Griff's aunt remarried. The sisters had agreed to take the secret of the illegal adoption to the grave, which Reginald's mother did. But when Reginald had begun his absurd anti-abortion campaign, Griff's mother decided her loyalty—both to the family's name and to her own son—trumped her promise.

"All I am trying to do is find out who his real parents are," Griff had explained. "If it's as I have been told, I may be able to put a stop to his ridiculous grandstanding. The tabloids will have a field day, and he'll be too embarrassed to continue."

Alexis wouldn't let him off the hook. "And—don't tell me—Grandpapa isn't going to allow Reg to inherit if he's not a legitimately adopted member of the family. Once this all comes out, you'll go to the head of the queue."

"As it should be. Bloodlines mean something where I come from."

The loud buzzer, signaling the end of the first calf-roping team's hopes, jolted Alexis back into the moment. "No time," the announcer had said quietly, as a crestfallen pair of cowboys rode out of the arena. She sat alone now with Rowdy who was cheering for the next team of ropers. Hank had gone to prepare for the bull riding event where he was one of the chute men. Alexis turned to look over the back of the bleachers into the parking lot. *Where the hell was Mesa?*

She was about to turn back to the calf ropers when she realized she had seen something she recognized: that same weird color motorcycle. It was hard to believe more than one beige motorcycle existed in Butte. Beige, *really*?

Or had she had one too many Coors and the light of the setting sun was playing tricks on her? She took her iPhone from her back pocket and took a quick snap. She would show Mesa and then maybe the Sheriff, not that he had paid much attention when she'd told him about the motorcycle earlier that day. He was inclined to dismiss the "shots fired" incidence at the parade that morning as "knuckleheadedness."

She felt Rowdy's elbow gently in her side. "Isn't that your compadre from the other night?" He gestured with his head toward the aisle that circled the arena.

Alexis saw Mesa walking in their direction. At least she'd put on some jeans and her boots, which accentuated her slender build. For once, she actually looked like she could jump on a pony and do a little barrel racing herself. For someone who'd spent half her life in Montana, Mesa could act like the least Western person in the state. Alexis put her fingers to her lips and produced a sharp whistle she knew Mesa would hear and recognize.

Mesa breathed in the pungent smell of cow manure and felt strangely relaxed. She thought about the summers on her grandparents' ranch before they'd moved to town. The ammonia scent that had wafted out of the chicken coop grossed her out, but the fermented-grass smell of cow shit had a strangely fresh odor, like new-mown hay. That said, any discussion of shit was appropriate for a day where she felt like she'd been slogging through it the whole time.

Her meeting with Macgregor at the *Mess* office had not gone well. She didn't think he actually expected to find Phade there. It was more like he wanted an opportunity to take out his frustrations on somebody.

"I got a call from the Hardcastle family that you were out at the house talking to Chloe," he had said as soon as they walked into the *Mess* office to find the lights on and Evan hard at work on the blog.

He'd quickly removed the Tootsie Pop from his mouth and shot a Mesa smile. Clearly, he was happy to see her, but then he shrank behind his computer screen when he saw Macgregor bringing up the rear. She introduced them.

"You the kid who found the phone?" Macgregor had asked.

"Yes sir," Evan said, looking owl-like, his eyes going back and forth, between Mesa and the detective.

How Macgregor knew this, Mesa couldn't be sure. Maybe Phade had mentioned it. In any case, the moment passed, and the detective simply said, "Good work."

Macgregor then proceeded to grill Evan. Did he often work at night? Did Phade? Were they often there together? Did Phade ever say where he was going when he left?

Mesa had come to appreciate in recent days how attentive Evan was to details. She suspected he had ideas about where Phade might be, and she regretted that she hadn't gotten to the office early enough to ask him before Macgregor showed up.

"Some-, sometimes, he goes up to the radio station," Evan said.

"What radio station? Up where?" Macgregor barked.

Evan stuttered again, looking at Mesa with a panicked expression as though maybe he was saying something he shouldn't. Mesa nodded to encourage him.

"The Community Radio station, KBMF—Butte, America," he said. "The studio's in the Union Hall. On the first floor."

"Across from the Courthouse?" Macgregor said. "What's he do up there?"

Evan shrugged. "Sometimes he's a substitute DJ. Or he helps the station manager with any digital editing projects."

"You got a radio?" Macgregor said.

"You can listen on the computer," Evan said and immediately pulled up the streaming website. Obnoxiously loud heavy metal music filled the room.

Evan jumped on the volume and then seconds later a female voice announced the music, "That was the mind-bending Axl Rose…"

Macgregor said, "Turn it off. Obviously, Phade's not subbing right now. When's the last time you saw him?" Macgregor asked in an accusatory tone.

Evan scratched his forehead and then reached out with his hands, placating, "Uh, I guess it was at the garden party on Saturday at Mrs. Ducharme's house."

"You haven't seen him today? You were at his house earlier."

"Right, I was, but he was already gone," Evan stuttered again.

Mesa felt sorry for Evan. Clearly, Macgregor was irritated and was taking it out on the kid.

"You'd tell me if you saw him?" Macgregor said.

Evan nodded.

"Okay, get out of here and go look for him."

Evan looked at Mesa. She nodded at him and said. "Call me, too, if you find him."

Once they were alone, Mesa headed into her office and said, "Was that really necessary? He doesn't know anything."

Macgregor followed her, saying. "Maybe not. I guess I'm a little frustrated. The Draganovichs are good people and they're worried. The investigation is going nowhere fast. I thought the least I could do was help them find their son."

Mesa sighed. She understood how he felt.

Macgregor balanced his oversized frame on the arm of the sofa and crossed his beefy arms. "Dr. Hardcastle is coming down to the station first thing in the morning. Wanna give me a head start and tell me what the two of you talked about?"

"I'd rather let Chloe tell you herself," Mesa said quietly.

"I'm sure you would," Macgregor said, "And I'm sure you wouldn't want to impede the police investigation either. Is there anything she told you that I could do something about tonight?"

According to Nana Rose, Butte was a small enough town that antagonism between law enforcement and the newspapers benefited no one. Mesa didn't necessarily agree but Macgregor probably knew that was the *Messenger* philosophy.

"The dead baby from Thursday—" Mesa said quietly, "belonged to Danica."

"From the Granite Street house?" Macgregor said, pausing for a second to take in the information. "I'll be damned." Then he added, "And Nathan Hardcastle was the father." Macgregor might be slow, but he wasn't stupid.

Mesa nodded. She didn't see any reason to protect that bastard.

"That's who she was going to meet on Friday," Macgregor said. "Well, that definitely puts a different spin on things."

Macgregor paused again and then said, "He was on our list of friends of Danica's to interview. Been out of town. He's on the list for tomorrow."

Mesa wasn't about to brag that she and Alexis had already tracked Hardcastle down. She knew the Butte Silver-Bow police department probably wouldn't have been paying Macgregor overtime to work a holiday weekend on a case that was a likely suicide.

"What else?" Macgregor said, his tone suggesting he knew Mesa was holding back.

"According to Chloe the baby was stillborn, which Danica never knew. The plan was to give the baby up to a family Chloe had found that was eager to have kid, ala Elsie's Babies, except without the price tag."

"That's some fairy tale," Macgregor said in disbelief. "But wait, so that's what Danica meant in the text, when she said she saw the story. She had just found out the baby had died?" He stood up, hands on hips, and said, "My God, that could have put her over the edge right there."

"And that's why she wanted to see Hardcastle on Friday. The GH mentioned in the text?" Mesa continued.

Macgregor had taken a small notebook from the breast pocket of his shirt and was taking notes. "Yeah?" he said.

"It's this place they used to hang out when they were all in high school. It's not actually a place anymore but there used to be a glass hut on top of the elevator equipment room on the roof of the Finlen."

"Right," Macgregor said, as if knew exactly what she meant even though apparently he hadn't put it together when he'd seen Danica's text, or if he had, he hadn't told anybody. "Part of the staircase is still up there. The owner, Frank Harper, you know Harp, don't you? Hell of a nice guy. Anyway, he was telling me they tore down the glass room when they remodeled in '79 but they left the staircase until recently. So that's where you think Danica and Hardcastle were rendezvousing?"

Mesa nodded. "He might have been the last person to see her alive."

Mesa drank deep from the can of Coors Alexis had given her. She felt like she'd drifted from one dust bowl to another all day. She took a deep breath and told herself to relax. Now that Macgregor saw the link to Hardcastle, she felt like a weight had been lifted.

She stared out at the rodeo ring and took in the atmosphere. She'd been going to rodeos all her life without really knowing much about what was going on. Alexis understood far more about the actual events. Still, Mesa loved the atmosphere and the time-honored traditions that didn't seem to change. Corny as it might sound, the rodeo really was the quintessential symbol of the American West.

The horses were nothing short of remarkable, some of the most beautiful Mesa had ever seen, well-trained and well cared for, the cattle too, particularly the bulls. The excitement that surrounded the contests, above all the bronc busting and bull riding, was palpable. The human competitors were equally hard to overlook.

On the drive to the rodeo grounds, Mesa had told herself that she deserved an hour of relaxation. Then she would head back into town to look for Phade. But Alexis, who was normally riveted to any sporting event that involved horses, wouldn't shut up about the Englishman. She was going on about talking to him at the hospital.

"He found the ledger," Alexis said, right as one of the chutes opened and the first bull, called Gobbler, threw itself and its rider into the ring. The crowd let out a thunderous roar, and the rider fell to the ground a nanosecond later.

"The ledger?" Mesa said, drawing a blank, and looked at Alexis whose face glowed with triumph.

Mesa began recalling her banter with Jones over the previous three days. When she got to their conversation at The Gun Room, before she'd left with Evan, she realized what Alexis meant.

"The ledger, he found Elsa Seppanen's ledger?!" Her voice had risen and she looked around to see if anyone had heard her, but everyone else was watching the next pairing which was already into the ring. A ferocious gray bull called Bad Medicine, spinning and tossing, threw its rider into the air like a rag doll.

Alexis could hardly contain her excitement. "He says it's proof that his aunt and uncle bought a black market baby in 1968. And it also names the birth parents. Turns out Reg's birth father was some traveling gambler and his mother worked in one of the brothels on Mercury Street.

"Jesus," Mesa said with a laugh, thinking of the speculations about what had been in that book and now hearing them come true.

"Griff's mother had found a midwife who was from Butte who got them the baby," Alexis continued. "He says he made arrangements to buy the ledger, or at least he thought he had, until there was what he calls a 'misunderstanding' about the price."

Mesa was impressed. She'd spent months asking around about the existence of the book without any success. How could Griff Jones have found it? "Who had it?" she asked Alexis, who was now cheering along with the crowd as a bull rider had managed to hang onto a jet black bull with the unlikely name of Gargamel for the entire eight seconds. At the rate they were going, the entire bull riding competition would be over in less than ten minutes.

"I haven't wormed that out of him yet. Thought maybe we could soften him up when we get him over to your Nan's tomorrow."

Mesa thought for a moment about what Sheriff Solheim had described to her, how the night before, when Griff was lying in that alley in danger of bleeding to death, he had called out. "Get my book. It's mine."

"Think that's what got Griff shot?" Mesa said aloud. So the attack wasn't random. But he had only been in Butte twenty-four hours. It didn't make sense unless somebody knew he was coming to town or someone knew he wanted the ledger, or both.

"Maybe we should ask his pal," Alexis said and pulled out her iPhone. "I think I saw his motorcycle in the parking lot."

Mesa took a quick look at the photo and then jumped up to the back of the bleachers to have a look for herself. Alexis joined her, pointing to the outer fence of the parking lot, not far from the north gate. Just then they saw someone approaching the bike. Mesa strained to see the guy who leaned on the seat, biding his time. She had only a vague recollection and a yearbook photo ten-plus years old to go on. It might be Gillette, but maybe not.

"Let's go down there," Mesa said. She and Alexis began as quick a trek down the steps as they dared. Cowboy boots were not made for sprinting, Alexis saying her goodbyes as she went. They'd taken two or three strides when they heard the announcer say, "That's our last bull rider of the night. Thanks everyone for coming out. Stick around for the Mud Creek Wranglers band. They're warming up to perform for you in the beer garden. Have a beverage and congratulate the competitors."

Suddenly the nearly empty aisles of the arena were filled with departing spectators. Mesa estimated the crowd at less than a thousand, but they'd been drinking beer all evening and were in no hurry. She led Alexis toward the exit farthest from where the faithful were gathering for the cover band's performance. Cars had already begun to move in the parking lot, the air thick with dust.

Mesa, with Alexis on her heels, dodged a horse trailer in time to see a metallic gray SUV pulling up next to the motorcycle. The vehicle stopped right in her line of sight but not before she got a clear view of what she thought was the same guy with mirrored sunglasses they had seen driving the motorcycle with Jones the previous afternoon. And not before she noticed a parking sticker on the SUV's bumper and the silhouette of the driver.

Now the pedestrian traffic had picked up as well, and Mesa and Alexis had to sidestep departing rodeo lovers carrying coolers, blankets, riding gear and the remains of half-finished twelve packs. One row of parked cars away from coming eye to eye with Razor Gillette—Mesa was sure—the silver SUV pulled away and the motorcycle followed, gravel flying in all directions. They roared out the north entrance of the parking lot and toward town.

"Damn it," Mesa said as she stopped in the middle of the parking lane, not fifty feet from where the motorcycle had been parked.

"My pickup's two rows back," Alexis said. "We can follow them."

Mesa shook her head, wiped the grime from her dry lips, and said, "They're taking the back way, probably cutting across Shoe String Annie Street. They'll be over to Harrison in no time and long gone. That SUV look familiar to you?"

"You mean like a thousand other silver SUVs between here and Dillon?"

"Yesterday at the Hardcastles' cabin, see one there?"

Alexis paused for a minute, pulled the tab on the last Coors which she'd brought along, took a sip, and nodded. "Now that you mention it, I believe I did."

Mesa took the can from her friend and truly wet her whistle. Then she pulled her iPhone from her hip pocket and phoned Royal Macgregor.

Chapter 16

With the actual 4th on a Monday, Chance knew the four-day week helping the Montana Folk Fest organizers would be a bear. Already a day behind in preparation, all across uptown, volunteers in red T-shirts were setting up tents, stages, and rigging for five different venues. Concrete barricades for street closures and an endless number of signs and smaller tents sprang up throughout the streets. Days were long, as the lack of sufficiently burly volunteers made for slow-going. Uptown Butte was miserably under siege.

For the fourth year in a row, Chance had taken off a week from his own projects, in this case the Park Hotel renovation, and volunteered to help with the festival site setup. And for the last three years he had recruited Nick Philippoussis. Not only because Nick was wicked strong, but because Chance despised waiting and time seemed to shorten with his buddy around. As long as no one died unattended or in an unexpected way, the assistant coroner could be counted on to regale everyone with an endless string of stories.

Now they stood in front of Hennessy's Market on Granite Street, waiting for some sound engineer, shipped in from Seattle, who was behind schedule to okay the speaker setup. Per usual, the guy was way more interested in the timetable for sound checks, particularly for his band, than the stability of the stage. His attention was more focused on finding out when his band would perform than whether the stage-left loudspeaker tower was properly rigged so it wouldn't topple over during the set and mangle part of the audience.

"So how was the rest of the weekend?" Chance asked, checking his watch for the third time in ten minutes.

"Near perfect—after Friday," Nick said, quietly. "Hard to get that one out of your mind." He shook his head and then added, "That image that they're not really dead is tough to shake. The wife knows the family, too. Guess the young woman had been outta the fold for the last few years, and they were glad to be having her home. Shame."

Chance listened, nodding his head at the appropriate pauses. While he hadn't seen Danica Draganovich lying dead on the roof of that SUV, he had heard plenty about it from Mesa. Now, three days later, he wondered how much they would ever really know for certain. Adrienne had explained about the stillbirth, but that had happened ten years before. He couldn't imagine that all these years later, Danica's guilt would have driven her to end her own life.

"Were you in on that baby on Granite Street?" Chance said. "It was hers, you know."

"No kidding," Nick said. "Well, that explains a lot."

"How do you mean?" Chance asked, listening with one ear and staring up at the half-constructed aluminum speaker towers on the Granite Street stage. The height of the towers always unnerved Chance, the lightweight aluminum piping never seeming sturdy or stable enough. The Granite Street stage was a temporary structure and nowhere near as well-built as the Original Mine yard's permanent stage. "If this engineer doesn't show up soon, I'm going down to the Finlen and drag him back here."

"You can tell a lot about how death occurs by how the body is disposed of," Nick said. "The poor little thing was wrapped in some kind of christening blanket and then laid in that dry cleaning bag, almost like they'd tried to fashion some kind of cradle."

"Still a crime though, isn't it?" Chance said, echoing Adrienne's concern.

"Hiding a body, you mean?" Nick said. "Not my department."

He had just made that declaration when Delilah Tate, the *Messenger*'s entertainment reporter came around the corner. Always easy on the eyes with her arty outfits that frequently included low-cut blouses, Nick greeted her warmly. They got a well-intended but overbearing lecture about how the Granite Street stage really offered the best sound of any of the festival stages. Its location between Main and Wyoming had been chosen because it formed a natural echo chamber for the music which bounced off the three-story buildings on either side of the street."

"Yeah, well it also creates a natural wind tunnel," Chance piped in. July thunderstorms could whip up thirty-five mile-an-hour winds easy. A faulty piece of rigging could get ripped apart and torn away in seconds.

"You need to relax or you'll never enjoy the music," Delilah said in her flirtatious way.

"Maybe you're right," Chance said, telling himself he could only do what he was told, and the rest was up to the music gods. That was kinda the way he felt about Danica and her baby. It was between her and God. "And what about you?" he said to Delilah. "Got any eye-opening stories you're covering"

"Mostly behind the scenes stuff with artists and performers. A couple of international filmmakers are supposed to be here, too. One of them is from England. You should tell Mrs. Ducharme. She didn't get to meet him last year. She had just had her heart attack."

Irita's call came exactly at nine a.m. Tuesday morning, following Mesa's standing order that if she hadn't called or appeared in the office by that reasonable hour, her assistant should roust her. "Where's Phade?" was Irita's first question.

Sitting half-way up in bed, Mesa quickly outlined the search for Phade. She and Alexis had left the rodeo grounds, keeping a keen eye out for Gillette and Hardcastle, and then made a concerted effort to find Phade. They had parked Alexis's honker of a pickup and taken Mesa's car. "If he doesn't want to be found, he won't be," Mesa explained to Alexis. "He may have driven to the coast. He loves to stare at the ocean. Which I can understand. I only wish he'd told someone."

They had stopped by the community radio station and talked to a DJ called Magic Mike. He said on occasion Phade was one of the guys who hung out at the recording studio at Len Waters Music Center. They'd driven over to Main Street and peeked in through the glass storefront, but the place was dark. On the door was a handwritten sign in red magic marker that read, "Check back. Open from time to time 'til Evel Days," which meant the owner had probably gone fishing for the next three weeks. Frustrated, they'd roamed the bars, drinking as they went, until closing time at 2 a.m.

Irita was none too worried. "Well, no sign of him here either," was all she had to say and then moved on to more pressing concerns. "I'm so tired of going into the garage and not being able to find what I want, and then going back two weeks later and having the same problem except then I find the thing I was looking for two weeks ago. I've decided to have a garage sale." Irita's mind flitted from thought to thought like bees on buttercups. "How's the Englishman doing?"

Mesa explained the bare details about Jones and his search for his cousin's connection to Elsa Seppanen, leaving out the tidbit about the ledger being found. She didn't want Irita alerting the whole town to that tasty morsel, with who knew what repercussions, until she had talked to Griff herself. "He's been talking to a guy name Razor Gillette."

"I need to go up to Insty-Prints and get some Garage Sale signs made," Irita was explaining, as if she had barely heard what Mesa had said. "When you coming in?"

"I'll be there in twenty minutes," Mesa said with a yawn and swung her legs over the edge of the bed. Irita was still talking.

"I'm being really cruel when it comes to clothes, too. I'm selling it all, and what I don't sell I'm giving away. If I haven't worn it in a year, it's going. I'm doing this for larger women everywhere. Try going to Goodwill and finding something in 2X."

Mesa held the phone away from her ear and headed to the kitchen. She walked past the other bedroom, peeked around the half-opened door, and saw that Alexis was sound asleep. "Okay, Irita, I can see you've got a plan."

"I just wanted you to know what I'm up against. Now, Evan is here and so is Cinch. Delilah is over at the Finlen looking for scrap on the performers coming in for the Folk Festival. Did you talk to your grandmother this morning?"

Mesa stopped for a moment. "Did she call?" Rose Ducharme liked her landline, and Irita remained her link to what was happening at the paper. Not that Mesa minded. Her grandmother wouldn't want to seem like she was breathing down Mesa's neck.

Reaching for the coffee in the freezer, Irita's comment reminded Mesa that Griff was being moved to her grandmother's house that morning. Thankfully Adrienne had agreed to oversee the ordeal. Then, as she recalled all that she'd heard from Alexis the night before and her suspicions about Gillette and Hardcastle, Mesa had a sudden wave of anxiety about Griff's presence in her grandmother's house.

"Good old Razor," Irita said, harking back to the previous topic of conversation. "He had a hard time, got knocked around more than most. Used to work at the Finlen, I don't know if he still does. For a couple of years there, he was fulltime at the Country Club."

Mesa thought about cutting Irita off. They could talk about all this when Mesa got to the office. But once Irita got going on one of her stories, it was easier sometimes to let her finish than it was to get her to refocus.

"He started out mowing lawns when his uncle was head of maintenance. Then when he died, Razor got that job. The hotel job was part-time to help get through the winter. But seems like I heard he was fired from the Country Club last summer for trying to scam some of the members."

Mesa was listening as she searched for a filter for the coffee maker. Irita had never been part of the country club set. She wondered how she knew so much. "How do you know all this?" Mesa asked.

"My next door neighbor's granddaughter, Kiley Ransenberg, worked as a cart girl out there for a couple of summers during college. Shoulda heard her talk."

"Like what?" Mesa said. Wasn't Hardcastle on the Board of the Country Club? Maybe Kiley had seen him in action, too.

"You know, the guys with three-hundred-dollar golf outfits, bragging about their perfect kids and vacation homes, meanwhile always trying to get in the cart girls' pants."

"Charming how some things never change," Mesa said, remembering how Tara McTeague, her best friend in high school, had complained about the same thing when she had been a cart girl.

"Oh yeah," Irita continued. "Kiley said these guys would drink a beer a hole, and yell if the cart girls weren't quick enough bringing refills. Regular Country Club douche bags.

"They liked to gamble too. I heard Razor got into it pretty heavy. He was real competitive and a sore loser who wouldn't pay up. Pretty soon nobody would even get on the putting green with him. Maybe that's why he got canned."

There was a momentary pause and then the footnote—and the bombshell. "You know, he was Einar Mortensen's nephew."

"The coroner back when?" Mesa said, stopped in her tracks, causing coffee grounds to spill across the kitchen counter. Suddenly, Razor's connection to Griff came into stark relief. Razor must have figured out where Uncle Mortie had hidden the book.

"Irita, I need to swing by Nan's before I come in."

The smell of scones filled Rose Ducharme's kitchen. "I don't really think it's necessary for Alexis to stay, though you are certainly welcome," she said and patted Alexis on the hand. Mesa sat with her grandmother and Alexis at the kitchen table drinking steaming, milky tea and eating the mouth-watering pastry. "Adrienne will stop by this afternoon to check on the patient. Vivian's coming by at lunch time to help with his tray. So you see, everything's sorted."

Mesa had been grateful for Alexis's offer to "hang with Nan" 'til they could get a better handle on Griff's plans to recover Elsie's ledger. Alexis had no pressing responsibilities at the ranch that her trusty foreman, Jesse, couldn't handle. So delaying her drive back to Melrose was no big deal. While Alexis could be a handful on a Friday night, in the light of day, she could also be a formidable presence, one that made Mesa feel more secure about leaving her grandmother with Griff in the house.

"Nan," Mesa countered, "we think the reason that Griff was shot has to do with Elsa Seppanen and the ledger she supposedly kept. Alexis says he claims to have bought it and then someone took it from him."

Nan put down her cup of tea as Mesa spoke. "Dear me," she said. "You really think someone found it? She's been dead for more than thirty years," she said. "Someone could easily be taking advantage of Mr. Jones." She shook her head. "The whole business is unsavory, I don't mind telling you. Every time there's a story in the newspaper or a magazine, it brings up difficult memories for a lot of people around town. No mother likes to think about giving up a child."

She paused and began to fold her napkin, a sign Mesa knew meant that her grandmother was gathering her thoughts.

"Now Mesa, I know you have strong opinions about women's rights, as do I, but when it comes to individuals' private lives, one must be careful. If such a book exists, its contents ought not necessarily be put on public display."

Her grandmother was already thinking about the impact of the ledger's discovery and whether that information could go into the newspaper. Mesa smiled briefly at her cagey grandmother and then said, "I understand your point. But first we need to find out where the ledger is and if it's the real deal."

"I do hope you'll not browbeat our guest," her grandmother cautioned. "I've invited him here to recuperate. It would hardly be hospitable if you start interrogating him."

According to Alexis, Griff maintained he couldn't remember how or why the ledger had disappeared, but he wasn't leaving Butte until he had retrieved it. But he didn't know about Hardcastle's involvement with Danica and the possible implications that relationship had on her death.

Mesa imagined Detective Macgregor might want to be informed about any communication between Gillette and Hardcastle. In any case, she wanted to be sure that if any contact occurred while Griff was at her grandmother's, she should be safely out of the way.

"Of course not," Mesa said, trying not to sound patronizing. "It's only that Griff's been in touch with a couple of guys in Butte that I'm not so sure are thinking as kindly toward him as you are. One is Einar Mortensen's nephew, a guy named Razor Gillette. Then there's Nathan Hardcastle. Do you know anything about either of them or their families that might suggest a connection to the ledger?"

"Well, the Hardcastle boy is one of Dr. Armistead's grandchildren. Of course, I know of him. Adrienne and I were talking about him last night."

Mesa was surprised by this. "In what context?"

"The Armisteads lived in the house on Granite Street where the dead child's remains were found. She was asking who might have been living there when that child would have been born."

Mesa looked up to see her grandmother's penetrating gaze.

"You don't think Dr. Armistead had anything to do with that child, do you? He could never do anything like that, I assure you."

"No, I didn't think he would," Mesa said, knowing that the story Chloe had told would come out soon enough. Right now she was more concerned with what connection Nathan had to the ledger. "But might he have known something about Elsie's Babies?"

"He certainly knew of Elsa Seppanen," her grandmother said with a sigh. "By the time I got here in the late fifties, all the doctors in town knew what Elsie did, as far I could tell. Wealthier doctors handled the unwanted pregnancies of married women, patients who could pay, and somehow that wasn't frowned on. If a divorcee needed a D and C, that didn't come with shame. But the poor women, the ones who were without husbands, they got sent to Elsie. Armistead was a good Catholic. I couldn't see him performing abortions. He'd be far more likely to suggest having the baby delivered by Elsie and giving the child to a decent family."

Nan continued to talk about the rumors that would swirl around Elsie and who did and did not avail themselves of her services, when Mesa got a call from Chance.

"I'm over here on Granite Street stage working on the rigging," he said, sounding slightly out of breath. "I saw Delilah. She's been down at the Finlen, talking to the Artist Hospitality coordinator about getting a press pass. Turns out they're expecting a documentary filmmaker and asked if she wanted to interview him." Here he paused and she could tell he was pacing himself toward a big crescendo. "Like they did last summer." He paused again. "The filmmaker last year was an Englishman named Griffin-Jones."

"He was here last year?" Mesa gasped half in surprise and half in irritation.

"Yep. Better add that to his string of lies," Chance said. "Think he's telling the truth about anything?"

Mesa felt her temper beginning to rise. She hadn't come back to Butte until Labor Day weekend last year so she could not have possibly seen Griff around town then. Even if she had been in Butte, the crowds at the Festival were in the tens of thousands. He would have had plenty of anonymity to begin hatching his little plan, damn him.

Chance had finally gotten the canvas stage cover connected to the speaker towers. With his fear of heights, Nick had stood at the base of each aluminum tower, holding it steady, while Chance shinnied up to secure the canvas. By tower number four, they were both ready for a break. They were headed toward the M & M for lunch when Royal Macgregor met them coming along Granite Street.

Royal might be maddeningly methodical for some, but Chance liked him. According to the Sheriff, who would confide these things in his quiet moments, usually after a few beers, Macgregor was his best detective. "He gets it right," Rollie would say.

"We're headed to the M&M for lunch. Join us?" Chance said after the three had exchanged greetings.

Macgregor declined. "Much as I would enjoy a juicy ground round burger with some fries and gravy, I gotta go down to the Finlen and follow up some details about the Friday situation."

"Anything new?" Nick asked, glancing at Chance who was muttering about Delilah's revelation.

"Contacted the Medical Examiner's office about the tox results. We might get something back by Christmas. But there's nothing obvious." Macgregor shook his head. "Just spent an hour with Nathan Hardcastle, self-righteous prick. Neither of you heard me say that."

Chance smiled and nodded cooperatively along with Nick.

"He claims he wasn't up on the roof and he has no idea what happened," the detective continued, nodding at Chance. "I think your sis is right that the Draganovich girl was going to meet him, but he's not going to cop to it. I tried to guilt it out of him, saying she was a nice girl and if he didn't want everyone to think she'd jumped from that roof, he needed to say something."

Chance thought that was a good approach. "How'd that work for you?"

"He said 'I can't help you, and can I go now'," Macgregor said and threw his arms in the air in mock disbelief.

Chance thought about what Adrienne had told him, the story that would eventually come out about the dead child. He wondered if Macgregor knew yet. "Mesa talked to you about Chloe Hardcastle and what Danica went through?"

Macgregor nodded and said, "Oh yeah. Guilt tripped him bad about that, too, her being so torn up about what he had done. That he stood to lose a lot of respect from people in the community when that story got out. How Danica must have been distraught when she read about the baby in the *Standard*. Of course, since the bastard's got a law degree, he's like, "Charge me or let me go."

Nick crossed his arms and rocked back on his heels. "Well, he's in a tight spot if he admits to being up there with her. Whatever he says is gonna get called into question. He's got nobody to back him up, right?"

"Exactly," Macgregor responded. "And to be honest, I'm not looking to pin anything on him. You probably know better than I do, there are no indications of foul play, defensive wounds, and such. But I do want to know what happened, for Christ's sake. We can't have people falling off roofs without knowing what caused it. I told Hardcastle I was going to talk to his sister so him denying everything is not going to last."

Macgregor looked at Chance, "I asked him about the shooting, too, of that English guy. Hardcastle says he didn't have anything to do with that either. Then I say I know he was with the Englishman at Georgetown Lake, which I don't, but again I'm going on what your sister told the Sheriff about seeing all those guys out there." He nodded Chance's way again.

Chance suddenly felt wary about Hardcastle's interview with the cops. How wound up would he have been when he left? And what if he decided he needed to see Griffin-Jones? The possibility of Hardcastle showing up at Nana Rose's front door did not sit well.

Mesa stared at the tray of scones Nan had put together for Griff, trying to decide what she would say to him, confused once again about how she felt. That he had misrepresented himself, if not outright lied, made her not want to talk to him at all. Nevertheless, he had been shot, and though he may have put himself in harm's way, she felt bad for him. The fact that she had not made time to see him at the hospital made her feel worse.

She carried the tray upstairs and when she walked in, Griff was sitting up, resting on several pillows set against the delicately carved, dark cherry headboard. His eyes opened as she approached, and he smiled weakly. "Oh Mesa, I was hoping it would be you. After my chat with

Alexis yesterday, I wasn't sure you'd want to see me again. She seems to tell you everything. I hope you'll let me explain."

His voice was muted, and he held her gaze for only a second before he started fiddling with the bedclothes. She put the tray across his lap, saying nothing. His hair was tousled, and he had lost that confident glow she'd been attracted to Saturday afternoon when he had worked Nan's garden party like an ambassador. "My grandmother made them especially for you, so eat up," she said perfunctorily.

He took a bite, sipped some tea, and then put the cup down, and what sounded like a well-rehearsed speech tumbled out. "Look, Mesa, I'm grateful to your grandmother, and I'm sorry I didn't confide in you about why I was here. When I met you, I wasn't sure who I could trust. I know now that was a mistake. I wish we could start over."

He paused and there was a silence that Mesa allowed to linger. He sipped his tea and then added, "Will you forgive me?"

Pulling up the upholstered mahogany side chair next to the bed, Mesa sat down and said, "Eat some more scones. I promised Nana I'd make you." She decided to let his little speech go unanswered. And instead, asked, "How are you feeling?"

"Physically, not that bad, I have to admit. Bit like being gouged in the side repeatedly with a cricket bat and chucked out a window." Then he returned to his original plea. "I'd feel a lot better if I thought you'd forgive me."

His conciliatory words were having their intended effect. She held her hands to her chin, her fingers intertwined. She wondered, later, if she had looked like she was pleading. "My grandmother is the most generous person I know. Promise me having you here won't put her in any danger."

Griff put the scone down on the plate and wiped his mouth. "Good God, no," he said in a contrite voice. "I am indebted to her for getting out of that hospital. I assure you I have no intention of doing anything but getting a day or two of uninterrupted rest, and then I shall be on my way. I'm hoping to be back in England by week's end."

"So you're not staying for the Folk Festival after all?' Mesa said, laying the sarcasm on. "Like you did last summer?"

She got up and walked to the window, leaving Griff to weigh what she was saying. "You know, this is a small enough town that charming Englishmen don't come around that often. You were here in Butte last summer. Turns out someone from the Folk Festival staff at the Finlen remembered you." She turned back toward him, his dewy eyes following her. "Why did you feel the need to lie to me?"

Griff rubbed his hands together and stared down at the tray, straightened its bits and pieces. She knew that for him, appearances were essential. That was what tempered his approach to the truth. Now she had caught him in another lie.

"Why all the subterfuge? Considering what Alexis told me, there wasn't really any reason to lie, at least not to me. Was there?"

He wiped his mouth with a napkin and then said, "I was only trying to simplify matters. It's not that I lied. I simply omitted that I'd been here before."

"So is that when you tracked down Razor Gillette and he told you he had the ledger?" She had to admit she was curious about how Griff had tracked down the elusive black book.

"Not exactly. We happened to meet in The Gun Room after he'd gotten off work one evening, quite serendipitously. I had asked several people about Elsie's Babies, and he claimed he knew all about Seppanen, including where he could get the ledger that detailed all her activities. Of course, I didn't really believe him. He wanted a finder's fee to put me in touch with the person who was in possession of the book. But nothing actually happened. I finished up the filming I had been contracted to do and went back to England, thinking I was really no closer to finding out what I really wanted to know."

"Which is that your cousin's birth parents would be an embarrassment to him."

"That's right," Griff said fervently. "And I'm not ashamed of that. He's been going across the countryside creating unnecessary turmoil, embarrassing the family in the meantime. I feel like I can finally shut him up. When I got an email from Razor in March, saying he had talked to the person who could get me the ledger, I didn't know he meant Hardcastle. I simply made plans to come back."

"I thought Razor found the ledger," Mesa said. "His uncle was the coroner I told you about the other day. You let me tell that story when you knew it all along."

Griff nodded and then said, "I am sorry. If I'd met you last summer, I might well have taken a different tack. But at that point, I was trying to get verification of Razor's story. The truth is I didn't know the particulars of how it came into Hardcastle's possession then, but certainly Razor understood the value of the book to me. The three of us were supposed to meet on Friday afternoon at my suite at the Finlen, except Hardcastle had made this other assignation, as it were."

"You were waiting for him in your room while he was on the roof with Danica?" Mesa asked in surprise. There was something surreal, thinking about those simultaneous events.

"I didn't know what had happened until afterwards," Griff said with a nod. "Nathan simply didn't show up. I don't mean to sound callous, but I never knew the woman. He left the hotel, and our business did not get concluded, which led to my continued presence. I had planned to leave as soon as I had the ledger." He paused and then said, "That's the one good thing about this mess: I got to meet you."

"Right," Mesa said, telling herself that she was immune to his charms at this stage. "And all those questions you were asking me about my theories about where the ledger might be when you knew where it was all along."

"I thought I knew," he corrected. "To be honest I was unsure about its provenance. I'm still not entirely certain. I've only had my paws on it for a few minutes. But Nathan seems to think it's real. He says he can recognize Elsa Seppanen's handwriting from birth certificates he's seen in the Archives. He also says he doesn't think his grandfather would have kept it if it weren't genuine."

"He got it from his grandfather?" Mesa said, surprised to hear that Dr. Armistead might have been involved. She realized she was suddenly more interested in what Griff knew than whether she liked him or not. He was back to helping her find out what had happened, like he had on Saturday.

Griff nodded. "I think Nathan must have found it in his grandfather's effects after he died."

"So Nathan left the Finlen with the ledger, without stopping to give it to you. And is that why you went out to Georgetown Lake on Sunday afternoon with Razor Gillette to finish your business?"

Griff nodded again. "At that point, we still had a deal."

Mesa sat back down, trying hard not to let her guard down, Jones's calculating attitude notwithstanding. "So what are your intentions as far as seeing your friends Razor Gillette and Nathan Hardcastle now? I'm assuming one of them now has the ledger." Which one of them shot you to get it back?"

"That misunderstanding that will be put to rights once I have the ledger." Griff put down his teacup. "I know I've lied to you and you think me unscrupulous, but I've done nothing illegal here. If it hadn't been for the death of that unfortunate young woman, I would have had the ledger and been on my way."

"Why don't you explain what you know about Danica's death?" Mesa asked. Even if Hardcastle had stood up Griff, maybe Razor had said something after the fact that might explain what had happened.

Griff held up his hands as if to stop Mesa's assault on his character. "I swear, Mesa, I had nothing to do with it. As far as I know, it was an unfortunate accident. I certainly wasn't involved. Gillette is who you want to talk to. He saw it and came back to my room and said there had been an accident and that Nathan had left. At that point, I had no reason to think he would lie."

"Except for the same reason he shot you," Mesa said, deciding to play her hunch. She couldn't see Nathan threatening Griff or taking his money. And he still needed Gillette, if in fact Razor had seen Danica fall. If this trio had a wild card, it was Razor.

Griff's reaction was telling. His expression went from thoughtful to agitated. "What do you mean?"

"For the money," Mesa said. "He wanted more than the finder's fee you originally agreed on. When you wouldn't give it to him, he decided to take the ledger. He knew you wouldn't go to the police. What were you going to say? That you argued over some silly book everybody thinks is one of Butte's urban legends?"

Chapter 17

"This Hardcastle character hasn't stopped by, has he?" Chance asked as he walked into his grandmother's kitchen. He sat down at the table with Adrienne and Vivian who were engaged in an animated conversation of their own and ignored him.

"I don't think he's a bad person," Adrienne was saying, "just calculating."

"The accent always gets me," Vivian said, nodding. "Plenty of people come into the Archives interested in their personal history. He could simply have asked me who or what he wanted to know. Instead, he spent his time convincing me he wanted to make a documentary."

Spooning up some apple crumble left over from lunch, Chance interjected, "You're talking about the Englishman."

Adrienne looked at him, gave him a quick peck on the cheek, and said, "I brought him over this morning. Why were you asking about Hardcastle?"

"I'm worried he might show up here looking for Jones. Gillette, too, with his six shooter and who knows what in mind." He then relayed what he'd learned listening to Macgregor and Nick's conversation.

"Hardcastle must be feeling the pinch. I wouldn't be surprised if he got all up in somebody's face."

Mesa entered the room, carrying a tray of empty dishes. "Where's Nan?" she asked, her voice tinged with caution.

Vivian stood up and took the tray from Mesa, saying, "She's fine. Alexis took her down to the Safeway to pick up some ground lamb for a Shepherd's Pie. What with all the Folk Festival hubbub around Hennessy's, your grandmother wanted to avoid it."

"Macgregor finally questioned Hardcastle about what happened Friday," Chance said and then added, "Said he couldn't get anything out of him, plus he claims he doesn't know anything about what happened to Jones." He looked pointedly at Mesa, "You still think it's a good idea to keep him here?"

"It wasn't my idea to invite him," Mesa said. "But I'm not sure Nana can be talked out of it, especially since he's already here. You think we have something to worry about?"

"Especially since we have three," Adrienne chimed in with a smile on her face, "soon to be five, capable women to watch over him."

"He's not the one I'm worried about," Chance said. "I'm gonna go have a word with Mr. Jones." And with that, he headed down the hall toward the stairs.

"Hold up, Chance," Mesa said quickening her pace to keep up with her brother. He was taking the stairs two steps at a time and was through the bedroom door before she could catch him.

Griff looked at Chance's thunderous expression and then at Mesa. "What's the matter? I thought we had come to an understanding," he said, sounding puzzled.

Chance rarely got angry, but his concern for Nana was one thing that could push him over the edge. He stood at the foot of the bed, his hands on his hips. "When was the last time you talked to your buddies? I don't want them sniffing around here, looking for you. So you better let them know that. You can take care of this ledger business when you're well enough to leave here. Got that?"

Mesa watched her brother trying to play the hard ass. It was almost comical. Despite his 6' 2" height and a rangy physique, he was too good-natured. Not that she hadn't seen him hold his own in a fight, but she knew he would rather negotiate. At best he came across as Gary Cooper on Valium.

"Chance, I think it should be obvious from my condition," Griff said, "I have no *buddies*, as you would call them. Thankfully I remain in your grandmother's good graces even if everyone else seems to think I'm some sort of reprobate. As I told Alexis, and your sister," here he nodded at Mesa, "I intend to get the property I paid for, which will likely make it necessary to see Mr. Hardcastle again. But as for Gillette, I have no use for the man. I want nothing to do with him. I only wish there was a way to have someone negotiate with the two of them on my behalf." He paused for a moment, looked at Mesa and then at Chance. "Perhaps, you could help me get this sorted out."

Chance looked at Mesa whose expression was still tense. "You set up a meeting with Hardcastle and tell him you're sending me as your emissary or whatever?"

"Wait a minute," Mesa said. She didn't like the idea of Chance getting that involved.

Chance ignored her. "That suits me. You won't have to deal with either of these guys and more important, they won't come here."

Griff nodded and said, "We can try it. I don't know if Hardcastle will be amenable. He was extremely jumpy when I met him on Sunday evening which is part of the reason I ended up in a struggle with Gillette. Of course, I've no way to get in touch with either one of them as my phone went by the wayside when this happened." He waved his hand from his head to his waist.

Before he could explain more, the doorbell rang. Mesa backed out of the bedroom and looked down the stairwell where she saw the back of Alexis, her blonde ponytail, long blue-jeaned legs, and boots spread in a wide stance. Across from her, the feet and legs of a man in khakis and boat shoes. It had to be Nathan Hardcastle.

"Damn it," Mesa muttered under her breath, and bounded back down the steps.

"Hello again," Hardcastle said to Mesa when she met him in the entry hall. Alexis stood with a grim expression, her arms crossed. This time Hardcastle seemed more tense than arrogant. He was walking right into the lion's den. She was pretty sure he knew that. In a way she had to respect him for that much.

"I'll only stay for a few minutes. I have some business with Griffin-Jones. I went over to the hospital, but they said he'd been released to you." His voice had lost its superiority now. Instead he seemed subdued, even anxious.

Mesa felt fairly sure no one at the hospital had released any details to him, but then she was sure he had his connections like she had hers. She let the moment linger, to let Nathan stew, and then she said, "He's upstairs."

She led Nathan up to the bedroom, looked at Chance as they entered the room, and gestured to him to stay where he was. "I think you probably know my brother from the Country Club," she said to Hardcastle who nodded. Chance had played in numerous golf tournaments there.

"I apologize for not calling ahead," Hardcastle said, an acknowledgment that Chance would take as a good sign. "Griff doesn't seem to be answering his phone."

The Englishman shook his head. "Do forgive me." Then he added, "Awfully good of you to come calling. It seems that since the last time I saw you, my health has taken a turn for the worse." Clearly Griff was not happy with Hardcastle.

"Look, I need to talk to Griff in private," Hardcastle said, looking awkwardly from one corner of the room to the other.

"Cut the crap," Chance said with uncharacteristic brusqueness. "We know why you're here. We know about Elsie's ledger, and we know about you and Danica. So you got nothing left to hide."

Hardcastle turned to Mesa with a look of anguish that surprisingly made her feel sorry for him. The attitude had melted away, replaced by the bags under his eyes and wrinkled clothes that suggested he might have slept in a chair the night before.

"I get that you have been through a lot these past few days," she said. "But Danica's family deserves answers, and you may be the only one who can provide them."

Hardcastle passed his hand through his hair, his body swaying ever so slightly. Mesa wondered if he might pass out. "Could I have some water," he said. "I haven't had much sleep."

Mesa motioned him toward the Queen Anne chair and then got him a glass of water from Griff's bedside table. She could imagine that being in the middle of two shit storms might be stressful. Of course, he'd put himself there, and she wasn't about to let him off the hook. "Tell us what happened to Danica. And then, we'll leave you to do your business with the patient." These last two words dripped with sarcasm.

Hardcastle drank the water down like a man rescued from the desert and put the empty glass back on the table. "I don't know exactly what my sister told you," he said and began to rub his thumb on the palm of the other hand. He looked at Mesa who was happy to let him wonder. Hardcastle seemed adept at getting around the truth of whatever she did say. Silence was her most effective weapon.

Finally, he began to speak. "It was never my idea for Danica to come up to the roof. If only I had made her meet me somewhere else. But she was like that. Once she had her mind made up, that was it." He paused and looked at his palm again. Then he said, "Danica had read the paper that morning about the baby." His voice became flat and then he said, louder, "our baby."

Mesa tried not to let surprise show in her expression. She hadn't expected Hardcastle suddenly to own up to his role in the baby's concealment, let alone as its father, not after all this time.

"I knew talking about it would be difficult, but I wanted to make her understand that I never meant for things to happen that way. It was an intense conversation." He paused and concentrated on rubbing his palm again, as if there were a spot he was trying to erase.

"There are these old wooden stairs on the roof. She'd climbed up to the landing to sit and was leaning on what was left of the banister rail. She was crying, and I was trying to comfort her, but she was having none of it. I reached out to hold her hand," he said, gesturing as he spoke, "but she drew away from me right as Razor came busting through the access door."

Hardcastle stopped talking, his hands quiet, his focus on his next words, as if he had thought about it over and over. "The noise startled her. She lurched back when she looked to see who it was. Her weight shifted, and she leaned back on the rail, looked at him and then at me. The railing cracked and she lost her balance." He took a deep breath and said with a sob, "And then she was gone."

"Steady on, old man," Griff said quietly, and looked toward Mesa with concern.

"I know it sounds bizarre but you have to believe me. That's what happened. Razor saw her fall."

He was saying it was an accident. "Why didn't you call the police?" Mesa asked, suspecting she knew the answer.

Hardcastle looked at her. "I panicked. You know about our history, Danica and me. Macgregor says my sister told you that much."

Mesa nodded, wondering how much of Hardcastle's story to believe.

"All I could think was that I wouldn't know what to say to my family, my parents. I knew I couldn't face it. Or at least I didn't think I could then. Razor was having none of it anyway. He said he was getting out of there and so should I. So that's what I did."

Chance, who had been leaning against the wall, stood up and said, "So why haven't you told Macgregor all this?"

Hardcastle shrugged and his voice became unemotional again. "Because I play it safe, that's why. I always have."

Mesa and Chance looked at each other, both feeling uncomfortable.

"I know what you're thinking. If I had been thinking of someone besides myself," he said. "None of this might have ever happened. Danica would be alive, maybe even the baby." His voice trailed off. Then just as quickly, he added. "I've got to find Razor before the police do. I want to make sure he backs my story, and then we'll go to the police when he has what he wants."

"Elsie's ledger?" Chance asked.

Hardcastle shook his head, wiped his nose with the back of his hand, and then said, "He already has the ledger. Didn't Griff tell you?" He glanced at the Englishman, who looked away. "Razor took it at gunpoint, and he's not giving it up until he gets another $5,000."

Chance whistled. "So it is about the money."

"It is for Razor," Hardcastle said. "He's got some serious debt, and that's all he cares about."

"Bugger," Griff said, and sighed. "This deal has been in the making for a year. He was going to get 20% of the $5,000. That was the agreed upon amount."

"That's what he negotiated," Hardcastle said, the lawyer in him coming to life. "That's not what I agreed to. As far as I am concerned the ledger was never for sale. Like I told you when we met on Sunday, I was always willing to share the contents of the ledger for a fee. I know now that was not what you had in mind."

"I need that ledger," Griff said, his voice becoming tense. "It's a far more convincing argument if I have the actual document. My cousin, and more likely his lawyers, could simply dismiss any copy I might show up with as some sort of cut and paste forgery."

Hardcastle continued rubbing his palm, harder, using that effort to regain his focus and avoid making eye contact with anyone. "Well, you may still get what you want. Razor's got the ledger, but he says if I don't help him get the other five thousand, he's not going to corroborate what happened on the roof. Actually, I think I'm going to need the both of you to help with that." He finally looked up at Griff and then at Mesa.

What did he mean by that, she wondered. Had Danica's death had something to do with the ledger? "Wait," Mesa said. "Did Danica know about the ledger? Is that the real reason you met up there?"

Hardcastle spoke sharply, "She was completely innocent. If she knew about the ledger, it was only because we used to joke about it when we were kids. We were all fascinated by Elsie's story, especially Chloe. That's part of what got us into the whole mess." He was sullen again, his memories clearly eating at him. Then he said again, "No, Danica was innocent."

Then he looked at Griff and said, "Razor wants his five grand. Of course, if I give it to him, the police will try to turn this into some kind of conspiracy, like I'm buying the little bastard off. If you give it to him, then we'll be square. Do this and you can have the ledger. Then, when the time is right, I'll pay you back." He paused when Griff said nothing. "I give you my word."

Mesa shook her head. She didn't know whether to believe Hardcastle. It was hard enough listening to him negotiate with Griff, all in the name of protecting the Hardcastle reputation. What was wrong with people? "What's to stop me from going to Macgregor and telling him everything you've told us," she said finally.

"Nothing," Hardcastle said with another shrug. "Go ahead. He can't arrest me without some physical evidence of a crime, or a witness, and all Razor cares about is the money. Even with him, it's my word against his. Macgregor knows that. So I'll take my chances."

"I meant what I said earlier," Chance said to Griff. "I'll act as your representative. I think the whole deal smells but I don't want Gillette in this house. You and Hardcastle decide where and what you want to do, and let me know." With that, Chance walked out of the room saying, "Time for some fresh air."

ఞ✌

"You really think that's what happened?" Adrienne asked Mesa later. She was still sitting at the kitchen table with Nana Rose. Vivian was drying dishes at the sink while Chance leaned on the counter, looking out the kitchen window and sipping tea.

"It's plausible, I guess," Mesa answered. "Detective Macgregor didn't share any information about a broken banister rail, but I'm assuming they can connect the dots. Maybe she had some splinters in her hand. I don't know." *What a waste* was all Mesa could think. *What an incredible waste.* She looked up at Adrienne whose expression pretty much mirrored her thoughts.

"Man, this sucks," Chance said. "I don't want to be around when somebody has to tell Phade about this. He's gonna go nuts."

Mesa knew her brother was probably right, wondering again when Phade would reappear. She went out onto the porch and called his girlfriend, Stella, who said that after she had texted him more times than she could count, he had finally answered and said that he was okay, that he would be home soon. "You understand how hard this is for him, Stella. I'm sure he recognizes that," Mesa said, realizing how under-appreciated the young woman must feel. Mesa thought about her own family and friends and how oblivious she must have seemed when they were trying to comfort her after Shane's death.

Stella didn't argue and said that Macgregor had been to the house and told Phade's parents that they were making progress and that suicide was no longer the likely cause of death. "You'll have him call me if you see him," she had almost pleaded.

Mesa sympathized with Stella, who liked to act free-spirited but was so clearly attached to her relationship with Phade. "I'll do my best," she said, knowing how difficult it could be to get him to do anything.

The mention of the detective spurred Mesa's decision to call him and let him know what she had learned from Hardcastle. She was hopeful that she could parlay her offer of information into an invitation to see the roof of the Finlen. She wanted to see for herself where the stairs to this glass hut had been and just how believable Hardcastle's story was.

Their chat the previous evening had clearly softened the big detective into collaborating, and he obliged. "Gimme an hour," he had said. "Meet you on the ninth floor of the Finlen at one."

Just enough time to swing back to the office and check in, Mesa thought. She was on her way back to the *Messenger* when she got another call from Irita. "You headed into the office yet?" she asked. "I need to go to Insty-Prints to see about those posters. Oh, and Phade just wandered in."

Mesa hurried through the lobby of the Finlen which was now a sea of red-shirted, Folk Festival volunteers, putting up tables and signs, scurrying around with supplies. At the desk, Mrs. Terkla gave her a quick wave as Mesa strode toward the elevators. She tried to flash a sincere smile, but her frustration at Phade had unsettled her. He seemed so self-centered at times and not even mildly apologetic about his absence. Had she been like that?

She punched the elevator button once, then again, and when it didn't open immediately, decided to take the stairs. Maybe the nine-floor climb would help her refocus. As she passed the second floor, where she and Griff had first encountered Macgregor, she thought about the detective. She had come to appreciate his approach. He had begun gathering facts right away and had clearly been covering the bases the last two days, though the holiday made that difficult, and he had shown a genuine concern for Phade's family.

When she had questioned Phade about where he had taken to, his reply was classic. "What's everybody so steamed about? I haven't even been gone twenty-four hours."

She had ushered Irita and Evan out of her office, shut the door, and tried to get Phade to understand. "Your family's been worried sick. Detective Macgregor was up here last night looking for you. Evan rode all over town. Alexis and I hit all your hangouts, trying to find you."

"Alexis should thank me," he said. "Bar hopping seems like her favorite form of exercise."

That comment had gotten to her. "Don't you dare say anything about Alexis," Mesa had shot back. "Even she wouldn't do something as self-centered as disappearing on her grieving family."

It was nearly ninety degrees outside, and the Finlen had no air-conditioning in the stairwells. At the third floor, Mesa leaned toward the open window to feel the breeze. She thought about Phade sitting on the sofa in her office, nonchalant as ever, acting as if he could care less that Mesa had lost her shit on him. "Where the hell were you?" she had finally yelled at him, only to be met in the end with his tear-rimmed stare.

Now, she looked out the hallway window to the street below. A couple of County pickup trucks were unloading extra trash bins for the festival, nothing like the scene three days before when some unsuspecting SUV owner had parked his car there, only to have its roof caved in by a falling body.

By the time she reached the ninth floor, the climb had sucked the remorse from her. Macgregor had already arrived and was leaning against the wall, arms crossed. He was surprised to see her coming up the stairs. "Catch your breath," he said and popped a couple of jelly beans in his mouth. "I took the elevator."

While she took his advice, Macgregor opened the hallway door to the roof. Inside, a couple of mops and a broom leaned against a plastic garbage can, the interior looking like a broom closet except for the three steps that led up to yet another door, which was locked. These last few steps Danica had taken before her life ended, through a broom closet, were so ordinary.

"Got these from Harp," Macgregor said, dangling a ring of keys, and then opened the door into a windowless room that housed the hotel's elevator controls, mechanical equipment, and Wi-Fi apparatus, its neon blue light casting an eerie glow into the dark space. Feeling a hint of claustrophobia growing in her, Mesa willed herself to talk.

"Phade's back," she said and followed closely on Macgregor's heels.

The detective stopped, flipped on a light switch, and put the keys into his pocket. "Thank God for that," he said. "Where the hell was he?"

"Would you believe editing some old recording of him and his sister singing together?" Phade had holed up in the studio in the basement of Len Waters Music Center after all. He had told Mesa how the music had helped take his mind off that last image of his sister, how he had needed to get back to thinking about her the way she was before. He had lost track of time, enveloping himself in the comfort of his memories while he worked on the CD.

"Musicians," Macgregor said with a shake of his head and then climbed another three steps to unlatch the final access, a wide door made of thick wooden planks that looked as old as the hotel. "As long as he's all right. Somebody called his parents?"

"Yes," Mesa said, recalling remorsefully the strong-arming it had taken to get Phade to call Stella.

Macgregor had to give this final door a shoulder. It flew open, and a rush of air flooded the small, warm room where they stood. "Here we are."

Taking a deep breath, Mesa let the cool air blow over her. The sudden switch from the dark interior to the bright sunlight took her off balance. She stepped cautiously out onto the roof, surprised by its off-white color and its suppleness. The sponginess underfoot felt like warm tarmac, only without the smell. No doubt it had been painted white to reflect the sunlight and minimize absorption of heat into the building during the long days of summer.

High above the street noise, the roof was eerily quiet. A wind came up, and she lifted her gaze to the spectacular, panoramic view—the mountains, the valley, the rooftops nearby and beyond, Big Butte to the north, Timber Butte and Red Mountain to the south, and all of the East Ridge. She could imagine the breathtaking nighttime canopy of stars, marijuana-induced or otherwise, and understood the appeal to anyone who had ever snuck up there.

Then, remembering the somber reason for her visit, she turned her attention to the physical aspects of the roof, comparing it to Hardcastle's description. Sinister elements appeared in a number of places. Three times as long as it was wide, the roof was dotted with a scattering of vent pipes that could easily have tripped someone at night, less likely in the middle of the afternoon. Around the edge of the roof on all sides, she could see the decorative brick and sandstone parapet. The wall acted as a protective barrier about two feet high, but it would not have been impossible for Danica to have fallen, or been pushed, over it.

The access door of the equipment room opened out on the north side with the streets of Walkerville visible in the distance. Mesa moved to the left toward the Wyoming Street side, where Danica had fallen. There, Macgregor stood looking at what was left of a set of stairs clearly constructed decades earlier. The wood— some kind of pine—was weatherworn and graying.

"This is what's left of the steps that went up to that observation deck," Macgregor said, pointing up to the roof of the equipment room. "The room was built out of glass, pressboard, and brick, as best Harp could remember, about eight by eight floor space. It got took down back in the mid-80s when they were remodeling the upper floors of the hotel.

"Harp said his dad's lawyer called it an 'attractive nuisance'. Probably on account of some people from a New Year's Eve party climbing up there to smoke dope and take in the Milky Way," Macgregor said with wide eyes.

Mesa imagined that was what the Hardcastles and their buddies had been doing when they were in high school. "Where exactly were the stairs located?" she wondered aloud.

He pointed up to the roof of the elevator equipment house, which had its own decorative parapet. "The observation deck had about a two-foot walkway all around it. I'm surprised nobody fell off that," he said, shaking his head. "Apparently they had three or four hundred volunteers coming up here 24/7."

Mesa smiled, thinking about the 1950s paranoia that had led to the federal government's decision to establish a nationwide organization of volunteer Skywatchers. "How did you find out about all this?" Mesa had to ask, impressed by how many details Macgregor knew.

"The Archives, of course. They got a whole file of photographs and newspaper clippings."

Mesa nodded, but she still couldn't imagine what the Skywatchers accomplished. "What did they actually do?" she asked, besides maybe calm people's fears and make them think the government was trying to be vigilant.

Macgregor shrugged, "They had binoculars and a book of plane silhouettes. They logged all the planes that came across the valley and sent that to Helena. If any weren't identifiable, they put in a call to the base in Great Falls. It's the same thing we did during World War II on the coasts."

Mesa shook her head and then looked at the pile of wood on the roof, faded and worn from sixty years of sun. She pointed to it with her foot. "So this is what's left of the stairs to get up to the hut?"

"There were two flights of steps with a landing in between," Macgregor answered, nodding. "I saw a picture in a *Standard* article from the 50s. That must be the lower section, I think, or what's left of it. They were attached to the outside of the equipment building here on the south side," he said and lumbered around to the wall opposite the access door. "The lower section of steps went up to the left, and the upper section turned back to the right of the landing with more steps up to the roof and the hut."

Mesa followed Macgregor around to the next side of the small square building. She made yet another mental note to ask Nana Rose what she knew about the whole operation.

Macgregor continued. "Some hotel employees, maybe Razor, detached the stairway away from the wall. Harp says it's on Razor's summer to-do list to finish the job. He's supposed to take the steps apart and remove the wood from the roof finally."

Mesa could see the holes drilled into the wall where the stairs had once been anchored to the building, and then said, "But you found what was left of the steps where they are now, when you first came up here?" She was trying to visualize what Nathan said had happened. The stairs stood like he had described, lodged against the parapet on the west side of the roof with the back of the landing facing the edge, as if there were a stairway leading off the roof. The perfect location if anyone wanted to take a swan dive to oblivion.

Macgregor nodded, looking down tentatively over the parapet. "It's straight up from the car where Danica landed."

She walked over to the stairs and reached out to touch the banister, thinking to test its sturdiness, when Macgregor stopped her and said, "Hold it, now. From what you're saying, that banister might be part of the investigation. Best not touch anything until I check with my evidence guy in case he needs to get back up here to take some more pictures. We may need to take that banister apart and send some samples to the crime lab."

Mesa nodded, drew back her hand, and stepped to the side of the stairs to look more closely. She could see some daylight between the edge of the post and the handrail, for sure.

"What do you think?" she said to Macgregor, who stood with his arms crossed, slowly chewing on several jelly beans. All she could think about was the tone of Nathan's voice earlier when he had said *and then she was gone.*

"Still no obvious signs of a struggle," he said and shook his head. "I don't know. I guess she coulda gone down like he said."

࿇

Turning down Idaho Street past the Knights of Columbus building, Chance parked his Land Rover across the street from The Motor Doctor, Sam Chavez's little handyman business. He took a deep breath, knowing that it was a long shot that Sam might be able to help find Razor. But at this stage, it was all Chance had. He sure didn't fancy sitting around and waiting for the nut job to reappear on his own.

Not long before his death, Grampa Ducharme had bought the one-story, orange brick building. Built by an imaginative pharmacist, Dr. Stajcar, the building had housed a full-service pharmacy that utilized one of the first drive-up windows in Montana.

Chance could remember talking to his grandfather about their concern for the many closed buildings in Uptown. Gramps thought they should try to make use of one of them again somehow, as an example to other investors.

Sam had done much of the work, remodeling the front half of the interior of the building. After gramps had passed away that fall, Chance remembered fondly how his grandmother had paid Sam to finish the job so the building could be rented, because she knew it was what her husband would have wanted. But the building had remained vacant, proving once again that flipping a property in Butte was a crapshoot. Finally, on Chance's suggestion, his grandmother had leased the building to Sam for a dollar a year and a small percentage of any profits from his business.

Now he used the front of the flat-roofed edifice for his workshop and lived in the back, where Chance had helped him refashion a modest living space. Sam had never had much but didn't seem to need much either, a simplicity that Chance admired.

On the south side of the building under the car port that had once proudly covered the drive up window, Sam's customers could leave their ATV's, lawn mowers, snow blowers, anything with a small engine that Sam could get to. If he could get to it, he could fix it. Chance found Sam under the carport doing a preliminary exam of a riding lawn mower. "It gonna live?" Chance called out as he strode up to Sam, glad for the shade. Sam wasn't much of a talker, but he had a well-developed sense of humor.

He looked up, beads of sweat across his mahogany brow, which he wiped away and then stood up. "Yep," he said with confidence.

"Need to ask you about somebody," Chance said.

Not only did Sam not say much, he wasn't a fan of idle chatter either. He kept his ears open, but he saw no need to add to the palaver unless something important needed to be said. "Water?" he offered.

Chance nodded. Even though this business with Griff Jones had him chomping at the bit, he reminded himself to be patient. If Sam had something to tell, he'd get around to it. They walked over to a small red and white cooler next to the side door that led into the shop. Sam pulled out an aluminum canteen, circa World War II, and offered it to Chance, who took a swig. He handed it back to Sam who did the same, only for longer.

Once the canteen had been returned to its rightful place, Chance asked his question.

"You ever have any dealings with Razor Gillette?"

Sam pulled a worn, red bandana from his back pocket and wiped his face and hands, using the time to gather his thoughts, no doubt. Then he nodded.

"Seen him recently?" Chance said, hoping to get lucky. He wanted the hand off of this ledger or book, or whatever it was called, taken care of before patience grew thin for any of the parties—Jones, Hardcastle, or Gillette—and possibly put his grandmother in harm's way, even if unintentionally.

Sam shook his head with a closed-mouth expression of apology.

"Don't suppose you know where he lives," Chance asked, knowing this was another long shot.

"Mebbe," Sam said. "Rode him home, while back."

Chance tried not to get excited. "While back" was one of those terms that could mean ten days or ten years, depending on the situation and the speaker. "When was this?"

Turned out Sam has known the "kid"—that's what he called Gillette—forever. They had worked together at Mountain Rental where Sam had gotten a job fixing rental tools that came back a mess. "Kid was smart but had an attitude," Sam said. "Work all day getting a fussy motor to start. Then leave a muddy trailer for somebody else to clean. He don't read good either," Sam added. "That why he ended up learning to fix stuff, kinda like me in the beginning."

Chance thought about how Nana used Sam as an example whenever he or Mesa had been lazy about schoolwork, saying how education had helped Sam to turn his life around. He had missed so much school as a kid, herding sheep and drinking wine with his dad that he had never learned to read. Once Nana Rose had taught him, he became a whiz around machinery.

"Dyslexic, he says they call it," Sam said. "Tried him here when I first open," he continued. "But he took some tools, never brought 'em back. Same thing happen at Mountain Rental. Got mad when I call him on it. Broke the antenna on my truck."

Chance thought about when he had seen Razor at the Country Club and how that attitude might have played out there. "I want to talk to him," Chance said, explaining his concern about Razor and Griff. "I want to be sure nothing stupid happens. Tell me where he lives. I'll pay him a visit."

Sam looked at Chance and then at the sky, as if he was taking a bead on the time. Then he said, "Razor ain't a bad guy, but unless it's about machines, he can frustrate easy. If he got reason to be in a bad mood, don't wanna go looking for him by yourself."

Chapter 18

Mesa sat at her computer at the *Mess*, her conversation with Phade spinning in her head. Why had she gotten so angry? The truth was, the whole situation was off-the-wall awkward. Flipping back and forth between fifty or so photos from the parade that Chance had uploaded the day before, she told herself that nobody really knew how to act around someone whose sister had fallen off a building.

But that wasn't the half of it. Phade looked to her as a friend, but she was letting him down, so much so that she had gone in the opposite direction, telling him that he needed to understand that she had to cover the story of Danica's death. That didn't mean she couldn't be his friend, too, only that the paper came first. But that was bullshit. The truth was it came easier—dealing with the story rather than the grief.

She continued to flip through the photos, putting her thoughts of Phade aside, and concentrated on which photo warranted the front page. Plenty of the Mess's readership, the older set as Nana liked to call them, had yet to enter the digital age. They preferred a photo they could cut from the newspaper and add to a scrap book or mail with pride to a relative.

Looking at photos took less brainpower than trying to write something, especially since she couldn't get the details of Danica's death out of her head. Once on the roof of the Finlen, she and Macgregor had walked through the series of events Hardcastle had described. The logistics of it were clearly possible, but something didn't feel right.

Mesa tried to imagine how Danica had felt—angry, hurt, betrayed, and not only by Nathan, but Chloe too. What had Danica hoped to accomplish by meeting Hardcastle? And why the roof? That might have been symbolic when they were in high school, but now, as adults? Did she think Nathan was that paranoid, not wanting to risk being seen with her? Was she still trying to protect his reputation?

Irita walked into the office carrying an armload of flyers. "I want to run an ad for my garage sale in next week's Mess. Cinch says I have to pay like everybody else, the tight-fisted old bastard."

"I'll talk to him," Mesa said, not looking up from the computer. Lately, there was no end to Cinch's crankiness. And at that moment, Mesa had little patience for her staff's petty conflicts.

"You hear if the sheriff got a line on whoever took those shots during the parade?" Irita asked as she headed toward the door, apparently not expecting an extended answer.

Macgregor had filled her in at the Finlen on the elevator ride down. "Only that they were most likely fired from the roof of the Auto-Parts store. One of Butte's finest was actually with his family on the street and thought he heard the direction the shots came from. Turned out a semi was parked against the back wall of the store, and it looks like the shooter climbed from the ground to the hood to the top of the cab and onto the roof, then reversed his tracks to get down."

"Could have been any one of a number of numbskulls, I guess," said Irita. "Everybody wants their fifteen minutes of fame these days."

Mesa looked up at the flyer Irita was holding and nodded approvingly. "Alexis was waiting for me on Sanders Street behind the Hampton Suites and happened to look across that vacant lot where the rodeo grounds used to be. She thought she saw a guy on a motorcycle like the one Razor Gillette rides."

"I'll be damned. Think it was him? What's he trying to prove?"

"Evan says he saw Hardcastle and his sister talking in front of the Montana Club during the parade. That's right across the street from the Auto-Parts store. Evan's theory is that the shooter was Razor and that he was taking pot shots at them, maybe only trying to harass them, but either way, it was a stupid thing to do."

"No shortage of stupid in some quarters," Irita said and took back her poster. "Especially in the Gillette family."

"Yeah, well, he's disappeared into thin air since."

Irita edged back into the office and sat tentatively on the arm of the sofa. "You know," she said, "The events committee has a storage unit on Longfellow Street, west of Harrison. You know those units were built by Razor's grandfather. I heard that somebody out there had gotten in trouble for living in one of them. Maybe it was Razor.

"When his gramps died, the cantankerous old fool divvied up the storage units between three different relatives. Caused all kind of hard feelings, but he didn't want to give 'em all to one person. I think he seriously enjoyed the idea that his family would be pissed. That's the kind of stock Razor comes from."

Mesa thought about this for a minute. She was big on simplicity as far as household furnishings were concerned, but even she would draw the line at living in a storage unit. "I guess you could live in one in the summertime. Come winter, you'd freeze for sure."

Irita shrugged. "I think he's got a girlfriend somewhere, mostly during the winter months, no doubt, so he can stay warm. That Razor's a piece of work. You name it, somebody in his family's done it to him. He's been jerked around by experts, locked in closets, beat with boards. He ran away from home so much, he's the poster child for Social Services. He's had to make do on his own for a long time. I wouldn't put anything past him. He learned it all at home."

Around four p.m., Alexis headed up to the sick room with a tray of tea and Nana's biscuits. Ever stealth of foot, a talent developed during a misspent childhood, her approach had gone unnoticed by Griff. Surprised when she heard his voice, she paused at the slightly opened door to listen.

"One can hardly make five thousand dollars appear like magic," she could hear him saying. "I'll have to get to a bank, for God's sake, and see if I can arrange for a money transfer. Otherwise, I'll have to call my uncle in San Francisco, which I really don't want to do. He can wire me the money, but he'll get suspicious and first thing you know he'll be flying into Butte and knocking on the door." Griff went silent, no doubt listening to the other side of the conversation. Alexis pushed the door open enough to see him sitting up in bed talking on a cell phone, which she suspected he must have gotten from Hardcastle.

She knew he didn't have one on him when he came to the house. After Adrienne had brought him upstairs, Alexis had gone through all his belongings. Mesa might have scruples about that sort of thing, but Alexis had none. If Mesa wanted to protect her grandmother, Alexis wanted to be sure the patient didn't have means to invite trouble.

"All right," Griff said, clearly exasperated, "Let's not get our knickers in a twist. I'll try calling this Mountain Bank manager directly. Perhaps I can arrange an Internet bank transfer."

Sensing the conversation coming to a close, Alexis walked into the room as Griff ended the call. "Now who might you be chatting with, and if you don't mind my asking, where'd you get the phone?"

Griff rolled his eyes when he saw her. "Bloody Hell, I didn't think that when I accepted Mrs. Ducharme's generosity, I had to give up my right to privacy. I feel like I've been taken hostage."

Alexis put the tray down on the table by the window and poured Griff a cup of tea, which she brought to his bedside along with a homemade shortbread biscuit. "If I didn't know better, I'd say you sound a tad ungrateful," she said, standing next to him. "Now where's the phone?" She started to root around behind the pillows.

"Stop," he said, "You'll make me spill my tea." Then he added indignantly, "I'm not in prison. I've a right to a phone."

"Don't make me pull back those covers," Alexis said, figuring he'd stuck the phone where he erroneously assumed she would have the good grace not to look.

Griff pulled the phone from under the covers, and then said, "What you should be more worried about is that Hardcastle is planning to meet Razor Gillette this afternoon, unfortunately without the money he wants. Seems Mr. Gillette's patience is running thin."

After Nathan Hardcastle had left the house, Mesa had filled everyone in on the newest revelations, not only about Nathan's confession about the baby, but also on the negotiations over the ledger that Elsa Seppanen had used as potential blackmail. Alexis knew everyone was serious about keeping Gillette from coming to the house. She held her hand out for the phone.

"And, so is mine," Griff continued and put the phone behind his back. "He's got that ledger, and I mean to have it." He looked at Alexis who had retreated to the tea tray for a biscuit herself. "You seem to understand my situation better than the others. This inheritance business can be frightfully complicated, as you well know. I don't suppose you could see your way clear to securing some cash I need. Once Gillette has his money, I suspect he'll be out of everyone's hair."

Alexis thought for a moment. Getting her hands on cash was never a problem. She kept a decent balance in her account at Cascade Bank where she had made a point to become friendly with the bank's president, a strategy she had learned from her grandmother. "Bankers like to keep their big account holders happy, especially the ones they know personally," her grandmother had explained.

"I'm surprised you didn't bring it with you," Alexis said, delighted to see the conniving Englishman squirm. "Guess you didn't think of everything after all."

"Let's be clear," Griff said. "I had everything under control. I brought enough cash to cover our original agreement, but then Gillette went mad and decided to change the terms." Griff shook his head. "So much for the code of the West."

Alexis smiled and shrugged. "What you see is what you get. That's what I like about Butte people, most of them anyway—no pretense. Did you really think you were going to put your hands on that ledger simply because Razor Gillette said he might know where he could find it? Sounds to me that you were hoping to pull one over on someone yourself."

"That's not true," Griff said, sounding hurt. "I fully intended to deal fairly with Nathan Hardcastle once I realized the limitations he imposed. I'd have flown him over to England with the ledger in hand if need be. Now he's keen to sell, I'm prepared to pay his price."

Alexis smiled, "Yes, but now he's selling to keep from going to jail. Sounds like you're the one taking advantage."

Griff sighed. "That's not a deal of my making. That's between Hardcastle and Gillette." Then he handed her his empty teacup and saucer. "It does seem to me that you might consider how to recover the ledger and get it back to its rightful owner, instead of brow beating me. Hardcastle is going to meet Gillette in a couple of hours with or without the money."

∽∾

Sam hung the *Gone Fishin'* sign on the front door of his shop and got in Chance's Land Rover with its steering wheel on the right side. They exchanged smiles at the curiosity of the World War II vehicle that Sam had helped Chance pull out of a rancher's field a dozen years ago. "Let's hope we find Razor in a good mood," Chance said and turned south on Montana Street toward the flat.

They drove under the Interstate overpass and made a left at the intersection by the Town Pump, soon following along the edge of the municipal golf course, which Chance eyed absently. Since Adrienne had come into his life, he seemed to play less and less.

They turned into a neighborhood of small houses and then onto Longfellow Street. Sam pointed to a series of identical buildings. "That's them on the right," he said. "Dropped him in front. It was night so not sure where he went, but I hear he live in one of these little places."

Chance looked skeptically at the setup but parked. Long, blue metal buildings, with rows of silver garage doors on each side and at the ends, stood in three rows. Chance found it hard to believe that anyone could live in a space that might be ten by twenty at most. "Sure this is right, Sam?"

Sam shrugged and then said, "It was dark, but it wasn't that dark."

Chance smiled and said, "You think anybody could live in one of these?"

"I've lived in worse," Sam said.

"Right," Chance muttered. Sam had lived in a hobo camp by the tracks behind the Civic Center ball fields. Chance had heard Gramps talk about Sam's drinking days and silently cursed himself for drawing attention, even unintentionally, to those hard times.

They walked down the aisle between two of the buildings. Beyond the row of storage units, Chance could see an empty field crisscrossed with dirt paths made by kids on motor bikes, no doubt imitating Evel Knievel. In the distance, the valley sprawled out in front of them. Summer in Montana meant getting out of town—not a person in sight anywhere. Even traffic was minimal.

Chance was about to turn around when Sam held up a hand and whispered, "Radio." Chance couldn't hear a thing. He looked at Sam whose face was alert with certainty and couldn't help wondering if Sam had such keen senses because of his Indian blood or just exceptional patience.

As they moved forward, Chance began to hear faintly what he thought was a sports commentator's banter. Was it a baseball game? Almost at the end of the second building, Sam raised a hand, tapped his chest with his hand, and mouthed, "Let me go first."

Chance hung back as Sam turned at the end of the building, saying, "That you, Razor?"

"Sam Chavez, what brings you round here?" came the reply in a calm, unassuming voice.

"Hey, Razor," Sam said. The exchange seemed neutral enough.

"How you been?" Sam continued, "Brought a friend to talk to you."

Chance turned the corner of the building to take in the two open doors on the storage units at the end of the building. He was surprised by how well thought-out the small spaces were. Shelves of canned goods with all the labels turned toward the front stood next to a small refrigerator with an old-fashioned hot plate sitting on top of it. In the back corner was an assortment of plastic bins that contained clothes and household items, dishes and pots and pans. Even a bed next to an inner wall and a floor fan nearby, plugged into a light socket. But all the organization in the world wouldn't withstand twenty below temperatures come winter.

In front of the second unit where the sand denim motorcycle was parked inside, Chance recognized Razor Gillette sitting on an upturned plastic bucket. He was tinkering with the motor on a small airplane, the kind that flew by remote control. A slender boy of about eight stood next to him, watching the work. Razor looked up at Chance, who smiled quickly.

Razor had lost the boyish expression that Chance remembered from the golf course in years past. He had often seen Gillette on a riding lawn mower or with a weed whacker trimming around a green, an underling who worked while others played. Now his face was grim, his blue eyes suspicious, and his unshaven face made him look not only older but harder.

"What you do that for, Sam?" Razor said, pulling the boy closer, his voice turning sour.

"It was my idea," Chance jumped in. "Sam owed me a favor, that's all." Which wasn't true but the last thing Chance wanted was to get Sam in hot water.

Sam looked at Chance and then stepped back as if to say, *Up to you.*

"You remember me," Chance said to Razor, "from the golf course. I don't get out there much anymore."

"Me either," Razor said, and snapped the cowling back on the engine of the miniature plane and gave it to its young owner.

Chance looked at the boy standing next to Gillette and said, "That's a fine looking boy. He yours?" He was reaching—trying to establish rapport with the guy who may well have pushed a woman off a roof, shot the Englishman, and taken pot shots at Hardcastle and his sister.

Razor stared directly at Chance, giving no indication that they might know each other. "What's that got to do with anything? What you want?"

"I'm not looking to get you jammed up or anything," Chance said, deciding not to press the issue of the police's *attempt to locate*, "but I met this English guy who wants the ledger you have. We've talked about getting you the money you want. I was hoping we could work out how to do that."

Razor looked at Chance and then at Sam. "I don't need your help," he said and got up, pulled down the one storage unit door. Then he pushed his motorcycle out of the other, and closed that door as well. "Get going, Jackie. Tell your mom, I'll be in touch," he said to the boy, who turned and ran to a small bicycle at the end of the other row of storage units and pedaled off, a miniature of his father.

Razor carried himself with an attitude Chance didn't remember at the Country Club. He was still thin and wiry but tougher somehow. He was done being pushed around.

"Wait," Chance said, "At least, hear me out, Gillette. I can get you the money you want."

"Unless you got it to give me right now, I got nothing to say to you." He didn't even look up.

Chance could see that Nathan's partner, if that's what he was, had no interest in any intermediary, and so he held up his hands, in a *never mind* gesture.

"That's what I thought," Razor said, then fired up the Harley and left them standing in an eddy of dust. He steered the motorcycle through an open panel in the fence at the back of the property and fled across the open field.

Moments later, a police cruiser pulled up at the entry to the storage lot, and Macgregor got out.

Mesa paced in her office at the *Messenger* while she talked on the phone. She had spent much of the afternoon putting finishing touches on that week's edition, the photos and a short article about Danica's death. She was almost done when a call from Chance about the run-in with Gillette and then Macgregor interrupted her. And now Alexis.

"Griff says that Nathan and Razor are supposed to rendezvous this evening to discuss the money handover, if you can call it that," she explained.

Alexis was talking fast which always meant that she was thinking about making a move, something Mesa wasn't sure was a good idea. Not that she had anything against getting into the mix, but not without her.

"How did you find this out?" Mesa asked. Had Nathan returned to the house after she and Chance were gone?

"I heard Griff talking on the phone. Apparently, Hardcastle snuck one to him during your tea and roses talk about what happened to Danica."

Damn him, Mesa thought. Just as she had suspected, he had concocted a plan all along but had purposely hidden it.

"Trouble is, as usual," Alexis said, with an audible smirk, "Nobody can come up with the cash quick enough. Griff even asked me to lend it to him."

"Are you going to?" Mesa said, curious. Alexis could always get her hands on cash. "The way I look at it, ole Razor is not gonna care where his money comes from. I don't see why I can't buy the ledger from him."

Damn, Mesa thought, when you least expected it, Alexis could come up with some curious ideas. "But why would you do that?" Mesa asked. There were usually consequences for Alexis' largesse. "You wanna do something with that ledger?"

"Yes and no," she said. "You wanna know what's in it, right? So do I. Plus, like you're always saying, it's part of local urban legend, so the ledger should stay in Butte. And, I like the idea of giving Griffin-Jones a run for his money. Don't get me wrong, I'd lend the ledger to him so he could chuck his brother. Wouldn't mind seeing how that all goes down either."

"Why do I think there's a *but* in there?" Mesa asked.

Alexis's tone of voice was reminiscent of all the times she had worried about having to talk her grandmother into something she was probably not going to want to do. "Jones is making noise about how that's not the deal that was agreed to, selling to a third party. He thinks Hardcastle may not go for it."

"According to what he said earlier," Mesa interrupted, "he doesn't have much choice. Unless he mischaracterized Razor's threat, Nathan needs cash to buy his old pal off. Why would it matter where it comes from?"

"Griffin says Chance agreed to make the trade," Alexis continued. "I think that's a good idea. Of course, I want to be there too."

"Now wait a minute," Mesa said. "Chance met up with Razor earlier and said the guy is wound tighter than a golf ball." Her brother had also endured a browbeating by Royal Macgregor, who had hoped to corner Gillette at his hidey-hole. The fact that Chance and Sam had beaten the detective to it had not set well. Macgregor had warned them to "stay out of police business." If they saw Gillette again, they were to tell him to come into the station immediately so the police could question him as a material witness.

"I think the fewer people Razor has to deal with the better. When and where's the big meet?"

"Nathan is supposed to text Griffin," Alexis said, sounding petulant. "Though probably not in the light of day, since apparently Razor isn't ready to go to the police until he has the money in hand. No one knows where he is."

Mesa thought about this. Razor would have to go to the police station to give a statement that would corroborate Nathan's story. What was to keep Razor, once he had the money, from leaving Nathan high and dry?

"Who's at the house now?" she asked. Her own plan was to return to her grandmother's right after work. She still felt uneasy about Griffin's presence there.

"Vivian's here and Adrienne is going to come over so that I can go to the bank and get the cash. I think Nan's safe enough."

"I'll see you a bit after five then," Mesa said. Irita poked her head in Mesa's office door just as she was putting her phone down.

"You got a visitor," Irita said, her eyebrows poised expectantly over her red cheater glasses. "Chloe Hardcastle."

Curious, Mesa got up from her desk followed Irita out to the lobby on her way home. She said goodnight and went out the door after casting an inquisitive glance Chloe's way.

Chloe sat on the Naugahyde couch, small and compact, despite her considerable height and long legs, as unpretentious a human being as Mesa had ever met. The woman devoted to saving babies in Africa was literally as plain and quiet as a church mouse, not like any doctor Mesa had ever met. She even wore a gray dress, albeit well-designed. It was as if some part of her wanted to be invisible.

Mesa spoke softly, careful not to disturb the mood, and invited her visitor into the inner sanctum. Unable to ply her with food or drink, Mesa offered her a seat on the office couch and retreated to her desk chair. She wanted Hardcastle to feel comfortable, but it didn't seem possible. Despite the fact that she, no doubt, faced death regularly in her job, she bore the added burden of her own grief over Danica's death.

Chapter 19

"I'm worried about my brother," Chloe said, almost in a monotone voice. For a woman who was probably used to being in charge, the last few days seemed to have undermined her confidence. She sat on the couch in Mesa's office, her hands in her lap, her expression worn. "I've come from the police station. Detective Macgregor says he has to talk to the County Attorney. She'll decide what, if any, laws have been broken.

"He also says he hasn't talked with all the parties involved. That includes Razor Gillette, who the police can't seem to get hold of." Sarcasm laced this last statement as if Chloe wasn't surprised that Gillette was avoiding the police. "Not that he had anything to do with the death of the baby."

"So how is it that Razor got involved in all this in the first place?" This was a question that had Mesa confused from the beginning.

Chloe sighed. "It's not so much Razor as the ledger."

"Aha," Mesa said under her breath, mentally giving props to Alexis who had suggested three days ago, that the two deaths, the baby and Danica, were connected. "This sounds like the beginning of a long story. Sure you don't want that coffee?"

"Maybe it would help," Chloe said, rubbing her shoulders as if she were trying to will some energy into her body.

Mesa darted into the newsroom's makeshift kitchen, a utility sink next to a long table with a set of cupboards above it. She could see Phade sitting in his carrel staring at his computer monitor, well past quitting time. Why he was at the office, maybe to see her, tugged at her heartstrings. She regretted being so hard on him earlier. She thought about offering him some coffee, but she didn't want to risk Chloe's leaving.

Should she invite him to sit in on the interview, to let him hear how Chloe felt about Danica? No, bad idea. She didn't yet know what Chloe was going to say, and Phade knew nothing about Danica having a baby. That would be a shock in itself. She needed to break that to him privately.

"That coffee drinkable?" she said, resorting to timid small talk, rather than ignoring him altogether.

He nodded. Mesa found a clean mug, filled it, and then paused for a second at his carrel. "Why don't you go home, Phade? I promise I will come by this evening. I have some things I want to tell you."

He eyed her with such a dead stare, she felt uneasy. Suddenly, Evan was at her elbow. "Phade and I are gonna go down to the radio station and do some editing."

"Yeah," Phade said. "Don't worry about me."

Mesa could tell by his tone he didn't mean it. But she nodded and returned to her office anyway, telling herself that she would see Phade later.

Once Chloe began to drink the coffee, she loosened up. "I don't know about you, but we had one of those perfect Butte childhoods," she said.

Mesa sat down at her desk, wondering if she would hear about the twins running around the slag piles and alleyways. To Chloe's credit, the narrative was far more revealing.

"We were peas in a pod, always somebody to play with. The kind of brother that made me look good. He could always make me laugh, and we'd stick up for each other. When he would get into trouble, I would get him out, or cover for him. I never minded. We lived two doors from our grandparents up on Excelsior, and they doted on us," she said.

"My grandparents moved when we were in seventh grade," she said. "Life got a little bleaker then. Mines closed. Nathan struggling in school. Me trying to help him keep up. That was when he started hanging out with Razor."

Mesa was trying to keep her perspective, but she couldn't help warming to Chloe whose guard had clearly dropped. "I'm surprised to hear they had that much in common," Mesa said, moving from behind her desk, closer to Chloe.

"They didn't, except for the fact that both of them could barely read." Chloe looked at Mesa and must have seen the look of surprise on her face.

"Most people have a similar reaction. Everybody thinks Nathan is bright, and he is good at his job, in his own way," she emphasized. "But he's dyslexic. It wasn't diagnosed until he was sixteen, when he had trouble passing the Drivers' Ed. test. In grade school, I would read aloud to him. I helped him memorize whole passages of books to help him compensate. But by the time junior high rolled around, we couldn't keep it up. We got put in different classes. He had to get by on his own."

"Did he get put in a special class?" Mesa asked. "Was that where he met Razor?"

Chloe shook her head. "There were no special classes or learning disability teachers then, at least not in Butte. Not until after we graduated. He mostly got put in the back of the room, out of the spotlight, so he didn't get embarrassed. That's where he met up with Razor."

Imagining Nathan's humiliation, especially being compared to his whiz-kid sister, Mesa felt a twinge of sadness for him. She and Chance had a hard enough time with comparisons, and they weren't even twins. "Misery loves company, you mean?"

Chloe nodded, equivocally. "Nathan wasn't dumb. He knew he had certain advantages—family, money, people who cared about him. Razor didn't have any of that. His father was long gone. His mother was barely around and rarely sober if you believe the gossip.

"Razor made Nathan tougher, while my brother looked good next to Razor's rough edges. It halfway worked."

"Halfway?" Mesa said, wondering if this was what Brendan had alluded to, that Nathan's friends didn't understand what he saw in Razor.

"The whole Skywatcher thing grew out of this English class we all had, where we did this group research project. I'm sure my parents told the teacher how much Nathan relied on my help, so she put him with us—with Brendan, Danica and me. And where Nathan went, so did Razor.

"By then Razor had been helping his uncle out at the Finlen. He was the one who eventually got us up on the roof. The only problem was that Danica could not stand Razor, which was unusual for her. She was sweet to almost everybody, but she disliked Razor. He would make fun of her all the time, teasing her about 'itches and vitches' and getting to celebrate two Christmases. Junior-high stuff, but it got to her."

These were taunts that Mesa knew Phade could be sensitive to. Sometimes he would laugh it off, saying that you couldn't have a name like Draganovich and not expect somebody to crack on it. But one day, he and Cinch had almost drawn fists. How it was taken seemed to have a lot to do with who said it and in what tone.

Mesa could see how Razor might have developed a personality that got under people's skin. According to Irita, he had been kicked around by everybody. Nathan was probably one of the few with sympathy for their common struggle.

"So whenever anybody wanted to go up on the roof," Chloe continued, "we had to find Razor to let us up there. At first he would come along, but at some point Nathan simply paid him to get lost so Danica wouldn't end up going home in tears."

Most people outgrew their teenage resentments, but maybe not Razor. Had that been what fueled his plans about Elsie's ledger? "So do you have any idea how Razor got involved with the plan to sell Elsa Seppanen's black book?"

"The detective asked the same thing. I knew almost nothing about the ledger, at least until Nathan started talking about it last night."

Mesa wasn't surprised. She hadn't even thought to ask Chloe about the book when they had met previously.

"I didn't realize, until Nathan told me, that he found that ledger the night he hid the baby's body."

So that was where the book had been? Mesa picked up her notebook. "Can I take a few notes," she asked and tried to act nonchalant.

Chloe nodded and then said, "I'm tired of all the secrets. That's why I'm here. Apparently my grandfather bought the book because our Uncle Andrew's name is in it."

"Ah," was all Mesa said, though "Holy shit!" was what she was thinking. She concentrated on her note-taking to avoid revealing her eager expression.

Chloe explained that Nathan had found the ledger when he had wrapped the baby's body in the wardrobe bag. The book had fallen out of a pocket in their grandfather's tuxedo jacket, along with a ticket to the 1995 Winter Ball. Nathan had given it only a passing glance, not even realizing what was in the book. He put it in the pocket of his parka and only looked at it several weeks later when he was back at school in California. Danica was the one who realized what the ledger was. Nathan had found it again when he was clearing out the trunk of his car, and he showed it to her."

"So Danica did have a connection to the ledger," Mesa said aloud.

Chloe nodded. "She read it to him. That's when he realized that our Uncle's name was in it. Nathan asked her to keep it for him because he wasn't sure what to do with it, and he wasn't sure who to ask. He never told me about it, partly I think because of its association with the baby's death, and by then we weren't talking much anyway. He told me we could never talk about what happened again. In his mind, I had abandoned him. We were never really close after that."

"Your uncle was a client of Elsie's?" Mesa asked, trying not to sound surprised. So Griff's cousin might not be the only revelation to come out of Elsie's ledger, Mesa thought excitedly. How many more might there be?

Chloe nodded. "I think that's why my grandfather ended up with the book."

"Elsie was already dead by then," Mesa said. "She died in the seventies. He was in no danger of blackmail by her."

"Not that gramps or my uncle would have cared," Chloe said. "Uncle Andy was no stranger to scandal. We used to get sent out of the room when my parents and grandparents talked about him. He'd been married three times and then fathered a child with a model half his age that he met in Vegas. He died from a heart defect when he was sixty. That's why I think gramps probably wanted the book."

"In case somebody came forward," Mesa said, "looking for clues to their birth parents for medical reasons." It made sense. At least one of Elsie's Babies had said that medical problems had triggered her search for her biological parents. "Danica had the ledger for the last ten years?"

Chloe nodded. "I guess so. Until Nathan told her he needed to make a copy of the page that had our Uncle's name on it. He says she gave him back the book when she got back to town three weeks ago."

Mesa's mind was spinning. Had her knowledge about the book gotten her killed?

"But Griff Jones said Razor Gillette was the one who claimed to know where the book was. How did your brother get involved?"

Chloe shook her head in a *go figure* way. "Nathan and Razor's lives intersected again over the ledger. According to Nathan, he and Razor were at the clubhouse at the Country Club drinking beer. This was about three years ago. Razor got on a rant about how he could have been rich if his uncle hadn't sold Elsie's ledger."

"Einar Mortensen," Mesa said with a smile, her pet theory again.

"You've heard of him then?" Chloe said.

Mesa nodded. "He's notorious. I always thought it was possible he had gotten his hands on the ledger when Elsie died."

"I guess so, and then he sold it to my grandfather. Probably at that Winter Ball."

Sitting on the sofa in Hardcastle's house, Chance and Alexis listened to their host talking on the phone in the nearby kitchen. Nathan was leaving an animated phone message, and Chance suspected Razor would not be happy to hear it.

Alexis and he pretended not to be eavesdropping by looking out the picture window in the front room. They exchanged a furtive glance when a Butte Silver Bow police patrol car drove past the house for the second time in five minutes.

Hardcastle came back into the room, clearly agitated. "He said he would be here at six. I left him a message to call me so we can decide what he wants to do now. "

It was half past. "He probably saw the beefed-up police presence in your neighborhood," Alexis said.

Macgregor had been steamed about losing the opportunity to talk to Razor at the storage unit earlier in the day. The detective had let Chance know how unhappy he was. "What the hell you doing? Why didn't you call me if you knew where he was?"

Chance had done some fancy backpedaling. "We went out here on a hunch. I was as surprised to see him as I was to see you." Which was entirely true.

Macgregor was not mollified. "Well, I'm done fooling around. If you see him again, you better call me ASAP. Got it?" He had punctuated this last question with a finger to Chance's sternum.

"I think Alexis is right," Chance said. "Maybe we need to negotiate another location."

He looked at the leather shoulder bag Alexis held in her lap. Sitting next to five thousand dollars in cash felt unnerving. "Did you tell him we have the money?"

"Not yet," Hardcastle said. "The more information Razor has, the more likely he is to do something stupid." No sooner had the word stupid come out of Nathan's mouth than his cell phone pinged, signaling a text. "He wants to meet at the Napton across from Hennessy's."

"Why the Napton, I wonder?" Chance said and looked at the other two. "I thought it was boarded up."

"His girlfriend has a place there."

୬୦ଏ

By the time Chloe left the *Mess* office, the wind had picked up from the west and the threatening, gray sky seemed ready to explode. Mesa did not like the idea of getting caught in a downpour halfway through the walk to her grandmother's. Butte's mile high altitude produced summer storms with cold, pelting rain which made her shiver to even think about. The ten-minute walk to her Granite Street duplex seemed equally uncertain.

She called Adrienne for a ride. While she waited, she noticed a text from Alexis asking for a callback. Mesa returned the call but got no answer and swore under her breath. Five minutes later, Adrienne pulled in front of the *Mess* office as the sky began to spit rain.

Adrienne had put down her cell phone when Mesa got into the car.

"What?" she asked. The two women knew each other well enough that Mesa knew something was amiss.

"That was Vivian. The power's out at Nan's house. She's hoping we're on our way home."

Mesa nodded. "Nan's got plenty of candles, not to worry, right?"

Adrienne sighed. "I had a quick call from Chance when I was getting in the car. He and Alexis went out to Nathan Hardcastle's home to meet with Gillette and get the ledger. Only he didn't show, so now they're on their way to the Napton to make the exchange."

"Damn it," Mesa said. "Alexis said she was going to let me know when the rendezvous was supposed to happen." She took her phone from her bag and sighed. "I got a text from Alexis earlier when Chloe Hardcastle was in my office pouring her heart out. I ignored it."

The two women looked at each other. Mesa mused aloud. "I wonder if somebody told Macgregor."

"Let's check on your grandmother, and then we can decide what to do next."

ೞ

"Why is it that when it rains in the mountains, the clouds seem to stand still—and dump all their moisture in one place?" Alexis said. She and Chance were standing in the arched entrance of the Napton, wiping the rain off their faces, and waiting for Hardcastle to arrive. They had barely turned the corner onto Granite when the clouds had opened up, necessitating a sprint through pounding, cold rain the last fifty yards.

Chance rubbed his arms, trying to warm himself. The streets were empty, with most of the Folk Festival workers having halted work in mid-stride and taking shelter until the storm passed. Finally, he walked up the several steps to the two oak and glass doors of the building, peering through the glass. "Maybe Hardcastle beat us here." He opened the door on the right. Cool, stale air wafted toward him, and he instinctively held his breath for a split second. Then he walked into the hallway, dark and hushed.

"Does anybody actually live here?" Alexis asked, following close behind.

"Beats me," Chance said, looking at the rubble that had been swept into one corner. The door to one apartment had been taken off its hinges and leaned next to a wall with peeling wallpaper. "I'll be happy if we can just find Gillette."

Suddenly the sound of a couple of voices reached them. "Sounds like that's him," Alexis said.

The two inched toward the other end of the hall where they could see the shadow of two figures. "That's them." Chance stopped and looked at Alexis. "You'll hold onto the cash until we actually see the ledger, right? I don't trust Razor as far as I could toss him."

"Do I seem like that kind of pushover, Chance?" Alexis said. She sounded genuinely offended.

"No ma'am," Chance said. "I only wanted to be sure we were on the same page. I have no doubt you'll do exactly what you need to do when the time comes." He didn't add that he hoped it would be the *right* thing to do.

When Alexis and Chance met the men, nearly two-thirds of the way down the hall, Razor wasted no time on small talk. "Let me see the cash," he said.

"Not until I see what I'm buying," Alexis said her voice firm and calm.

Razor reached into the left pocket of his wind breaker and pulled out a package wrapped in a plastic shopping bag. He withdrew a black leather-bound book about the size of a small paperback, maybe half as thick.

"Let me see it," Alexis said and reached her hand out.

"No way," Razor said, "Not until I have the money. Tell her, Nathan. It's the real deal." He put the book back in his pocket.

"That's it," Nathan said with a nod. "Let's get this over with."

Nathan sounded nervous, and Chance looked toward Alexis and nodded. He could see that Razor was in no mood to chat, which was just as well. Making the exchange meant that Nathan and Razor could get to the police station and satisfy Macgregor.

Alexis had positioned the strap of her satchel over her head and across her chest, so it couldn't be easily pulled from her shoulder. She unbuckled the purse's flap to reveal ten bands of fifty-dollar bills inside.

Like a bolt of lightning, Razor reached into the purse to snatch the bills.

Impressively, Chance would say later, Alexis grabbed his wrist in the same second. She had been ready for him. Sadly, none of them were prepared for the .22 pistol which Razor promptly pointed between her eyes. "Let go," he growled at Alexis.

"What the hell are you doing?" Nathan cried, his voice echoing in the hallway. "Not again. We got a deal going here."

"Shut up," Razor said and jerked the purse's leather shoulder strap up around Alexis's neck, and yanked her toward him. "I'm tired of you telling Jones that I'm just some creep with money problems. Nobody ever gave me one damn thing, not like you two bastards. Jones would never have even known about that ledger if it hadn't been for me. Now it's my turn to catch a break. I'm gonna sell it for big money. Maybe even *People Magazine*."

Chance looked at Alexis who was pulling at the strap with both her hands to keep from choking. She looked more angry than afraid, but Razor was definitely making her uncomfortable, the pink color in her cheeks deepening. He pulled her down the hallway toward the back of the building. Unsure what Gillette might do next, Chance took a step toward them while Nathan spoke.

"You said you'd vouch for me with the police," Nathan said, his voice pleading.

Razor shook his head. "You chicken shit! We both know they were going to believe you over me. Go ahead and tell them I pushed her. It was her own damn fault. She wasn't gonna let go of that ledger for love nor money. Ha, ha," he said.

Chance looked at Alexis whose was struggling to keep the strap from crushing her windpipe. Had he heard right? Did Razor say he had pushed Danica? "Let Alexis go," he said to Razor and took another step toward them. "You don't need her. Take the money. You've got the ledger. Just go."

"You shut up, Dawson. I'm done with people like you telling me what to do."

Chance could hear the years of welled-up resentment for all the golfers who had ever ordered Razor around or, worse yet, treated him as if he were invisible. Chance would have liked to think he wasn't in that category.

"Get down on the floor, now!" Razor said. "You too, Nathan. You know I'm not afraid to use this." He pointed the gun at Alexis's temple.

"Okay," Nathan said. "Okay." He got down on the floor and Chance followed suit.

"Come after me and she's dead," Gillette said and pulled Alexis, stumbling, toward the back stairs.

Chapter 20

As soon as Mesa got to her grandmother's house, she ran upstairs to talk to Griff. "What the hell is going on?"

She could see by the look in his eyes, he was worried, too.

"I don't know," he said, stuttering. He threw up his hands and said, "I spoke to Nathan twenty minutes ago. Alexis was to go to the bank and then to Nathan's house with your brother. The exchange was to be made there, only Razor hadn't shown up. Nathan wanted to know if I had talked to Gillette which, of course, I hadn't."

Mesa gave him a cold stare. He might not be lying, but that didn't stop her from wanting to choke him, no longer blinded by infatuation. Things were spinning out of control, and he was in the center of it. He'd been in town a grand total of five days and wreaked havoc at every turn, ducking responsibility all along the way.

"You better hope nothing happens to my brother or Alexis," she said, and took her cell phone from the back pocket of her jeans and dialed Macgregor who answered right away.

"Nice of you to call," was the detective's sarcastic greeting. Mesa knew she and Chance had both pushed the edge with Macgregor, and she wasn't proud of it.

"I had a patrol car out at Hardcastle's, thinking Gillette might show up. The officer said he saw your brother and some woman go into the house instead. Now, apparently everybody's gone."

"You're not going to like this," Mesa said, holding the phone away from her ear. "They're meeting with Razor Gillette at the Napton."

"What?" the detective snarled. "I told your brother to stay away from that guy and to call me if he saw him again!"

"I know, I know," Mesa said. "But Razor is supposed to come into the station as soon as he and Nathan get this business with the ledger straightened out. At least that was the plan. So you should see him before the day is over."

"I'm sure as hell not waiting around here for that to happen," he said and then hung up.

Mesa felt her frustration boiling over. She looked at Griff and said, "Why couldn't you have told me the truth from the beginning?"

Griff shot back, "You only want the truth when it suits your purposes." He turned away from her. "I'm going to use what's in that ledger to shut up a narrow-minded politician who also happens to be my cousin. He's the single biggest backer of the anti-abortion movement in the UK. At least give me some credit for that."

"I don't know what to think about you," Mesa said, saying out loud what she had felt since she met the Englishman. "All you can think of is your own selfish reasons. You have no idea about the people who have struggled for years to find their parents. They need to see that book. They've spent their lives trying to get some closure. You've been so busy trying to feather your own nest, you forget there are other people that are a part of this story."

"How is that different from your wanting to play the heroic journalist? Fine. Once I get the ledger, I'll commission you to write the exposé on my cousin. I'm sure *The Sun* or one of the other English tabloids will print it." Then Griff chuckled. "He's not my cousin anymore. He doesn't even know he was adopted. I've been tormented by this bastard my whole life. I can't wait to see the look on his face."

Chance jumped up the minute Alexis and Razor had disappeared out the back of the building. "Call 911," he yelled to Nathan and then followed down the steps and out to the alley. He was just in time to watch Razor speeding away to Quartz Street on his motorcycle, through the access that led north directly behind the Napton. He could see Alexis, smeared with grime, where Razor must have thrown her to the ground, sprinting after him in the driving rain.

A patrol car came to a quick stop on Quartz Street and blocked the end of the access way. The officer got out of the car, walking toward Razor, who screeched to a stop, the back wheel of the bike careening away from him.

With a building on one side of the narrow lane and a lot filled with piles of staging equipment for the festival on the other, he had two choices: turn around and run the gauntlet between Adrienne and Chance or try his luck through the maze that was the corner lot.

Razor regained control of the Harley and began threading the warren of spools of cable, pedestrian guards, garbage cans, and safety posts. Chance veered across the lot after him, hurdling a set of sawhorses as he ran.

Alexis, pissed and gaining on Razor, picked up a roll of orange plastic fencing, thick as a log, and hurled it like a Scottish Highlander, barely missing Gillette. He turned onto Wyoming Street to head north but quickly shot onto the sidewalk when a second patrol car appeared at the top of the street.

Thunder cracked overhead, and the motorcycle engine roared as Chance lost his footing on some rain-slick plastic sheeting. When he pulled himself up, he could see Razor heading across the lot where crews had begun to set up the Copper Street stage tent. A semi was parked broadside on Copper, blocking the patrol car's pursuit. Chance shook his head. Did Razor really think he could escape up the hill into Walkerville and over the mountain?

Alexis seemed to have lost steam after her near miss with the plastic missile. Chance stopped next to her, and when he asked if she was hurt, she let go with a string of expletives. He saw Razor headed toward the giant tent, which was only partly anchored down. The crew had retreated in the intense wind and rain. Two pools of rainwater were forming on the top of tent, causing it to sag, and the guy wires had come loose from their tethers, the wind tossing them wildly.

Seeing no choice but to leave Alexis to nurse her bruised knee, Chance called to the cop who was running toward the tent. Every summer the Folk Festival Operations director warned the site volunteers about overhead utility lines. A 7500-watt distribution line ran diagonal across the Copper Street lot. Ten feet above them, it was swaying in the wind like a loose clothesline.

Chance crossed to the street and saw the concrete barriers already in place on the far side of the lot and blocking Razor's escape. Razor spun his wheels, turning back. His rear wheel must have caught on some of the tent wires or the cables on the ground, but he persisted, determined to get out of there. Suddenly one of the supporting aluminum poles inside the tent began to wobble.

Mesa drove across West Granite, trying to avoid the streets blocked by the Folk Festival set up, trying not to dwell on her last words with Griff. She couldn't believe she'd ever found him attractive. She had just pulled into the Wells Fargo Bank parking lot on Main Street, intending to pull into the alley behind the Napton, when what she thought was a massive bolt of lightning struck. In all the mountain storms she'd sheltered from, even when the lightning felt like it was directly overhead, she had never seen the whole sky turn indigo and electric blue as it had just done.

Momentarily disoriented by the storm's assault on her senses, she hesitated but then decided to pull farther into the alley to see if she could get inside the Napton. Out of nowhere, a patrol car had beaten her to it. "Damn it," she said and banged the steering wheel with her hand.

All at once a half dozen sirens, police, EMS, and fire trucks seemed to descend from every direction. The cop in front of her was waving at her to back up which she did. Nothing seemed to be happening at the Napton, but she could see people at the other end of the alley running up Wyoming Street toward something.

The rain had slowed, and as much as she hated getting out in it, she abandoned the car in the bank parking lot. She trotted up Main and when she got to Quartz and an ambulance blew by her, she knew she was headed in the right direction. She picked up her pace, pulling out her cell phone and speed dialing Chance who didn't answer, as usual, and then Alexis who picked up immediately.

"What's happened? Where are you? Where's Chance? Are you hurt?"

Mesa slowed to listen to Alexis's answers.

"I'm standing in front of the Capri. I'm fine. Chance is fine, maybe a little frazzled." Her voice sounded tinny, strangely detached, and Mesa wondered if maybe her friend had been near the lightning strike and was in shock.

"Sit down somewhere," Mesa said. "I'll be right there." And she was. Moments later, she had crossed Wyoming Street and found Alexis sitting in front of the motel, wet and cold, jeans torn, dirt on the side of her face, and she still looked good.

Firemen were tripping over themselves to offer her raincoats and blankets. One of them miraculously came up with a cup of coffee. Chance was standing between two cops, and when he saw Mesa, he came toward her.

Emergency Response people were milling about everywhere. "What's happened?" she asked her brother, who was soaked through, his dark hair curling into ringlets that reminded her of Saturday night baths when they were kids.

He cleared his throat. "*FUBAR* as they say in the military. The whole place went up in 240 volts of gigantic blue flash. Rainwater poured through a breach in the tent and lit up like a thousand electric eels."

Mesa listened, suddenly aware of the smell of smoke and burnt hair, while Chance described how Razor Gillette had been electrocuted when his motorcycle dislodged a tent pole that then made contact with a distribution line overhead in the middle of the driving rainstorm.

"You sure you're alright?" Mesa said, after hearing the harrowing story. She thought her brother's eyebrows seemed a little bushier than usual.

He nodded and then went to sit by Alexis. Mesa asked, knowing she would sound like an ambulance chaser, "Did you get the ledger? Where's Hardcastle?"

Both of them looked at each other, acknowledging silently that Hardcastle did seem to have disappeared. Chance explained what had happened in the Napton and that Razor had taken had taken both the cash and the ledger.

"I'm not leaving 'til someone tells me where and when I get one or the other back," Alexis said. "I paid for the damn book. It's mine."

Was it? Mesa wondered, pulling her fleece vest collar close to her neck. The rain had stopped, but the clouds were still thick and the temperature had dropped twenty degrees.

It sounded to her like Razor had stolen both ledger and cash and that it was still Hardcastle who needed to decide the ledger's ownership.

She looked around again, toward the Napton then back to the commotion around the tent to see if she could find Hardcastle. She saw Macgregor ordering people around and popping jelly beans. Clearly Razor would never give any statement that would help to exonerate Nathan. When she mentioned this to Chance, his response stunned her. "Not a problem. Razor admitted he pushed Danica. Alexis and I both heard him."

"What?" Mesa said, thinking of Phade. She also thought of Hardcastle and the story he had told that morning. Why hadn't he said what really happened? Was he that worried that Razor would claim the opposite—blame it on Hardcastle? She silently cursed that she had missed out on Razor's confession.

After twenty of minutes of grousing and the arrival of Sheriff Solheim, Alexis and Chance were finally permitted to go home and get into warm clothes. They both agreed to appear at the police department in an hour's time to give statements.

Mesa drove them to Nana Rose's house, glad that Adrienne was there to give them the once over. Once she declared the pair no worse for wear, Alexis and Chance left for the police station. Mesa was sure Griff was upstairs fuming about not being included, and she went to his room. Somehow, the storm had cleared the air.

He was sitting on the edge of the bed wearing a pair of Chance's sweat pants that Adrienne had given him and pulling on a tee shirt. "Not so fast," Mesa said. "Where do you think you're going?"

Griff looked at her with the expression she now took pleasure in, frustration, and resignation. "I'm not deaf. I thought I would come downstairs and find out what's going on."

Mesa moved the tray of empty dinner dishes onto the Queen Anne chair and sat down on the bed.

"Something bad has happened, hasn't it?" Griff said, his voice suddenly dead serious. "Your brother's all right? Alexis?"

Mesa nodded, appreciating that Griff had at least asked about the people she cared about. "Razor Gillette is dead."

"Razor popped his clogs?" the Englishman said, clearly surprised. "But how?"

Mesa sighed at the futility of all of it. "He tried to get away with the ledger, as well as Alexis's cash. Ended up wrapping himself around an aluminum pole and a utility wire in the middle of the storm."

"Crikey," Griff said, bringing his hand to his mouth. "I didn't care for the man. He did shoot me, even if he probably didn't mean to. But that's seems a terribly hard way to go."

"Adrienne said it was instantaneous."

"How did Hardcastle take it?" Griff asked. "They were childhood chums, after all."

"Don't know," Mesa said. "He seems to have faded into the woodwork. Don't suppose you've heard from him?"

Griff shook his head quickly and then picked up the phone on the bedside table to show Mesa. "Scouts' honor."

"You'll let me know if you do…" she said.

"Immediately," he said. Then he sighed and said, "I suppose you'll think it insensitive to ask, but what's happened to the ledger?"

"Police station, amazingly, it didn't burn up. Macgregor has it," Mesa said. "But not to worry. Alexis is on it. So back in bed where you belong."

Mesa was halfway down the steps when her phone pinged. She read a text from Evan.

Trouble brewing – can you come to Len Waters?

Mesa followed Evan down the steps into the basement, lit dimly by a couple of bare bulbs and smelling of old newspapers. A recording studio had been tucked away here, thirty or forty years ago at least. She could see tacky metallic wall tiles through the glass that made up the top half of the downstairs wall.

The long room was separated in two with the larger space serving as a session room. A couple of pianos, a drum set, and a line of guitars, along with music stands, speakers, and microphones, provided enough equipment for a dozen musicians. So this was where Phade had snuck away to. At the end was a smaller room, also with a half-windowed wall, for the technical side of productions. A long mixing board and an array of sound meters and other controls filled the smaller room. Like so much of Butte, if you squinted you would think you were back in the seventies. He'd gone back in time.

"He's locked the door," Evan said and started pounding, calling to Phade to let them in. "I'm with Mesa. Come on, Phade, let us in."

Through the window, Mesa could see Phade pacing back and forth in the control room, stopping in mid-pace to yell. "He's in there all right," Mesa said. She could also see someone sitting in an upright chair with his back to the window. She was fairly sure it was Hardcastle. What confused her was why he was sitting there while Phade clearly was going off on him.

Evan had come over to the window to see as well. He cupped his hands around his eyes trying to improve his view through the other glass pane at the far end of the room. "I think maybe he has him tied up," he said and looked at Mesa with distress.

Phade's anger and grief had gotten the better of him. And Mesa felt partly responsible. She might have been able to help him let off some steam, but she was too busy trying to figure out what had happened to Danica, and the ledger. All her attention had gone toward putting all the pieces of the story together—not helping her friend. "What do you think he's trying to do?

"How did he even get him in there?" Mesa said, thinking aloud. Out of the corner of her eye, she saw Evan's head drop. She looked at him and said, "What?"

"If I'd known what he was going to do, I wouldn't have gone along with it."

"Gone along with what?"

With another great sigh, Evan explained that he and Phade had run up to Len Waters after work to do some editing for a piece Phade was putting together for his sister's funeral service. "The owner is on a fishing trip up in Alaska, but he lets a bunch of us use the recording studio," Evan explained. When they heard the sirens, they had stood in the portico of the store, watching and listening. "Hardcastle came walking down Granite Street in the pouring rain. When he crossed the street and turned down Main, Phade called to him."

Evan explained how Phade had literally pulled a disheveled and disoriented Nathan Hardcastle into the empty store. After a few words, Hardcastle had tried to leave, and Phade let him have one in the jaw. "I helped Phade carry him downstairs and put him in the chair," Evan said.

"Phade said he was sorry he had to involve me, and then he told me to get lost—but nice like. He called me 'kid'. You know, 'Get lost, kid'."

"Oh Evan," Mesa said. What people will do sometimes to belong. "What did you think he was going to do?"

"He said he wanted to talk to him privately—*man to man*, he said."

Mesa did not like the sound of it. "He doesn't have a weapon, does he?"

Evan shook his head. "I know where I can get a key to this door," he said. "The radio station manager has one, and I think he's over at the Carpenter's Hall."

That was at the other end of the block. Mesa was nodding her head, "Go, go," she said quickly. "I'll stay here and keep an eye on things." She felt certain she could defuse the situation if only she could talk to Phade. She pulled out her phone and called him. It went right to voice mail. "Damn," she said aloud, frustrated and worried. She stared through the large wall window, alternately banging on it and waving her arms. Then she called Chloe Hardcastle.

The phone conversation with Chloe had been short. She was up on Excelsior visiting old friends, and she had agreed to come to see if she could help. Then Mesa texted Chance and told him to come to Len Waters Music once he was done with the cops. She didn't say why. Then Evan was back with the key.

"The second door doesn't have a lock," Evan said.

"Okay," Mesa said. "Once you unlock the door, I want you to go back upstairs and wait for Chloe Hardcastle."

"But, but," Evan protested.

Mesa shook her head. "I can handle Phade, but I think he's going to want to hear from Chloe, too. You need to get her down here."

Evan started back up the stairs, and Mesa quietly opened the first door, and then gingerly closed it behind her. Inside the soundproofing, she could hear Phade's voice.

"You piece of shit! You killed my sister and broke my parents' hearts!" he yelled, half sobbing. "You bastard! Tell me why you did it!"

She couldn't hear Hardcastle's response, but she hoped he would distract Phade enough so that Mesa could sneak across the studio floor to the second door that led into control room.

"Stop saying you didn't do it!" Phade was yelling. "You got her up on the roof. That's as good as killing her."

Several more quick steps and Mesa could hear Hardcastle.

"I never meant for anything to happen to her, I swear. I loved her. I always loved her."

Mesa gently pushed the door ajar. She didn't want to startle Phade into doing something even more drastic. Nathan was tied to the chair with electrical cord. Hopefully, those cords weren't connected to anything else. She'd already had enough of an example of what electricity could do to people.

Phade looked up when she stepped into the room. "Get out!" he said, his voice vicious. He wiped tears from his face with his forearm and then said, "You've done enough. I'm taking it from here."

Mesa was stung by the tone of Phade's voice. "I know you're mad at me, Phade, but don't let that fuel what's happening here."

"I'm not mad at you," Phade said. "This has nothing to do with you, or that stupid ledger. This is about this piece of shit and what I want!" he said and backhanded Nathan across the face. Then he looked at her again and growled, "If you don't want to see this, you should leave."

Mesa felt a bit of panic. Had she overestimated her ability to get through to Phade? At least, she had to try. "Phade, Nathan didn't kill Danica. It was Razor. He admitted it. Chance heard him say so," she said and took another step closer to Phade.

"But this guy is the one who got her up there." Phade looked at Nathan and yelled, "Why?! Why did you make her go up there?!"

"It was her idea. She was upset," Nathan said, tears streaming down his face. "I only wanted to explain what had happened, to comfort her. How could I know Razor would go off on her?"

"You bastard!" Phade said, crying now, too, and slapped Nathan again.

"Please, Phade, there's more to it than you realize," Mesa said. "She went up to the roof to see Nathan because she was upset about the baby."

Phade looked at Mesa. "What baby?" He was stunned.

"My boy," Nathan whispered.

"The baby I delivered."

Mesa turned to see Chloe Hardcastle standing in the doorway. She seemed taller now than an hour or so ago. She walked right past Mesa and stood between Phade and her brother.

"I've been trying to decide when would be a good time to talk you, Phade," Chloe said in a quiet voice. "You remember me, I know. Danica and I used to babysit for you. We'd play soccer in your backyard and then eat ice cream. You were so sweet. Danica loved you so much."

Mesa watched Phade's expression soften, and Chloe put her hands to his shoulders. She turned him toward the couch in the corner and looked at Mesa. "Untie Nathan. Then we can talk this through."

Mesa was amazed at how quickly Chloe was defusing the situation. She sat next to Phade who sat with his head in his hands, resigned. Nathan got up and brought over his chair and sat down. Mesa stood by the door, partly to keep the conversation from being interrupted, and because she didn't want to miss a word.

"I know you only want the truth, Phade," Chloe said. "God knows I've wanted to tell it. I only wish Danica could be here, too." She reached over and touched Nathan on the knee. Then she looked back at Phade and said, "The main thing to know is that Danica loved her family so much and would never have done anything knowingly to hurt any of you."

During the next half hour, Chloe explained about their time in California, the pregnancy and the decision to have the baby and find a good home for it. All the while she painted a picture of Danica as a woman who wanted to do the best she could do for the baby in that situation.

With Chloe there, Nathan seemed to recover some composure. He talked about the panic he felt when he realized the baby was dead, the fear that Danica might die, too. "I've wished so many times that I had walked out into that snow with the baby and never come back."

Phade sunk back into the sofa, looking back and forth between Nathan and Chloe as he tried to take in all that was being said. He seemed to believe Nathan when he said, "I knew I would tell Danica someday what had happened to the baby. I wanted to wait for the right time. I would never have wanted her to find out the way she did."

Once he began to describe the scene on the roof, how she and Razor had fought over the ledger, Mesa looked for signs that Phade's anger might return. Nathan explained that he had met with Danica when she first returned to Butte three weeks before. She told him then that she felt it was crucial to protect the names of the people in the ledger. That they should find a way to share it with the people who were looking for their birth parents, but not make it public. "That's why I told Griffin-Jones that I had no intention of selling the ledger. Danica died trying to protect Elsie's Babies."

Chapter 21

Chance lay next to Adrienne, watching her sleep. As usual she lay on her back, motionless, her breath calm and even. Some nights he was fairly sure she didn't turn over a single time. Clear conscience.

He stared out the tall window at a star-filled night, storms finally gone. For the third night in a row, he was having trouble falling asleep, a record, at least in recent memory.

Sunday night they'd been up 'til all hours talking to the Sheriff about the Englishman's shooting. Monday night there was the aggravation around the shooting at the parade, and then tonight Chance was waiting to see if he would glow in the dark.

The death of Razor Gillette had been harsh. Not a way he would wish anyone to go, no matter Adrienne's assurance that all that voltage would have shut down his brain almost instantly. "It was more painful to watch, I'm sure," she had said to comfort him.

Razor must have been at the end of his tether, talking about pushing Danica Draganovich off that roof. He was almost bragging about it—one last slap in Nathan Hardcastle's face. Chance couldn't put the look on Razor's face out of his mind, the resentment he must have felt his whole life.

Then another flash of that monumental arc of electricity, the macabre blue and purple light show came back to him. He ran his fingers though his hair which still felt like it was standing on end.

"Awake again?" came a sweetly inquiring voice next to him. Adrienne lifted up on her elbow and leaned toward him.

He pulled her close, her head resting on his chest, her warm skin soft and welcoming. "You know Razor had a son?"

"He did?" she said and turned so he could tell she wasn't falling back to sleep.

Nodding, he said, "About eight, I would say. Sam and I saw them together out at that storage unit. "

"Feeling bad that Razor will be missed?" Adrienne said.

Chance shrugged. "Fathering a child and raising one are two distinct activities. A lot of guys are more inclined to do the first than stick around for the second."

"So what's really keeping you awake?" Adrienne asked.

"I can't figure out why Danica wouldn't give up that ledger. If Razor was gonna go after her for it, why not let him have it?"

෴

On Friday morning, July 15th, Mesa got to the office first thing. The summer's normal pace had returned. The Folk Festival had come and gone, and Butte would have a short respite until Evel Days at the end of the month.

Considering the visitors she would see that afternoon, she was looking forward to a block of uninterrupted time afterward to devote to the story she would write.

Mesa had taken Nana Rose to Danica's funeral on Friday, one week ago. The church's old world feeling had embraced them—the chanting, the aroma of frankincense, and the magnificence of the church's frescos, detailed images with dark blues and reds, accented with gold. The depth of their ancient Orthodox faith and the intimacy apparent in the warmth of its congregation had formed a deep impression on her. These were people who looked you in the eye, filled with the church's call to be in the present, making Mesa glad to be there when they called Danica home as Father Jovan explained during the service.

Mesa had read about the church's iconography project, but to see the work up close was spectacular, not just in its design—the color and the visual images—but also in the expressions of devotion on the faces painted there. They possessed an other-worldly quality, a spiritual presence that drew Mesa in. She realized that this directness, this presence, was what had drawn her to Phade from the beginning.

The service, the *a cappella* music Phade had recorded, singing with his sister, and the reception that followed, meeting the parishioners and seeing the tender care they gave the Draganovich family lingered in Mesa's mind. She had found Phade, and they had hugged tightly but with tenderness they still shared when he returned to work.

On Sunday, Nana Rose had asked her to stop by. Mesa was pleased and only mildly curious when she saw Vesna Draganovich sitting with Nana in the parlor.

Maybe Mrs. Draganovich was still concerned about Phade.

Mesa could see from the tea service that the two women had been there awhile which was no surprise. Nana had a soft spot for anybody who had come to Montana from Europe, as she had done from England. They shared firsthand how hard it could be to adjust, to feel accepted.

The three exchanged greetings, and Mesa waited for her tea to be poured to find out the topic of their meeting. She knew her grandmother would not rush. Vesna seemed to have more color in her cheeks since the funeral and certainly since that evening, nine days previous, when Mesa had brought Phade home after Danica's death.

After a sip of tea, Nana said, "Now Mesa, Vesna has a concern that has to do with this ledger that belonged to Elsa Seppanen. She's come to me for help, and I've told her I feel that you should be part of our discussion about what to do."

Mesa sipped her tea, even more curious. Vesna put her cup down and adjusted her wire-rimmed glasses before speaking. Mesa thought of Phade's gentle teasing, that his Baba spoke with an accent, but there was no difficulty in understanding what she said, at least not because of how she spoke. What she said was another matter.

She looked at Mesa, making direct and prolonged eye contact, and then said calmly, "I believe my name is in the book."

Mesa put down her teacup and looked at her grandmother and then back at their guest. To say she was stunned was an understatement. Surely, there was some confusion about which book they were talking about.

"That's why Danica wouldn't surrender it," Vesna explained. "She was trying to protect me." She put her fingers to her lips like Mesa had seen her do at the funeral after she had leaned over her granddaughter's body and put a Last Kiss on her forehead.

After Razor's death the ledger had been taken into police custody. Once the County Attorney had decided no charges would be filed, a decision that had only just been made public, the ledger had been released to Nathan. At Chloe's suggestion, he wanted Mesa to help him set up guidelines that would follow Danica's wishes that the ledger be kept in the Archives with precise and strict stipulations about who could see it.

Nathan had agreed to allow Mesa to take photographs with the assurance that she could not publish the name of anyone living, who was listed in the book, without their permission. Mesa had thanked him for the trust he placed in her. "Before Chloe left, she told me she thought you had the best interests of those involved. I think Danica would have liked that."

Of course, Mesa had agreed. Nathan had allowed her to take the ledger for an afternoon, and she had closed herself up in her office, spending several minutes studying the feel and smell of the book's pages. Unlike the other black marketers Mesa had researched, Elsa Seppanen had kept meticulous records, her cursive handwriting clear and concise. Mesa could imagine her each night, recording the transactions that had made her so controversial. No doubt, she felt the record was the only protection she had, and so her notes were extensive.

The book contained seventeen entries, one for each of the births. The date of the birth, the name of the biological mother with her date of birth, a column labeled "father if known," and then the client who paid for the delivery. Elsie also identified the relationship of the person paying. Often it was the "child's father;" sometimes the "mother's parent;" in two cases, the madam of one of the houses; and sometimes by the new parents.

On the opposite page came the child's name and sex as it appeared on the birth certificate, on which Elsie had provided her signature as the attendant at the delivery in her same distinct handwriting. Finally the names and addresses of the adoptive parents, sworn to secrecy, came last. On the bottom of this page were any notes that Elsie needed to remind her of the pertinent details that might prove to be helpful when she got hauled into court.

Every entry was its own story. The first one she studied was Andrew Armistead. That entry's date, on the left page, read:

January 8th, 1966
Mother's name—Annie Flick
Father's name—Andrew Armistead
Service pd for by father
Child's name—Aaron Story (male)
Parents—Mr. and Mrs. Jasper Story, Port Angel,
    Oregon
Father is son of Dr. Armistead
Annie Flick works at the Dumas

Mesa realized that, like Rabid Reg, this baby's mother was a "soiled dove."

The entry for Reginald Griffin-Jones was slightly more exotic. Dated 1970, that entry read:

Mother's name—Belle Ingraham

Father's name—Chicago Joe Arnos, Las Vegas, Nevada

Services pd by father (labor and delivery) and child's new parents

Child's name—Reginald Griffin-Jones (male)

Parents—Mr. and Mrs. Simon Griffin-Jones, current residence Washington, D.C., British citizens—father works at British consulate

Contact—Millie Lemuel, midwife working in Three Forks

Belle Ingraham works at the Windsor

Chicago Joe—professional gambler, Vegas

When Mesa asked Irita about the couple, she had confided that Belle and Joe were a well-known pair. The father played the tables in Butte in the summers to escape the Nevada heat. Eventually the mother had left the trade and moved to California, where she had gone into the porn industry, the accounting side, information Mesa had shared with Griff before he left.

Beyond those two, Mesa had not had time to study the other entries in any detail.

She had assumed the Griffin-Jones revelation would be the most dramatic until Vesna's disclosure. She certainly had not seen Vesna Draganovich's name anywhere.

"You needed the services of Elsa Seppanen?" Mesa said, finding the possibility almost beyond comprehension.

"Some sixty years ago," Vesna said and gave the details of her circumstances.

While Phade's grandparents had met, love at first sight, at the Orthodox Christmas services in Butte, sadly that was not Vesna's first visit to Butte. She had immigrated from war-torn Yugoslavia in 1954, orphaned and pregnant, the victim of a brutal rape by a Croatian soldier. Sponsored by a Serbian fraternal organization in Canada, she had been taken in by a family in Lethbridge, Alberta. Young and desperately fearful about having the baby, she was unable to consider the alternative. Her Serbian sponsor-family understood, and reached out to a woman they had heard about in Butte, Montana, no doubt through someone in its large Serbian community, who could help.

As Vesna spoke, Mesa tried to recall the photographs she had taken of each page of Elsie's ledger. Digital images were actually more legible than photo copies, but she had only studied the pages that pertained to Griffin-Jones, Nathan's uncle, and the three women from Belgrade who were coming to the *Messenger* office on Friday.

"Do you have your copy of the ledger," Nana Rose asked when Vesna had finished.

Did she have it? Mesmerized by the impact of its contents, she hadn't let it out of her sight since Nathan had let her take photos of it. She reached for her backpack, and the three women moved into the dining room where Mesa flipped through the pages, which were in chronological order.

Finally she saw the two entries in 1954. The second entry was dated August 4.

> Mother's name—Vesna Milenko
> Father's name unknown
> Service paid by K. Begovich (employer)
> Child's name—Anthony Grosfeldt (male)
> Parents—Mr. and Mrs. Stanley Grosfeldt,
>   Bellevue, Washington.
> Mother—teen aged victim of rape. Referred by
>   Ruby Yelenich in Lethbridge

So Vesna had given up a child as well. Mesa was both stunned and impressed with the older woman's dignity.

Vesna nodded stoically, with Nana by her side, as Mesa read the details aloud. When she was done, Nana had Mesa explain the circumstances under which the ledger was now being housed and that Vesna alone could release that information, but only if she chose to. "I would never write about your story without your permission," Mesa assured her.

"I am not ashamed of what I did, but this is between me and God, as it was for Danica," Vesna said... Then she paused and finally added, "I only wish I could have told her how I understood what she went through."

After Vesna left, Mesa and Nana Rose talked about the ledger and Mesa's plans to do a feature on the discovery of the ledger and on any of Elsie's Babies who chose to come forward to talk with her. "These are stories that need to be told," Mesa said, "wherever possible. Otherwise, people become victims of their secrets—like Danica did."

Nana wasn't so sure. "I don't know, Mesa. Your generation acts out its life as if on a stage. On Twitter and Facebook and Insty-Print."

"Instagram, Nana. It's called Instagram."

"Whatever it is, so many young people think the whole world wants them to be out there in public. But for my generation and many younger, what you're talking about is an invasion of privacy."

"What about Rock Hudson?" Mesa said, knowing Nana had always been a big fan. "He put a face on AIDS, and that's what started changing people's attitudes." She tried driving home her point, arguing that getting difficult subjects like mental illness, sexual identity, adoption, and violations of women's rights out in the open allows people to learn. "Remember Vivian's story in the *Messenger* last year? It opened a lot of minds around town about homelessness and the mental health system."

"You make some good points, Mesa, and I know your heart is in the right place, but Butte is a small community and the people whose names are in that ledger ought to get to decide if they want their origins to be made public. Promise me you'll abide by that, not even any veiled descriptions that could potentially identify someone even if you don't mention their name?"

Of course Mesa had agreed, respecting Nan's opinion and glad to help protect her friend. After all, she had more than enough to write about. That wasn't what had kept her awake.

Lying in bed that night, she relived her last conversation with Griff. He'd gotten his money returned and settled for a digital copy of the ledger, along with a sworn affidavit from Nathan as to its authenticity. By the time he was ready to fly home, a week after he'd arrived, Mesa had even driven him to the airport.

"I feel I can't apologize enough for imposing on you and your family. If I had to do this all over again, Mesa, I would have taken a completely different approach. An honest one."

"Getting mixed up with Razor right out of the gate was an unfortunate twist of fate," Mesa said, having rethought the situation herself..

Griff shook his head. "It would be easy enough to lay it off on a dead man, but I'm not that big of an ass. I could have investigated more thoroughly, asked more questions. I let my emotions rule my actions."

"How very un-English of you," Mesa had teased.

Griff had laughed but then continued, "More than that, I said some things to you that were bloody. I had no business criticizing you or your work. Butte is your home and I see now how dedicated you are to the *Messenger* and to your community. They are both lucky to have you."

He stuck out his hand to say goodbye, but Mesa opted for a hug, gingerly at first and then they had both hugged a tad tighter. Then he flashed his toothpaste smile one more time, and he was gone. On the drive back uptown, Mesa realized she had been hard on him. The same with Nathan. She'd seen both men not for who they were but for who she wanted them to be, through the lens of her own experience. The same with Evan and Phade. Her perspective definitely needed work.

Now, on this Friday morning, the women from Three Forks who Mesa had interviewed for her first Elsie's Babies story back in January were finally going to get to see the ledger. Mesa had prepared a special folder for each with the digital images of the pages on which their names appeared. They were going to discuss their efforts to discover more about their real parents' lives and any possible new family members, something they'd been wanting to do their whole lives. Mesa shared their excitement.

She picked up the files and spread them out on the coffee table, trying to make things look special, and sat down at her desk to await their arrival and to contemplate the title of the current feature she was working on, "Distant Revelations: The Power of Secrets." Moments later, Irita popped her head around the door and said in a conspiratorial whisper, "Elsie's Babies are here."

The End

Author's Note

While this is a work of fiction, the story of Elsie's babies is inspired by the real life journey of Gertie's babies, particularly Mable Dean, Sherrie Keller and her new-found half-brother, Michael Kello. I am indebted to them for their cooperation in the writing of this novel. This group of adult adoptees have spent years trying to uncover their origins. Their search is ongoing, and any new information, even the smallest detail would be welcomed. To learn more about their personal stories or how to contact them, go to www.gertiesbabies.com.

Acknowledgements

The streets of Butte teem with inspiration for any writer, and its inhabitants are beyond generous in sharing their knowledge and stories. All-around great story tellers Molly Blinn-Kirk, Barb Jeniker, and Coroner Lee LaBreche provided details that brought the ideas for this novel to life. Ronda Cogill talked to me about bullet wounds and at-home births; Karen Sullivan, Barbara Jozovich, and Diane Snyder provided perspective on Gertrude Pitkanen's work. Big thanks also to Denise Horne for background on Holy Trinity Serbian Church and its wonderful community; Joan Porter and Dianna Porter, for sharing their experience growing up in Butte in the 50's, Dianna in particular for her experience as a volunteer for the Ground Observer Corps; Jessie at the Mother Lode theater; Frank Taras for allowing me up on the roof of the Finlen; Josh Peck for Folk Festival nightmares, and Sheriff Ed Lester and Detective George Holland of BSB Law Enforcement. Also Butte Archives staff are a gold mine.

Once the story is on the page, the tedious hard work remains. I am especially thankful for my NY editor, Margaret Diehl, copy editor extraordinaire and BFF, Lynn Robbins, who rose to the challenge of correcting all my comma splices, and once again to super reader Amy Kuenzi, biology professor and mystery lover, whose nose for a good story keeps me honest.

About the Author

Marian Jensen has lived in Kentucky, West Virginia, and Ohio and, more recently, in Butte, Montana, since 1999. *Mortal Wounds* is the third novel in her series, Mining City Mysteries. Trout fishing on the Big Hole River is still her favorite place to be.

HELP! Pass the word if you think this book is worth a read. While full-page ads in the NY Times may be ideal, that's out of reach for us. Surprisingly, perhaps, word of mouth is the next best thing! So, even if it's only a few lines, consider leaving a review where you purchased your book. The Mining City Mysteries thank you!

Not feeling so literate? Visit us on Facebook at Mining City Mysteries and like our page. Or read our blog at www.miningcitymysteries.com.

Made in the USA
Charleston, SC
04 June 2016